DARKNESS FALLS

DARKNESS FALLS

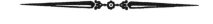

Margaret Murphy

 St. Martin's Minotaur ♏ New York

www.minotaurbooks.com

Library of Congress Cataloging-in-Publication Data

Murphy, Margaret, 1959 Apr. 14–
    Darkness falls / Margaret Murphy.—1st St. Martin's Minotaur ed.
        p. cm.
    ISBN 0-312-32851-6
    EAN 978-0312-32851-1
    1. Women lawyers—Fiction. 2. Kidnapping victims—Fiction. 3. Cheshire (England)—Fiction. I. Title.

PR6063.U7337D37 2004
823'.914—dc22   2003070098

First published in Great Britain by Hodder and Stoughton, a division of Hodder Headline

First St. Martin's Minotaur Edition: June 2004

10 9 8 7 6 5 4 3 2 1

For Murf

ACKNOWLEDGEMENTS

A number of people have been more than generous with their time and expertise in helping me with the research for this novel. Dierdre Maguire allowed me to follow her work schedule, and gave me valuable insights into a barrister's work. Inspector David Griffin has provided acres of information into police procedure, patiently explaining and clarifying points of particular relevance to the story. He also introduced me to several of his colleagues who could not have been more helpful. For their tolerance of what must have seemed at times odd questions, I am grateful. Sally Griffin showed me around the children's interview suite, and went through the interview procedure in some detail. My special thanks go to Glynn Hughes, of the Cheshire Constabulary HOLMES team, who gave up a morning to go through the intricacies of the system with me. To Val Rowbotham and Dave Bourne, Senior Medical Technical Officers at Macclesfield General Hospital, I promise the word 'morgue' features nowhere in this novel.

Factual accuracy in the story is thanks to the good-humoured assistance of those mentioned above. Any errors in procedural detail I claim as my own.

DARKNESS FALLS

Chapter One

A clear drop falls onto her cheek. It glistens for a moment, plump as a pearl, then is drawn into the soft powder of her make-up, and its lustre fades. She does not stir. He touches his face: he is crying. Crying because she is so beautiful and yet she does not stir when a tear falls, warm on her skin. Is he sorry for her or for himself? He cannot bear it. She was his. She belonged to him for too short a time, but it was the purest pleasure he had ever known. Now she is gone. How will he ever find another like her?

He looks again at her lovely face. Her eyelids have a shadowy look, blueish, bruised, and her lips are pale and bloodless, for he has kissed away the lipstick that she had so carefully applied, only hours earlier. He smooths a stray hair from her face – *God, she's so beautiful!* He closes his eyes against a pain that is real, physical. She was everything to him – everything he wanted, everything he could ever imagine. A moan escapes him and he puts his fingers to his lips to stop their trembling. He kneels beside her and sits back on his heels, for a while losing himself, rocking slowly back and forth, comforted by the repetition.

This can't go on. There are things he must do – for her, and for himself. They say that rituals help us through difficult times; that the conventions of mourning and burial help us to accept both the fact of death and the need to carry on. He believes this, and although he has no religion, he still has faith in its rites: the old hymns, the smell of incense, and the murmured responses of a congregation retain their soothing power over him. He wipes his eyes.

He will not bury her. She hated the dark — was in terror of being shut in. And anyway, how will they find her if he puts her under the ground?

He finds a quiet place, upstream from the bandstand, hidden from the prying eyes of insomniacs and the occasional drunk, weaving home across the footbridge over the River Dee. Still deep water, black and inscrutable, far from the treacherous pull of the weir that, given the opportunity, would drag her too soon into the glare of publicity. Before he has had a chance to clean and disinfect, to re-establish order from the disarray her preparation and death have caused.

She is heavy. Heavier in death than she ever was in life. It is as if her life force bore her up, defying gravity's pull. In life, she was quick to learn not to oppose his will, but now that conscious resistance is beyond her, she obstructs him with her inertia. He quells an angry impulse to punish her — she is beyond that; and he is no lunatic — he won't disfigure her: she came to him unblemished, and she will leave the same way.

He takes one last look at her body, perfect in its vulnerability, then lowers her into the water. He gasps in shock at the icy chill and looks quickly into her face. It is untroubled. She feels nothing — he almost envies her that because he is in turmoil: he has embarked on a course of action from which there is no going back. She slips, unprotesting, under the surface. For a moment her hair drifts out in an arc, framing her face, then she rolls and turns, sleek as an otter, and disappears into the depths.

Chapter Two

Lunch-time. He has to escape the crass, mundane gossip of his co-workers or he will go mad. He is grieving and yet he has to appear unaltered, as calm and purposeful as he always is.

Eastgate Street is crowded with shoppers. In the shop windows, notices for seasonal staff: the Christmas rush is gaining momentum. He stands in the lee of the archway under the clock tower, facing the Grosvenor Hotel. He smokes a cigarette huddled against the cold, watching more from habit than hunger.

In a crowd, his eyes slide over and past the overweight and the ugly. It's not merely that they do not interest him — they simply do not exist. The rest, he categorises using an instinctive, almost unconscious system of classification, rising in status from the too-young, to the too-fair, to *the type*. For preference, she will be over thirty — but definitely not older than forty. Confidence is crucial: he finds confidence in a woman alluring; it presents a challenge to him. He likes a challenge and where is the challenge in a woman who is submissive from the outset? He looks for poise — a woman who knows how to move and is aware of her effect on men, who enjoys her femininity without revelling in it; the type who can cause a frisson of sexual tension when she walks into a room, but who will not always feel the need to exploit it.

He stares into the constant surge of bodies, his eyes unfocused. There! By the hotel colonnade. She dresses well —

fashionable without being brash. She walks at an unhurried, measured pace, elegant, sure of herself, unselfconscious. Her hands are gloved, she holds an umbrella rolled and sheathed in one hand. She is wearing camel-coloured cashmere, with a dash of red at the throat; her boots match her gloves.

She smiles and he feels his lips draw back as if in answer. She moves out into the street into a sudden blaze of sunshine, and it is as if she has stepped onto a stage, into a spotlight. His heartbeat accelerates. She is moving towards him! A man steps into his line of view and he feels a spark of annoyance, leans off the archway and grinds his cigarette under his heel. She greets the man and the spark flares; he feels the heat rise into his face. The woman slips her arm through the man's. He reaches across and pats her hand. They walk away, smiling.

His fists clenched, he follows them a few steps. *For God's sake! What do you think you can do about it? She's* with *someone*. He slows and stops, staring after them until they turn, ascending the steps to one of the Rows, and disappear into the shadows.

He shrugs, half smiling to himself — it's just a bit of nonsense, a game he sometimes plays in an idle moment — why get upset over it? He returns to his station for another ten minutes, relaxing into the task. A girl — she is sixteen, perhaps, or seventeen — stops to ask him the time. Asks him the time with the great iron clock thirty feet above them, ready to chime the hour. He stares at her until she blushes and backs away, afraid. He feels buoyed by the encounter. Watching the woman in cashmere has brought back some of the excitement he had felt when he had first chosen Eleanor. He would get over her. She will not be the last.

Chapter Three

Pippa dashed into the kitchen, already late for breakfast, and plonked her new Barbie in front of her, immediately engaging it in conversation.

'Not on the table!' Clara groaned, rescuing the toy from a milk spill.

Pippa wailed.

'Do you really want her spoiled before you've had the chance to show her to your friends?' Clara Pascal stared down at her daughter's head and couldn't resist planting a kiss on the glossy crown. 'Stop pouting and eat your breakfast.'

She sat down briefly to sip at her coffee and crunch a piece of toast, pretending not to notice the fact that her daughter had folded her arms and was refusing to eat, while Hugo pulled faces at Pippa, trying to bring her out of her sulk.

Clara glanced up to see the two of them sticking their tongues out at each other and making exaggerated grimaces. *God, it's like looking in a mirror! The same gestures, the same china-blue eyes, the same straight black hair. She even has the dimple in her chin.*

She stood and brushed herself down, aware of Hugo's appreciative glance. Their eyes met and she favoured him with a slow smile.

'I suppose you absolutely *have* to be at chambers early?' he asked, wistfully.

'Nine o' clock sharp,' she said, slapping away his hand. 'Can you see to Madam – make sure she's ready for Trish?'

Pippa gave a little shout of protest. 'I want *you* to take me, Mummy.'

'I wish I could, but I can't, darling.' She launched into an explanation to her husband over the top of her daughter's head, justifying herself to him, knowing that no explanation would satisfy Pippa. 'I've a PDH at ten. The plea is straightforward – matter of minutes, but it depends on the running order, and Peter Knight's prone to run over time.'

Hugo raised an eyebrow. 'Peter Knight. I hope you've done your prep., Ms Pascal.'

Clara smiled. Justice Knight wasn't nicknamed The Headmaster for nothing.

Pippa squirmed in her chair. 'Mummy, I want to come with you.'

'I'm seeing the police witnesses for a quick rehearsal this afternoon,' she said with heavy emphasis.

'Oh,' Hugo said, understanding immediately. 'About the um . . .'

'The case at the end of the week,' she finished for him. She pressed a hand to her midriff and took a deep breath: even a mention of the Casavettes case made her nervous.

Pippa stopped agitating for a moment and looked from her mother to her father. 'You always say it's rude to whisper. Well *I* think it's rude to talk in code,' she observed.

'You may be nine today, but it's still too young to be pompous,' Clara told her.

'I'm not being pompous,' Pippa replied, stung by the implication, though evidently unsure what it meant. 'I just want you to take me to school.'

'Daddy will drive you, then.'

'I don't want Daddy, I want *you*.'

'Mummy will be back in time for the party,' Hugo said.

'Absolutely.' Clara solemnly crossed her heart.

'Mummy!'

She looked down into her daughter's face. She really was so like Hugo. 'Trish is coming for you, darling.'

'I don't *want* Trish. You *never* take me to school!'

'That's because I have to be in whichever court is hearing the case by nine-thirty, and that could take me—'

But Pippa was not in the mood for explanations. 'All the other girls' mummies take them, but you never take me,' she shouted. 'Even on my birthday.'

'Darling, I'd have to drop you at school at eight-thirty. You'd be in the freezing cold for half an hour.'

'I don't care! I *like* the cold!' Her eyes filled, her lower lip began to tremble and Clara had to concede defeat.

'All right,' she said. 'All right! I'll take you to school. You've got ten minutes.'

Confused by the sudden and unexpected capitulation, Pippa shed a tear before realising she had won. She jumped up from the table.

'Don't come near me with those sticky hands!' Clara warned, shielding herself from her daughter's hug with a chair. 'Ten minutes and I expect you to have brushed your teeth and washed your face – all shiny and clean and neat.' Pippa ran to the door, her sulks forgotten, and belted for the stairs, her footsteps clattering down the hallway.

Clara turned back to find Hugo smiling broadly.

'The lip-quiver argument,' she said with a slight lift of her shoulder. 'Gets me every time.'

Hugo laughed and opened his arms. She slipped into his embrace, sitting on his lap, savouring the warmth of his body through his shirt and the tangy scent of his cologne. 'Will you square it with Trish?'

'Too late to phone – I'll talk to her when she gets here. She'll understand.'

Sometimes she thought Trish understood their daughter better than either of them. She had cared for Pippa, first as a nanny and latterly as a child-minder, since Pippa was six months old. It was unworthy of her, she knew, but Clara found it hard not to feel a little envious, even resentful of their relationship.

She broke the embrace reluctantly and began stacking the breakfast dishes in the dishwasher.

'Leave those – I'll do them,' Hugo said, standing and taking the breakfast bowls from her. 'You know you're gorgeous, don't you, Counsel?' he said, stooping to kiss her on the lips. Clara was tall, but at six feet four, he still towered above her. She responded to the kiss, wrapping her arms around him, letting her hands travel to his buttocks, pulling him hard against her. Pippa's footsteps pounded down the stairs and they separated.

Clara smiled apologetically. 'Duty calls.' She tore off a piece of kitchen roll indicating the lipstick smears on his mouth.

Pippa came in, hair smoothed and tied back, her blazer bristling with metal badges from her birthday cards.

'You won't be able to wear those in school,' Clara warned.

'Annabelle Forrest did and it wasn't even her birthday – her birthday was on Sunday – and nobody told her off.'

'Annabelle Forrest leads a charmed life,' Clara remarked dryly. She picked up her briefcase in the hallway. Pippa had set her Barbie shoulder bag next to it and scooped it up primly as she passed.

'Don't I get a kiss?' Hugo asked.

Pippa spun round and hurled herself at him, her face beaming. He caught the shoulder bag, parrying it before it could do serious injury, and crouched to kiss her.

'You smell nice,' she commented, then ran to the door.

'Just what I thought,' Clara said, this time making do with a chaste kiss on the cheek. 'Oh, God,' she said, pulling away and looking into his face, suddenly stricken. 'I forgot to ask about Melker.'

'Don't worry,' Hugo soothed. 'It's not today. He's in France, sussing out a new property. But he says he'll definitely have an answer tomorrow.'

Clara reached to wipe away a smudge of lipstick he had missed. 'You'll get the commission,' she said.

'Car keys, Mummy!'

'You think?'

Pippa made a swipe at the key ring in Clara's hand, but she held them just out of reach answering, 'I know.'

'How do you know?'

'He'd be mad not to.' She didn't need to add, 'He *has* to' — they both knew how important the Melker contract was to Hugo's business.

'Mummy!'

'You driving?' Clara asked.

Pippa giggled.

On the journey to school, Pippa chattered on about who she had invited to her party and what she thought her friends would buy her.

Clara thought through her morning's work. Her client, who had been charged with a Section 18, had agreed to plead guilty to a Section 20. The lesser charge of GBH without the intent gave her the opportunity to put forward various factors in mitigation. She would have to go through the summary transcript again before going into court. It shouldn't be necessary to do more than agree the transcripts with her opponent at this stage, but Justice Knight took pleasure in catching out Counsel in poor preparation at Plea and Direction Hearings.

She pulled off the main road into the winding lane that led to Pippa's school and skimmed the notes from memory. Was there anything the defence might object to? Her left hand went automatically to her briefcase, nestled in the well of the passenger seat, and she glanced across at her daughter.

'Pippa,' she said, noticing for the first time the dark pink ribbon in her hair. 'Where did you get that?'

Pippa coloured.

'If you've disarranged my papers —' She slowed for a tricky

bend and came face to face with a milk float. The milkman grinned and drove around her, mounting the pavement.

'I didn't, Mummy. I just took the ribbon off. I didn't even take them out of your bag.'

'You know you're not to touch my papers. Those ribbons aren't for decoration.'

Pippa looked so astonished at such a crazy notion that Clara had to bite her lip to stop herself from laughing out loud. 'I could get in serious trouble if any of the documents are missing.' An exaggeration, but it could certainly cause her serious embarrassment.

Pippa blinked. 'Sorry, Mummy.'

'And you know you're only allowed blue ribbons in school.'

'But, Mummy it's my—'

'Birthday.' Clara sighed. 'I know.'

She swung the car into the side road leading to the school. The primulas lining the edges of the private drive to the back of the school were lightly dusted with frost. A few cars were parked in the teachers' bays next to the entrance to the building, but otherwise the school looked deserted. Clara parked opposite the end of the drive and checked her watch. Eight twenty-five – she could walk Pippa to the playground and still make it to Chambers by nine o'clock.

She unclipped her seat-belt and opened her door.

'You can drive in,' Pippa told her. 'Everyone does.'

Clara left her door unlocked and held out her hand. 'The rules are there for your safety, Pippa. If "everyone" drove into school, there'd be chaos.'

They trudged down the drive, Pippa stopping to break a thin glazing of ice on a puddle with her heel. 'But there's nobody here, yet.'

'Yes there is.'

Pippa turned and scanned the road. Only a few of the residents' cars and a van, sputtering and coughing, sending out uneven puffs of pale blue exhaust into the chilly air. 'Who?' she asked.

'You.' Clara smiled and planted a kiss on her daughter's forehead. 'Don't leave the playground,' she warned. 'And don't go hiding around the back of the building.' She handed Pippa her shoulder bag. 'Oh, and have a lovely day.' She pressed one of the badges on Pippa's lapel and it began playing 'Happy Birthday'.

Pippa giggled joyfully and opened the gate, stepping into the protective confines of the playground. Clara left her with some misgivings. Nobody on duty, she thought. There really should be someone on duty.

At the bend of the road, Clara heard the playground gate's complaining squeal, but she was already rehearsing her court presentation in her head and it registered only distantly. The van had parked in front of her car. The back doors were open and the driver seemed to be rummaging for something.

Clara reached for the door handle as the man turned to face her. She jerked back, startled. He wore a red ski mask and his breath came in misty bursts, as though he had been running. Clara recovered, half smiled, turned away, embarrassed that she must seem so jittery.

The man moved fast. He grabbed her from behind, his left arm around her shoulder, right hand covering her face. Clara struggled, tried to scream, but he had taped something over her mouth. His finger and thumb pinched her nose. She tried to free her arms, grabbing and reaching behind her, trying to pull free. Her vision began to cloud from the edges and she knew she was going to pass out.

A shrill scream made the man ease his grip momentarily. She drew in a lung full of air through her nose and worked her jaw against the suffocating constraints of the tape. It tautened but did not give.

The man held her fast and, horrified, Clara saw that Pippa had followed her out onto the road. She shook her head, trying to tell Pippa to go back, but she came onward, onward, as the man dragged her to the van.

Finding new strength, Clara kicked backwards and heard him groan and swear, then he slammed her hard against the side of the van, winding her. She fell to her knees and he pulled her arms behind her wrapping something tight around her wrists, then he threw her inside and slammed the doors shut.

Clara kicked at the doors, using both feet, hearing Pippa's screams, frantically trying to distract him. *Dear God, please, not Pippa. Don't take her!*

Chapter Four

The sun sparkled on the frost melt as DI Steve Lawson walked the fifty yards from the road block at the end of the road to the blue-and-white police tape the responding officer had set up within minutes of arriving at the scene.

Robins battled it out for territory in a musical slanging match, incongruous against the backdrop of flashing police lights and the beep and crackle of car radios.

A PC approached Lawson, arm raised as he ducked under the tape, but she dropped it when he flashed his ID.

'DS Barton is co-ordinating, sir,' she said, stepping aside.

A stocky, balding man glanced up from his conversation with a white-suited forensic scientist and nodded recognition. He spoke a few more words, then strode over to Lawson.

'Good to be working with you again, Boss,' he said taking Lawson's offered hand.

'Phil! Christ! How long has it been?'

'Four years, thereabouts.' Lawson had done a stint in the Firearms Support Unit and later moved to Crewe CID, while Barton had remained in Chester.

'Bloody hell – what happened to the hair?'

'Fatherhood.' Barton grinned, rubbed a hand over the close-crop of what remained.

'You're a dad?'

Barton's smile broadened. 'A lad. He's eighteen months, just coming up.'

'Congrat-u-bloody-lations!' When they last worked together, Phil's wife had been going through fertility tests. The two men walked side by side to where the Scene of Crime Officers were working.

'So what's the secret of your eternal youth?' Barton asked, 'Picture in the attic?'

Lawson laughed. 'Lost a bit of weight,' he suggested.

'And the rest—' Barton narrowed his eyes, scrutinising the inspector. He clicked his fingers. 'You got rid of the face-fungus!'

'It's bad enough going prematurely grey – adds insult to injury when the beard goes white as well.'

'What's this about *prematurely* grey?' Barton asked slyly.

'Good to know you're as insubordinate as ever, Sergeant.' They stopped by the narrow driveway leading to the school and Lawson surveyed the scene. 'What've we got?'

Barton sobered immediately. 'Daughter saw her being dragged off. Bastard knocked her down trying to get her mother free.'

'She okay?'

'Shaken up, otherwise . . .'

They watched a group of scientists, looking like giant larvae in their white overalls, working inwards on their hands and knees in a small arc towards the front end of a BMW parked opposite the school drive.

'Who is she – the abductee? Do we know?'

'Clara Pascal.'

They made eye contact, then Lawson gave a low whistle. 'Bloody hell.'

'Wasn't the Casavettes trial due to start this week?' Barton asked.

'Friday. They had to postpone because of intimidation of witnesses.'

There was a silence while both men considered the implications of this. A black, square-heeled shoe lay on its side at the front of the car. Lawson watched as a member of the forensic team picked it up carefully with gloved hands and sealed it in an evidence bag.

'Forensics are doing fibre lifts, dust samples, tyre treads and imprints, but this thaw isn't helping.'

A white suit joined them. 'We need to achieve seizure of the child's clothing ASAP,' he said in a low voice, aware of parents at the boundary of the tapes, craning to see what was going on.

Lawson gazed in the direction of the school. Beyond the playing field the bell in the church tower chimed ten o'clock. 'I'll do what I can,' he said.

'Another hour or two and any fibres she picked up in the contact will be lost.'

'The girl's welfare has to come first,' Lawson said.

The SOCO seemed ready to respond angrily then he nodded, continuing in the same low, measured tone with which he had greeted them: 'Sure. But don't forget the mother in your concern for the daughter, eh, Inspector?'

Lawson turned back to look at him. The man had a point, he had to admit. 'Got anything?' he asked.

'Enough fibres to knit a woolly sweater, but since hundreds pass this way morning and afternoon, I'm not sure how much of it will prove useful. The fibres on the girl's clothing really are our best bet.'

Lawson sighed. 'Okay, I'll talk to her father. Is he here yet?'

'On his way,' Barton replied.

'And a nail scrape,' the SOCO added, apologetically.

Barton explained: 'She fought with him briefly.'

'If we can get a skin sample – DNA typing—'

Lawson threw Barton a questioning look.

Barton shook his head doubtfully. 'I wouldn't bank on it, Boss. She was pretty distraught when they took her in . . .'

'I'll see how she is now. What about witnesses?'

'Nothing so far. Uniform are knocking on doors, but most people have left for work by half eight.'

Lawson did one last sweep of the area. Although the road was narrow, the houses were all detached properties and widely spaced. Only a couple of them would have a view of the end of the school drive, where Mrs Pascal parked her car. Here, a low sandstone wall bordered a large ramshackle garden with an old and raddled orchard nearest the wall and a garage next to the house – no windows through which an interested neighbour might watch the comings and goings of school traffic.

He looked down the road and caught sight of a damaged Renault. 'Was that involved?'

'All done and dusted, Boss,' Barton said. 'Photographed, sampled – they've even swept up the bits from the rear light.'

Lawson grunted. 'You've done a good job here, Phil – thanks. Let me know when the husband arrives.'

Barton stared over his shoulder. 'I think this could be him now.'

They turned to watch a man, flanked by two police constables, striding towards them. He dwarfed both the officers and Lawson got a sense of tremendous physical strength as well as uneasy control.

'Big bastard, isn't he?' Barton breathed.

One of the officers lifted the tape and the man had to bend almost double to get beneath it, the tails of his grey wool overcoat momentarily trailing in the dust.

'Are you in charge?' he asked Lawson without waiting for introductions. He was very pale and a muscle worked in his lower jaw.

'Mr Pascal?' Lawson asked.

He nodded, irritated by the question. 'Where is she? Where's my daughter?'

He took a step towards the school driveway, but Lawson put a restraining hand on his arm. 'I'd like to ask you a few questions first, Mr Pascal. I am Detective Inspector Lawson.'

Hugo stared at him uncomprehendingly for a few seconds, then shook free. 'That can wait,' he said. 'Pippa—'

'Is in safe hands,' Lawson said, with implacable calm. 'You might have information vital to our investigation, sir. When your daughter sees you, she's going to be upset. It could cause a delay . . .' *And what about your wife, Pascal? Aren't you going to ask about her?*

Hugo hesitated a moment, seemed to be bracing himself for an argument, then his face crumpled and his shoulders sagged. 'All right,' he said. 'Where?'

They conducted the interview in the junior school library, surrounded by trolleys of paperback novels and shelves of faded encyclopaedias, under posters of Harry Potter.

Hugo sat uncomfortably on a plastic chair more suited to someone half his size, answering the inspector's questions in a distracted, incoherent way.

'Worried?' he repeated, as if it were a concept alien to him. 'What would she be worried about?'

Lawson raised his shoulders. 'Work? Was she anxious about any of her cases?'

'No. She thought she might be kept waiting at court this morning, but . . .'

Lawson waited, half expecting Pascal to mention the Casavettes case.

'It's her birthday, you know.'

'Mrs Pascal's?'

'Ms – She likes to be called Ms,' he corrected automatically. 'No, not Clara, Pippa. It's Pippa's birthday. She was so excited.'

Lawson tried again. 'You or your wife might have noticed something out of the ordinary over the last few days,' he said. 'Cars parked in the street outside your house. Unusual phone calls, letters—'

'I'm worried about her party, you see,' Hugo went on. 'She's been so looking forward to it.'

Barton and Lawson exchanged a look. 'I don't think your daughter will . . .'

'No, of course not. She's upset. Bound to be.' He looked anxiously into their faces. 'Do you think I should cancel?'

Lawson left Mr Pascal with Barton and found his way back to the reception desk. A small boy arrived, clutching a note from his teacher as Lawson reached the hatch. The boy gawked at the inspector with unabashed interest when he asked to see Pippa. As Lawson was led to an office off the main corridor he heard a piping voice ask the secretary, 'Is he taking her to jail?'

The head teacher's office was simply furnished: a desk with a captain's chair, two upholstered easy chairs — not matching — for guests, a set of metal shelves crammed in one corner of the room and stuffed with folders and box files. There were blinds on the windows, tilted open at the moment, looking out onto the school playground.

The head teacher crouched next to Pippa, talking quietly. On her desk a laptop computer stood open and, next to it, a pile of mail. She rose and greeted Lawson, asking if he would like her to leave.

He urged her to stay and then turned his attention to the two figures seated in the armchairs. The plump, kindly-looking woman sitting opposite Pippa he recognised as Sarah Kormish, a member of the Child Protection team. She stood, leaving her chair free.

Pippa Pascal was her father in miniature: her face was more oval and her hair was cut in a neat fringe across her forehead, but she had the same creamy white skin and glossy black hair, the same intelligent blue eyes. She seemed calm and still, except for her hands twisting and fretting at a damp tissue in her lap.

'Pippa?' Lawson said. 'It is Pippa, is it?'

She lifted her chin bravely and answered him in a whisper.

'I am Inspector Lawson.' He held out his hand. She stared at it for a moment and then took it with solemn formality; her hand was ice-cold.

'How are you now?' Lawson asked.

'My back hurts a bit. And my throat.'

She swallowed and Lawson realised it wasn't shyness that made her whisper: she must have screamed herself hoarse, seeing her mother taken away like that.

'Is my daddy here yet?'

'You can see him in a moment.' Lawson sat next to her, anxious not to make her nervous by looming over her. 'Do you think you could tell Sarah what happened?' he asked, smiling over at the DC, who had stationed herself behind the child's chair.

She twisted in her seat, first looking up at the Child Protection officer, then frowning down at her hands and biting her lower lip. Sarah spoke up: 'Only if you feel up to it, love,' she said. 'But it would really help us if you could.'

The frown deepened and the little girl swallowed again before speaking. 'Will my daddy be with me?'

'Oh, yes,' Lawson said, in answer to Sarah's quick, questioning glance. 'Daddy can go with you.'

The child seemed puzzled. 'We have a special place,' Sarah explained. 'It's really nice. I'll show you round, if you like.'

'When are we going?'

'Just as soon as you've had chance to change out of your school uniform,' Lawson said.

Troubled, Pippa turned once more to Sarah for explanation. 'You don't want to be out and about in your school uniform on your birthday, do you?' she said. 'And you did get a bit mucky when you fell over . . .'

Pippa rubbed self-consciously at a grubby mark on one white sock.

'Thanks, Pippa,' Lawson said, taking her hand gently in his. 'You've been a very brave girl.' He stood to leave.

'You will find her, won't you?' she asked, her eyes bright with unshed tears.

'Oh, yes, we'll find her,' Lawson replied, with more conviction than he felt.

'Do you know who took my mummy?'

She looked guilelessly into his face. He took a breath. 'No.'

She bit her lip. 'D'you know where she is, then?'

Trust a kid to cut through the crap. He fixed his gaze on her face. 'No,' he said. 'But we will find her.'

She turned away and looked out of the window onto the deserted playground. A pied wagtail tumbled and skittered onto the tarmac, then darted back and forth, tail bobbing, in search of food.

'I told her to drive in,' she muttered, a tear brimming on her lower eyelid. 'But she wouldn't.'

Lawson called in to the library before he left. Pascal was sitting in the same chair, bent forward, his hands clenched between his knees. Lawson looked askance at Barton, who gave a brief shake of his head – he hadn't given them anything useful in the DI's absence.

'We'd like Pippa to talk to a Child Protection Officer,' he said.

He looked up, instantly protective of his daughter. 'I don't want her going to the police station.'

'No, of course not. We have a special interview suite for children.'

Hugo repeated the words distractedly.

'But we need her clothing first.'

He stood, toppling his chair. 'What are you saying?'

Lawson realised his mistake and raised both hands to reassure Hugo. 'It's all right,' he said.

'What did he do to her?' He leaned forward, flushing dark red, his very outrage a threat in the confines of the cluttered space.

'Nothing,' Lawson said, firmly. 'Your daughter is unharmed.' He waited a moment for this to sink in. 'But she may have had brief contact with the abductor and there could be forensic evidence on her clothing.'

Hugo turned away, bumping into one of the book trolleys and gripping it as though he needed it to stay upright. 'I thought you meant—'

'No . . . Your daughter witnessed the abduction. She tried to stop the man—' Hugo stiffened and he added, 'I'm sorry to have distressed you, sir—'

He let out a sharp bark of laughter. 'Distressed,' he repeated bitterly. '*Distressed* doesn't even begin to describe what I'm feeling.'

Lawson felt for the man, but he had a job to do and the quicker they got moving, the more likely they would bring Clara Pascal home unharmed. 'With your permission, Mr Pascal,' he said, 'we'll put a trace on your phone.'

'Yes,' Hugo faltered. 'Anything . . . anything to – I just want her back safely.'

At last – some concern for his wife. 'Someone will meet you at your house. Sergeant Barton will accompany you and collect the clothes.' Lawson didn't relish what he had to ask next. 'While the forensic scientists are still here . . . Perhaps you could ask Pippa if they could take a – a sample – from under her nails.'

The creamy skin turned paper-white.

'I'm sorry, sir, there's no easy way to put these things.'

'No. No, I suppose not.'

But neither was it easy for a father to think of his nine-year-old daughter grappling with the man who had just kidnapped his wife. Hugo let go of the trolley and swayed a little, then he made his way unsteadily to the door. 'Let's get it over with, shall we, Sergeant?'

Chapter Five

Clara kicked hard at the door, the walls, the floor of the van, using the foot that was still shod, making as much noise as she possibly could. The man drove crazily, careering along the side street to the T-junction and swerving onto the main road; he raced down the hill and turned right, away from the city, onto the A483, heading towards Wrexham.

He had driven the route many times, rehearsing the turns — across the A55, then left to Rossett, off onto B roads, along the unmarked road to Cuddington, running parallel with the River Dee, taking a straight line, where the Dee coiled and twisted, ravelling like intestinal loops. He drove fast, attracting attention, creating as many sightings as he could away from his base, then he would quietly double back, mingling with the rush-hour traffic on the A41, matching his speed with the rest, easing back into Chester City's boundaries.

'Shut it!' he screamed. This was no good. She would attract more attention than he wanted. He needed to be seen, but he didn't want to bring the police down on him. Didn't want to risk being stopped. 'Shut your bloody noise!'

A few hundred yards on, he slewed to a halt in a lay-by and climbed into the back.

Clara froze. Cars and lorries zipped past, but she was aware only of her own breathing, thin and urgent; she felt she was suffocating. He bent over her, still wearing the ski mask, his eyes glittering with such unreasoning fury that she thought he would kill her there and then.

She held still, waiting until he was closer, close enough, then she brought her foot up and kicked hard. He grunted and staggered backwards. Clara scrambled for the door on her knees. It wasn't fastened shut — she might just make it—

He grabbed the collar of her jacket and yanked her backwards. She fell to the floor of the van with a thud. If she thought he was angry before, it was nothing compared with the look in his eyes now. The fight went out of her. All she wanted was to survive the next few minutes.

He stood over her until his breathing steadied a little, then he reached into the pocket of his jacket. *Blue, padded, red piping down the front*, she recited to herself, despairing of ever having the opportunity to pass on her careful observations to the police. *Blue eyes*, she thought. *He has blue eyes.*

He tore open a square, flat packet and took out a pink eye-pad. He grabbed her by the hair, wedging her head against his chest with one elbow. He smelled of damp and mould — then a whiff of antiseptic, reminiscent of childhood, and he pressed the pad against her left eye. He ripped open the second packet and repeated the process on her right eye.

He took her by the shoulders and forced her face down onto the floor of the van. He grabbed her ankles. She struggled but he held her and she felt her legs secured with the same soft fabric that bound her wrists.

'Now,' he said, his voice still harsh, breathless. 'Make another noise and I'll kill you.' Slowly, quite deliberately, he lay on top of her, his stomach to the curve of her back. She was assailed with the smell of nicotine overlaid by the musty, damp odour. She heard her own desperate cries of revulsion, muffled by the tape on her mouth, but she was too afraid to move. His hand travelled along her arm to her shoulder. She shut her eyes tight, felt tears squeeze between the eyelids and wet the eye-pads. *Now*, she thought. *This is where it begins.*

But he brought his hand around and up to her face, her mouth. He cupped her chin in the palm of his hand, closing finger and thumb over her nose. Too late she realised what he was doing. *Was this it?* Would the last memory her daughter had of her be seeing her dragged off by this maniac? Thinking of Pippa gave her the courage to fight; she kicked and bucked, straining against him, but he was strong and she weakened fast. The faint red light filtering through the eye-pads blackened; she felt herself slipping away, but was powerless to stop it.

Slowly, he reached over his head and pulled off the mask — there was no need for it now. He felt suddenly weary, but he had only just made a start. He had entered into a pact with Clara Pascal and he had to see it through, at least as far as he had planned it.

He prodded her, testing the unprotected concavity of her abdomen with the point of his shoe. Clara Pascal wouldn't cause him any more trouble.

Chapter Six

Pippa pressed close to her father as they mounted the steps to the house. Barton saw Pascal reach down and squeeze her shoulder reassuringly as he turned the key in the latch. Sarah made straight for the stairs when he switched off the alarm, seeming thrilled by the prospect of being introduced to Pippa's collection of porcelain pigs.

Barton began to speak, but Hugo silenced him with an irritable gesture and led him across the wood-block floor to a room on the left of the hallway. 'Forgive me,' he said, closing the door after them. 'I'd rather my daughter didn't hear any of this.'

Barton nodded. 'Mr Pascal,' he began without preamble. 'Did you notice a water authority van outside the house as you came in?'

Hugo nodded.

'That's one of ours. It's fully equipped with a communications room.'

Hugo went to the window and looked out. A man in blue overalls slouched with his hands in his pockets next to a couple of others, who were digging through the tarmac on the far side of the road.

'The van will remain outside for the duration,' Barton went on. 'There are several ways the kidnapper may make contact.' He counted them off on the fingers of one hand: 'Phone – land-line or mobile – post, courier or email.' He left out the possibility of direct contact, on instructions from DI Lawson.

'I rarely use my mobile,' Hugo told them. 'I keep forgetting to charge it.'

'Good, that simplifies things.' He kept his tone direct, unemotional. He wanted Pascal to remember what he was saying. He also wanted to break through the man's stupefied apathy. To make him think.

'The phone-tap is being put in place as we speak. You'll get a call in about ten minutes, just to check everything is working as it should – so don't be unduly alarmed.'

Hugo looked over at the telephone, sitting on an antique table with spindle legs, as if it were a vile creature crouching there. He thrust his hands into the pockets of his overcoat and shivered. 'This wasn't supposed to happen.'

Barton tensed. What the hell did *that* mean? He waited, but Hugo stared resolutely at his hands. 'Sir?' He kept his voice neutral. Still Hugo did not reply. Barton shifted his weight to attract Hugo's attention. A frown creased the big man's forehead. He blinked.

'You said this wasn't supposed to happen . . .'

Hugo seemed startled, as if he hadn't realised he had spoken aloud. For a moment he was flustered then he said, 'I – it was supposed to be an ordinary day. Clara was supposed to come home early, in time for the party . . .' He shook his head.

'If there's something you need to tell me . . .' Barton said, leaving things wide open.

Hugo stared blankly at him. 'Like what?'

Barton said nothing, only looked at Hugo a little longer. Hugo fetched a juddering sigh. 'I wish I could think of something else,' he said. 'I really do.'

'Well,' Barton said. 'If anything does occur to you . . .'

'Yes, of course, I'll call you straight away.'

'All right,' Barton said. 'Now, if you forget everything else I say, remember this: the priority is to get your wife home safely. Don't do anything to jeopardise that.'

'Do you really think I need to be told?' Hugo demanded angrily, facing Barton.

'You're confused,' Barton said, unperturbed by Hugo's outburst. 'And frightened. You would like to hit out at something — someone. In such situations we sometimes say things we regret.' He saw a flicker of recognition and shame in Hugo's face.

'If you get a call, stay calm. We'll be listening. Keep them talking as long as you can. Ask to speak to your wife. Ask,' he said, holding Hugo's gaze, 'for proof that she is alive.'

Hugo looked away and paced again to the window. Barton surveyed the room, giving Hugo time to compose himself. Abstract watercolours, vibrant and fresh, decorated one wall in a cluster — the four paintings were evidently a themed series. Two long sofas in pale green linen stood at right angles. Bookshelves had been built into the alcoves, a gleaming marble fireplace laden with logs, ready to be lit, dominated the centre of the wall.

Hugo pushed his fingers through his hair, his hands trembling, the tension evident in his neck and back muscles.

'You have absolute discretion, Mr Pascal,' Barton said. 'Act as you see fit.'

Hugo shot him a disparaging look.

He thinks I'm lying, Barton thought. *He doesn't believe me.* 'Ms Pascal comes home safe — that's a result for us,' he said.

'Well, let's hope you get your "result", Sergeant,' Hugo replied.

Behind him, in the street, Barton saw the surveillance team erecting a canvas shelter.

'Do you have—' The door opened, interrupting his request for a photograph of Clara Pascal. Pippa stood in black hipsters and a short, lime-green woollen top, her feet bare. Sarah stood in the doorway, looking embarrassed.

'Why do they want my clothes?' Her voice was high and panicky, her face chalk-white.

Hugo Pascal bent down to his daughter. 'They think—' He was at a loss to explain.

'We use a microscope to look for clues,' Barton intervened, understanding at once that the idea of someone picking over his little girl's clothing, searching for fibres, hairs, flecks of skin or blood from his wife's abductor was repugnant to Mr Pascal.

'But *I* haven't done anything wrong,' Pippa wailed.

'No, darling!' Hugo hugged her to him. 'Of course not. It's just so that the scientists can look for – for clues,' he said, latching on to Barton's word. 'To find Mummy.'

She squirmed away from him and stared solemnly into his face for a few moments. 'But my other uniform skirt is in the wash,' she challenged. 'What will I wear tomorrow?'

His smile was a grimace of pain. 'We'll worry about that later.'

She frowned, determined to have it out now.

Hugo sighed, his massive frame shuddering. 'I might need you here tomorrow,' he said at last. 'And if you really want to go in to school, I think we can work out how the washer works between us. Okay?'

She thought about it for a moment, then nodded, not quite convinced. ''Kay.'

Hugo knelt a few moments longer after she had left the room, as if the effort of standing were something he had to brace himself for. When he got to his feet, he moved to the bookshelf on the far side of the room.

'Is this what you wanted?' he asked, handing Barton a framed photograph.

Clara Pascal had a pretty, oval face, her hair a mass of unruly, dark-brown curls. 'She's very fair-skinned,' Barton remarked.

'She wears a hat in summer, otherwise she's a mass of freckles.' Hugo stopped, mortified that he had told Barton more than he wanted to know.

Barton looked back to the photograph. Clara's was an open, friendly face, her expression one of a woman who had known little anger and was disposed to good humour.

'How do you think she'll react, Mr Pascal?' he asked. 'I mean, how will she cope?'

Hugo took back the photograph, scrutinising it to avoid looking at the bag of clothing on the sofa. 'She'll talk,' he said. 'She'll try and bring him round to her way of thinking. Disputation is a game to her – an excuse to show off her adversarial powers—' He broke off. 'That sounded critical. It wasn't meant to be. I meant that Clara isn't easily intimidated. But she's not insensitive, either,' he added. He reacted to something in Barton's expression. 'I'm trying to give a clear picture of my wife.' He sounded belligerent, defensive. He shrugged, even managed a rueful smile. 'I'm afraid I'm not doing her justice. What I'm trying to tell you is, if she can convince him to let her go, she will.'

If she can, Barton thought. *If he lets her.*

She's heavy. Why does that surprise him? He is familiar with the expression 'dead weight', and has even had cause to test the accuracy of the term himself. He has backed the van into the driveway, intending to carry her into the house, holding her in his arms, the way they did it in the films: her head flung back over the crook of his arm, exposing the pale white vulnerability of her throat. But it's not as easy as they make it look.

Her body folds in the middle – it won't lie flat in his arms, and anyway, she's too heavy to lift. He steps down from the van onto the mossy driveway. There's no one about; the street is deserted, as he knew it would be – he chose the house with great care.

He grabs her by the ankles and drags her towards the back of the van. Her hair has come loose in the struggle; it trails after her, picking up flecks of rust and dirt from the floor. Her legs reach the edge and fall. He looks into her face. A brownish shadow of bruising has appeared either side of her nose. It will deepen, smudging to blue and purple as it ripens.

He feels a sudden rush of hatred; sullen, ugly and unreasoning. He takes hold of her jacket lapels and pulls her up. Her head snaps back with an audible *click*. For a full minute he is undecided. The shallow flicker of her carotid pulse is maddening: it would take very little to finish the job.

But that's not why he brought her here. Not now. At least, not yet.

For a few more seconds he stares into her face. With her eyes and mouth covered by tape, she is blank – featureless. He places his palm close to her mouth, close enough to feel the faint warmth of her breath stuttering uncertainly from her nostrils.

It isn't compassion that stops him. Or pity. Clara Pascal deserves neither. He has gone to a lot of trouble to bring her this far and he wants more from her; so much more. He lets her live because she doesn't deserve to die unaware, peaceful.

Chapter Seven

The electricians had been at work on the second floor of the Bridewell Museum, attached to Diva Street Station, since ten o'clock. Two hours on, grey cable ran like a ribbon from one end of the Major Incident Room to the other. Surface-mounted electric and phone sockets were fixed to the walls and telephone cables were being tacked in place.

Lawson's team of eight carried their own tables and chairs from a removals van parked outside the old police station. He passed a rather frail-looking DC on the stairs, carrying an overhead projector, who laughed at his suggestion that he might help her.

Personal computers, phones, a fax machine followed in procession – the filing cabinets and heavier items they would leave to the professional shifters.

Barton arrived as two joiners manoeuvred a large whiteboard through the side door leading to the museum.

'Which way, Boss?' the older man asked.

'Second floor,' Lawson replied, waving them past. 'Just follow the noise.' He flattened himself against the wall to let them through and Barton trotted up the stairs to meet him. He was carrying a handful of evidence bags.

'The girl's clothes?' Lawson asked.

Barton nodded. Each item of clothing was bagged separately

and Sarah Kormish had also carefully folded and bagged the brown paper sheet the child had stood on. 'She's gone with DC Kormish to the Carsley Interview Suite.'

'Good. Get those to the exhibits officer, he'll arrange for Scientific Support to pick them up. What about a photo?'

'I've sent the photo for duplication, but they let me have a few colour photocopies for now.' He dug in his breast pocket and brought out a bundle of highly coloured replicas of Clara's photograph.

'Attractive woman,' Lawson commented, turning back the way he had come.

On the first floor, Barton exclaimed at the sight of a mannequin dressed as a Victorian bobby, pointing the way to the main museum exhibits. 'Is this the best they could do?'

Lawson shrugged. 'There's a couple of other major enquiries going off elsewhere in the county. We need a HOLMES team to manage the data and we're pushed for space.'

'What about the sterile room at HQ?'

'Unusable.' Lawson's tone was dismissive. The Home Office Large and Major Enquiry System was not economical in terms of space: computers, printers, telecommunications and facilities for filing were indispensable. When the Chester HOLMES Room was set up in the nineteen-eighties, it comprised only a few computers and staff, but the narrow office conversion was now inadequate to house the modern system with its team of eight or nine trained officers, together with their computer equipment.

Barton was outraged. 'It's not on, though, is it — Joe Public coming and going while we're trying to conduct an investigation?'

'The choice is, hike out to Ellesmere Port for the facilities or bring them here. At least based at the Bridewell we're local to the incident. The SIO wants us all here for briefings, not developing ulcers in snarl-ups morning and evening on the M53.' He pushed through the fire doors onto the main corridor of the second floor. The sound of hammering and electric drills grew a notch louder. 'The museum isn't that busy this time of year, but if the public get too nosy, we'll close it.'

'Are they going to be long?' Barton asked, wincing at the racket.

'I bloody hope not,' Lawson said with feeling. 'DCI McAteer's due any minute and he'll want to get the briefing under way.' He led Barton a short way along the corridor to a smaller room which, only in the last hour, had been cleared of mouldering junk, some of it a century old. 'Exhibits room,' he said, leaving Barton to check in the bags of Pippa's clothing.

The HOLMES team was based a little further on. Lawson stood in the open doorway of the cramped office. Small oblong windows, high up, let in a little diffuse light, the rest was provided by fluorescent tubes. The Office Manager had arranged the Receiver's and Action Manager's desks at right angles to each other, with the Receiver's desk directly opposite the doorway. This left only a five-foot-square corral in which officers could stand when they delivered their completed actions or were allocated new ones. Lawson approved: the fewer distractions the HOLMES operatives had, the better.

The other work-stations were set up back-to-back, nine of them in all; the CPUs hummed quietly and two indexers clicked away at their keyboards, typing in data from questionnaires completed from the door-knocking earlier in the day. Another member of the team fiddled with a paper jam in a printer. The serenity of the scene – and the relative quiet – was almost restful. But already a pile of pink message slips was stacked up on the Receiver's desk: she looked up and smiled, then continued reading through the flimsy sheets, endorsing, sorting, prioritising, passing the more urgent lines of enquiry directly to the Action Manager. More slips had found their way into in-trays around the room, littering desks, stacked next to the photo-copier, ready for duplication, building inexorably to what would be barrier-level within a week.

Detective Chief Inspector McAteer appeared at the stairwell doors just as Lawson and Barton re-emerged into the corridor.

McAteer had a jowly, serious face. He was a vain man and years of squinting at documents, rather than admit that he needed reading glasses, had carved a permanent frown into the space between his eyes. His hair was suspiciously dark for a man in his fifties and the suits he'd had made at Gieves & Hawkes in Chester no longer hung quite so flatteringly on him has they might have done five years ago.

He shook hands with both men, then nodded towards his office. 'A few words before we begin, Steve?'

Barton took his cue. 'I'll sort out the Incident Room,' he said, jerking his head in the direction of the continuing clamour. 'Get rid of the civilians.'

When Lawson and McAteer came through a few minutes later, the room was quiet. The workmen hadn't needed much persuasion to take an early lunch and the eight officers drafted in as the nucleus of the enquiry team seemed rather lost on the expanse of floor space. Rows of sixty-watt bulbs, set high in the ceiling under metal shades, cast only dingy pools of brownish light, absorbed by the cracked dull red oilcloth on the floor.

The desks were set in uneven huddles at odd angles around the room, awaiting their final places when the wall sockets and phone points had been completed. Monitors and CPUs sat, disarticulated, their cables dangling, keyboards balanced on top of monitors, boxes, any space available.

The hum of conversation died down as Lawson and McAteer strode to the far end of the room. Lawson outlined the case so far so that everyone was clear what they were dealing with, while Barton handed out bundles of Clara's photograph to each officer. It wasn't necessary to explain Clara Pascal's involvement in the Casavettes trial: it represented the biggest drugs case the county had ever seen.

'Everyone has an equal right to put forward suggestions,' Lawson went on, looking at the younger members of the team.

'You might think you don't have much experience, but a fresh look at these things can be helpful. Any ideas you have, give them an airing – but since we don't all know each other, perhaps you'll introduce yourselves if you do chip in.'

McAteer took over. 'My dilemma is this,' he said. 'Keep the investigation low-profile and risk having the victim turn up in a bin-bag in the River Dee or go the shop-front way and maybe panic the abductor – with same result.' He scanned the faces as though looking for some indication of the right way to go.

'I've decided to give it twenty-four hours. If by this time tomorrow the abductor hasn't been in contact, we'll go public.'

'Pascal has been informed of the covert surveillance on his house,' Lawson said. 'And he's sanctioned the phone tap. But he doesn't know that we're doing mobile surveillance as well.' He turned to Barton and spoke in a lower voice, 'I'll need two more officers to help out the regular team.'

Barton nodded, already sussing out the right personalities from the job.

'Is he a suspect, Boss?' someone asked.

McAteer stared piercingly at the officer. 'I don't want to clutter up this investigation, but let's put it this way: I want Mr Pascal positively eliminated as soon as possible. I want to know more about him – a lot more. His work, finances, his relationship with his wife – and the woman who gave him his alibi—'

'Trish Markham,' Barton supplied.

McAteer continued: 'The obvious link is the drugs case,' he said. 'And I'll be talking to the SIO in charge of Operation Snowman later today, but we don't want to get hung up on that.'

'It could be someone with a grudge.' The DC who had laughed at Lawson's offer of help to carry the overhead projector. Sallow-skinned, with less flesh over her high cheekbones than looked comfortable; nevertheless, Sal Rayner had a clear, steady gaze. Realising her omission, she apologised and gave her name.

'Her chambers might be able to help with that,' McAteer

suggested. 'But go gently. We've no right to demand anything of them – it will all be down to goodwill. Whatever they can give us, we're grateful.' Rayner nodded. 'I'll want someone to talk to the husband as well.'

'Call me old-fashioned, but what about a straightforward ransom-kidnap?'

Lawson peered towards the back of the room, where the shadows gathered. 'Stand up, will you.' Adding dryly, 'And don't be shy.'

'Dave Fletcher.' A corpulent figure emerged with indolent reluctance from behind a clutter of computer hardware piled on a desk near the door.

'In my experience,' McAteer said, 'Ransom-kidnaps are never straightforward.' He inclined his head a little. 'But you may know better, Constable Fletcher.' McAteer might be vain, but he was no fool: he had Fletcher pegged right from the start.

Fletcher shifted uncomfortably.

'If it is a ransom the abductor's looking for, then until he makes contact, we have to rely on eyewitness statements to give us something to work on,' Lawson added.

Fletcher was about to take his seat again, but Lawson called out. 'Like I said – don't be shy. Come and join us.'

The team waited in silence while Fletcher made his way slowly to the main group of officers and perched on the edge of a table already groaning with the weight of boxes and electrical gadgetry.

'A Renault was damaged in the getaway,' McAteer went on, when Fletcher had settled himself. 'Scientific Support have got paint samples from it, but we've also had an eyewitness report that the van was involved in a second collision – with a grey Lexus. We need to trace the Lexus: the driver might have a description of the kidnapper or even the van's index number.'

'Who's the informant?' Rayner asked.

'One of the residents. He was in an upstairs room – couldn't make out the plates.'

'I take it the Lexus owner hasn't called in?'

Lawson shook his head.

'You'd think he would, if only for the insurance,' Rayner commented.

'So maybe the car was stolen or maybe the driver had to get to an urgent business meeting and didn't want to tie up the morning talking to the police. Whatever the reason, we have to find that car.'

There were nods all round.

'Repair shops, panel beaters, dealers – we try the lot,' Lawson said. 'The HOLMES Room has generated some actions, so we can make a start immediately. Make it your first port of call when this briefing is closed.'

McAteer added, 'When you've followed through, I want the forms properly endorsed and returned promptly. Any questions?'

'Any chance of a few more bodies on this?' Rayner again. She was voicing what all the others were thinking. One or two muttered their support.

'With the best will in the world, you're asking a hell of a lot, Boss . . .' Barton added. He was a good team rallier, Barton. He knew exactly when to back up his officers.

Lawson looked at McAteer.

'You're right, Rayner,' he said. 'And I'm happy to tell you that we have more officers on standby. If this isn't sorted by morning, there'll be thirty more at tomorrow's briefing.' This was greeted by murmurs of approval.

'Anything else?'

'A bit of heating wouldn't go amiss.'

Fletcher, trying to be ironic, but sounding resentful instead. He wore grey slacks and a cinnamon-coloured anorak over a blue jacket; he zipped up the anorak, as if to emphasise his point.

'There's an air-lock in the system,' Lawson said. 'The heating engineer's calling by this afternoon.'

'Well three cheers for Mr Fixit,' Fletcher muttered under his breath, hunching down into his overcoat. Lawson didn't catch what he said, but the officers near him did. One, a newly trained DC, smiled nervously, the others stared ahead, unconsciously shifting their upper bodies the merest fraction away from him. Lawson sighed inwardly, hoping that the thirty extra officers drafted in would be enough to dilute Fletcher's air of malcontentment.

McAteer checked his watch. 'Debrief at seven-thirty this evening,' he told them. 'And the press are to be told nothing – so if you've a pet journo on the local rag, forget it. There is a blanket embargo on this case.'

'I could do with one of those meself,' Fletcher grumbled, shivering theatrically. This provoked laughter. McAteer let it pass.

'DS Barton will assign duties,' he finished. 'There will be a lot of tedious T.I.E.s on this one, but it's a necessary evil.'

'It must be nice to be *right as Rayner*,' Fletcher sneered as Sal passed him on the way out.

Rayner turned to see who had spoken, her face showing little interest and no offence. 'Fletcher,' she said, as if that explained everything. She carried on through the second set of doors and down the stairs, on her way to Clara Pascal's chambers.

Fletcher, put out by her lack of reaction, began remonstrating with Cath Young, the newly trained DC, as they waited for the Allocator to hand out actions. 'When I started out in the job, the "D" in "DC" stood for "detective". Human beings did the thinking, not computers.'

Young flushed, unsure how to respond, and DS Dawn Tyrell, the Office Manager, peered over the head of another officer picking up an action. 'To be able to think, you need a brain, and "D" can also stand for "dickhead",' she said. The officer laughed, picking up his computer printout of the afternoon's work. Dawn beckoned Cath forward.

'You know how this works?' she asked.

'I Trace, Identify and Eliminate,' Young recited dutifully. 'Endorse the form and bring it back in to be fed into the system.'

'You'll do all right,' Tyrell said, giving her shoulder a friendly shake. 'Now, Mr Fletcher,' she said, beaming. 'What can we find to tax those little grey cells of yours?'

Chapter Eight

Darkness. *Pippa!* Her first thought. Then more, crowding in, unbidden, unwanted: Pippa advancing, shouting, fearful, refusing to turn and run. Her own sick fear, as suffocating as the tape over her mouth. She felt herself falling; though she lay on the cold ground, her body seemed to plummet, spiralling out of control. She took a huge, cold draught of air, realising with relief that she was no longer gagged. The skin around her mouth and nose felt tight and sore — bruised, perhaps.

She forced herself to reason, to think what she had heard and seen in the moments after the attack. Pippa screaming, the man yelling. Then he was in the van. In the van and driving, hitting something, once — twice — the groan of metal on metal. And Pippa? Yes! Pippa sobbing and screaming, her screams fading as he drove madly down the narrow street. *He didn't take Pippa!* She gasped in relief, then held her breath.

The darkness seemed to throb with danger and for a while she lay still, listening. Her face rested against a smooth, slightly slimy surface; stone, rather than concrete. Her eyes were still covered and beyond the patches she sensed an intense, unforgiving darkness. How long had she been unconscious? She strained for the slightest sound: the whisper of clothing as her captor moved; a cautious exhalation.

Nothing — only the rapid thud of her own heart. But he

might be there, waiting for her to awake. It took an act of courage to try and sit up. Her wrists and ankles were still bound tightly and she cried out as pain shot from her thigh to her knee. Her cry fell flat; she was in a smallish space, then. If her kidnapper was with her he would have spoken up by now. She grew more daring.

'All right,' she whispered. 'A stone floor and . . .' She felt behind her. The walls were uneven, with that same cold sweat of dampness that seemed to ooze from the stone flags.

She tried to stand, but her ankles were bound so tightly that the bones ground against each other. She cried out and sat back down heavily. A ripple of movement followed the rush of air upwards, a whispering, fluttering sound and Clara ducked, panicking, half expecting some creature to sweep down on her out of the inky black. The ruffling settled as quickly as it had started and she thought, *Paper. There's paper on the walls.*

She could not reach the binding around her ankles. She would have to kneel up and then sit back on her heels. Taking several deep breaths, Clara rocked to give herself the momentum to come up to a kneeling position. The binding cut viciously into her flesh and the pressure of bone to bone was almost too much. She bit back another cry. 'Come *on* Clara!' she muttered. 'You can do it.' And she did, after two more tries, grunting with pain and sweating with the exertion.

Sitting back on her heels sent sharp arrows through her ankle bones, but she persevered, walking her fingers down the binding, testing, probing, pulling at the material. One finger found a small gap and she worked it inwards, straining against the bindings on her wrists, ignoring the discomfort in her ankles and shoulders.

The gap widened and she felt two distinct surfaces, one furry and soft, the other rough, barbed like a cat's tongue. *Velcro?* she wondered. Her finger worked with greater urgency. She tugged and pulled, stopping only to stretch her hand as it was gripped in an agonising cramp. Finally, panting with the effort, she heard the familiar tearing sound as the two surfaces pulled apart and her feet were free. She waited a few minutes for her circulation to return before trying to stand. She was unshod and the stone beneath her was freezing, but the maddening pins and needles that the return of circulation brought were far more unpleasant.

She eased herself into a sitting position and waited for the throbbing, itching pain to ease a little. The wall behind her was smooth, except for one U-shaped loop of solid metal bolted a couple of centimetres above floor level, like a stay for a hook, she thought. A hook for a door? To stop it swinging to?

Slowly, using her hands against the wall behind her to ease herself up, she rose to a standing position, determined to find out more. Paper. There *was* paper on the walls. She felt a spurt of triumph at discovering even this small thing about her prison. Exploring with her fingers she found that the paper was tacked loosely – sellotaped – and there were different textures. *Newsprint*, she thought, and the thin, glossy feel of magazines, like the pictures of her favourite pop stars, soap stars and football heroes that Pippa pinned up on her bedroom walls. Clara's eyes started to water and the back of her nose flooded. She stopped for a moment, her back braced against the wall and took a few deep breaths.

She had to find out where she was. Crying wouldn't achieve anything. Afraid, but determined, she paced out the dimensions of the cell. If she came up against a solid wall, her hands were tied – she had nothing to protect herself. One, two, three, four – each step made gingerly, slithering one foot in front of the other, feeling with her toes, nervous of steps or obstacles. Twitching and flinching at imagined sounds, the feathery touch of a spider's web.

What does he want?

He wants you, Clara. Why do you think he went to all that trouble? Cold, hard reason demanded.

But why does he want me? And is it me in particular or . . .

Or any woman?

He didn't rape me.

45

Didn't he?

I don't want to think about it.

You'll have to, sooner or later.

I'll face it when I have to.

What makes you so sure it hasn't already happened?

Because I don't feel—

What? The cold, cynical part of her demanded. *You don't feel violated? Would you? You were unconscious, Clara.*

'No!' If she could have covered her ears, she would have. *I can't think about this any longer.*

Unyielding reason spoke up again, in the voice of one of her tutors: *The secret of a good defence is preparation.*

Clara felt her way down the wall to the far end of the room. 'All right,' she said aloud. 'All right. I don't *think* he raped me.' Not allowing the menace of the word 'yet' to tack itself on to the end of the thought.

She came back to her original question: what *does* he want? She began again her cautious pacing from the centre of the end wall. One, two . . . If she knew what he wanted, she would know how to negotiate with him, what to offer – as inducement or threat. Three, four . . . She made herself consider a link with the Casavettes case.

For the last week, the men in Chambers had tried out jokes varied on a theme of horse heads under bedclothes; once, in the lift, heading for the chambers library, one of them had leaned over her shoulder and whispered in an approximation of Marlon Brando's *Godfather* wheeze: 'You mess wid da Fambly, you gonna pay.'

She had laughed, because that was what was expected of her, but now she had to take it seriously. On prosecution evidence Ray Casavettes could go away for fifteen years.

Five, si—She stubbed her toe against something hard and almost fell forward. A set of steps, wooden by the feel. She took one riser at a time, feeling for the height, testing it before putting her full weight on it. There were seven steps to the top, then what felt like a metal door. No handle on the inside, but turning around and using her hands to seek it out, she discovered a keyhole. She felt her way down again and sat on the bottom step, grateful at least not to be sitting on the freezing stone floor.

Casavettes had plenty of motive. She had met him face to face only once – at his Pleas and Directions hearing. She knew what he looked like, having seen his police mug-shot and photographs in the papers, but nothing could have prepared her for that meeting. He was remanded in custody and two beefy Securicor guards had brought him up. There was a brief silence after he was called, then the panelled door leading to the stairs below the courtroom opened and Casavettes appeared. He paused at the top of the steps, taking his time, getting his bearings.

Clara had met a few people – only a few – whose very presence seemed to suck the air from around them. Casavettes was one of them. Without intending to, she turned to look at him. He stared at her, memorising every line and contour of her face with such an intense, cold hatred that she gasped involuntarily.

Casavettes wasn't a one-man-band; as the Superintendent in charge of Operation Snowman said, he was the foundation of a whole rotten dynasty. He had family who not only cared about him, they relied on him to keep their business running smoothly. And they had enough hired muscle to make things happen.

But what would Casavettes gain from kidnapping her? Delaying the trial? To what end – they would soon find a replacement for her. *Face, it, Clara, he's already intimidated witnesses.* With the trial delayed, he could lean on them again. Just knowing that she had disappeared might be enough to silence some of them. And if she stayed disappeared . . . *After all, Casavettes makes people disappear all the time.*

Her breathing came fast and hard, her heart beat thickly in her throat, until, dizzy, she dropped her head between her knees. Clara was almost grateful to make the discovery that terror, if it continues long enough, has a numbing effect. She waited for her

47

breathing to return to normal, felt each wave of fear a little less overwhelming than the last, until finally, she was ready to go on, to try out another theory.

Ransom demand. If it's a ransom they want, Hugo will pay it and you'll go home. It sounded so simple, until she remembered how much Hugo had sunk into his business in the last year. Buying out his partner had taken every last penny of their savings. He was depending heavily on landing the Melker contract. 'He'll get it,' she told herself. 'Hugo will find the money somehow.'

Clara jumped up as, behind her, the door rattled and a key was turned in the lock. She hadn't heard him approach. She moved away from the steps, facing her captor blindly. She felt a draught of warmer air as the door opened; a footfall, then silence.

Her chest rose and fell, rose and fell. She knew how frightened, how vulnerable she must look to him, knew also that she must try to establish some degree of control, however small. 'What do you want?' She wanted to sound reasonable, even curious, but she heard the panic in her voice, knowing that he would, too.

'I see you've made yourself comfortable.'

'Comfortable? You bastard! Untie me.'

He didn't answer. Her vulnerability made her defensive and her defensiveness made her angry. 'Did you *hear* me? Are you *deaf* as well as stupid? What the hell were you thinking? Don't you know they'll be looking for you?'

'I know that.' He seemed unmoved by her impotent rage. 'But who are they going to look *for*? You don't know me. How are "they" supposed to know?'

The van! They'll look for the van. Clara felt a spurt of triumph. Her mind raced. If he stole it the police would know what to look for: the registration, colour, make. And it would lead them to her.

And what if he bought it cash in hand, no questions asked?

'Getting you here was just the start.'

She turned her head, startled by his voice — it was closer, more threatening. In the silence that followed, she sensed him willing her to follow his line of thought. It took her down dangerous and dark alleyways. He wanted her to think of sex — no — he wanted her to think *rape*.

She took a couple of steps towards him. 'Untie me.'

He was silent.

She kicked the rough wood of the staircase. It shuddered. 'Untie me.'

'Why?'

She hadn't expected this. 'Why? Do you need a reason why?'

'It's how you earn your living, after all. You should be able to come up with a convincing argument.'

She wasn't going to play this game for his amusement. 'Go to hell.'

'Oh, I've been there. Didn't like it. But then I didn't have company . . .'

Was he crazy? Some incipient schizophrenic she had defended — or prosecuted — in the past? What was he implying? *Maybe you'd like to come with me, this time?*

'Untie me,' she repeated. 'Please.'

A pause. 'No.'

A strong voice. A man's, rather than a boy's. But how old? It was difficult to tell. Accented. Cheshire, she thought, but she lacked Hugo's talent for mimicry and could never discriminate between the Chester and the Crewe accent, between Northwich and Frodsham.

'I'm cold,' she said.

'Are you?'

Mocking? Or was he simply uninterested in her physical comfort? She couldn't discern his meaning from his tone. *You're handling this badly*, she told herself. *Establish contact, make him talk.* 'My name is Clara P——'

'Oh, I *know* who you are.'

Clara took a step back, shocked by the force of feeling; there

49

was no mistaking the hatred in his voice. His first genuine response to her and it crackled with danger. She steadied herself, then said as evenly as she could, 'If you know who I am, then you'll know that by now a major investigation will have been launched.'

'You said that before. You see, I'm not deaf . . . Not stupid, either. Maybe not clever by your standards, but definitely not stupid. I know "they're" out looking for me – a woman like you warrants a major investigation,' he said.

There was, she thought, an edge of accusation in his tone and she hesitated, unsure how to proceed.

'They've pulled out all the stops. Surveillance. A twenty-four-hour guard.'

Her heart seemed to stop for a beat. Surveillance. Of Hugo and Pippa? Was he watching her house?

'Stay away from my family,' she warned, her voice harsh, desperate.

'Family,' he echoed. 'When it comes down to it, they're more dear than life itself.'

'My family has nothing to do with this,' she said, carefully.

He laughed, a mirthless chuckle that bounced off the walls and fell dead in the damp air. Then he was next to her, his breath on her cheek, that stale smell of cigarettes and damp on his clothing. He took her by the shoulders and spoke in her ear. 'It's *all* about family,' he said.

Oh, dear God! Casavettes! Casavettes has set this up! The man released her and she stumbled backwards.

Stay calm, Clara. Take it slow and easy. She took a few moments. Tried to sound reasonable, assured.

'I can help you.' She turned her head. Was he still there? 'I – I understand the judicial system.' What was she doing, offering advice to a man like Casavettes on how to subvert the system? *I don't care*, she thought. She would do whatever it took to keep him away from Pippa and Hugo.

'My family has already been tried and sentenced.'

Her breath caught. He *was* still there. And he was listening. Of course he was right: the evidence against Casavettes was irrefutable.

'But with my intervention . . .' She finished the thought aloud.

'And they'll believe you when you vouch for my good character.'

He continued up the steps. He was leaving. He was leaving and she still didn't know—

'Pippa,' she said, knowing it was the wrong thing to say, but unable to stop herself. 'My daughter. Was she—'

'*Hurt?*' he finished. She could tell he was smiling, imitating the high, frightened pitch of her voice. She heard the door creak slightly as he began to close it.

She called out again. 'Is she—'

'*All right?*' He shut the door and turned the key in the lock.

Beyond the door, he leaned against the wall and gasped. His hair and face were damp with sweat. He hadn't expected rage. Tears, yes. Pleading – but not this. *Are you deaf as well as stupid?* The violence of her response had taken him by surprise. He paced the bare boards of the hallway. She was supposed to tremble. She was *supposed* to beg. Instead she had threatened him – impotent, empty threats, it was true – but blindfold and bound *she* had threatened *him*. *Stay away from my family.*

He strode back to the cellar door. He would *make* her afraid. He stared down at her and she turned once more to him. Her face upturned, her head on one side. For several minutes he struggled with the urge to hurt her, to make her feel in a real tangible way just how much power he had over her. His emotions as he watched her were complex. He was pleased even to have got this far. Excited? Yes – why not? He had sought her out, trapped her, subdued her, got her here without being detected.

The rest, he could wait for. After all, there were more ways than one to skin a cat – different kinds of terror: the terror of being dragged off the street by a total stranger and bundled into a van. The terror of thinking you're dying as you fight for breath. The terror of waking alone, bound and blind in a cold, dark place. The terror of not knowing if your daughter was safe . . . He could make her cower without laying a finger on her, given time. Hadn't he already? Oh, yes, there were more ways than one to strike fear into the heart of a woman — he knew that well enough.

Chapter Nine

Jericho Chambers was housed in a late Georgian building in a quiet cobbled square near the Crown Court. DC Rayner had managed to dodge the showers that blew in squally succession from the Welsh hills and pressed the intercom buzzer with a feeling of good omen. Parking had been easy, just a flash of her warrant card and she was waved through the barrier into the walled courtyard at the rear of the building. She noted automatically that the doors on the fire escapes all had swipe-card entry and the car park was CCTV monitored; the front door, too, had a small camera trained on the doorstep. The door clicked open without her having to show her ID a second time. The wind was whipping up and she hurried inside. A second door gave onto a spacious circular atrium below a glass-panelled cupola; the architect appointed to refurbish the building had been inspired by the inner and outer circle of the old Crown Courts: the waiting area formed the inner circle and a series of glass block and solid ash partitions screened the outer circle which housed the chambers' admin offices.

The reception desk, a wide sweep of curved blond wood, fronted the main office, an open-plan area, which was humming with ordered activity when she arrived. The senior partner was still in court and since nobody else was willing to risk talking to her without his say-so, she was invited to help herself to coffee while she waited. She killed a few minutes of time choosing between the various combinations of caffeinated, decaff, espresso and mocha available, then positioned herself on a blood-red leather sofa adjacent to the reception desk, hoping to pick up the odd piece of gossip.

The receptionist also worked the telephone and two of the incoming calls were for Clara Pascal. These were fielded with the bland statement that Ms Pascal was 'not available', but the receptionist was helpful in suggesting alternatives.

Directly opposite, through an opening in the glass block wall, was a series of smaller offices and, leaning to one side, Rayner caught a glimpse of a kitchen work-surface and a sink. It was to this room that the office staff started drifting at around one o'clock. Most used the cover of the curved partition so all she heard were disembodied voices, more relaxed now, talking about plans for the weekend, laughing, teasing each other, mild flirtations between the men and women sharing the cramped kitchen space. The clink of coffee cups accompanied the deepening rumble of a kettle approaching boiling point.

A movement at the periphery of her vision made Rayner turn to her right. A small, dark woman was hovering just outside the low gate into the main office area. She started and blushed as Rayner looked at her. For a moment, it seemed she would speak, then, frowning, she hurried past, her head down and turned slightly away from her.

She disappeared into the little kitchen and someone greeted her with 'Coffee?' Rayner heard a murmured reply, the voice surprisingly deep and husky.

'So what's going on with Ms Pascal, then?' This was quite distinct, then a flurry of whispers and one of the men actually popped his head around the kitchen entrance to get a look at Rayner. She stared gravely at him and he jerked back inside as though someone had tugged him hard. After that, the conversation stopped entirely and they trooped out in silence with their hot drinks and packed lunches to another room, out of her line of sight and – more frustratingly – well out of earshot.

Julian Warrington arrived five minutes later. He paused in the foyer to ruffle some hailstones from his hair, then made his entrance.

He glanced at her from the corner of his eye as he walked past, but didn't acknowledge her. Rayner was fairly sure that Chambers had warned him of her presence, because she had heard the receptionist mention her name in a call, but she allowed him his little charade.

He greeted the clerk to the Chambers with a bluff pronouncement on 'Lady justices who *will* dither over empanelling jurors who might have a little difficulty arranging child care.'

The clerk sympathised.

'I can't see us getting to jury selection before three this afternoon at this rate.'

Another consolatory murmur.

'Any messages?'

The clerk raised his voice and enunciated clearly, performing his role with dutiful assiduousness. 'Nothing urgent, Mr Warrington, but there is a lady detective here – a Miss Rayner. She would like a word about Ms Pascal.'

Rayner clenched her teeth at the label of 'lady detective' and wondered what it had taken Clara Pascal to get her male colleagues to call her 'Ms'. She crossed to the bin and disposed of her coffee cup, then turned and smiled across the desk at the barrister.

'Mr Warrington?'

It took him a moment to arrange his features into what he thought conveyed the dual sentiments of welcome and concern. 'Miss Rayner.' He reached across the reception desk and enclosed her bony hand in his meaty grip.

'I'd like to talk to you about Ms Pascal's workload, sir.' She felt Warrington stiffen slightly, then he let her hand drop. She lowered her voice. 'We're trying to establish possible motives for her abduction.'

He inclined his head courteously, but made no comment. 'Could we go somewhere more private, sir?' Rayner asked, impatient, but for the moment remaining civil.

His eyebrows shot up and he gazed at the empty lobby. 'There's only ourselves and my staff,' he said, adding smoothly, for the benefit of the clerk, 'In whose discretion I have complete confidence.'

Oily bastard! DCI McAteer had warned her of the need for diplomacy and in retrospect she would regret not having taken the time to flatter him. She tried to smile, but her face felt stiff and unwilling to comply.

'The Casavettes prosecution—'

'Ah, yes,' he interrupted. 'I expected you to make that assumption. But Mr Casavettes is on remand.'

'We are aware of that,' Rayner replied. 'But his family is very much at large.'

'The Mafia connection.' Warrington tapped the side of his nose with mock solemnity.

Rayner chose to ignore his drollery. 'Did she seem anxious about the case?'

He smiled apologetically. 'I don't see that much of my colleagues on a day-to-day basis, Miss Rayner. I travel the country, from court to court, as do all the members of Chambers.'

'Well, perhaps you would have heard if Ms Pascal had received any threats?'

He raised his eyebrows. 'Threats? Miss Rayner, this is not Italy.' His tone was amused, gently reproaching.

'No, sir. But Ms Pascal *is* missing. And she *was* forcibly taken.'

He considered this for a moment, then nodded, accepting the point. 'And it *will* delay the trial. But another senior barrister is at this moment preparing to take over the prosecution, should Ms Pascal be . . . further detained.'

He made it sound like she'd overrun on a dental appointment. Rayner opened her mouth, closed it, took a breath and began again. 'Perhaps you'll allow me to speak to her clerk,' she suggested, keeping the lid on her anger. But Warrington had seen it flare before she clamped down on it.

'My point is,' he said smoothly, 'There would be nothing to be gained in Mr Casavettes abducting or conspiring to abduct Prosecuting Counsel, since it will cause no more than a minor delay in the trial.'

'I see,' she said, allowing him a small victory in the hope of getting him to agree to her earlier request. She couldn't see any mileage in arguing with him about the advantages to Casavettes of a delay and the silencing effect Clara's disappearance would have on witnesses for the prosecution.

'I'll tell you what,' he said, brightening considerably. 'Why don't you have a word with the superintendent who ran Operation Snowman – he's been in meeting after meeting with Ms Pascal over the past few weeks. I'm sure he could tell you more than I.'

He swept his arm in the direction of the door, gallantly dismissing her. Rayner refused to be rushed. 'We are looking into that, sir.' It went against the grain, but she tried a sheepish grin. 'Truth is, we're fishing about, hoping we'll turn up something useful, so if her clerk is available—'

'There are issues of client confidentiality to consider,' he interrupted, seeming rattled for the first time.

'And what about the issue of life or death for your colleague?' It was out before she could stop herself. She caught a brief look of outrage, then his face closed. She had overstepped the mark by a long way.

'We owe a duty to our clients.'

Rayner matched his clipped formality. 'I appreciate that, sir. But we have to establish possible motives as a matter of urgency.'

He moved swiftly to the door. 'Let me know when you have,' he said. 'If you can demonstrate a link with one of Ms Pascal's clients, we will be more than happy to assist – given the proper paperwork, of course.'

He opened the door and as she left, gave a curiously formal bow.

Proper paperwork! Meaning the bastard expected a warrant before he would release any records. She stormed back to her car in a fury. He knew damned well they wouldn't get a warrant without proving a link between Clara's disappearance and one of her clients. And how the *hell* were they supposed to do that when they didn't even know who her clients were?

It fell to DS Barton to talk to Mr Pascal about his wife's caseload. He drove into Grosvenor Avenue as the last few stones of a ferocious hailstorm pinged off the roof of his car. Barton was grateful: he cared about such things far more since his hair loss.

While he locked the car, an elderly woman with a rain hood tied securely over her good felt hat appeared from one of the houses opposite and remonstrated with the surveillance team.

'. . . because if you are,' she told him, 'you are required to give notice.'

'If we need to cut off your water, you'll get twenty-four hours' notice, love,' the officer replied.

'In writing.'

'Card through the door,' he assured her.

Barton walked to the gate. She sniffed, adding as a parting shot that she did not like to be referred to as 'love'.

Hugo answered the door before Barton had time to lift his finger to the bell-push.

He was wearing the same suit and tie he'd had on that morning, but the tie was loosened and he had popped the top button of his shirt. His hair looked tousled, as if he had been constantly pushing his fingers through it. 'Any news?' he demanded.

'Not yet.'

Hugo's shoulders slumped.

'Can I come in, sir?'

'What? Oh, yes.' Hugo stepped aside and glanced quickly up and down the street before closing the door and leaning against it as if to hold back the horror outside.

'Hugo?' A woman came into the hallway. She was mid- to late-thirties, by Barton's estimation. Her hair was cut into a shoulder-length bob. She finished wiping her hands on a towel and then rolled down the sleeves of her blouse.

'Police,' Hugo said in explanation.

Barton introduced himself.

'I'm Trish Markham,' she said, glancing quickly at Hugo.

The child-minder. Barton acknowledged her greeting with a nod. 'I need to ask you some questions, sir,' he said to Hugo.

Hugo didn't respond and Trish took the situation in hand. 'Why don't you two go through to the sitting-room and I'll keep an eye on Pippa.'

Hugo hesitated.

'I'll take any phone calls,' she urged. 'If it's important, I'll fetch you, I promise.' she smiled at Barton. 'Coffee, Sergeant? Tea?'

'No, thanks.'

Hugo remained at the front door, his hands pressed flat against it in that defensive posture. Trish went to him and touched his shoulder. She was average height, but she had to stretch to make the contact. He shuddered, then eased himself away from the door, as if fearful it would be battered down without his protective presence.

'How's Pippa?' Barton asked. 'I mean after the interview — was she all right?'

Hugo shut the sitting room door. 'Pippa?' he repeated as if he had never heard the name before. 'Oh, yes. Sarah was . . . was very good with her. She—' He seemed to lose his train of thought, opening the door again and leaving it slightly ajar.

'You had some questions,' he said, seating himself on one of the pale linen-covered sofas, inviting Barton to do the same.

As Barton began an explanation of the purpose of his visit, the phone rang and Hugo jumped. He reached the phone extension in two strides and picked up, listening in.

Trish called through from the hall: 'It's all right, Hugo. One of Pippa's friends.'

'It hasn't stopped ringing since we got back,' he said, replacing the receiver and staring at the phone with a mixture of horror and revulsion. 'Pippa's friends, Clara's Chambers – I didn't think to tell them, but apparently your people had already been in touch . . .'

'Chief Inspector McAteer thought it wise, sir, with the trial and so on . . .'

Hugo wasn't listening. He went again to the door, only returning to his seat when he was satisfied that Pippa had rung off.

Barton fell silent and he glanced over, abashed. 'I'm sorry,' he said. 'You were saying something about the trial.' Barton began to answer and immediately Hugo interrupted. 'That bloody trial! She said it could do her career a lot of good – Christ! Some good it's done her!'

'You didn't want her to take the case?'

Hugo frowned at his hands, balled into fists in his lap.

'What makes you think your wife's disappearance is connected with the trial?'

Hugo made a small movement, a slight twitch of the shoulders. If he knew something about Casavetttes' involvement, he wasn't saying.

'Sir.' Barton spoke firmly, willing Hugo to look at him. When, finally, he did, Barton said, 'We don't know who has taken your wife. We're trying to find out. But we have no proof that Casavettes—'

'What proof do you need?' he burst out.

'We are investigating a possible connection, but there may be

60

other people — someone with a grudge against your wife. If we fix on just one thing, we might be ignoring important lines of enquiry.'

Hugo gave a cautious acknowledgement of the truth of what Barton said.

'She may have mentioned something,' Barton went on. 'Someone who frightened her or made her uneasy.'

Hugo laughed harshly. 'She deals with scum I would cross the street to avoid. She sits opposite them and calmly works out a convincing defence for them.'

'You don't approve of your wife's work?'

Hugo seemed perplexed by the question. 'Clara doesn't require my approval. She defends with as much rigour and passion as she prosecutes. She leaves it to the jury to decide innocence or guilt. As if they have the wisdom of Solomon conferred on them when they're sworn in.'

'You're saying she's naive?'

'No. But, like Justice, she can be blind.'

'I'm afraid I don't get it, sir.'

He sighed. 'She can see when the evidence is stacked up against her client, but she's happy to leave the decision as to innocence or guilt to the jury.'

'That's the law, sir,' Barton said, gently. He couldn't make any sense out of what Pascal was saying. On the one hand he seemed desperately worried about his wife and on the other, he seemed to blame her for what had happened. 'Can you think of any recent cases where the decision went against the evidence?' he asked.

Hugo ran one hand tiredly over his face. 'We didn't discuss it that often. We have other things to do — our lives to get on with.'

Barton was not convinced: this had the feel of a deep and well-aired difference between Pascal and his wife. 'All right,' he said, deciding on a different tack. 'These people you would cross the road to avoid. Was there anyone in particular?'

'No . . .' Barton thought for a moment that he was going to drift off again and he shifted impatiently. 'Well,' Hugo muttered, half to himself. 'There was that man . . .' he looked at Barton. 'A rapist. Clara defended him, but even she was pleased when he was convicted.'

'Do you have a name?'

He shook his head. Simultaneously, the phone rang. This time Trish got to it well before him. 'For Pippa,' she shouted through.

Hugo frowned. 'He made her uneasy. She even asked to be taken off the case, but there was no one else – at least no one he would have. Yes,' he mused. 'He frightened her.'

'Do you remember *when* it was?'

Hugo stared fretfully at the door. 'What?'

'The trial,' Barton repeated. 'When was it?'

Hugo opened the door and called, 'Pippa, get off the phone, darling.'

'Sir?'

He turned back. 'When? Recent. Fairly recent.' He broke off. 'Pippa!'

'*Okay*, Daddy!'

His brow furrowed with concentration. 'November – no, slightly earlier. October, maybe. Last year.'

Barton was about to ask where the trial took place, but Hugo was in the hall. Through the open door, Barton saw him snatch the phone from the girl and bang it back on the hook.

'For God's sake, Pippa! Stay off the bloody phone!'

Pippa looked shocked. As her father towered over her she seemed almost to shrink. She began to tremble and he put out his hand in tentative apology.

'No!' she screamed. 'Don't you touch me! I hate you!' She fled upstairs, crying and Hugo made as if to follow, but Trish stopped him.

'Let me,' she said.

On the journey back to base, Barton reflected how easily Hugo had acquiesced, how much in charge Trish seemed to be in his home.

Chapter Ten

He returned to watch her, but refused to reply to her questions. Stubbornly mute, he stood at the top of the wooden steps in silence. She strained her ears for some sound – a slight scuff of his shoe on the boards as he shifted his weight, a sigh, even for the sound of his breathing – but he was silent as a cat and infinitely more cruel.

If she tried to walk about, he ordered her to stay still. Once, exhausted by the constant tension, she drifted off, waking moments later with the smell of him in her nostrils, his breath on her face. She gave a cry of disgust and pushed back with her feet, catching the base of her spine against the metal loop jutting from the wall.

'Sleeping?' he said. 'Did I say you could sleep?'

His fingers dug into her shoulders. Clara struggled, but he held her fast. She turned her head away, but she could still feel his breath on her neck. A sharp stab of discomfort reminded her that she needed to urinate. 'Leave me alone,' she groaned.

'And what did you do to deserve to be left alone?'

Suddenly angry, she yelled at him. 'Why are you *doing* this?'

'Why not?' He spoke close to her ear, his smell like an aura around him. It wasn't sweat or dirt, but a pervading whiff of decay. 'You'll have to do better than this.'

'Better than *what?*'

'Where are the arguments – the blistering counter-attacks we've come to expect from Chester's favourite female counsel?'

What was he driving at? Frustrated, Clara realised just how much she relied on non-verbal signals in her judgements: of people, of situations. A gesture, a facial expression told more than words ever could, with their shades of meaning, their capacity to lull and persuade, to fabricate and falsify. It was harder for her clients to misrepresent the tiny gestures, the subtle body language that told the truth while they lied in earnest.

She felt a rush of air and a slight ripple of sound, a whisper of paper as he ran his finger over the cuttings tacked to the walls. 'We're waiting to hear some of that legendary wit, the adversarial powers of Defence Counsel Ms Pascal.'

We, she thought. *We, the Casavettes family? But he said Defence Counsel.* Was it a case she had lost?

Another sharp reminder of her full bladder sliced into her groin and she closed her eyes behind the patches. She didn't want to ask him, but she had learned, even in this short time, that he wouldn't anticipate her needs – that he made a policy of forcing her to ask for the smallest thing.

She chewed her lower lip. He had moved further away from her and the smells of tobacco and mildewed clothing faded somewhat. He didn't prompt her, but she could sense he was waiting. Would he grant her request – or make her wait until she could no loner ignore that tightening, tearing pain – would asking simply give him something else to humiliate her with?

To hell with it! She took a breath. 'I need the lavatory.' She lifted her chin defiantly. No reply. 'Did you hear me?'

'You told me you need the *lavatory*.' He mimicked her accent.

The pain, now she had spoken, was becoming more insistent. A sudden movement – a draught and a rustle of paper – made her flinch, then he was walking up the steps. He was leaving.

'Please!' she called after him, but he was gone and she was talking to an empty room. 'Bastard,' she muttered to herself. For the moment, she couldn't contemplate relieving her discomfort, but she knew it was only a matter of time.

She heard a metallic note, gentle as a wind-chime, then his hands were on her. She struggled, repulsed by his proximity, by the odour of decay that surrounded him.

'Keep still!' he warned.

Clara heard a tearing sound, then her hands were free. She fell forward, carried by her own momentum. Her chest and shoulders felt torn and bruised and she cried out, then hugged herself, massaging the strained pectoral muscles. Despite the pain, she experienced a moment's soaring optimism, even excitement: he was willing to give her some dignity.

Another soft musical *chink!* of metal on metal and she turned her head, seeking out the source of the sound. He grabbed her right ankle. She kicked with her left. He slapped her, open-handed, and her head cracked against the wall. He snaked the chain tight around her ankle and she heard the click of a padlock. A second click and she knew the chain had been secured to the wall. She yanked at it; it sang against the metal stay, but held fast.

'No!' she screamed, her heart racing with fury. Mind and soul she rebelled against the injustice of what he was doing to her. She felt sick with the pain in her groin and the blow to her head, but more than anything she was sickened by the humiliation. She leapt to her feet, swinging wildly and connected with flesh. He slapped her away, then pinned her arms behind her; she cried out at the renewed strain on the muscles of her shoulders and upper arms. The unshaved stubble of his chin scratched her face.

'Don't make me hurt you.' His voice was ugly with hate. 'I want to – believe me, I want to. And if I start, I might not be able to stop.'

These words froze her. She gave up struggling and he let her go. Clara swayed for a moment, sensing a distance between them. He stood a little way back, just out of reach, panting slightly.

'Take this thing off me!' She sounded tearful, but she couldn't help it. 'I know you're there, you coward!' Still no reply, only the sound of his laboured breathing. 'All right.' She began tugging at the edges of one eye-patch.

'You see my face, I'll have to kill you.'

He sounded calm, but Clara knew with chilling certainty that he meant what he said. Carefully, so that he wouldn't mis-interpret the action, she lowered her hands. When she spoke, her voice was not as steady as she would have liked.

'Take — the chain — off.'

'I thought you said you needed the *lavatory*,' he said. 'Even important lady barristers have to go to the toilet. Now, how do you think you'd do that with your hands tied? Of course, I could help—' He took a step closer and she crouched against the wall.

'I'm not an animal!' she blurted out.

She felt his scrutiny of her. What did he see? What was he looking for? A victim? She tugged at her skirt, pulling it lower over her thighs.

'You think you're better than this, do you? Think you're better than me — than *my kind*?'

'I know it.'

'Because I dragged you off the street and tied you up and locked you in this cold damp hole in the ground.' Something in his voice stilled her. 'And you would never wish that on another woman.'

She turned in the direction of his voice. 'Of course not.' Her eyes, open behind the patches, were hot.

'You wouldn't swap places with little Pippa, for example.'

Clara's eyes flew wide and she felt a squeezing pressure around her heart. 'I told you — this has nothing to do with my family.'

'I asked you a question.'

'Leave her alone.'

'Or?'

There was no 'or'; they both knew it — Clara was in no position to make threats.

'Leave her alone,' she repeated. 'Please.' The threat to Pippa made the pain and the fear for her own safety unbearable. She began to weep.

'To your left,' he said. 'A bucket.'

She reached out. A laundry bucket, with a lid. She wiped her nose with the heel of her palm. 'How will I know you've gone?'

'You won't.'

She pushed the bucket away. 'Then I don't need this.'

'You know you do.'

'All right, I do. But I won't use it. Not while you're here. I'd rather rupture!' And for that moment at least, she meant it.

'I'd give it five, maybe ten minutes at the outside.'

She didn't answer and she sensed a shift in his attitude in the silence that followed. The stand-off lasted a few minutes.

'I'll close the door,' he said, at last. 'Will that do?'

For a little longer after the door clanged to, she waited, her bladder screaming for relief. There was no sound, no shuffle or sigh, not even a creak from the wooden steps.

He removed the bucket without comment, but refused her request to be allowed to wash her hands. He returned soon after, standing at the top of the steps, and Clara turned her face blindly in that direction, tilting her head to catch any tiny sound. Listening to him watching.

Clara Pascal was used to people listening to her. When she spoke, people paid attention. Eager to please her, they would try to anticipate her needs. He would train her to think differently — she would learn to anticipate *his* needs, *his* moods, and to flinch at an angry word from him.

She thinks she can manipulate me. She thinks she can persuade me. It was almost pitiful to watch. He wondered idly how long it would take. He shifted his weight from his right hip to his left and she lifted her head, tilting and rolling it to try to catch the sound of his breathing. He lit another cigarette. He saw her nostrils flare as the scent of tobacco reached her.

'This is what it's like, Clara. To be powerless, friendless. Alone. I bet you've never been truly alone in your life – with your circle of influential friends, your family connections.'

She opened her mouth to speak.

'Shut up.'

That was enough. She fell silent. He nodded to himself, taking a deep, satisfied drag on his cigarette. She was already adjusting to her new situation. Their eagerness to learn was both the strength and the weakness of intelligent women. He exhaled, watching his breath condense and disappear more quickly than the plume of blueish smoke from his cigarette. It wouldn't take long: the cold, the privations he subjected her to, and the lack of food, would quickly eradicate the illusion of authority. Clara Pascal would soon be just another frightened woman.

Chapter Eleven

'Target is on the move.' Those few words from the surveillance team outside Hugo Pascal's house caused a flurry of activity. The three cars on mobile surveillance scrambled for action. There were three routes he might take to the main road out of the estate and each was covered. The cars had the favoured male/female combination and the drivers were ready to slip into pursuit at an unobtrusive distance.

'He's heading towards Queen's Park Road.'

'That makes us the lead car,' Fletcher said. He had struck gold with this duty: the action Tyrell had given him took less than an hour to complete and he had been assigned with Cath Young – her of the long legs and wide blue eyes – to tail Pascal if he decided to go out. He had spent the last two hours explaining the difference between a good investigative officer and a training school clone, incapable of thought. Here was an opportunity to show her how an experienced professional worked.

He dumped the dregs of his coffee out of the window and shoved the cup at Young. 'Hi-Ho Silver,' he murmured, smiling to himself as he fired up the engine, adrenaline banishing all the tiredness and frustrations that had accumulated since morning.

Pascal passed them in his BMW, but Fletcher held back for a few seconds before pulling out. 'Fletch with eyeball target,' he said, then as an aside, 'Got a nickname, have you?'

She shook her head.

'Everyone's got a nickname, love.' He pulled in to the side of the road as Pascal gave way at the junction. He flipped her a quick glance. She was blushing. 'If you don't like the one you've got, you'd better make something up, quick or you'll be stuck with a handle somebody thinks up for you.' He pressed the 'speak' button on the hands-free radio. 'Turning right, right, onto Handbridge.' There was a tailback of ten or fifteen cars waiting for the lights to change and allow them single-file over the narrow bridge. He dropped back to allow two cars between his and Pascal's and turned to face Young.

'Shirley,' he said.

'What?'

'As in Temple.'

'Who's she?'

'You've never heard of—?' He shrugged. No point in a wind-up if it meant nothing to the intended target. 'What about "Baby", then?'

'Baby.'

'Young — Baby. Or Babe.'

'Very original,' she said.

'Just a thought.' He'd definitely got a reaction on that one. 'Lights.'

They edged forward, nose-to-tail.

The signal changed to amber. 'What if he goes through?'

'Don't panic, Babe . . . You'll just have to leg it after him.' He glanced at her worried face. 'Traffic's only moving at walking pace anyroad.'

The BMW stopped and he turned to grin at her. 'You're off the hook, this time,' he said.

On the next cycle, Young and Fletcher squeezed through after Pascal.

'The others aren't going to make it,' Young said, seeing the lights turn amber again as they reached the bridge.

'I'll give them directions,' Fletcher said. 'They'll catch up.'

'Straight on into Lower Bridge Street,' he informed the team, 'at ten – that's one zero – miles per hour.' He kept one car between himself and Pascal. When the other cars caught up with him, he would peel off and let one of them take the lead for a bit. Pascal slowed and indicated right. 'Turning right, right, into Pepper Street.'

The BMW passed Habitat and squeezed into the turn right lane. 'He looks like he's going into Pepper Street car park,' Fletcher told the team. The central reservation prevented their cutting across directly into the entrance; instead, they followed Pascal, past the car park exit, driving three sides of the block, ending up by the old almshouses with no covering car between them and the BMW.

'He's bound to clock us,' Young said anxiously.

'Relax,' Fletcher said. 'Smile.' He caught the look on her face and said with a grin, 'Purely in a professional capacity, sweetheart. Why d'you think they put a man and a woman in the car? Look like you're chatting.'

Young thought about it for a moment, then swivelled in her seat and flashed him a smile that fair took his breath away. He informed the other members of the team of their location, then, returning Young's smile, he followed Pascal's BMW back onto the main road and into the car park.

'Follow him on foot,' he told Young, as they spiralled upwards passed ranks of solidly parked cars. 'If he takes the lift, use the stairs. I'll stay in the car and wait to see if he doubles back.'

He parked one level up and Young watched to see where Pascal headed before leaving the car. She ran down the stairs two at a time, leaping the last set of five and reaching the bottom just as Pascal emerged from the lift. She turned towards the city centre, while Pascal went to the kerb and waited to cross. Traffic was heavy on Pepper Street and Young considered stopping to fiddle with her shoe to avoid losing him, but then she saw one of the surveillance cars twenty yards up the road, facing in Pascal's

71

direction and carried on walking, though she slowed her pace. Seconds later she was past him and there was no way she could turn and check to see where he went without drawing attention to herself. She would have to rely on the officers in the car ahead maintaining eyeball with him. It was beginning to rain in spattering bursts and she hunched her shoulders against a biting wind.

'Where the hell are you, Babe?' Her tiny earpiece produced a sharp and dizzyingly clear signal; she flinched.

A second voice chimed in. 'Nev has eyeball.' One of the officers in the car parked across the street. 'He's reached the central reservation. Having difficulty crossing.'

A minute later, Pascal had entered an office building across from Habitat. Young doubled back and checked out the plaque inside the plate glass front door. 'It's his office,' she said, turning away from the building and talking into the microphone pinned to her lapel. 'Number seventeen, Pepper Street.' She crossed over the road and stared at the reflection of the door opposite in Habitat's window for the next hour, wishing she had dressed for the weather, rather than to make an impression. Maybe if she hadn't worn a skirt Fletcher wouldn't have decided to call her 'Babe' and she knew for sure that if she had worn her waterproof instead of her leather jacket she would be a damn sight warmer and dryer.

When the hour was up, Fletcher told her to meet him outside the solicitors' offices, ten yards down from Pascal's building. Almost immediately, Pascal emerged and turned right towards the city centre, heading directly for the two officers.

' 'Scuse me,' Fletcher murmured. He grabbed Young around the waist and pulled her to him. 'Darling!' he exclaimed. 'You're drenched!' He planted a kiss on her lips. 'Really, you shouldn't have waited.'

By this time Pascal had passed them. Young shoved him off and wiped her mouth. Fletcher grinned. 'Welcome to the wacky world of surveillance, Babe,' he said.

'There was *no* need for that,' Young said angrily.

'You almost got spotted by the target,' he said. 'You almost blew your cover.'

'Piss off, Fletcher!' She turned towards the centre of town.

'Where d'you think you're going?' he demanded.

'Following Pascal,' Young said.

'Do me a favour!' Fletcher exclaimed. 'You look like a drowned rat. You'll only draw attention to yourself. Go and dry off in the car. I'll take care of this.'

The rain had abated and a patch of dazzling blue sky opened up overhead. Fletcher smiled to himself at the sight of Young making her way despondently towards the car park. He set off after Pascal, pressing the speak button taped to his wrist to make contact with the rest of the team. By the time they reached the corner of Pepper Street, two more officers were positioned in Bridge Street and Grosvenor Street.

Pascal turned right again, into the pedestrianised area of Bridge Street. The crowds were dense, so he kept close, but he crossed over, ready to turn away or even to duck into a shop, rather than be seen. Pascal hesitated at the Cross and Fletcher held back, then he took another right into Eastgate Street and stopped near the corner of the crooked road leading to St Werburgh's Cathedral.

'Fletch with eyeball target,' he said, keeping his voice low, continuing the stream of information he had been feeding the other members of the team. 'He's gone into the middle telephone box. That's the centre box.' He mounted the stone steps onto the raised wooden walkway of one of the rows and, using the shadows for cover, he watched over the black-and-white railings as Pascal took a slip of paper from his pocket and dialled a number. He left five minutes later without a backward glance.

The throngs of shoppers closed in around Pascal, but he wasn't hard to pinpoint, standing head and shoulders above them, moving purposefully towards Foregate.

A woman about to step inside the telephone box gave a cry of dismay as she was caught by the elbow. She subsided when the officer wordlessly showed her his warrant card. He went into the box and used his mobile to contact *BT*.

Fletcher elbowed his way through the crowd and barged down a narrow set of steps further along the row. Pascal was headed for the ornate archway which would take him out of the bounds of the city walls. Fletcher hurried after him, almost bumping into the target, who had slowed to negotiate a crowd gathered around a street performer, wobbling on a tall unicycle and juggling skittles.

Pascal walked on, beyond the pedestrianised area, to a bar with a plate-glass window and pillar-box red woodwork. On the other side of the road, Fletcher stopped in a bus shelter and waited. At first he though Pascal would go in to the bar, but he went instead to the door to the right of the window and pressed the doorbell.

'No go.' The DC's voice sang in his ear with such clarity, it seemed to be *inside* Fletcher's head. '*BT* can't trace the call without prior notification.'

'What're you going to do, mate?' Fletcher demanded with heavy sarcasm. 'Seal the bloody phone box and call in a SOCO team to dust for prints? We know who dialled out—'

'Yeah, Fletch,' he replied, angrily. 'And if I hit the "LNR" button, someone's gonna pick up and they're gonna want to know who the hell I am.'

Fletcher swore under his breath. 'So hang up before it connects. You can memorise a few numbers, can't you? We haven't got time to prat about, mate!'

The officer pressed the button, grumbling quietly to himself. He hung up before the Last Number Redial completed the connection, memorising the number from the liquid crystal display, noted it, then dialled the operator. Minutes later they had a name; within ten minutes, an address.

*　　*　　*

74

McAteer invited Lawson to sit. He had managed to scrounge a couple of leather easy chairs; they were scuffed, but better quality than the steel-framed chairs in Lawson's office and such emblems of status were important to the Chief Inspector. They sat sipping coffee and reading through copies of returned actions.

'What do you make of Rayner?' McAteer asked. Her action return had criticized Mr Warrington's lack of co-operation.

'She's direct,' Lawson said, 'But I think she'd know when to go gently.'

'We need Warrington's co-operation, Steve. The husband's worse than useless and we need to know just how much of a threat this rapist is – right now, we don't even know if he's still banged up.'

'We could find him through court records,' Lawson suggested.

McAteer snorted. 'Which court? She's on the circuit: Liverpool, Chester, Rhyll – in fact the whole of North Wales – and tracing him via his defence lawyer could prove difficult, given that she's vanished without trace.'

Lawson considered the options. 'Give Rayner another crack at it. If she draws a blank, then we do it the hard way.'

McAteer nodded, 'Okay. Now what about this Markham woman?' He was skimming through Barton's action report.

'The child-minder . . .' Lawson sipped his coffee thoughtfully. It was seven-fifteen and he had lost count of the number of half-drunk cups he'd had during the day; his stomach told him it was far too many. 'She's been with the family for ever,' he mused. 'It's her job to take control of situations – particularly if they involve the child.'

'But . . .'

'But.' Lawson wasn't sure about her role within the family, any more than Barton was – or McAteer, for that matter. And it wouldn't be the first time a husband had got rid of his wife to make room for his lover. 'Move that one up to priority?'

McAteer thought about it for a moment. 'I'd like to know who I can trust in this, Steve.'

Lawson smiled, surprised by the mild distress in the Chief Inspector's tone. 'Yeah, wouldn't that simplify things?' he said.

Officers had been drifting back to base for the last twenty minutes; filing reports, chatting, grabbing a coffee from the machine that had been shipped in late in the afternoon.

The Incident Room was still incomplete and the heating was off, but the Admin Officer at HQ had allowed the electricians and joiners overtime and they would be working through to eleven p.m. to try and put things right.

After Pascal's walkabout, some of the reserve team who had been due to start in the morning had been drafted in early and team numbers were up from eight to fourteen. Several were refining and redrafting their reports from notes taken in the field.

Young had dried off, but looked bedraggled and cold in the outfit she had so carefully chosen that morning. Fletcher tutted. 'You do look a sight,' he said. 'Now me, I could have stayed in that bus shelter all afternoon, if need be. Perfect cover.'

Young looked so miserable that he relented a little. 'Cheer up, Babe. Even old hands like me come a cropper sometimes.' He glanced round, including a few others in his yarn-spinning. 'I was following a villain on a drugs case, once. He stops at a caff – I'm across the road, using the reflection in a shop window to keep an eye on things. Ten minutes later and I'm bored. So I actually look inside the shop and I've been staring at a window full of naked shop dummies!'

The others laughed obligingly.

'Surveillance has its perks, eh, Fletcher?' Rayner squeezed past the knot of men to a free chair.

Young was grateful. *But why can't you stick up for yourself? Why're you letting other people fight your battles for you?* She glared resentfully at Fletcher. *Next time.*

The superior officers came in and people quickly settled down: they were all keen to make a start, either to tell the others what their investigations had unearthed or, for the less successful, so they could go home and gather strength for another day of hard slog.

Rayner and Barton each gave a brief account of their afternoon's work. Rayner was still fuming at Warrington's obstructiveness.

'Should've flashed him a bit of leg,' Fletcher muttered.

She glared at him and he flipped her a quick, appraising glance, then stared intently at the whiteboard, already filling with details of the investigation. His mouth barely moved. 'On second thoughts . . .' he breathed.

McAteer addressed Rayner. 'I want that followed up.'

'I'll give it another go, Guv.'

Fletcher was on next. He summarised Pascal's trip to work, the telephone call and the meeting in the office above Ryan's bar in Foregate Street.

'Safe Hands Detective Agency,' he said. 'Divorce, adoption enquiries, forensic analysis – you name it, they do it.'

'And the phone call?' Lawson asked. He knew the answer, but this was for the rest of the team.

'Same address.'

'So which particular service was Mr Pascal inquiring about?'

'D'you want us to talk to the owner, Boss? Find out?'

Lawson shook his head. He and McAteer had discussed it before the briefing. 'But I'd welcome ideas.'

'If they do missing persons, he might've asked them to help find Ms Pascal.'

'Maybe he thinks someone in his office is on the fiddle.'

'If they're a dodgy set-up, the agency could be implicated in Clara's disappearance.' This was from Barton.

'It's happened in the past,' Lawson agreed. 'But with the new regs it's less likely. Let's do a background check on the firm, see if they've got any black marks on their record.'

McAteer nodded his approval. 'We've no right to stop Mr Pascal exploring every avenue in trying to find his wife.'

'But if it puts her at risk—' Fletcher put in.

'Then we'll intervene. But not before.' He moved on briskly: 'Child Protection have interviewed Pippa Pascal – the daughter,' adding for the benefit of the new team members, 'She witnessed the abduction. What have you got for us, DC Kormish?'

Sarah Kormish stood up. Lawson thought she looked nervous, but she was a veteran of such briefings and he knew her to be a thorough and experienced officer: if the child had come up with anything of interest, Sarah would have picked up on it.

'She was still pretty shaken, but she'd given a good description of the van,' Sarah began. 'White, probably a Transit-type. Old – a lot of rust on it. The windows were blacked out. It's probably in poor shape mechanically – she said the exhaust was smoky.'

'That concurs with the sightings we've had in so far,' Lawson said.

'Don't suppose she got a registration number?' Fletcher asked.

Sarah widened her eyes at him. 'She's nine years old, Fletch. She'd just seen her mum dragged off the street by a man in a mask. Anyway, she was side-on to the van.'

'What about the assailant?'

Sarah gave a description of the man, adding, 'She said he smelt funny.'

'Nothing more specific?' McAteer asked.

'Sorry, sir. She couldn't tell me any more than that.' The interview had lasted over an hour, with a fifteen-minute break half way. She had taken it very slowly, beginning with the events of the previous week, circling the event, spiralling gradually inwards to the attack on Pippa's mother.

She'd had to back off several times, talking on safer subjects, sensing that the child might break down. Through her earpiece, her colleague in the studio on the other side of the glass suggested questions, asking for clarification and, more than once, she heard Mr Pascal exclaim in distress.

'Had she noticed the van before?' someone asked.

'No. She didn't notice anything strange during the past week. But she did confirm that her mum was worried about something.' A smile touched the corner of her mouth as she remembered. 'Said her parents kept talking in code.'

Lawson looked around the room. They were all focused, all thinking, all trying to come up with questions, ideas, everyone – even Fletcher – hungry for a result. He felt a spurt of excitement. A major investigation depended on team synergy, and this team was beginning to mesh.

At nine o'clock he called in at the HOLMES room for one last update. A night shift of four had been organised to man the phones in the Incident Room and follow any leads that couldn't be done during the day, but the HOLMES team were finishing for the night.

'Mind if I take a look at the actions for tomorrow?' Lawson asked.

'Feel free.' DS Tyrell looked about all in. 'I've had copies run off for you and the DCI.' She handed him a stack of thirty or more computer print-outs. 'I hope you've got more bodies coming in, because house-to-house will generate another wagon-load.'

Lawson took the bundle and assured her that by morning they would have the staff to do the job. She locked up as they left and Lawson went down to the Incident Room to see if anything new had come in. The joiners hadn't yet returned and the room was deserted except for Barton who was sitting alone, bundled up in his overcoat against the intensifying cold. He pored over a set of reports, absently rubbing one hand over the stubble on his scalp.

'Didn't know you were on nights.'

Barton looked up, startled.

'Go home, Phil,' Lawson said. 'Put your lad to bed.'

Barton checked his watch. 'Too late for that.'

'Well, tuck him in then. Give him a goodnight kiss – give *Fran* a goodnight kiss.'

Barton laughed.

'There'll be plenty of times when late nights will be unavoidable,' Lawson said. 'This one's a sticker, I can feel it.'

Barton yawned and switched off his lamp. 'Know what you mean, Steve. Too many variables. Too many people with a reason to want her out of the way.'

'D'you include her husband in that?' Barton had seen more of Pascal than anyone else and Lawson was interested to hear his view. He hadn't been able to shake the unease he had felt that morning in Pascal's presence. Barton thought it over.

'He's in shock,' he said. 'You have to take that into consideration.'

'Okay. Taking that as read . . .'

Again, Barton's hand went again to his head, rasping the stubble. 'It's like he can't make up his mind if he admires her or despises her for what she does. He's really pissed off she took the Casavettes case. And he's convinced we should look no further than the Casavettes family.'

'Did he have anything to back that up?'

Barton raised an eyebrow, his mouth twisting into an ironic smile. 'He seemed to think that was our job.'

'He has a point,' Lawson agreed. 'We should have the chance to suss out Casavettes ourselves with a bit of luck: the boss is trying to set up a meeting. But we've got to get past Operation Snowman, first.'

Barton snorted. 'And there I was, thinking we were on the same side.'

Marie was curled up on the sofa when Lawson got home, a bottle of red wine on the coffee table beside her and two glasses, one empty. She had a sketch pad on her knee.

'Still working?' he asked, bending to kiss her. She tasted of berries and warm spices.

'Commission for a cleaning firm. They want an original image that will encapsulate the attributes of honesty, friendly service, thoroughness and old-fashioned values – all for next to nothing and by next week, *if you please.*'

Lawson flopped onto the sofa next to her and she straightened her legs, resting her feet on his thighs. He poured himself a glass and topped hers up. 'Pull something off the computer,' he suggested.

'I've trawled our database – we haven't got anything suitable.'

He took a gulp of wine. 'So charge them extra.'

She raised her eyebrows. 'Just like that.'

He sighed. 'Unrealistic – margins are tight and you can't afford to lose the commission.'

She gave him one of her shrewd looks. 'Bad day?' she asked.

'A real stinker. Abduction.'

'The lawyer?'

'Lawyer?' He sat up, jostling her arm and she spilt wine onto her sketch.

'*Shit*, Steve!' She jumped up, dripping wine onto the floor.

'How the hell do you know about that?'

Marie dabbed at her drawing with a wad of tissues. 'I watch the news,' she said angrily. '*Goddamnit!*'

'It's not so bad,' he said, handing her a couple more tissues.

She snatched them from him scowling. 'Not so bad!' she exclaimed. 'It's ruined!'

'Look, I'm sorry,' he said. 'But the media aren't supposed to know – Oh, hell!' He stood and strode to the door.

'*Now* where are you going?' she demanded.

He dipped his head apologetically. 'Got to phone my boss.'

'Who was it, Lawson?' McAteer demanded. 'Who leaked the story?'

Lawson switched his mobile from his right to his left ear and used his free hand to open the fridge door. The chances of finding something he could grab and eat on the run were slight: Marie believed in cooking meals properly or not at all. If he wanted snack food, he had to buy it himself.

'It's a big team, Boss — even without the extras you've drafted in for the morning. D'you want me to come back in?'

McAteer sighed. 'No. the Press Office have given them a statement. I've called a conference for tomorrow morning. I'll ask them for help — if we can get them on-side, we might even get something useful out of them.'

'Anything I can do?'

'No. I've asked the night team to phone around, tell people not to respond to questions — we're bound to be inundated in the morning.'

'What about the Pascals?'

'They've been warned off, but there's no saying what some of the tabloids'll do. If this is a ransom-kidnap, I don't want hordes of bloody hacks door-stepping Pascal.'

'Well, you'll get the chance to put that to them that tomorrow.'

McAteer gave a non-committal grunt; he evidently had little hope of persuading the tabloid press of their moral responsibilities.

Chapter Twelve

Clara shivered and the chain clinked hideously. Over the last few hours her mood had swung from fury to despair. It was pointless talking to this man: he wouldn't leave her alone and he wouldn't communicate.

She remembered a conversation she'd had with an old university friend. Michaela O'Connor had worked for a few years in Leeds after qualifying, dealing mostly in family law. Now she ran an office in Chester, specialising in women's issues. When she first began to practise at the Bar, Michaela's slight frame and pixie features had earned her the rather obvious nickname of 'the leprechaun'. It didn't stick for long: her reputation for ruthless cross-examination spread quickly, and although she was always painstakingly civil as she demolished her opponents' arguments, nevertheless, most came out of a tussle with Michaela feeling they had been savaged. She gained few friends, but a degree of grudging respect on the circuit, and she was quietly amused to hear that she was now referred to as 'Mitch the bitch' though not to her face — *never* to her face.

They last met for lunch in early July; Michaela was at the Crown Court, defending a woman accused of the attempted murder of her abusive partner. Blushing with shame, Clara recalled saying that if women communicated more effectively

— if they *talked* instead of becoming aggressive or submissive, they wouldn't become victims.

'What if their men don't want to talk?' Michaela demanded. 'What if they want to slap and punch and kick and rape instead? What if degradation is more *fun* than talking?'

Clara could feel the emotional temperature rising and she tried to cool things down a little. 'I know it's no pushover getting through to that type—'

'You're telling me!'

Clara felt a little spark of anger: Michaela evidently felt that her varied workload, which took in aspects of family, civil and criminal law, didn't qualify her to comment. 'I have dealt with a lot of violent men in the course of my practice,' she said, stiffly. 'And for the most part, they have been reasonable.'

'Well, they would be, talking to their lawyer, wouldn't they?'

'Some of them get angry,' Clara said, aware that she was on the defensive, but Michaela's altruistic pursuit of justice always made her feel that she was practising law for all the wrong reasons. 'I've been frightened on occasions. But I always managed to talk them round.'

Michaela laughed. 'Oh, well, congratulations! You managed to persuade them that it isn't a good idea to thump their defence counsel. And don't forget, you always have a solicitor's clerk as a witness in case they forget their manners. These women don't have witnesses or chaperones — sometimes I don't think they even have the law on their side.'

'I'm not saying it's easy for them—'

'You're damn right it's not easy! You try reasoning with a man who's just itching to give you a good kicking. You try finding the right words when he's already made up his mind that whatever you say will be wrong. They're masters of taking the innocent remark and twisting it — not that they need an excuse. They're so bloody good at mind games, they can make the victim feel like she's the one at fault.'

They had parted on bad terms and she hadn't spoken to

Michaela since the summer. Clara wondered with a pang of fear and regret if she would ever get the chance to apologise.

Clara thought that she now understood what her friend had been trying to tell her: she relied upon rules, she lived by them — the rule of law, rules of social exchange. Here, there were no rules — at least none that she understood. Here, *he* decided what was allowed, what was acceptable. For an instant, the recognition of the dire nature of her situation froze her; she could neither think nor speak, but she knew she had to try to get through to him. She couldn't just wait for him to decide what to do with her. The need in her to communicate was too strong to ignore; she couldn't simply switch it off.

'Are you there?' she called. No reply. The darkness seemed to intensify, threatening to suffocate her. She spoke loudly, beating back the silence, holding off her fear with words. 'This silent treatment isn't achieving anything,' she said.

'You don't think so?'

It's got you right where he wants you, Clara — frightened, anxious to appease him.

'It doesn't make sense,' she went on, ignoring his mocking tone, trying to ignore the voice in her head that undermined her best efforts to stay in control. 'If you want something, you're going to have to tell me what it is.'

'I don't *have* to tell you anything, Counsel.'

That was true enough. 'No,' Clara said. 'You don't.' She had to keep him talking — at least she had to try. 'But if you want me to co-operate—'

'D'you think *what I want* is yours to give or hold back? D'you think I *need* your co-operation?'

Clara felt a pang of alarm.

'Maybe I've got what I want, right now.'

Did he mean her imprisonment achieved his intention, or did 'right now', mean for the moment? *Only one way to find out.* She braced up and turned to face him, determined to know.

'So what you want is me chained up in a basement — that's it?'

He laughed softly. 'It's so much more than that.'

She forced herself to go on, to bring the confrontation to a head. 'I'm cold and hungry and afraid. Is *that* what you want?'

The staircase creaked as he shifted his weight. 'It'll do for now,' he said.

Hugo had carried Pippa to bed after two o'clock. He sat in a chair, with the phone within arm's reach until, at around 4 a.m., he fell into an uneasy sleep, in which he dreamed that Pippa was climbing the scaffolding on a tower block, treading the narrow planks unconcerned while something dark and ugly loomed behind her. He tried to warn her but he was held back by a grinning mannequin who tied him up with ribbon.

He woke with a shout. Above, coming from Pippa's bedroom, he heard a high keening sound, eerie and not quite human, coming in short terrified bursts, increasing in volume.

'Pippa?' he muttered groggily. '*Pippa!* He was out of his chair and in the hall in seconds. 'Pippa!' he called, running and stumbling up the stairs. 'It's all right! Daddy's here.'

Trish appeared on the landing in her pyjamas. She looked frightened and disorientated. He took her by the elbows and moved her out of the way, aware dimly of the warmth of her skin through the silk.

Pippa was sitting up in bed, her eyes wide open. That terrible shrill sound was rising to a scream. Hugo sat on the bed next to her. 'Pippa – darling – it's all right. You're having a dream.'

She began to babble: 'The man – the man – horrible mask – Mummy! He's got Mummy. Spiderman's got Mummy! He's in the garden!' she shrieked. 'He's climbing up the wall!'

Hugo felt the hairs stand up on his neck. He shook Pippa and she gasped and seemed to come to. For a moment she stared at him, then she broke down, sobbing. He hugged her to him. Her feverish warmth, her terrible distress, were almost unbearable and he struggled to keep from crying himself. He shushed and soothed, stroking her hair, rubbing her back, but she would not be comforted. At length, Trish came to the bedroom door. He gave her a helpless shrug and, taking this as an invitation, she came in and touched his shoulder lightly.

'Let me,' she said.

Hugo peeled Pippa's hands from around his neck. She clung to him for a moment, then threw herself on Trish.

'I tried to stop him, Trish! Honest, I did!'

'I know darling,' Trish soothed. 'I know you did. You were very brave.'

'He — he pushed me on the floor and I h-hurt myself,' the child wailed.

Trish shushed and crooned, while Hugo hovered uncertainly near the door. 'Go to bed. Try to get some rest,' she said over Pippa's head. 'I'll be along later.'

Chapter Thirteen

Two police constables had been posted at the museum door to keep back the droves of reporters that had appeared overnight. Scores of them waited expectantly at the entrance, cold, but eager for news, stamping and breathing clouds of vapour into the frosty air. For the most part, they stood quietly, but when the local hacks recognised one of the officers, there was a flurry of activity and they crowded in, yelling questions, jockeying for best position, shouting and shoving and clamouring for a useable quote until their target disappeared inside the building. Then they would settle again, grumbling, the photographers squabbling about who had pushed who. Lawson elbowed his way through the crush and ran up to the Incident Room.

'Bloody hell!' he exclaimed. 'This is a bit of a turnabout.' He was taken aback by the sheer volume of officers.

'Not a bad turn-out,' McAteer remarked, with the ghost of a smile.

In a matter of hours, it seemed that this cold, empty hangar of a room had shrunk and was barely capable of containing the extra numbers. Greetings were being exchanged: officers meeting friends and acquaintances they hadn't seen for some time. The high, airless room jangled with the noise. It was noticeably warmer than the previous day and the central heating system made occasional judders and groans, as if eager to convince that it too was working flat-out.

Lawson noticed a few nervous faces among the younger members of the team – uniform division, probably, on training. He had vivid memories of his own first placement with CID: he remembered thinking that even in civvies his uniformed status must be obvious. He was right, but it had been his youth and inexperience that had singled him out. He'd made some corking errors on that first outing.

McAteer called the room to order and forty or more faces turned towards them: some eager, some earnest, a number unreadable. He made eye contact with individuals, moving from one section of the room to another.

'First of all,' he began, 'I'd like to welcome the new members of the team. We needed a few more on board.'

An ironic cheer went up from the original team members.

'Nobody has contacted Mr Pascal overnight,' he said. A DC made his way self-consciously towards McAteer from the far end of the room. 'But house-to-house reports that residents heard *two* impacts when the van shot off down the road. One – a Renault – has already been accounted for. A damaged grey or silver saloon – possibly a Lexus – was seen driving away from the scene. We need to trace the owner. And we've got several more sightings of a van fitting the description of the suspect's vehicle in Grosvenor Avenue in the days leading up to Clara's abduction.'

'D'you reckon he followed her from her house then, sir?' Young asked.

The DC handed McAteer a note.

'I mean,' Young went on, blushing slightly, but evidently determined to have her say, 'there's been no sightings outside the school, barring yesterday. And her mum didn't usually drop the little girl anyway – the child-minder did.'

While McAteer scribbled a reply on a scrap of paper, Lawson took over. 'That's a good point, Young,' he said. 'If this van is the suspect's vehicle, we could get his description from one of the neighbours. As for the van itself, we've no index. We do know the driver was a man and we have got a description. Forensics are working on DNA samples of scrapings taken from under the daughter's nails.'

'If he's in the records, we'll find him,' McAteer added, handing his reply to the constable.

'Now. For those of you who are new to a major investigation,' he said, looking at no one in particular, 'You need to keep detailed notes; any notes you do make will have to go to the disclosure officer at the end of this enquiry.'

'Anything you *do* say, will be taken down and may be used in evidence . . .' Fletcher intoned, his face turned slightly away, so McAteer could not see who was talking.

'So, to avoid embarrassment, buy yourselves a decent-sized notebook and keep it up to date.' He slid the original message along the table for Lawson to read.

It was what they had both been waiting for. *And about bloody time, too*, Lawson thought.

'I don't know how the Press got hold of this,' McAteer said, leaving the implied 'yet' an unspoken but almost tangible threat. 'But you will have noticed a sizeable contingent outside the building as you came in. I'm assuming someone in her chambers gave them the info.' He regarded the group steadily. 'That *is*, unless or until I'm proved wrong.' The warning was enough to make one or two people shift uncomfortably in their seats. Fletcher, Lawson noted, was one of them.

'I'll be giving a press conference later this morning. My comments and the official bulletins issued by the Press Office are the only information I want to read in the papers. Do I make myself clear?' He waited until he had an acknowledgement from the team. It came in a ragged chorus of 'Yes, Boss', and grunts of 'Guv'.

'With media co-operation we might get information vital to

the search. So be prepared for a big increase in the number of actions going out this afternoon. I want them completed with all speed, but without compromising standards — I don't want important lines of enquiry missed because one of my officers confused speed with efficiency.'

A queue formed outside the HOLMES Room immediately after the briefing. Tyrell was on the phone and she turned her back and stuck her finger in her ear to block out the noise.

The Actions Manager handed a computer-generated form to each member of the team. Some were given follow-up or linked inquiries from the previous day's work. The rest were new actions. Officers compared actions, eager for a chance to shine and spirits were high.

'What've you got?' Rayner asked Young.

Young ducked her head, answering in a low voice. 'Perv, creeping around the school last week. What about you?'

'Back to Clara's chambers — see if I can charm anything out of the delightful Mr Warrington.'

Young envied Rayner's easy, confident manner. She felt she had made a bad start — why else had they taken her off surveillance? She walked with Rayner to the Incident Room, but hesitated at the door.

'What's up?' Rayner asked, holding the door open. She glanced into the room. 'Fletcher?'

Young lifted both shoulders. 'When he finds out I've been taken off surveillance . . .'

Rayner let the door swing to and, taking Young by the elbow, edged her a little further up the corridor, out of earshot of the officers queuing up for their actions. 'You don't want to get so het up about what Fletcher thinks,' she said.

'I don't!' Young replied, indignant that her dread of what Fletcher might say was so apparent.

'You don't?'

'No.'

They locked gazes, then Rayner added, 'So next time Fletch the Letch calls you "Babe", you'll tell him what you think of sad, fat, sexist gits who get their jollies harassing female officers – am I right?'

When they went into the Incident Room to pick up their coats, Fletcher broke off from a tirade against DS Tyrell and her 'computerized bloody robots'.

'Hey, Babe!' he called.

Rayner glanced questioningly at Young, but she looked away, avoiding eye contact.

'Don't be like that, darling. We're partners, aren't we?'

Young shot Fletcher a look of impotent fury and he laughed, clasping a hand to his wounded heart. 'After all we've been through . . .'

She went to fetch her waterproof from the chair where she had left it, anxious to get away.

' 'Fraid you're on your own today, Doll,' he persisted. 'Bloody Tyrell's pulled me off surveillance. Now just you remember what I taught you. It's all in the lip action.'

He puckered up and Young felt her cheeks burn with embarrassment. They were laughing and she didn't know what to say to him. *Say something, for God's sake, Cath. Say anything!*

'I'm not on surveillance.' *Shit, Cath! You're playing right into his sweaty hands. Say something about his crappy performance yesterday – tell him that's why he's off the rota.* But she couldn't, because for one thing, she was the one who had gone back to base sodden, her hair in rats' tails, not Fletcher, and for another, she knew how he would respond: 'You didn't have any complaints about my "performance" yesterday, Babe.' Then he would drop a broad wink to his mates and that would be it: wolf-whistles and catcalls whenever she showed her face here or in the canteen.

While she fastened her waterproof, dithering about what to say, he swooped on her desk and carried off her action slip.

He clicked his tongue. 'I don't like the look of this.'

'Give it back, Fletch,' Young said.

'You're not going out alone, are you?'

'Why the hell not?' She made a grab at the slip but he snatched it out of reach.

He swivelled his head, garnering his audience before going on. 'She's tracking down a perv,' he said. 'Hanging around the school gates.' A few of the men smiled, the women frowned or pretended to be unaware of what was going on. 'If this feller's got a thing for little girls, you won't be safe, Babe.'

'Fletch—' She made another swipe at the slip, almost in tears with frustration. 'Give it to me.'

'Only if you promise not to take sweeties from the nasty man. 'Cos perverts might seem nice and sometimes they look normal—'

'And sometimes they're big fat slobs who pretend to be professional police officers.' Rayner plucked the slip from between his fingers and handed it back to Young.

Fletcher bristled momentarily, then relaxed, shrugging off her remark.

I should have said that, Young thought. *I should have put the fat pig in his place.* In reality, she knew it had already gone too far for her to claw her way back to a proper place on the team.

'What you got, Fletch?' Thorpe asked, pulling on a Benny hat as he made for the door.

'Someone taking snapshots in the Pascal's street,' Fletcher answered.

Thorpe laughed. 'Probably some old codger tripped over a cracked flag and hit his head. Suing the council for compo.'

Young stuffed the slip of paper into her jacket, grateful to Thorpe for taking the attention away from her.

'What you got then?' Fletcher threw back. 'Something *important* is it?'

His friend raised his eyebrows, his expression was one of

modest contentment. 'Car parked outside the Pascals' off and on over the last few weeks.'

'I bet Babe'd swap you for her perv.'

Young left before he could start in on her again.

Lawson handed back the slip of paper McAteer had passed to him during the briefing. 'I'd like to take this one, sir.' The news was that permission had come through for them to see Casavettes in Breck Moor Prison.

'I've already arranged it,' McAteer said. 'I'd like to have a pop at Casavettes myself, only I've got this press conference and—' He tapped the pile of paperwork that had appeared on his desk since the previous evening. 'Operation Snowman has cleared the visit, but they would like a debrief when you get back. Liaise with their SIO.'

Lawson nodded. 'Fine. I'll take Barton with me, if I can get his actions reallocated.'

McAteer sighed and took off his jacket. He hung it carefully on a wooden hanger behind the door, then reached into one of his desk drawers and pulled out a cardigan.

Noting Lawson's look of amused surprise, he said, 'Heating's bloody useless.' With another sigh, he sank into his scuffed leather office chair and took the first sheet from the pile.

As Lawson turned to go, McAteer spoke without looking up. 'Of course,' he said, his tone dry and unquivocal, 'Before you liaise with Operation Snowman, you'll be sure to liaise with me.'

Lawson grinned. He had learned a long time ago never to underestimate McAteer.

Rayner shivered and turned up the car's heating. Driving the long sweep of St Martin's Way on the outer rim of the city, she saw that there was snow on the Welsh hills. And although the sky was a clear, shimmering blue, the clouds massed on the horizon were forecast to reach Chester by the afternoon.

She couldn't see Mr Warrington having a sudden change of heart overnight and she had decided to try a more creative approach. Barton had got the name of Clara's clerk from her husband and Rayner had a strong suspicion that she was the little woman who had hesitated before crossing the foyer the previous day — why else would her colleagues have quizzed her about Clara?

Traffic was backed up at roadworks near the junction of Watergate Street and Rayner squeezed, cursing, into single file to avoid the coned area. It was already eight-forty; if she missed the clerk, she would have to try to coax her to talk over the phone and she didn't fancy her chances against a moratorium imposed by the firm's senior partner: Mr Warrington struck her as a man who wouldn't like to see his orders flouted.

Cars turning right slowed the flow even further and by eight-fifty Rayner was sweating. She swung into the inside lane and hurled up to the roundabout near the Roodee, racing ahead of the cars queuing to turn right and nudging into the turn right lane to a furious outcry of blaring car horns.

The convenience of Jericho Chamber's car park was out of the question: she couldn't risk Mr Warrington hearing about her visit. Finding a speck on the public car park opposite the racecourse would add precious time to her journey. *Sod it!*

She turned immediate left after the roundabout and under the grand archway of County Hall. The attendant flagged her down and she showed her ID, smiling, racking her brains for a case that was due to go to trial. She needn't have worried: he waved her on to the already half-full car park and she pulled into the nearest slot, locked up and headed at a run for Jericho Chambers.

Careful to avoid the security cameras at the front of the building, she positioned herself on the opposite side of the square and waited. A few people were still drifting in to work;

some drove round to the back, some arrived on foot, but Rayner had the sinking feeling that Clara's clerk was the conscientious type who arrived early and left late. A second, more depressing thought followed on from this: what if she had driven in and used her swipe card on one of the doors at the rear of the building?

Then, from her left, she heard the busy tripping clip of stilettos on cold stone and the little dark woman turned the corner, her head bent and her fist bunching the lapels of her coat closed against the freshening wind.

Rayner took a step forward and she started, evidently recognising her. With a quick glance around to ensure that no one was watching, the woman crossed the square to where Rayner stood.

'I can't talk to you,' she said immediately.

'Nesta, isn't it?' Rayner said. 'I'm afraid I don't know your surname.'

'Lewis,' she answered. 'But Nesta will do.' Rayner was again struck by the deep timbre of her voice. 'And I *still* can't talk to you.'

Her accent was as rich and mellow as the rolling hills of South Wales.

'Come on, Nesta. I saw the way you looked at me yesterday.'

'Mr Warrington has given strict instructions. If he even saw me talking to you—'

Rayner could imagine. 'We'll go somewhere,' she said. 'Anywhere. You name it.'

The little woman checked her watch. 'I'm going to be late. I'm never late.'

'There's a first time for everything,' Rayner said. 'Tell them you overslept. Tell them the traffic held you up – tell them what ever the hell you like!'

'There's no need—' Nesta began.

But Rayner wasn't listening. 'A woman's life is at stake and all you're worried about is your bloody punctuality record!'

Nesta looked shocked and hurt.

Rayner closed her eyes briefly. 'I'm sorry, Nesta. I'm sure that's not true. I know you care about Clara. But we've got to act fast. She's been missing twenty-four hours already and I can't get anyone in this place to take it seriously!'

'All right,' Nesta said, taking her by the elbow and guiding her towards the city centre. 'But keep your voice down, for pity's sake!'

They went to a coffee bar in the Rows and sat near the back. Nesta chose the chair facing the entrance, darting anxious glances over Rayner's shoulder when new customers came in.

Rayner went through Hugo's description of the rapist Clara had defended. 'He said she was nervous of this bloke. Found him intrusive. Any idea who it might be?'

'Farrell Smith,' she said, without hesitation.

'You seem pretty certain.'

'Ms Pascal defends a lot of rape cases,' she explained. 'Solicitors like to get a lady barrister to defend their clients. Ms Pascal doesn't scare easy — she's not the nervy type, but that man—' She shivered involuntarily.

'Describe him.'

She thought about it, focusing on a point in the middle distance, as if staring at the man himself. 'He's got a rugby player's build. He's not tall — more average, really, but he's physically imposing. Takes up too much space — you know the type.'

Rayner knew the type all right.

'Confident,' Nesta went on, adding with some reluctance, 'Good-looking, I suppose. A bit of a charmer. But he makes you edgy, you know?'

They paused while the waitress took their order.

Nesta folded her hands on the table in front of her, her dark eyes fixed on Rayner's. 'He would stand too close. He'd lean across the counter when I was checking to see when Ms Pascal was free, reading the diary, looking at the entries. I saw him pick a hair off her jacket once.' She shuddered. 'Made me go cold, it did. Intrusive – that's what he is.'

'Okay.' Rayner could see how that would make a woman feel vulnerable. 'Ms Pascal defended him on a charge of rape—'

'Not at first,' Nesta interrupted. 'The original charge was stalking.'

Rayner felt a thrill of excitement. *Stalking.* What if he had fixated on his barrister?

'Vile sod said he was trying to protect her – the girlfriend, that is. "You know how it is, Clara," he said. "You're not safe in your own home. I mean, where do you live?" Damned creep! Wanted to know the ins and outs of her family and everything.'

'And did she? Give him the ins and outs, I mean?'

Nesta gave her a pitying smile. 'Of course not. But she told me he was the sort of bloke made her flesh crawl. "I get the feeling," she said, "I'll be having dinner in a restaurant one night and he'll be sitting at the next table." ' Nesta shook her head. 'When she found out he'd been arrested for rape . . .' She glanced quickly around to see if anyone was eavesdropping. 'Ms Pascal wanted to hand the case over to someone else, but Mr Warrington wouldn't hear of it.'

'Smith was convicted of the rape . . .'

'Oh yes,' Nesta said with some satisfaction. 'That was one of Ms Pascal's happy failures.'

Rayner tilted her head in question.

'That's what she calls it when she loses a defence she ends up wishing she was prosecuting.'

'Just so I'm clear on this,' Rayner began, wondering how to phrase it so that she didn't seem to be accusing Clara of misconduct. 'Is there any chance that—' She stopped. There was no subtle way to put it. 'I'm wondering if Ms Pascal maybe didn't try quite as hard as she normally would, for this bloke Smith.'

Nesta stared at her, scandalised. 'Ms Pascal always does everything in her power to present the best case for her client,' she said furiously. 'It's *unthinkable* that she would ever do anything less than her best.'

Rayner apologised. 'Farrell Smith,' she went on. 'Is he still inside?'

Nesta shrugged. 'They don't tell us.'

'Okay.' Rayner marshalled her thoughts: it was important to get as much out of this meeting as she could. If Mr Warrington got wind of it, or if Nesta had second thoughts, this could be her only chance to find out about Clara's workload. 'Can you think of anyone who may have threatened her? Anyone who was dissatisfied with a verdict?'

'Ms Pascal has a very good relationship with her clients,' Nesta answered stiffly. She hadn't, it seemed, forgiven Rayner for the implied slur on her boss's professionalism and she evidently wasn't ready to indulge in further speculation.

Rayner was grateful for the arrival of their coffee. She poured, eyeing Nesta, who stubbornly refused to meet her gaze. Rayner waited until she had taken a sip or two before asking, 'What about her opponent's clients?'

This stopped Nesta mid-sip. 'People she's successfully prosecuted, you mean?'

'Or someone complaining that she got a guilty party off,' Rayner suggested.

'Last year,' Nesta said, 'There was a man – a dad. Just couldn't accept that his daughter was . . .' She coloured slightly, glancing round at the other tables and lowering her voice. 'Well, that she put it about a bit.'

'Another rape case?'

She nodded. 'But it turned out to be consensual sex. The girl had second thoughts when her dad found out about it and she accused the bloke of rape.'

'He got off?'

'He was found not guilty,' she corrected tartly.

Rayner gritted her teeth and asked evenly, 'And the dad couldn't accept the verdict?'

A curt nod. Rayner took a breath, but Nesta cut in: 'And before you ask, I can't remember his name. I'll look it up when I get back.' She stood, bringing the interview to a close. 'I'll phone tonight.' Then she was gone, leaving her coffee barely tasted and trailing a faint whiff of Chanel No. 5 in her wake.

Chapter Fourteen

Eleanor would always be special to him; the first of any experience always is: first cigarette, first kiss, first drink, first car, first lover, first kill . . . Those that followed would suffer by comparison with Eleanor, and he wished now that he had kept her longer: a week, a month — he was already thinking of refinements. But it had taken a great deal of self-control to wait as long as he had, to watch her, to have her near and yet to hold back. Although she had been pliable, and he could have enjoyed hundreds of little . . . considerations from her, had he kept her, he suspected that he did not have the tolerance to prolong the pleasure: he relished the kill too much for that.

He mourned the loss of Eleanor, insofar as it directly affected him. The confluence of their lives (and her death) was a chance event — she came along at the just right moment, or rather right for him, but the worst possible moment for her. He saw a certain melancholy irony in that, but he could not feel sorry for her. All the spiteful rejections and imagined slights of his adolescence seemed meaningless now. Her pain and fear, her willing compliance with his demands — no, with his *wishes* — cancelled out the awkwardness and loneliness of his childhood, if only for a fleeting moment; and for that moment it didn't matter that he made women uneasy, because *this* woman could not back away or turn her face from him. She was — literally — naked before him and his preparations had wiped away the revulsion he always sensed when a woman got close to him. Revulsion was a primal reaction, like lust or hate; when he got close, women withdrew, putting physical distance and emotional barriers between them. He had removed that option and had taught Eleanor to fear him instead.

Repugnance was hurtful, but their fear excited him.

The new woman was a distraction, but he was troubled: this one had been less carefully planned. Because he had taken less time, to watch her and film her before he took her, the experience was less satisfying. And he had taken unnecessary risks – things he would not do next time. He would try and keep the next one for longer – he owed himself at least that much; he had put in a lot of effort, placed himself in danger more than once – it made sense, after all the work of training and conditioning, to keep them as long as possible. But not this one. She would be expected home soon; when she failed to appear, people would come looking and if they found her they would find him. Moving her alive could also prove hazardous. No, the sensible course of action would be to finish this one as soon as she was ready and start afresh. It occurred to him that changing his behaviour would have the added benefit of confusing the police. They might even think that they were looking for two killers.

Chapter Fifteen

Lawson and Barton headed out of Diva Street Station for Breck Moor Prison in the promise of bright sunshine. Barton took the nearest route to Hoole Road, to pick up the M53.

'Think he's got something for us, Boss?' he asked. 'Or is he just pulling our plonkers?'

Lawson didn't quite know where to begin with that one: he hadn't seen Casavettes in a long time and he was apprehensive at the prospect. He shrugged. 'He's probably as well informed about this enquiry as we are.'

Barton glanced across at Lawson. 'His brief will have given him the basic outline – with the delay on the trial, but . . .'

'He's allowed his phone calls – he can phone who he likes.' Lawson waited and sure enough the penny dropped.

'You're saying he's got someone in his pocket?'

Lawson exhaled. 'It's possible. He hooks them with something minor: an address he needs, a bit of help getting a club licence renewed – and he pays well.'

'But it doesn't stop there.'

Lawson stared through the window as Barton slowed for the roundabout that would take them onto the motorway. He hadn't told this story to anyone, outside of Complaints and Discipline, who had investigated it, after it all blew up in his face. But Casavettes would use it to unsettle Barton, he would imply that

Lawson was in some way bent, working on his credibility, and weakening their ability to act against him. Barton had to know everything.

'Ten years ago – I was still a sergeant then – I was working on a drugs case. Casavettes was manufacturing crack in disused warehouses around Runcorn and Widnes.'

Barton eased into the outside lane to overtake a line of lorries doing sixty nose-to-tail.

'We had someone on the inside,' Lawson went on. 'A guy called Porter. He had a cocaine habit that was spiralling out of control. Casavettes gave him whatever he needed, in exchange for moving a few consignments. We caught him – he'd been shifting the stuff in a fleet car, for Christ's sake! We persuaded him to try and find out when the next big shipment was due. You see, they'd set up for a week – two at the outside – make what they needed and then dismantle before we'd cottoned on to it.'

He fell silent for a few moments, remembering. On either side, farmland sparkled, damp in the golden sunlight of late autumn. 'Porter did well. He overcame Casavettes' initial reluctance and swore he wouldn't touch the goods.'

'But he couldn't keep his fingers out of the sherbet.'

'No,' Lawson said. 'It wasn't like that at all. He was as good as his word. Casavettes trusted him enough to take him along on a reccy of a new site. They break in and start checking the layout: power points, gas supply, water and so on. The way it works is, if there's any security in place, Casavettes pays them off. They disappear for a week and when they get back, the only sign that anyone has been in the place is a few empty sandwich bags and a faint whiff of cooking.'

He paused, taking a breath before going on. It had been ten years, but he could still see it as clearly as he saw the road ahead. Something he thought he had left behind for good.

'Casavettes sends Porter to check out an office – the lights are on. Porter crosses the factory floor. He's not bothered. He knows the system: Casavettes' men will have checked ahead.

Security just forgot to turn off the lights in their hurry, he reckons. So he goes into the office.' He exhaled.

'He finds two security guards. Both shot. One in the head, the other's got two bullet holes in his chest. They'd been playing poker. The one with chest wounds is still breathing.' He glanced across at Barton. 'Then Casavettes comes in.'

'He shot Porter?'

'Oh no,' Lawson said softly. 'Casavettes has much more imagination than that. He knew right from the start that Porter was working for us. Now I don't know if he set up the murders just to make sure Porter was finished for good – and Porter isn't about to say – but Casavettes arranged it so Porter would be there and he made sure he couldn't leave.' He swallowed, tasting acid at the back of his throat.

Barton knew that Lawson was no pushover, nor was he a yarn-spinner. He was telling this story for a reason and he was clearly finding it hard going. He waited. To the right, the grey complicated landscape of Ellesmere Port slid past. The whiff of petrochemical products pervaded the air today, trapped by a cold inversion layer over the mudflats of the Mersey estuary.

'Casavettes hands Porter the murder weapon and Porter takes it. He knows it's empty – Casavettes isn't going to hand him a loaded gun – but he takes it, because he doesn't have a choice. Then Casavettes gets three of his men to hold Porter while he nails him to the floor.'

'*Jesus!*'

Lawson cleared his throat. 'I got a tip-off. A call direct to my home. Not my work number. Not even my mobile – that's Casavettes' trademark, Phil: he gets you right where you live. I went straight to the factory. Found Porter in the office with the two dead men. The second guy must have died listening to his screams.'

'*Fuck*,' Barton breathed. 'What happened to Porter?'

'He said he was out of his head on crack. Didn't know what he was doing. Pleaded guilty to the double murder.'

'Oh, come *on!* He had a frigging nail through his foot!'

'Self-inflicted, so he said.' Lawson shook his head in disbelief. 'He said he was overcome with remorse.'

For some minutes they drove in silence.

'I was his mate, Phil. We went through training together. Our first placement was in the same nick in Warrington. We walked the beat for two years together.' He hesitated. This was something he would rather not think about, but if he was going to tell the story he might as well tell Barton everything. 'It was me persuaded him to turn in Casavettes. And because of that, he's been banged up for the past ten years, in the company of nonces on a segregation unit.' He glanced over at Barton. '. . . Well, what else are they going to do with a copper?'

'He made his own choices, Steve,' Barton said. 'He was in with Casavettes long before you got wind of it.'

Lawson looked down at his hands. 'He was a good mate – a good officer.'

'He let Casavettes get away.' Barton slowed to forty as the motorway ended, dropping to thirty as they approached the toll booths for the Wallasey tunnel.

'Don't judge him, Phil. His career was finished. He was out of the force no matter what. The drugs charge was enough to get him a five-year stretch, but at least he wouldn't risk falling foul of Casavettes. He tried to do the right thing. He tried to help us, but Casavettes had the whole thing sewn up and we played right into his hands. Porter had a family before Casavettes got to him. He's got kids, he *had* a wife.'

'He bottled out.' At the barrier, Barton threw a few coins into the basket and they drove on.

They didn't speak for the rest of the journey. The road out of the tunnel onto the Liverpool shores of the Mersey were grey and depressing, despite the sunshine. They drove past rows of grimy shop-fronts. Some of the shopkeepers hadn't bothered to raise the shutters and presumably conducted business in gloomy artificial light. The narrow clutter of County Road gave way to the brief respite of playing fields and parks either side of Breeze Hill and within ten minutes they had arrived at Her Majesty's Prison, Breck Moor.

'Casavettes will count on my not having told you about Porter,' Lawson told Barton. 'He's a thug, but he's clever with it. Don't believe anything he says and don't let him try his mind games on you.'

He could see that Barton was unimpressed and he wondered, only fleetingly, if he had overplayed Casavettes' intelligence or his propensity for evil. All he had to do was remember the look on Tom Porter's face when he'd visited him the previous day. *I'd rather cut my tongue out than testify against Casavettes.*

Casavettes appeared at the far end of the corridor as the door clanged shut behind them. He was escorted by two warders. Lawson bridled at the way they kept their distance, not touching the man, showing him a deference that spoke of nervous respect.

He had hardly changed in ten years. The hair was as dark and thick and he moved with the same loose-limbed athleticism. The beard was new; trimmed to a thin bar down the centre of his chin and cropped close to his jawline. His moustache was neatly clipped. A sharp image of Casavettes snipping and preening with a pair of nail scissors flashed into Lawson's head and he was certain it was accurate.

The prisoner walked fast, forcing his escort to hurry to keep up with him. Barton tensed beside Lawson and knew that he had sensed the danger that seemed to follow Casavettes like a shadow. As he reached the door of the interview room, Casavettes spread one hand, inviting Lawson and Barton to enter ahead of him. *First point to Casavettes.*

As they got closer, Lawson forced himself to slow down and to maintain eye contact. He *had* changed. Cruelty was etched deep in the lines from his nostrils to his mouth and the empty, dead look in his eyes marred the good looks that had snared so many women in his youth.

Lawson waited for Casavettes to go into the room, then he nodded to Casavettes' escort and they left without having spoken a word.

'Sit down, Mr Casavettes,' Lawson said, waiting until he was seated before pulling out a chair for himself.

Casavettes leaned back in his chair, his legs apart, one hand resting comfortably on his thigh. 'You've done all right for yourself, Mr Lawson. *Detective Inspector* . . . Who'd've thought . . .' His voice was low and measured, slightly nasal, with a broad sardonic edge.

'We'd like to ask you a few questions,' Lawson said.

'You haven't introduced me to your colleague.' Casavettes had been given the names of both officers before he had agreed to see them, but Lawson went through the pantomime of introducing Barton anyway.

Casavettes spoke over the last of the introduction, addressing his question to a dusty corner of the interview room. 'Got any smokes?'

'You know we're not allowed—'

'Afraid of corrupting me, are you?' Casavettes interrupted. He cocked his head. 'It'd take more than that to tempt me.' He knew why they were there. His brief would have told him of Clara's abduction and he was looking to capitalise on it. Manipulating the situation, trying to gain control.

'You'd have to convince me you've got something I want,' Lawson said.

'I might have something for you,' he said, after a brief pause.

'I'm listening.' Lawson was careful not to show any eagerness.

'So am I.' He leaned forward, his eyes flitting constantly from Lawson to Barton, as if looking for some chink, some weakness to exploit.

'You know we can't make promises,' Lawson said.

'Be a shame to lose such a promising lawyer, a pillar of the Law Society, just because you felt you had to stick to policy.'

Lawson snapped forward, leaning across the table, nose-to-nose with Casavettes. 'And we don't respond to threats,' he snarled.

Casavettes didn't so much as blink. 'That policy an' all, is it, Mr Lawson?' He sat up, increasing the distance between them. 'Trouble is, general principles don't always work on an individual basis, eh, Sergeant Barton?'

Barton fixed him with a stony stare. 'Why don't you stop pissing us about, Casavettes?' he said.

Casavettes jerked his head in Barton's direction. 'Don't they teach pyschology in police training these days?' He asked Lawson. 'You'll never win my confidence talking to me like that, Sergeant.' He let his gaze linger on Barton for a moment; Barton held it, making no effort to hide his contempt for the man. Casavettes switched his attention back to Lawson. 'I mean, you're not above bending the rules, when it suits you, are you, Inspector? Speaking of which, have you seen Tom lately?'

It hadn't taken long for him to get onto the subject of Tom Porter and in a curious way, Lawson was relieved: that he had told Barton as much as he had and that Casavettes' behaviour could be predicted — even predictable.

Casavettes turned courteously to Barton. 'We know each other from way back,' he explained. 'Tommy got nailed for a double murder.' He winced. ''Scuse the pun.'

'Get off the subject, Casavettes,' Lawson warned, marking up a point to himself that Casavettes hadn't heard about his trip to see Porter the previous day. 'If you've got something to say, get on with it.'

A muscle twitched at the corner of Casavettes' mouth. 'It's not that simple, is it? I tell you what I know — as a gift. Where's the guarantee you won't just take it, say, "Ta, very much", and walk away, leaving me right where I am?'

'It's a risk you'll have to take,' Lawson replied.

Amusement, quickly suppressed, flitted across Casavettes' face, as if Lawson had inadvertently said something funny and Casavettes was too polite to laugh. 'No deal, no information,' he said, with a finality that was almost believable.

Lawson and Barton stood. As Lawson turned to the door, Casavettes began speaking in a low, urgent tone.

'White Ford Transit. He was wearing a red ski mask, blue anorak, padded.' The two policemen turned back. This information wouldn't go out on the news until lunch-time. 'He got into a tussle with the little girl.' Casavettes looked up suddenly, a glint of pure malevolence in his eyes. 'Pretty little thing . . .'

Lawson turned back.

'And spunky,' Casavettes went on, slowing down now, relaxing, confident that he had their attention. 'She bashed her tailbone when he threw her off.'

'Who told you this?'

Casavettes went on as though Lawson hadn't spoken. 'Her mum was more worried about her than about herself. You're a family man, Mr Barton. You'd understand that. They take everything you can give. Every ounce of love, every penny you earn, but you give it gladly, and more. Look at Tom Porter, he's given his life for his kids.'

Lawson's breath caught in his throat. This was the closest he would ever get to an admission that Casavettes had threatened to harm Tom's children. He took a step forward and Barton put a restraining hand on his arm.

He stared at Casavettes and suddenly it all seemed devastatingly simple to him: the Lexus — no wonder the accident wasn't reported — Casavettes' men had been watching Clara. 'Got a Lexus in your fleet, have you Ray?' Casavettes was momentarily shaken, but he quickly recovered. Lawson nodded to himself: it was acknowledgement enough. 'My guess is it was involved in an accident on Wednesday. I bet your apes saw the whole thing. Of course it wouldn't occur to them to butt in and help.'

Casavettes smiled, showing small, white teeth. 'What can I

say?' he said. 'Sometimes you just get lucky.' He gazed coolly at Lawson. 'Why don't you see what you can come up with, Inspector? And I'll do the same. But don't leave it too long – this offer is valid for a limited period only.'

Chapter Sixteen

She heard voices — several — raised in animated conversation, then laughter. Clara jumped to her feet, yelling, 'I'm in here! Help me!' The chain chafed her ankle, but she continued shouting. The voices got closer, booming and fading, their chatter unaffected by her cries. Suddenly, recognising the sound, she groaned in despair. A radio. He was listening to a radio.

Frustrated, furious, she tore down handfuls of the flimsy paper, determined to destroy every scrap.

'What the f—?'

Clara turned to face him, her eyes, though blind, seeking out the spot where he stood. With slow, deliberate defiance, she tore and scattered the paper in her hands, letting it fall at her feet.

The radio dropped with a clatter. He ran down the steps and seized her by the shoulders. 'You bitch!' he roared, shaking her violently. 'Look what you've done!'

She screamed back, 'How can I *look*, you bloody lunatic?'

He flung her away and she hit the wall with a thud. The impact winded her and she sank to the floor, gasping for breath. Gradually her breathing eased and she sensed him standing opposite her, watching. He was breathing hard; angry, but also distressed. He made short, choking sounds. *My God — he's having a heart attack!* For one absurd moment she was anxious for him, then she experienced a savage, soaring joy. *Die, you bastard! Die in agony!*

But he didn't die. And if he was in pain, it wasn't physical, because a few minutes later he walked heavily up the stairs and out of her cell. The radio had fallen flat onto its speaker, but she could still hear the programme: clear confident voices, raised in good-natured argument, occasional laughter, the authoritative intervention of the presenter. It made her want to weep.

She never knew for sure that he was watching her, but she thought that he often left the door open when he slipped out into the main body of the house. He gave her drinking water in a plastic bottle, but Clara couldn't remember when she had last eaten. Or rather, she knew very well: it was the morning she had snatched a round of toast at breakfast. Pippa's birthday. But she had lost track of the days and now she wasn't sure how long she had been kept here.

Shivering, suddenly shaky after her outburst, she clasped her arms around her kneess and hugged herself.

She knew that voice. '*You bitch!*' She had heard it before. Heard those very words. No, she thought. No. I can't do this. The terror of knowing almost overwhelmed her. *Yes, you can. You can do it — you've got to, if you want to get out of here alive.* She feared that if she recognised him, she would be all the more afraid. He'll see it in my face, I know he will! *No he won't. You've been pretending you're not afraid all your life. You perfected the art when you were called to the Bar. Lying is just as much a way of life to you as it is to some of your clients. Establish his identity and you'll maybe find some leverage, something to give you an advantage.*

He returned. The musty odour that had been so noticeable on his clothes at the beginning no longer troubled her; most likely it had seeped into her own clothing — the house must be furry with mould. The other, stale nicotine stench was explained by his almost constant smoking. No sooner did he stub out one cigarette than she would hear the click and hiss of his lighter and the quick hot fizzle of his first drag on the next. He was smoking now, the smell drifted down the stairs, reminding her obscurely of a November night in her student days. She had left the Crown

Court at five o'clock, after watching a murder trial. Journalists huddled in groups in the gathering gloom, shuffling their feet on the cold flags, lighting cigarettes and inhaling gratefully, waiting for the accused to be brought out.

This time *she* was the accused – at least, she felt that she was being punished – and this man wanted more than a good story. Clara held her breath. He set the radio upright and a burst of talk followed. He came down the steps and she braced herself, determined she would not cower from him. A faint rustle and then she heard the *rip* of tape. She tensed: would he gag her again?

She thought about Michaela; how she had calmly told her friend that you simply have to appeal to the rational in these men. *Well, why don't you rationalise this madman into accepting he's done a bad thing, Clara?* she asked herself, with none of the compassion that Michaela would have afforded her. *Calling him a lunatic – that was a good start – really intelligent psychological technique.*

He said one word, his voice flat, emotionless: 'Move.'

She obeyed instantly, her toes curling inwards against the cold of the stone beneath her feet. A faint sparkle of light flared in the blackness behind her eyes and then the dizziness passed. She heard the crackle of paper, then the tearing of another piece of tape. She stood out of his way, as far as the chain would allow, while he tore off strips of sellotape and stuck paper to the walls.

'There's hundreds more,' he told her, when he had finished. Repeating 'hundreds,' in a low voice that made her tremble with apprehension. She would not – *would not* – let him frighten her like this.

'Hundreds of what?' she demanded, with as much authority as she could muster.

Instead of replying, he touched her ear. She flinched.

'Struggle if you like,' he said. 'I'll tear it out if I have to.'

He wanted her earring. 'I'll do it,' she said, batting his hand away, while trying to assess what this meant, quelling an irrational surge of optimism: was he going to ask for a ransom?

'No,' he said. 'I'll do it.' He was quite calm, but Clara was convinced he would carry out his threat to tear the earring from her ear if she resisted.

His rules, she thought bitterly. *You're on his territory now; he decides what goes.* And so she submitted, her eyes stinging with tears at the humiliation of being touched – *handled* – by this man. She tried to focus on something – anything – rather than his ham-fisted attempts to unfasten the clip. The pips for the one o'clock news sounded and Clara listened while the newsreader spoke in sombre tones of the kidnap of a leading barrister from outside her daughter's school.

He took only one earring. At the top of the stairs he said, 'You can take off your eye-patches, now.'

'I don't want to see your face,' she said unsteadily.

'You won't see anything I don't want you to.'

She didn't move for several minutes, paralysed by a terror that this was a trick to give him an excuse – a justification – to kill her, because she would be able to identify him to the police. She heard a sigh and he retreated, taking the radio and closing the door behind him with a deliberate *click*.

Clara worked on the patch over her right eye. Her tears had loosened it over the cheekbone, but she winced as it tugged at her eyebrows, pulling out hairs as she peeled off the last tacky corner. Her eye felt suddenly cool and free, despite the impenetrable darkness, and she repeated the process on the other eye with greater eagerness.

There was no light. Not even a gleam from under the steel door. A new horror seized her. Was the room sealed? Was that why he left the door standing open during the day – so that she wouldn't suffocate?

'Hey!' She heard the panic in her voice and forced herself to stop and get control. She yelled again, and this time the door opened and a faint grey light seeped into her cell.

He was silhouetted in the door and instinctively, she closed her eyes.

'Look at me,' he said.

She kept her head turned away from him.

'Look at me.'

The tone of command was impossible to resist. She looked. The light was very poor, but she could just make out that he was wearing the mask once again. 'I want some light,' she said. 'Give me some light.'

He was silent. She sensed that he was weighing up the situation, deciding whether to grant her request.

'What's the point of allowing me to take off these bloody things if you don't give me light?' She threw the eye-patches to the floor.

He retreated, locking the door after him and she stood, blinking, imagining shapes, movement at the edges of her vision. Was this a new, subtle torment he had devised? To restore her vision, but deprive her of light?

Five minutes passed, ten, then she heard the scratch of the key in the lock. She saw a faint gleam: the dim light beyond the doorway; her eyes went to it hungrily. The man was silhouetted against the shimmering greyness. And he was carrying something. She caught a glint of reflection; was he carrying a torch?

'You want light?' His voice cracked and he was breathing heavily. He flicked a switch and fear slipped swift and cold as a knife into the pit of her stomach.

'Is that enough light for you?'

She gazed in horror as the torch swung wildly, lighting up one picture then another and another.

'Do you see?'

She saw, wishing that the darkness would swallow up what she saw. Faces, all young, all pretty. Smiling, sweet faces, full of hope, innocent of fear. Clara recognised many of them – faces from the newspapers – the faces of dead girls; girls raped and murdered. More of them, torn and crumpled where she had thrown them to the floor, their faces twisted into grotesque shapes by the impotent fury she had vented on them. She screamed.

She went on screaming while he let the light play on their faces for another thirty interminable seconds, then he left her to the darkness and her imagination.

Chapter Seventeen

Barton stepped into Lawson's office. Lawson looked up from his paperwork, his nerves tingling. Something had happened. 'What?' he demanded.

'A body's turned up.'

Lawson felt suddenly cold. 'Have we got an ID?'

'Not yet. She was dumped naked. She's been in the water some time.'

'Shit!' Lawson hissed. If she had been in the water, any external forensic evidence would almost certainly have been washed away.

'Get hold of Pascal, will you? Where's the body?'

'The Countess of Chester mortuary.'

Lawson nodded to himself, calculating how long it would take to get there, working out the quickest route. 'I'll meet you in the car park. Five minutes.'

As they drove to the hospital mortuary, it struck Lawson that McAteer's concerns had been prophetic: he had left it twenty-four hours before bringing in the media, and they had found a body in the Dee. Lawson had no strong religious beliefs – he had seen too much suffering in his career to believe in the bene-volence of an omniscient god; he had come to the conclusion that God, if indeed He did exist, was indifferent to the struggles and the cruelty inflicted by man on his fellows.

Despite his cynicism, Lawson did pray, from time to time. He prayed now, for Clara Pascal, not entirely sure who he was addressing his prayer to – God or a more corporeal power, equally indifferent to the preciousness of this one life among so many. He prayed that it wasn't Clara's body awaiting identification in the mortuary and since pragmatism told him that there were few other possibilities, he prayed that if indeed it was Clara, she had died swiftly and with little pain.

By the time they reached Liverpool Road, the rain was coming in great drifts, the clouds low enough to bring a misty pall down over Chester.

'Dr Lathom is doing the PM,' Barton said, as he pressed the buzzer for entry.

The intercom crackled and a voice asked them their business. Lawson gave their names and ranks and the double doors swung open. A mortuary technician stood inside, ready to show them in, checking their warrant cards before leading them to the post mortem room.

'When is Pascal due?' Lawson asked. They followed the technician, turning right before the visitors' suite, towards the business end of the place.

'He hasn't been told yet,' Barton said.

'Hasn't been told?'

'He's been off on his travels again.'

'Isn't that why we've got surveillance on him?'

They passed tall fridges, with their four-high stacks of shelves and Lawson noted that only one was full, every slot in the door was labelled: there were four people in chilly repose here, waiting to be claimed.

'They know where he is,' Barton said, 'but McAteer told the team to leave him be. He doesn't want Pascal to know he's being followed.'

They were in a wide corridor with a bed lift on one side and standard personnel lift on the other. In an office nearby a radio was playing at a low volume. The air was heavy with a sweetly scented disinfectant, which made Lawson's stomach roil in anticipation.

'What's he been up to?' Lawson asked.

The technician handed them both gowns. 'Overshoes and caps are on the rack to your left,' he said, before he disappeared into the post mortem room. Barton waited for the doors to swing to after him.

'He was supposed to go in to work,' Barton went on. 'His secretary's been phoning his place all morning. Apparently, some big cheese has been trying to contact him about a leisure complex Pascal is designing.'

'So where is he?'

'All over the place. He drove out to Tarvin. Every street, like he was drawing an OS map.' He looked Lawson in the eye. 'I think he's looking for her, Steve.'

Lawson hadn't been expecting that. 'Poor bastard,' he remarked, tying his overalls.

Barton nodded. 'But he won't find her like that.'

Maybe not, but Lawson thought he would do the same, if it was Marie who had gone missing. Doing *something*, no matter how fruitless, was always better than doing nothing.

A SOCO Lawson recognised from the previous Wednesday put her head round the door. 'Dr Lathom wants to know will you be much longer – he'd like to get started.'

Inside, despite the constant downrush of air from the ventilation system, the room was rank with the unmistakable whiff of decay. The body lay, grey and vulnerable, naked and cold on the steel table, and Lawson was almost overwhelmed by a sense of sadness for the woman, robbed of her life, and now viewed with curiosity by strangers. He had dreaded coming here; at the same time he had hoped that they would know for certain: either it was Clara Pascal or it wasn't. He tried to make some comparison with his mental image of Clara, using the photograph they had circulated as a reference point, but the body was bloated and discoloured, the skin almost soapy in appearance. Even her husband would have difficulty recognising this woman. She was married – at least she wore a wedding-ring – and she had dark, shoulder-length hair. He was no wiser and he pitied any man having to identify his wife from this.

'Gather round,' Dr Lathom said.

Lawson and Barton moved closer. The SOCO, already gowned up, stood at the end of the table and got a shot of the face, then she moved next to Lawson to take another. The businesslike, unemotional way in which she worked seemed somehow indecent, the bright flare of the camera flash a further offence to the dead woman's dignity. He had never got used to the clinical pragmatism of a post mortem.

'How long has she been in the water?' he asked.

Lathom gave him a comical look. 'To the hour?'

Lawson had attended enough post mortems to know that estimating time of death was an imprecise science. 'A rough idea will do,' he said. 'Days?' If the body had been in the water for days it could not be Clara. Adding reluctantly, 'Less?'

Lathom peered at the inspector over the rim of his glasses. He understood. 'Judging by the degree of saponification . . . Several days – and that *is* an estimate, mark you.'

'Right.' Lawson was aware that his voice sounded tight. Not Clara – not *likely* to be Clara, he corrected himself. Despite the uncertainty, his sense of relief was huge. It seemed perverse to be relieved by the news: a woman was dead. That fact was immutable. She had been dumped like offal into the river, left to rot. But the fact that it wasn't Clara meant more to him than he would have expected, perhaps more than it should, strictly within the bounds of professional objectivity.

Lathom continued his visual examination of the corpse, his gloved hands clasped firmly behind his back, as if he feared that exuberance for his task might lead him to touch the body and disturb some crucial evidence. He gave a short sniff and glancing up at the officers, indicated with his little finger. 'There's some bruising around the nose and mouth.'

Lawson stared into the face of the woman; he saw nothing but a faint shadow beneath the pale, waxy coating over her skin.

'This—' Lathom pointed to a dark smudge on the right side of her nose '– is almost certainly a thumb-print. There's more bruising under the chin,' he said, tilting the head back a little. 'As if he's cupped her chin in his palm and covered her mouth with the rest of his hand.' He demonstrated on the corpse. 'Pinching her nostrils closed.'

Lawson swore softly.

'What's up, boss?' Barton asked.

'Something the little girl said.' All his misgivings returned with the force of an express train. 'The man grabbed Clara from behind. And put his hand over her mouth and nose.'

Barton exhaled, a long, regretful sigh.

Lathom looked from one man to the other. 'We won't know for sure whether she was suffocated or drowned until after I've completed the organ analysis. And if it *is* bruising around the mouth, it will be more visible when I cut into the tissues. So,' He rubbed his hands briskly. 'Shall we make a start?'

Pascal's entire body quivered. He hung back as if standing in the visitors' room doorway would prevent the inevitable. Barton watched closely as the pathologist placed a small, sealed plastic bag on the table in front of Pascal – visual identification of the body was out of the question. The bag contained the one personal possession the killer had left her, a wedding-ring. Pascal's face showed signs of strain and the blood vessels in his temples throbbed visibly. Barton moved closer, ready to catch him if he fell.

He touched Pascal lightly between the shoulder-blades – the barest touch – and the big man stumbled forward through the open door as though he had been shoved. Suddenly Pascal's body seemed to jerk as if electrocuted and it was a moment or two before Barton realised that he was crying.

'Mr Pascal,' he said. 'Is this—'

That was as far as he got, because Pascal turned and barged past him into the corridor and was violently, wretchedly sick.

The radio was playing quietly in the staff room when he went in. It was too small for the four of them, but they took their breaks two at a time, to maintain minimal staffing, so it wasn't generally a problem.

'Listen to this,' Lynn said, turning up the volume.

He couldn't concentrate: the clutter distressed him. Unwashed mugs on the narrow table and boxes of brochures stacked up on the floor. One or two of the brochures had found their way on to the staff-room table and were spoiled by coffee rings and grease spots. He began clearing away, clattering the crockery to drown out her prattle. The radio commentary continued, but she spoke over it.

'Leave that for a minute – this is important.'

He paused, glancing across at her. Lynn's eyes glittered with the greedy excitement of a sparrow at a picnic table. '. . . body of a woman found in the River Dee has been identified as Eleanor Gorton, a financial advisor . . .' he heard.

He looked away quickly, into the sink, piled with plates and dishes from lunch-time.

'Isn't it horrible?' Lynn said.

'Disgusting.' He was talking about the mess. How could people live like this? He rolled up his shirt sleeves and began running hot water into the bowl. It hadn't taken long to identify her. A client, perhaps, reported her missing when she failed to turn up for a meeting. Worried she had skipped with their investment portfolio.

Lynn tutted impatiently. 'Don't you remember? She was in here. Booked a short break – the Canaries, I think.'

He shrugged, feeling the tension between his shoulder-blades.

'Poor thing. She could've been sunning herself on a beach, lazing by a pool instead of –' She waved a hand in front of her face as if to dispel the harrowing image of Eleanor's body in the chilly waters of the River Dee.

Shut up! He scoured the tannin-stained interior of a mug with the cloth. Eleanor was nothing to do with her. She was spoiling what they'd had together, talking about her, claiming some ownership of her.

'D'you think I should call the police?'

The mug slipped from his hand and fell with a clatter into the sink. Hot water and suds splashed onto his shirt. Lynn looked up, startled. He brushed himself down, thinking how to frame a response.

'The police'll be busy enough without every shopkeeper who served her in the past two weeks jamming their phone lines.'

Lynn looked disappointed. 'D'you think so?'

He turned back to the sink. 'It's up to you,' he said, injecting a note of doubt into his voice, knowing that Lynn would need encouragement to follow this one through – Lynn was not a woman to have the courage of her convictions.

'I wouldn't want to waste their time,' she said, echoing his tone. 'Surely you remember her, though?'

He gritted his teeth.

'Late thirties,' she went on. 'Long dark hair. Curly. Not bad for her age.'

Why won't she shut up! She was imposing her image of Eleanor onto his memory. He didn't want it – the very idea repelled him. He tried to recall the woman he had known. He could not. He had spent hours with her – days – he had shared intimacies that only a husband or lover should. He had even recorded and watched her final moments until he knew every nuance, every word, every gesture, and yet he could not see her face.

Eleanor Gorton was becoming distant to him, a fading

memory, even though it had only been a few days since he had slipped her, silent as a fish, into the icy waters of the Dee. It seemed slightly obscene, that Lynn should bandy her name about. Insensitive — embarrassing — like mentioning an ex-wife in the presence of the new bride. He had moved on. His heart and soul and mind were dedicated to preparing the next. But for the police, for the media, for a public eager to hear the sordid details of death, this was new — a breaking story. They would examine her last known movements, trace her associates, looking for likely suspects. They would shake their heads sadly over the dangers of women in careers that took them into the homes of strangers, out of the safe circle of a husband's strong arms. Psychologists would advise on safeguards, how to minimize risk. When all the time she had been in the safest possible place.

'Think it'll be in the early *Echo*? Lynn asked.

She wants to smile, but she knows it would be inappropriate. He shrugged again, worried that if he spoke, she would hear his contempt behind the words. There would be photographs, of course. He would keep the press cuttings for his album. He focused on a fleck of food on a plate, rubbing it, listening to the squeak to blot out Lynn's voice.

He made another effort to remember what Eleanor looked like. Dark hair, of course, and slim, but these were only general descriptors. Her features, her skin, the shape of her mouth . . . He tried to concentrate, but Lynn's description and her constant chatter intruded. He would get the album out tonight, maybe watch the video.

'Think I might go out — see if I can get a paper.'

He grunted non-committally.

'See what they say about it. I mean, I might have been the last to see her—'

'This is really making you *wet*, isn't it, Lynn?' The words were out before he could stop them.

Her eyes grew round and shocked and her mouth dropped open. Ugly, ugly bitch.

'*What?*' She stood up. '*What* did you say?'

He turned away, shutting out the ugliness of her poorly disguised lust for salacious details. Hypocrite!

'You take that back!' she shouted. 'You take that back, you horrible man!' Her voice rose to a shriek.

Shouldn't have said that. Shouldn't have let her see what you really think of her. Shut her up before the others come to see what all the noise is about. She carried on yelling and he felt a flutter of panic in his chest.

'You're right.' He looked away from her. *Tell her it's upset you. You didn't know what you were saying. Apologise!* 'It must be . . . scary — being a woman — when something like this happens.' His voice sounded false, metallic to his own ears, but he hoped he was saying the right things, what she expected to hear. He wouldn't look at her, because she would see what was behind his eyes and he knew from experience that it frightened them. 'It's the randomness of it. It seems so . . . senseless.'

Lynn was staring at him. He could feel her gaze hot on the skin of his neck. She waited a moment, then gave a sniff to show that she wasn't entirely appeased. 'You can't feel safe in your own home,' she said, her tone defensive, almost accusing.

But they had. That was the point. They *had* felt safe and that was why it had been so easy.

Chapter Eighteen

For a while there was nothing. She did not faint, but the screams – her screams – died away and with them the fear, the cold and the pain, for the chain had bruised her ankle, and it hurt to move. Even the faces of the girls faded from her mind, disappearing for a time into the darkness, allowing her a brief respite.

It was as if she had left her rational self and escaped to a refuge where nothing and no one could touch her.

When she returned, it was not all at once, but a gradual coming back, a coming *to*. She first became aware of an ache, not physical, but a profound sadness as strong and debilitating as physical distress. Once she had identified the emotion, she was able to recognise her own bodily condition. She was sitting on the floor, her hands clasped around her shins and she was rocking slowly backwards and forwards, her forehead pressed hard against her knees and her breath warm against her inner thighs.

Slowly, as slowly as she rocked, thought became possible. Unforgiving reason asserted itself despite her efforts to stave it off. Fear and hunger worried at her insides, the one indistinguishable from the other, both demanding a place in her consciousness.

The silence became a roar in her ears. She discovered that she was cold and she became aware once again of the fusty damp smell of her cell. She was back.

In the inky blackness that surrounded her, enfolding and oppressing her, Clara knew that scores of faces stared down at her, each one a chilling reminder of her own fragile mortality. And in her heightened emotional state, she felt their sadness, imagined their fear.

'No!' Her voice fell flat in the close silence, but it helped her to tear her thoughts away from the terrible spiral of despair and panic she was in danger of giving way to. She made an effort to imagine what Hugo and Pippa would be doing now, on a normal Thursday. Was it Thursday? She wasn't sure and in this suffocating dark she couldn't see her hand in front of her face, let alone the dial of her watch.

She tried hard to convince herself that Pippa was at home, safe, with Hugo.

But how can you be so sure, Clara?

If she wasn't, this man would have taunted and tormented me with it. He hasn't missed an opportunity yet. She's safe. Of *course* she's safe.

She paused, half expecting her harsh inner voice to raise some objection, to find fault with her reasoning, but for once it was silent and for this, Clara was grateful.

How were they coping? She couldn't bear to think of Hugo sitting by the phone, waiting for a call Clara feared her abductor had no intention of making.

There's hundreds more, he'd said. Am I to add to the number? She closed her eyes and felt again the presence of the girls smiling down from the walls around her, felt also a creeping sense of guilt and shame that their young lives had ended so brutally.

'I prosecute cases as well as defend them,' she said, just audibly.

As well? Who are you trying to kid, Clara?

'I've put a few away.'

Yes, and you've got a fair number off.

She was crying. 'I've never knowingly—'

Oh, now, come on! These men are manipulators and charmers who can rape a woman one night and attend their daughter's confirmation the next. Men like this guy. Think he's a family man?

The key scraped in the lock and she hurriedly wiped her eyes and stood up. This time she did not flinch from looking at him. He was impossible to read, his face a red mask, his eyes dark sockets in the dim light from the room beyond.

He did not speak and after a while she sat down again. Her tights were torn and her ankle bled a little where the chain chafed. She rubbed it absently, trying not to look at the photographs on the walls, but they were difficult to ignore. An occasional draught would stir them and the rustle of paper was like the hushed voices of girls in whispered conversation.

Clara felt tension building in her like steam in a pressure cooker. The more she tried to block him out, the more she grew hot under his blank stare.

Suddenly, she could stand it no longer. 'What do you want?' she screamed. 'Tell me what you want!' No matter how terrible the answer, it must surely be easier to deal with than this agonising silence, this awful guessing game.

'Are you brave?' It was a challenge.

Her breath caught in her throat and she felt a jagged stab of fear. She pushed it away and forced herself to answer calmly: 'Do I need to be?'

He laughed softly, as if she had missed the point and she had again that disconcerting sense that he was testing her, and that she had failed.

Mr Creggin, her pupil-master, had asked such questions. Booby-trapped questions that had no right answer. Closed questions that demanded a forthright yes or no, neither of which was sufficient answer. A yes, and she was puffed-up, conceited, vainglorious; a no would expose her as shallow, her modesty an affectation.

'No false modesty, Clara,' he would say, a mocking smile in his eyes.

She learned from Mr Creggin the trick of answering questions with questions, the knack of evading an honest answer with a reply to some other, unspoken question.

'I don't know why you're doing this,' she said wearily, when a few more minutes had elapsed.

'You know what fear does?' he asked.

Oh, I know all right, Clara thought bitterly. It degrades and dehumanises. Is that what he wanted to hear? She wouldn't give him the satisfaction.

But he required no answer. He had all the answers. 'It softens you up, breaks down your defences, whittles at you till you'll do anything, just for the promise of getting away alive. Even if you know it's not going to happen, the promise is enough, because it lets you have hope, and without hope, you might as well be dead anyway.'

'Get on with it,' she said, suddenly sick with weariness. 'Whatever you intend to do. Get it over with.'

He laughed again, softly, almost sadly. 'Don't be in such a hurry,' he said.

She closed her eyes to shut him out. She couldn't stay here. She would go insane if she stayed here any longer. When she looked again, he was shaking his head.

'It's not enough,' he muttered quietly, half to himself. 'It's not nearly enough.'

He left her, with the grey light filtering reluctantly from the room beyond the steel door; a place she had never seen and could not begin to imagine. The light, though pale and cold, was sufficient to show, in black-and-white, the pictures of the other victims. Clara checked herself. *Other victims.* She would not allow herself to become another victim. But she had made a painful discovery over the hours and days of her captivity: it isn't lack of resolve that makes a victim, it is the seizing of control by another. And that, more often than not, is down to sheer bad luck. Despite her resolve, Clara felt she was losing her individuality, was becoming what he wanted her to be.

Here, in this damp, chilly pit, he decided who and what she was. She saw for the first time in her life that her standing as a human being, her dignity as a woman, depended upon men obeying unwritten rules of conduct. This man had no moral code and she was no more distinctive to him than a department store mannequin.

God, help me, she thought. I'm never getting out of here.

Chapter Nineteen

Overcoats and weatherproofs, draped over the backs of chairs, dripped onto the blood-red lino of the Incident Room. Rayner was talking in a low voice into the telephone, but most officers had handed in their reports and were ready to finish for the night. A few huddled around the clanking radiators, deriving meagre comfort from the lukewarm pipes.

The rain had continued without let-up all afternoon and into the evening. Young came in, shaking water from her hair.

'You know, Babe, whenever I see you, you're always drenched,' Fletcher said. 'In years to come, when I think of you, I'll always think "wet".'

'You're remarkably dry, considering you were supposed to be knocking on doors today,' Rayner observed coolly, hanging up the receiver.

Fletcher smiled, unruffled. 'It's all in hand. I've narrowed it down to a couple of streets. Local newsagent reckons he's a regular customer. Goes in for his *Daily Mail* every morning.'

'Early start for you tomorrow, then.' Thorpe had just come in, still wearing his Benny hat. He swept it off and wrung it out on the floor, evidently relishing the exclamations of protest it provoked.

'I take it you didn't find your perv, then, Cath?' Rayner asked.

'All bloody day,' Young grumbled. 'Chasing my tail.'

'Now *that's* a job I'd volunteer for,' Fletcher put in. A few of the men laughed.

Young glanced over at them and back to Rayner. What *am* I going to *do*?

'Ignore them,' Rayner said, as if she had read her mind.

What Young most wanted was to go home and weep, but she had to get through the debrief. She desperately wanted to learn from this investigation and she wasn't going to do that by hiding in a corner, trying to be invisible.

'So what's the story?' Rayner asked.

Young flushed a little, feeling awkward with Fletcher's eyes on her. 'Turns out they were interviewing for a new class teacher last week. One of the candidates travelled by bus — arrived early and decided to have a stroll around the perimeter, rather than bother the staff when they weren't prepared.'

'You sure it was him?'

She nodded. 'The Neighbourhood Watch called out the local uniform. He took a name.'

Fletcher laughed. 'Goose, wild and chase come to mind,' he said. 'But not necessarily in that order.'

'At least she eliminated him from the enquiry — which is more than you can say for your snappy-happy peeping Tom.'

Fletcher smiled. 'Slow but sure, that's me.' He looked her up and down. 'And slow's better than full stop, eh, Rayner?'

'I wouldn't know, Fletch.'

'Well, how far did you get with Clara's boss?'

She gave him a tight smile. Whatever Fletcher said, it sounded like innuendo. 'I'm following a couple of lines of enquiry.'

'Defensive, Sal,' he said, wagging a finger at her. 'You're sounding defensive.'

McAteer and Lawson arrived and the officers quickly settled in any available chairs or leaned against radiators and desks, eager for the update or for their chance to put forward an idea. As the room stilled, the excitement was palpable.

'Some of you will have heard about the discovery of a body this morning,' McAteer said. 'I won't keep you in suspense. It wasn't Clara Pascal.' There was a collective outrush of breath. 'But there are . . .' He paused, wondering how best to proceed. 'There are . . . similarities that lead me to think that Clara may have been abducted by Eleanor Gorton's killer.'

Lawson explained the post mortem findings – the method of suffocation which bore a striking resemblence to the way Clara's abductor had tried to subdue her.

The dismay on his officers' faces made McAteer rally. 'This isn't over,' he said emphatically. 'We can't say with absolute certainty when Eleanor was taken, but she was last seen about ten days ago. The body was in the water for two – maybe three – days. Which means he kept her alive for up to a week before he killed her. I needn't remind you that Clara has been missing for nearly two days, so we may have only a day or two before . . .' He couldn't bring himself to say the words. 'We have to find her fast,' he finished.

'Who's dealing with the Gorton killing?' Thorpe asked.

'We are.' There was a muttering of complaint for the team. 'I know, for preference, it would be one dog, one bone, but if there *is* a connection between the two women, we're more likely to spot it if the one team works on both cases.'

'So,' Lawson said. 'We're looking for mutual business or social contacts. Did they get their cars serviced at the same garage, do they go to the same gym, share the same dentist – anything that could put them together – maybe not at the same time, but in the same place.'

'What about Pascal?' Barton asked. 'I mean, his reaction when he realised the dead woman wasn't his wife—'

'People can react strangely, under stress,' McAteer said. 'If he's up to something, he'll give himself away sooner or later. Rayner, what've you got on the rapist?'

Rayner stood up. 'Prison Service are still tracking him down, Guv. But he stalked his last victim,' she explained. 'Ex-girlfriend.'

'What's taking so long?'

'He's a bit of a trouble-maker — gets moved about a lot. He was in Lancaster, but they've shifted him south — he's got a court appearance in Devon tomorrow. They think he's en route.'

McAteer nodded. 'Let me know when you find out.'

'There was another threat,' Rayner added, wondering if she was making too much of it. 'The father of a rape victim. Clara's clerk looked up the name for me. I could call in before I knock off.' Maybe Fletcher was right: maybe she *was* on the defensive.

It was nearly nine p.m. when Rayner pulled up outside a neat, nineteen-forties semi. She had been on duty since the briefing at seven-thirty that morning, much of the time spent in the drenching rain or in the freezing cold Incident Room.

A small chink of light escaped through a gap in the curtains of the front room and in an upstairs room, she saw the tell-tale blue flicker from a television set. Rayner turned up her coat collar and hurried to the kerbside. The houses were set back from the road; three-foot-high brick walls formed a barrier between the pavement and the well tended gardens. Rainwater stood in gleaming beads on the newly painted wooden gate. Rayner reached over and lifted the latch, turning her face away from the fine mist of drenching rain and as she walked quickly down the path to the house, she heard the gate close against the sandstone gatepost with a solid *thunk*.

A man answered. 'Brian Kelsall?' she asked, showing her ID. 'DC Rayner.'

'No.' The man seemed surprised.

'Do you know when Mr Kelsall will be back?'

'No. I mean . . . He doesn't live here.'

Rayner flicked through her notebook to check the address Nesta Lewis had given her.

'Oh, I'm sorry,' he said. 'I meant to say he *did* live here, but he doesn't any more. He moved.'

'Are you the new owner, sir?'

'Yes.' He seemed relieved that she at last understood him. 'Alan Meller.'

'Would you happen to have a forwarding address, sir?'

'Sorry,' he apologised again. 'We never actually met Mr Kelsall, you see his sister did all the negotiations.' A thought struck him and he brightened. 'You should try the estate agent.' He darted indoors, leaving Rayner on the doorstep in the rain.

Her coat was soaked through and the reek of damp wool caught at the back of her throat. Her feet ached and her head throbbed. She wanted to be at home in a hot bath with a glass of whisky within easy reach.

As she reached to ring the bell again, he returned and seemed to notice for the first time that she was drenched, but he didn't invite her inside; instead, he thrust a business card into her hand. 'That's the lady who sorted us out,' he said. 'She'll be able to help you, I'm sure.'

The hallway light glowed gold through the frosted lights of the front door. A shadow flitted from the kitchen across to the front room. Marie. Lawson experienced a moment of exhilaration, anticipating taking her in his arms, taking her to bed.

He opened the door and heard laughter and he realised with a pang of disappointment that Marie had company. Cheryl, he judged, by the raucousness of the laugh. He hung up his coat and popped the top button on his shirt before going into the sitting room. Music played, a soulful guitar riff which they talked over, rather than turn down the volume. The room was overheated and Cheryl's heightened colour warned him to be on his guard. Cheryl had the pale complexion of a redhead, which quickly turned florid when she was excited or angry – or when she had been drinking.

Marie turned to him, her movements loosened by a little

more wine than she was used to. 'Hi,' she said, not quite focusing on him.

'Hi yourself.'

Marie reached up and hooked her hand around the back of his neck as he bent to kiss her.

Cheryl looked at him over the rim of her glass. 'The Lone Ranger returns,' she mumbled into her drink.

He smiled.

'Long day.' It was meant as a criticism, a comment on the long nights Marie often spent alone.

'He works too hard,' Marie said, leaning her cheek against the sleeve of his jacket.

'It's a tough job, keeping the forces of evil at bay, isn't it Steve?' Cheryl said nastily.

'Driving home, are you Cheryl?' he asked.

She hammed up the careful enunciation of an inebriate. 'Got a breathalyser hidden in your jacket pocket have you, Ossifer?'

'Be nice now, children,' Marie chided.

Lawson decided he was too tired to deal with Cheryl sober and it was too late for him to try catching up now. 'I'm off to bed,' he told them.

Cheryl opened her eyes wide and clasped her free hand to her breast. 'Who will keep the city safe while the intrepid inspector sleeps?'

'Do leave him alone, Cheryl,' Marie said. Cheryl made a hobby of baiting Steve, but she laughed despite herself. Cheryl always did have the knack of making her laugh at him.

'Goodnight, Cheryl,' Lawson said.

'Don't go.' Marie caught his hand. 'Sit with us. I'll pour you some wine.' She made a grab at the bottle, miscalculated and knocked it over. Steve caught it and set it upright.

'I prefer mine in a glass,' he said.

Marie giggled. 'Action replay of last night, huh, Lawson?' She slapped the sofa next to her. 'C'mon. Don't be such a grouch.'

'I'm tired,' he said. 'And I have to save the world again tomorrow.'

Cheryl snorted into her wine.

Always leave them laughing, he thought as he wearily climbed the stairs. Cheryl's jibes needled him more than he liked to admit, but she was Marie's best friend and he felt obliged to maintain at least a semblance of goodwill.

'I've upset him, haven't I?' Cheryl said.

Marie shrugged. 'It's this case he's working on. You know they found a body today?'

'Oh, shit. Me and my big mouth.'

'It's all right, it wasn't the barrister — God, what am I saying?' Marie shook her head, trying to clear it. 'It was all over the news. Didn't you see?'

Cheryl sipped thoughtfully at her wine. 'Steve's a good, kind, decent man.'

'He is,' Marie agreed, nodding so emphatically that wine sploshed onto her sweatshirt.

'So why do I always want to get a rise out of him?' The question was rhetorical.

Cheryl left twenty minutes later and Marie poured an extra glass of wine and took it upstairs. The bedside light was on. Lawson was lying on his side, turned away from her and she sat on the bed next to him. 'Nasty old Cheryl's gone. She says she's very sorry, but your good nature brings out the devil in her.'

Still no response. She went to his side of the bed. He was asleep. Perhaps it was as well: Cheryl would be more embarrassed by the notion that Steve had heard her apology — even second-hand — than by her rudeness earlier on.

Marie made a clumsy one-hundred-and-eighty degree turn and almost lost her balance, bumping into Lawson in the process.

He grunted, putting out one hand in a reflex response.

'Whoops!' Marie giggled. 'Watch the wine!'

Lawson sat up, looking rumpled and sleep-sodden. She offered him a glass and he took it, asking, 'Aren't you being a bit heavy on this?'

She raised her eyebrows. 'How would you know?'

'Ouch,' he said.

She took a sip of wine and glanced blearily at the flickering red digits of the alarm clock on the bedside table next to him. 'I'm celebrating,' she said.

'The cleaning company commission?'

She tilted her head in acknowledgement.

He frowned, still sleepy, trying to make sense of what she was saying. 'I thought that was small beer.'

'It is. But the owner was so impressed that she's recommended us to her husband's firm and *they've* just won a big contract to supply organic foods to one of the big supermarkets. They want a new brand image.'

They clinked glasses. 'I'm sorry, Marie. It's just—'

'Cheryl. I know. But I needed someone to share this with.'

'And I wasn't around.'

'I won't sit at home, counting every minute late as a penalty point, Steve. I won't become a sour, bitter copper's wife.'

Like Lynn, he thought. Marie was reminding him how badly his previous marriage had gone wrong. He gazed at her for some time, wondering if she resented the frequent late nights, the broken promises, the missed dinner engagements. He took a breath. 'Marie—'

She put a finger to his lips. 'Shut up and kiss me,' she said.

Chapter Twenty

He thought she'd never stop. At first it thrilled him, her blind abandonment to the horror of her predicament. Then he had felt an uneasy irritation. He shut the cell door against it, but the sounds, though muffled, penetrated the steel barrier, sending shivers of anguish through the air.

It went on and on until he was convinced she had gone mad. He fled. Terror, he understood, and despair, but this went beyond reason into a dark and dangerous place he had no wish to explore.

He walked, head down, hands in his pockets, away from the house, away from the woman, afraid that the fear that consumed her would insinuate itself into his own mind. He couldn't afford to show weakness: she was trained to spot it, instinctively attuned to it. He returned, hours later, to a breathless stillness.

He wasn't given to fanciful notions, but as he grasped the doorhandle, for one terrible moment he thought that maybe she hadn't stopped at all. Maybe she had gone on screaming during the hours he had been away, that her screams, trapped like wasps in a bottle, would swarm out and overwhelm him as soon as he opened the door.

'Ridiculous,' he muttered, but all the same, he put his ear to the door and listened, half-imagining a faint buzz, a slight vibration through the solid metal.

For the first few minutes after he opened up, he could not speak to her. Not that he was afraid of her — that would be absurd — but he was in awe; such raw emotion *was* awesome to witness. He told himself that she had brought it all on herself, making demands — she'd wanted light — well maybe in future she'd be more careful what she asked for. Even so, he hadn't meant to push her over the edge: Clara Pascal didn't deserve the option of retreating into a comforting madness.

She had driven him away with her screams and he felt the need to reassert his authority; but he left her, as always, with the feeling that it wasn't enough, that she had upper hand — challenging him, demanding, always demanding things of him. Well, he would just have to think of a way of regaining advantage.

Chapter Twenty One

The atmosphere was tense in the Pascal household. Hugo and Trish had argued the previous evening and Trish had gone home when he desperately needed her to stay. She returned at seven a.m., letting herself in with her latch key, and looking like she hadn't slept at all. They ate breakfast in silence, except for the clink of a spoon against a cereal bowl and the occasional sigh from Pippa.

'Don't play with your food, eat it,' Hugo muttered.

Immediately, Pippa stopped eating altogether and her eyes filled with tears. Trish glanced angrily at Hugo, but he looked away, stirring his coffee with unwarranted concentration.

'I'm going to my room,' Pippa said.

'Finish your breakfast first.'

'I'm not hungry.'

Trish tried to catch his eye, to warn him off, but he went on. 'You didn't eat your dinner last night. You must be hungry.'

'Hugo—'

'I'm *not!*'

Trish glared at him and this time he registered her annoyance. He passed a hand over his face. 'All right,' he said. 'But stay off the phone.'

Pippa shot him a look of pure hatred, but she got down from

the table quietly and pushed her chair in with exaggerated care, closing the door softly behind her.

Trish got up to refill her coffee cup. 'Would you like more?' She held the jug over Hugo's cup, refusing to respond to his grunt in reply, until he was forced to look up at her. The contact was enough. He saw the hurt in her eyes and he knew he was entirely to blame.

'About yesterday,' he began.

'That's your business,' Trish said stiffly.

'No, Trish. I shouldn't have said what I did.'

'You're upset. It's understandable.' But it was plain she neither understood, nor forgave him.

'It was cruel.' When he had returned home in the early evening, she was upset, worried. She demanded to know where he had been all afternoon. He resented the question and replied with a brutal disregard for her feelings.

'Whiling away the hours at the mortuary.' He had said it to injure, but the look of horror on her face was terrible to see. It was no good retracting, explaining that it wasn't Clara; he had intended to frighten her — no, worse — to cause her pain, and Trish knew it.

'Trish, I'm sorry,' he said, reaching for her hand.

Trish was about to answer when the kitchen door opened. Pippa was dressed in her school uniform, looking pale but determined. She had plain blue ribbons in her hair and the only trace of the badges she had worn on her birthday were a few pin-holes in the lapels of her blazer. She looked at the two of them and, blushing slightly, Trish gently removed her hand from Hugo's grasp.

'Will you take me to school, please, Trish?' She said it with dignity, making a brave effort to keep the tears at bay.

Trish looked to Hugo. He shrugged, helplessly.

'I think you'd best stay home, pet,' Trish said gently. 'At least until after the weekend.'

The child set her jaw in a small-scale imitation of her father. Neither she nor Hugo looked at the other.

'I want to go to school.' She was calm for the moment, but she was on the brink of tears or rage, and it could go either way.

'But why darling?'

The phone trilled sharply and Pippa jumped, giving a little cry of alarm.

They all stared at the phone – only for a fraction of a second – less than a heartbeat, but the moment seemed to stretch, then Hugo lunged across the room, sending a chair skittering on its side.

'Remember what they said,' Trish shouted. 'Stay calm. Tell them you want to speak to Clara.'

Pippa stood trembling and she wrapped her arms around the little girl as Hugo pick up the receiver.

The emotions chased across his face so rapidly that it was difficult to separate them. Hope and terror in equal measure, then disappointment, and finally annoyance.

'I can't think about that now.' In the pause that followed, he looked over at Trish and murmured. 'My secretary.'

Pippa turned to Trish and clung to her, sobbing.

Continuing his telephone conversation, he said, 'He made *me* wait, didn't he? Let him wait a few days.'

Another pause, then, 'Well if he can't, tell him to stuff it!' He slammed the phone down.

Trish bent to Pippa and wiped her tears with the broad pads of her thumbs. 'You go upstairs for a minute,' she said, kissing the child on the forehead. 'I'll be up soon.'

Hugo stood glowering at the phone for a few seconds longer, then he went to pick up the chair he had knocked over, dropped it half way and kicked it savagely into the far wall.

Trish hesitated, but only for a second, then she put a hand on Hugo's arm. He sat down and covered his face with his hands. Trish righted the chair and sat opposite him, waiting several minutes before beginning.

'You're not helping us, Hugo,' she said.

He gave her a hurt, resentful look. 'I'm doing what I can, Trish.'

'Running away? Leaving Pippa — leaving both of us — to face this alone? Leaving me to try and hold things together?'

He didn't answer and Trish shook her head angrily. She saw an anxious look flit over his face and for a moment he looked ready to explain his behaviour on the previous afternoon, then he clamped his jaw tight.

'I'm trying to make things right,' he said.

'Then sort things out with Mr Melker. Give your child some security, even if you don't care about yourself.'

The houses on the main road through Boughton had the look of seaside chalets on a wet winter's day. Rayner drove slowly, looking for house numbers, hoping to catch Miss Kelsall's house without having to double back on herself.

Mist settled in the grey stretches of undeveloped land between the clusters of houses, places where brambles thrived and litter, caught on their thorns, fluttered in the winter gales, slowly disintegrating until eventually they were lost in the scrubby tangle of the new season's growth.

Rayner slowed to a crawl, ignoring a motorist who leaned on his horn and swerved around her. Three-seven-five. She had found it. A bungalow, recently painted in pale blue and white. The wooden sills looked pulpy and soft and the tarmac was pitted. Tufts of grass, now yellow and matted, had pushed through in places, but the garden itself was well kept. A beech hedge, cut square, provided some privacy from the houses either side, and from the roadway. The lawn was trimmed and edged and the borders, though sparsely planted, were weed-free. Rayner formed the impression of a woman who was struggling, but determined to keep up appearances.

Inside the house, she heard the buzz of a vacuum cleaner. She rang and waited. When it was clear the bell couldn't be heard, she knocked long and loud, rattling the door knocker till the clatter resounded through the house. Abruptly, the vacuum cleaner was silenced. She knocked again, then stood back.

Marjorie Kelsall was not what she expected. What she *had* expected, Rayner wasn't entirely sure. Someone older, certainly. This woman was barely forty; she wore her hair short, it was fine and greying and lay flat on her scalp, clean and well groomed, but strangely lifeless.

She held the door firmly, so that only a wedge of pale coral hall carpet showed. She seemed edgy, anxious to get back to her housework.

Rayner presented her ID.

'I need to speak to your brother.'

'Oh.' Miss Kelsall sighed. 'You'd better come in.' She led Rayner down the hallway, past framed family photographs, stepping around the vacuum cleaner and into the kitchen.

'You'll have to be quick,' she said. 'I'm due in work at ten.'

'Where do you work?' Rayner asked.

Miss Kelsall turned, her hand on the door handle, her eyes a pale, clear blue examined Rayner's face. 'Why do you want to know?'

'Just making conversation.' Miss Kelsall seemed on the defensive.

The kitchen had apparently been dealt with before the hallway: it was clean and wiped, no dishes on the drainer, only a dishcloth, gleaming white and wrung dry. The washing-up liquid was stowed out of sight. The cupboards were old, but well-cared for, the doors painted bright green, and the frames cream. The windows sparkled, the low winter sun didn't even show up a smear on the glass.

Miss Kelsall fell silent while she fussed over finding a plate and arranging an assortment of biscuits on it, then made coffee with quick, precise movements. Although she was solidly built, she moved well, with fluid, athletic grace.

She caught Rayner watching her as she turned with the mugs

of coffee. Rayner rarely blushed, but under Miss Kelsall's steady gaze she felt the blood rush to her cheeks.

Miss Kelsall placed the mugs on the kitchen table and waved Rayner to a seat.

'You want to know where Brian is?'

Rayner waited.

'Why?' Miss Kelsall asked.

'Why?'

'It's a simple question, Constable.' Her thin mouth set in a hard line.

'I don't think—'

'I'm his sister. His only living relative. Don't I have a right to know?'

'Routine, Miss Kelsall.'

'It may be, for the sort of people *you're* used to dealing with, but it is not part of *my* routine,' Miss Kelsall replied tartly. 'Police calling at nine o'clock in the morning.'

Rayner deliberated. She could kick up a fuss, threaten Miss Kelsall with obstruction, waste a few hours just to talk to a man who was, in all probability, innocent of anything worse than making an idle threat in the heat of the moment. Or she could take the line of least resistance.

'You've probably seen on the news, about the disappearance of Clara Pascal. She's barrister—'

'I know who she is.'

Rayner was startled by the venom in Miss Kelsall's tone. Since they were being honest, Rayner decided to be blunt. 'Your brother made a threat against Ms Pascal,' she said.

'Alex Martin raped my niece, Miss Rayner. He raped her, humiliated and terrified her into silence. Your *Ms* Pascal convinced the jury that Laura only made charges against him because she was frightened of what her father would say, when he found out.'

'I'm not here to discuss—'

That was as far as she got. Miss Kelsall's voice rose to a

shout. 'No, *you* listen to *me!* That animal got away with ruining a young girl's life. She couldn't be with people – her friends, even her family – after what he did to her. She couldn't function as a human being. If it was your daughter, how would you feel?'

'I'm not judging your brother, Miss Kelsall. I just need to rule him out of our investigation.'

Miss Kelsall gave a short, harsh laugh. 'You can rule him out, all right.'

Rayner was losing patience. 'I will, if I can. *After* I've spoken to him.'

'Are you a religious person, Constable?'

Sarcasm was about the last thing Rayner was in the mood for. 'Would you care to explain?' she asked.

Miss Kelsall looked at her through half-closed eyes, then abruptly, she stood. 'Wait here,' she commanded.

Rayner listened at the kitchen door. Miss Kelsall's footsteps retreated down the hall and then she heard them on the stairs. The house was unnaturally quiet; it felt as if the normal boisterousness of daily life had been stilled – there was no music, no radio, no sound at all, except for the quiet tick of the kitchen clock. Rayner opened and closed a few cupboards, but there was nothing out of the ordinary and she was just taking a quick inventory of the notice board when Miss Kelsall came back into the room, carrying a scrap book.

'Here.' She placed the book on the table, opening it at the centre. The photograph was instantly recognisable. Three railway carriages lay on their sides, the front two were burnt-out. A fourth had ridden over the top of the penultimate carriage and had come to rest at a forty-five degree angle to the others. Briefcases and clothing lay scattered around. The chaotic way in which the fire engines and ambulances were parked emphasised the disorder and horror of the event.

'The Crewe rail crash?' This picture, and ones very like it, had dominated the news for almost a week during October. Rayner looked up. Miss Kelsall's face was unreadable.

'I see. I'm sorry, Miss Kelsall. If I'd known this . . .'

'You'd have spared me.'

Rayner didn't react to the woman's needling tone. 'I wouldn't have troubled you.'

'Well, thank you for your concern. Now, if you don't mind, I've a job to go to.'

Rayner tipped her coffee into the sink and rinsed her mug, giving herself time to think how to phrase her next question. 'How did Laura take it?' she asked at last.

'Laura?' Miss Kelsall stared at her.

'How's she coping?'

Miss Kelsall took a breath, then she shook her head. 'Her father is dead, Miss Rayner, and the animal who raped her is still at large.'

That wasn't really an answer, but it seemed that Miss Kelsall wasn't given to providing straight answers to questions.

'I'd like to speak to her.'

'I told you, she's frightened of new people.'

'Even so.'

'What can you possibly want from her? What could she tell you?'

Rayner sighed. 'I'm going to have to insist.'

Miss Kelsall closed the scrapbook and set it to one side, then she picked up the dishcloth and wiped down the table unnecessarily. 'You won't get anything from—'

'Her address, please,' Rayner interrupted.

'You're wasting your time.'

'If you'd be happier, I've no objection to your being present . . .'

Miss Kelsall seemed horrified by the suggestion. 'I can't!'

Rayner felt sorry for the woman. Whether or not Laura had concocted the story of the rape, Miss Kelsall evidently believed it and now her brother was dead she must feel responsible for the girl. Yet something had happened that had estranged her from her niece; apparently all communication had been severed. She must feel she had failed them both. Even so, Rayner had to say: 'I'd still like to speak to Laura.'

With an exclamation of disgust, Miss Kelsall rummaged in a drawer and pulled out a notebook and pen. She hastily scribbled an address and tore off the sheet to hand to Rayner.

The house was a three-storey Edwardian property, the front garden of which had been concreted over and was tarry with oil stains. Now, only one car stood on the lumpy concrete, but Rayner could see from the black streaks that there were usually two more.

The front door stood open, and from somewhere inside, the dull thud of a dance rhythm pounded. Rayner rang the bell for flat six. There was no reply and after two more tries, she selected three from the bank of nine on the door panel and leaned on their bell-pushes. Doors opened and she heard a confused muddle of sleepy voices, swearing, demanding to know what all the noise was about.

A grey-faced boy with a prominent Adam's apple came from the flat to the left of the front door. He was barefoot, dressed in jogging bottoms and a sweater. Rayner stepped through the porch, into the hall. The original mosaic floor was visible through the worn brown lino; pink, tan and cream tesserae now cracked and worn.

'Fuck you want?' the boy demanded groggily, scratching his backside.

'Laura Kelsall.' The hall smelled of dust and bicycle oil.

'You her mum, are you?'

A face appeared on the first landing, ducking to get a good look at her. Rayner called up: 'Have you seen Laura?'

The face vanished.

A girl came out of the other ground-floor flat.

'What's your name?' Rayner asked.

'Who wants to know?' She had a snub-nosed, pugnacious

face and a swagger that Rayner suspected covered a whole mass of insecurities.

She flashed her ID. 'Officer Dibble wants to know.'

The girl sniggered, evidently surprised at a police officer sending herself up.

'Kerry,' she said, ruffling her hair, in case it was lying too neat and flat.

'So, do you two know Laura?' She glanced from Kerry to the boy, who stopped guiltily in the act of closing his flat door and stepped out into the hall again.

'I don't even know *her*,' he said, lifting his chin to indicate his near neighbour.

'And you are?'

'Dave Holbrook.' He said it with great reluctance.

'Dave, meet Kerry. Now, can I get a bit of co-operation, here?'

'Laura, you said?' Kerry, it seemed, had decided that Rayner was all right.

'Laura Kelsall.'

Dave and Kerry exchanged blank looks.

'Brown hair,' Rayner went on 'slim, five-five, hazel eyes . . .'

Kerry shook her head slowly. 'I've been here about three months. Can't remember anyone like that, can you, Dave?'

Dave shrugged. 'It's none of my business anyway.'

Kerry spread her hands in a gesture of regret, as Dave shuffled off, muttering to himself.

'Ah, well. I'll talk to a few of the others.' Rayner looked up the poorly lit staircase, half-expecting to see frightened eyes blinking at her, like creatures in a night forest.

'Who chose the colour scheme?' she asked. The gloom was exaggerated by the dark purple emulsion on the walls, slapped on over woodchip paper.

'The landlord. Hangover from the seventies. He told me this place used to be a hippie commune.'

'Sold out to capitalism, did he? What d'you call him?'

Kerry laughed. 'You don't want to know what I call him. But his name is Parks.'

'You wouldn't have a contact number, would you?'

'On my rent book, but it might take me a minute or two.'

They agreed that Rayner would call on her way out and the constable began the tedious business of knocking on doors.

There was no reply at four of the flats, the occupants of two others were less than helpful: they probably wouldn't have recognised their neighbours if they passed them on the staircase.

Chapter Twenty Two

The woman on the bed is naked and eager – anxious – to please. He only has to ask and she will do anything for him.

He asks.

For a time, he watches in silence all the things she did to please him, listening to her little kittenish squeals and the sucking, slapping sound of flesh on flesh. But the trickle of excitement comes from the fear in her eyes as she fawns over him, kissing, licking, using her tongue and lips as he requires.

He grows bored.

He presses *fast forward* and smiles a little at the comedic contortions she performs for him at high speed, faking enjoyment, faking lust. He knows precisely where to stop the tape, presses pause as she feigns her climax, her face contorted with pleasure and pain – an ambiguity that has always intrigued and thrilled him.

He takes a sip of cool white wine, then presses play again. He mounts her from behind, grasps her hair and pulls her to his chest. He remembers she smelt of shampoo and the scent he chose for her.

His free hand comes around to her chin. He cups it gently; his hand closes over her mouth, but still she does not resist. Thumb and forefinger pinch her nostrils and she bucks wildly. Now he is aroused, now there is more pain than pleasure in her eyes and this is real. She lifts one arm behind her to scratch his face, but he leans forward and she buckles under his weight. His orgasm coincides with the last twitch of her body, the end of her struggling.

The next tape edit shows her lying on the bed again, still and beautiful. He has filmed this too; he treats her with respect and he needs to remind himself of the reverence he feels for these women and the gratitude he feels for the pleasure they have given him. He has never forced any of them; he made requests and they obliged.

As the tape plays, he hears his own voice crooning, snatches of a lullaby, a line or two of a hymn from his childhood. He cleans every intimate crease and fold of her body and he weeps as he sees the tenderness in his gentle caresses. *Eleanor, Eleanor . . .* Next, he combs her hair. He uses a fine-tooth comb, working section by section, starting at the hairline and working back to the crown, down to the nape of the neck, until not a single strand of his own hair, not a flake of skin remains.

He shaves her bodily hair: sometimes he likes to keep a souvenir.

He rewinds the film, thinking about the woman in the basement, and he is tempted to bring her upstairs and begin a little early. The camcorders are ready, but he makes himself wait. The days building up to the climax are a kind of foreplay and foreplay is something he believes should never be rushed. He does like them to be ready and anxious to please.

Chapter Twenty Three

At nine-fifteen a.m., surveillance noted the arrival of the postman, twenty minutes later than the previous day. Within
seconds, a red Vauxhall Astra estate parked outside the Pascals'
house. The driver crossed the road and walked to a house four
doors down.

Thorpe got a call on his mobile and came to check out the
car.

The woman who had made the original report on the
presence of an unfamiliar car in the street was certain it was
the same one.

'Curly-haired fellow,' she told him. 'He wears a suit.' She
lowered her voice confidentially. 'But it's not very good quality.'

'You could tell from this distance away?' He looked through
the latticed windows to the car parked diagonally opposite.
He'd've needed binoculars.

'I happened to be in the garden on one occasion,' she said,
stiffly, resenting the implication that she had been spying on her
neighbours. 'I was tidying up.'

A scattering of leaves blooded the lawns of most houses in
the street, but here the borders were clear and the dense sward of
grass swept and trimmed.

She nodded in the direction of number thirty-four. 'Here he
comes, now.'

Thorpe peered through the window. The man was walking down the path of number thirty-four. Thorpe had removed his hat partly out of respect and partly from concern that he might frighten the old dear, but he had no such qualms about putting the fear of God into this character. He pulled his hat low over his brow and lumbered outside.

Later, in the Bridewell Museum café McAteer had commandeered as a canteen, Thorpe told the story with some relish. 'I ask him to explain himself and he claims he's been visiting the woman a couple of doors down from the Pascals. So I take him over. She gives him this ball-shrinking stare. "Yes," ' she says, like he's a brolly she's left on the bus. "That's my lover, Jason Viner."

'She was all for calling the husband, getting him to vouch for her curly-headed Casanova — I thought he'd piss himself.'

'He works for her *husband?*' Dawn exclaimed.

Thorpe gave her a regretful smile. 'The husband's having an affair with his secretary. She finds out, picks on the lowest ranking sales rep in his company and decides to up his commission.'

Fletcher laughed. 'I bet that's one investment she'd *want* to go down on her.'

McAteer was poring over 12 charts when Lawson went in. His cardigan was maroon today; his jacket, as before, was hung carefully behind the door. The main people and key events surrounding Clara's abduction were represented symbolically on the chart, red lines drew links to Hugo Pascal, while yellow was used to delineate Clara's legal connections. Eleanor Gorton had her own chart. As yet they had found no definite links between the two women.

Eleanor was a professional woman, busy, but socially isolated. Since the death of her husband a year previously, she had concentrated on her career; she had a network of business associates, few friends. For five days no one had missed her.

Lawson tapped a symbol on Clara's chart, representing a car. 'This one's been eliminated,' he said.

'Oh?'

'Turned out to be an amorous salesman, visiting one of the neighbours.'

McAteer took a marker pen and crossed out the connection, then he stood back. 'Anything come back on the detective agency?' he asked, noticing where Lawson's gaze had come to rest.

'It seems kosher. We could approach them in confidence — ask them why he consulted them.'

McAteer shook his head. 'They would have to pass that information on to their client and he would know we've been following him. My feeling is that we'll find out more from a covert position.'

'I can see the logic in that, sir, but if we sit and watch for too long, we could end up investigating a murder instead of a kidnapping.'

'Your objection is duly noted, Inspector.'

Lawson knew better than to push it — a fall-out would only make both their jobs more difficult. He scanned the chart, trying to find connections he hadn't previously considered.

Rayner sat on a linen-covered sofa in Tristram Parks's ground-floor flat, in a house less than half a mile from Laura's place, but this was altogether a more salubrious affair: the gardens were landscaped and Parks had exclusive use of the rear garden, which backed onto Grosvenor Park. The flat itself was bright, with modern decorations in bright greens and yellows, but the airy effect intended by the interior designer was compromised by Parks's squirreling habit. Every inch of shelf space was crowded with a confused clutter of shells, stones, feathers; the kind of beachcombing hoard a ten-year-old boy might be expected to treasure. Postcards were propped against paperback books, faded with age and sunlight, which in turn were jammed onto the shelves, stacked upright, sideways or any way they would fit, spilling onto tables and, when they were full, piled on top of a litter of newspapers and magazines.

'Laura always paid four weeks in advance,' the landlord told Rayner. 'She didn't like to wait in on a Thursday for me to call.'

'Why's that?'

He grinned, showing teeth yellowed from smoking roll-ups all his adult life. 'Laura didn't like to wait in *any* night. She was a party animal.'

'Did she bring men back to the flat?'

'What if she did?' He tapped his fag-ash into a seashell and stared at her, amusement curling the corners of his mouth. When she looked into his eyes, Rayner realised that she had over-estimated his age by at least ten years. His skin might be lined and grey from all the chemically induced, mind-altering fun he'd indulged in over the last forty years, but his eyes were clear and an intelligent mind worked behind them. That one look challenged her beliefs, her values, her assumed right to judge others. Rayner saw the justice of it and felt a contrary resentment against Parks.

He raised his eyebrows and a flash of intuitive inspiration made her say, 'I don't believe it! You with a nineteen-year-old girl?'

He smiled. 'It wasn't what you're thinking.'

'Yeah?' Rayner said. 'What am I thinking?'

'Dirty old man knocking off a girl young enough to be his daughter, in exchange for a couple of weeks rent-free.'

She felt a grudging respect for the man: it seemed he had no illusions about his age or physical allure.

Parks took a pull on his cigarette, squinting at her through the haze of heat and smoke. 'Laura liked younger guys,' he said. 'Enjoyed their energy. But an older man appreciates a woman for who she is, as well as how she looks, and he isn't in such a hurry to satisfy his own needs.'

Rayner couldn't decide if he was justifying himself or coming on to her.

'You're telling me Laura didn't mind who she fucked,' she said bluntly.

Parks winced. 'Judgements like that are so dated – and inaccurate. Laura liked sex, it gave her pleasure and she gave pleasure to others. What's wrong with that?'

'When did she leave?' Rayner suspected that if she got involved in a discussion on morality with this man, she would end up defending a position she didn't necessarily hold herself.

He frowned, scratching his eyebrow and dropping ash onto his trousers. 'It was just after the trial.' He shook his head. 'Man, that changed her. She was terrified to go near the guys after . . .' He shrugged. 'After what happened.'

'Do you know where she went?'

He shook his head.

'I thought you were close.'

His smile was apologetic. 'Not *that* kind of close. I just got there one day and her flat had been emptied out.'

Rayner slipped her notebook into her pocket and Parks said, 'If you find her, can you let me know?'

'Missing her, are you?'

It wasn't meant kindly and he looked at her, surprised, and a little hurt. 'Yeah,' he said. 'I miss her. And she's never going to get better hiding away.'

Chapter Twenty Four

'Sir?' DS Barton stood in the doorway of Lawson's office. 'We've had a call from Pascal.'

Lawson held his breath. 'The abductor's made contact?' he asked.

Barton frowned. 'Could be. Pascal found an earring on his front doorstep. His wife was wearing it when she was taken.'

'Convenient, that – Pascal finding it,' Lawson mused.

'Think he's dug it out of her jewellery box and dropped it on the step?' Barton asked.

'I don't know,' Lawson said. 'But we'll soon find out.' He reached for the phone. 'I'll get Surveillance to run through this morning's video tapes. If he dropped it, they'll see him.' While he waited for a reply, he tapped his pen irritatedly on the pile of papers he had been reading. 'This leisure thing Pascal's designing. The developer's name is Melker, isn't it?'

Barton nodded.

'See what you can find out about him. How's he financing the development? Find out if he has any links with Casavettes. If his wife shops at the same supermarket as Casavettes' mother, I want to know about it.'

An hour later, they were in the Incident Room, watching a section of video selected by the surveillance team. The postman walked up the driveway, a bundle of letters in his right hand, ready to post through the Pascals' letter box. He posted the letters, sneezed, wiped his nose, then turned and began walking back down the drive.

Lawson rewound to the point where the letters were dropped in the box. He let the video play for a second or two. 'There,' he said.

'I don't see it.' Barton peered closely at the screen, holding his cup of coffee by the rim to avoid scalding himself.

Lawson rewound a second time, then advanced the picture frame by frame. 'See?'

As the postman put his handkerchief back in his pocket, something fell from it.

''S' pose it could be . . .' Barton said doubtfully.

'It is.' Lawson had spent fifteen minutes asking Surveillance to prove it to him. 'The enhanced stills show it clearly. He dropped the earring.'

Barton's eyes gleamed with anticipatory zeal. 'When can we have a go at him?'

Lawson ejected the video and replaced it in its sleeve. 'Right now,' he said.

Keith Dent was still in uniform. He plucked at his shirt collar and took a hefty pull on his cigarette as Lawson and Barton entered the interview room. Lawson started the audio tapes and went through the formalities.

'You understand that you can have access to a solicitor at any time?' he repeated.

The postman shrugged, but his attempt at nonchalance was unconvincing. 'Criminals need lawyers,' he said. He had small dark eyes that shifted constantly, resting on something in the sparsely furnished room for a second or two, then moving on.

'Where did you get the earring?' Lawson asked.

'What earring?'

In answer, Lawson placed a still from the video tape in front of him. The earring had just left his hand; the diamond and ruby setting caught the light.

Dent reached out tentatively, then snatched his hand back, actually pushing his chair away from the table, as if to distance himself from the picture.

'I'm showing Mr Dent a photograph, evidence number 01/ A1/3872. Now, would you like to explain how you came to have Ms Pascal's earring in your possession?'

'Bloke gave it me.'

'A bloke.'

'That's right.'

'What bloke?' Barton asked. Dent raised his shoulders in answer.

'Where?' Lawson demanded.

'Applyards Lane. He stopped me on my round.'

'What did he look like?'

'Ordinary.'

'Height? Age? Eye colour? Come on, Mr Dent – make an effort.'

Dent shifted in his chair. 'I don't know. Average height – maybe five-ten. How the hell do I know how old he was? He wasn't old, but he wasn't young, either.'

He lapsed into silence and Lawson had to prompt him again. 'What colour were his eyes?'

'Blue, I think. Not dark, anyway. And before you ask, he was wearing a hat, so I don't know what colour hair.'

'Describe the hat.'

He seemed irritated by the question. 'Black. Wool. The sort of thing the kids wear these days.'

'I thought you said he wasn't young.'

'He wasn't – I'm just giving an example.'

'What about his build?'

'Hard to say.'

Lawson exclaimed in exasperation.

'He was wearing a big anorak thing!' Dent protested. 'Quilted. You couldn't tell.'

Lawson took a breath and made an effort to calm himself. 'What colour was it?'

'The jacket?' He saw Lawson's expression and added, 'Okay! Just getting it straight. It was blue. Light blue, with red stuff down the middle.'

'Red stuff? He's a messy eater, is he, sir?'

'No!' Dent exclaimed. 'Sewn in, down the edge.'

'Piping,' Lawson said. 'Now we're getting somewhere. What about rings, jewellery – or tattoos. Did he have any tattoos?'

Dent shook his head. 'I was looking at the seventy-five quid in his hand.'

'Seventy-five quid?' Barton repeated. 'Think it was worth it?'

'Look,' Dent said. 'He told me he'd nicked the earring. Felt guilty. Wanted to give it back, but didn't want to be seen near the house.'

'I bet he didn't,' Barton muttered.

'You were doing him a favour,' Lawson said.

'That's right.'

'For seventy-five pounds.'

Dent shrugged and started picking at his fingernails. They were bitten to the quick and he looked like he was itching to have a go at them now.

'Know your round well, do you, Mr Dent?'

'I've worked that round twice a day for eight years,' he said, establishing eye contact for the first time in the entire interview.

'So you knew which house you were going to with the earring.'

He looked away.

'Watch the news, do you?'

Dent began to shake his head, 'No, come on, mate,' he said. 'I know what you're driving at, but you can't get me on that. I just did like the guy asked. He told me he wanted to put things right.'

'And it didn't occur to you that he might have a more . . . sinister motive?'

'All right, I admit it should have. But it didn't.'

'You just took the money and put your brains in your trouser pocket with your wallet.'

'Now wait a minute—'

Lawson spoke over his objections. 'If you had reported this we might have caught him. But I don't suppose that occurred to you, either.'

'No! All right?' Dent shouted. 'It didn't occur to me.'

They wrapped up a few minutes later. It was clear Dent wasn't going to give them anything useful. As he was being led out of the door, Lawson called him back.

'Right now, you're an accessory to kidnapping,' he said. 'If anything happens to Clara Pascal, you could find yourself facing charges relating to murder. You might reflect on that, see if it jogs your memory.'

Lawson and Barton sat for a few minutes in silence, the interview tapes in front of them. Barton cleared his throat and Lawson looked at him.

'Don't say it, Phil.' He pressed both palms into his eye sockets to try and alleviate the dry burning behind his eyelids. 'I know . . . He's just a greedy dupe who didn't think past the notes the guy wafted under his nose.'

'Chances are it wasn't the abductor, anyway,' Barton consoled him. 'Mr Average was probably dropped a couple of hundred himself.'

'I don't know, Phil. The jacket could be the one Pippa had described, which means it was our man. And would he risk bringing another unknown into the equation?' Barton offered no answer, but then Lawson hadn't expected him to. 'Ah, sod it.' He dragged the two tapes towards him and stood up. Every joint ached and it was only then that he realised just how tense he had been. 'It's the closest we've got to him and we missed the chance.'

'Come on!' Barton exclaimed. 'He stopped Postman Pat half a mile away. Our surveillance is good, but . . .'

Lawson nodded, tiredly. Barton was right. Beating himself up over this wouldn't help Clara. 'What about Casavettes?' he asked. 'Did you find anything on him and Melker?'

They made their way out through the custody area into the street: the doorway from the police station into the old Bridewell had been bricked up for security reasons and the only way to reach the museum was from the street. They hurried, their heads down against the rain and as they turned the corner, a shout went up and they were mobbed by photographers and press. Lawson flinched. 'Shit!' He had forgotten the press.

'Any leads, sir?'

'Has there been a ransom demand?'

'Is it true a man has been arrested?'

Lawson gritted his teeth and carried on.

'Are you any closer to finding Clara?'

Then, unexpectedly: 'What about the earring, Inspector?'

He turned to face the man who had asked the question. How the hell did he know about the earring?

One or two asked, 'What earring?' Then the man finished with the line that would be broadcast on radio and TV throughout the nation that night: 'Does the earring belong to Clara?'

Lawson shouldered through the museum doors and they started up the stairs.

'Who d'you reckon leaked *that* to the press?' Barton asked.

'Casavettes?' Lawson slammed the wall. 'Shit! McAteer will burst a blood vessel over this.'

At the top of the steps, Barton said, 'You asked about Melker.'

'Anything?' Lawson asked, eager for some tiny snippet of good news.

'Sorry, Boss. So far he checks out. Nothing on the PNC check. He's an upright citizen. Even pays his income tax. But the finance side of the leisure complex is a bit hazy. There might be something in that. I'll let you know as soon as I hear anything.'

Chapter Twenty Five

The rain was still falling when Barton finally got home just after ten. Sheets of cold hard rain from a black sky. A northerly wind drove it in rattling bursts, overwhelming the drains and sending the overflow in swirling rivulets down the street.

Abandoning any idea of parking in the garage, Barton grabbed the road map from the back seat and, using it to keep the worst of the rain off, he ran to the house. His fingers were numb with cold and struggling with the door key, he vowed, not for the first time, that next summer he would build them a porch.

Once inside, he dumped the map on the floor and tilted his head, listening. A faint murmur of voices told him that the TV was on in the sitting-room. This, he took to be a good sign. Timmy had been cutting new teeth this last week and he was cranky and difficult to get off to sleep.

Fran took the brunt of it, at home all day with him, and it had pained Barton to see her increasing exhaustion. He tiptoed to the front room and eased the door open. The slightest sound and Timmy might wake and in all probability it would take half the night to get him back down. The room was empty. So much for a romantic evening cuddled up on the sofa. Fran must still be struggling to get Timmy off or else she was so flaked out that she had gone to bed early.

He went through to the kitchen. A post-it note on the

microwave read, '*Heat on high for three-and-a-half minutes*.' Smiling, he tapped in the setting and time on the keypad and rummaged in the fridge for a beer with the hum of the microwave a comforting background noise.

Fran must have done a big shop, because the shelves were crammed with goodies. He bypassed a bag of mini-Snickers and found two bottles of lager jammed behind vacuum-wrapped packets of cooked ham and jars of various Italian pasta sauces.

He opened the first bottle as the microwave bleeped. Whatever it was, it smelled wonderful. He took a glug of lager then lifted the plastic tray out with his fingertips. Something Chinese. Duck maybe. Pre-packaged – Fran had given up on trying to keep home-cooked meals edible for him when he was on a major investigation.

He grabbed a fork and spooned in a mouthful, burning his tongue in the process.

Simultaneously, the phone rang. 'Shit!' They had moved the phone from the hall into the sitting-room because of the number of times it had woken Timmy and ruined their night's sleep. If this was the Incident Room, it was the worst possible timing. He ran to the sitting-room and picked up. 'Barton – and this had better be good.'

A moment's silence, then, 'Sergeant Barton . . .'

The voice was familiar and although he couldn't quite place it, his spine tingled and he felt instantly wary.

'Who is this?'

'Now, come on, Phil. Don't be coy. You've been asking questions about me half the day.'

Momentarily confused, Barton thought it might be Clara's abductor. But the confusion was replaced with a cold certainty. 'Casavettes,' he said. 'How the hell did you get my number?'

Casavettes laughed. He might well have asked how Casavettes had access to a phone in prison at this late hour. Men like Ray Casavettes knew how to buy or barter just about anything they wanted.

'Look out the window, Phil,' he said, in a low, carefully moderated tone that conveyed threat far more effectively than if he had raised his voice.

Barton carried the telephone to the window with a feeling of sick expectation. Across the street, as he knew it would be, was a car. A light-coloured Lexus saloon. It was in darkness, but the driver struck a match — he saw the flare and then the softer glow as he lit his cigarette. The man's face was indiscernible in the sheeting rain. One of Casavettes' men. Casavettes had his unlisted phone number and his address. How many hours had they been parked outside with Fran and the baby inside, alone, unprotected?

He felt a tearing sensation next to his heart. He dropped the phone handset and let it bounce off the sofa to the floor. Fear and dread almost overwhelmed him in the walk to the front door. By the end of the driveway he was soaked to the skin and his fear had turned to anger. The rain hissed on the pavement, it rushed and gurgled, bubbling madly at the drains, threatening to swamp the entire road.

The driver saw Barton in the second before he reached for the door handle. He just had time to take the cigarette out of his mouth, then Barton yanked the door open and dragged him bodily into the street. The man was bigger than Barton and stronger, but he didn't resist. Barton slammed him backwards against the side of the car.

The man threw down his cigarette and said quietly. 'Before you make a total tit of yourself, there's something you should take a look at.'

Barton's right hand was bunched into a fist; with his left he held the man back against the car, but the assurance in the man's tone made him hesitate. The man reached across Barton's restraining hand and fished in his inside pocket. He came out with a brown envelope.

Barton looked at it stupidly for a few moments, blinking rainwater out of his eyes, then he took it and tore it open.

Already sopping wet, the envelope came apart like tissue paper in his hands. Inside were glossy photographs.

Fran pushing Timmy in his pram, that intense, distracted look on her face that she always wore when she was absorbed by her own thoughts. Fran at home – the picture taken through the front window. She nursed Timmy on her shoulder and she was patting his back, soothing and placating. Barton shuffled the picture to the back. The photographs were tacky with the rainwater. The final, chilling image was Fran smiling as a man helped her to carry the pram down some steps. It was the man in the car, the man standing in front of him now.

'What the fuck d'you think you're doing?' His voice was hoarse with emotion and he felt suddenly weak and afraid again.

The man straightened up, leaning away from the car, confident that Barton no longer posed a threat. 'Me?' he said. 'I'm just doing my job, mate.'

Barton didn't know what to say to him. He stood with the rain coursing down his face, stupefied by the horror of what was happening.

'Go back inside,' the man told him. 'Listen to what Mr Casavettes has to say.'

For a moment Barton didn't respond, only stared numbly at the man. But when the stranger moved to touch his arm, he jerked away violently.

'Touch me and I'll deck you, I swear,' he warned. There was the briefest of pauses, then he turned and started the long walk back to the house.

The laughter from the American sit-com on television was muted, the volume turned low. Barton picked the handset up from the floor. 'You still there?' he asked.

'I'm a patient man,' Casavettes replied.

'You'd better be, because you're going to do a hell of a lot more time because of this.'

'Brave words, Sergeant Barton. And I'm sure Fran would be proud to hear them. But look at the hours you work. Look at all the time Fran spends alone with little Timmy.'

Barton flinched at his son's name. It seemed obscene, coming from this man's mouth. And infinitely more terrifying than anything he had said so far. His teeth started to chatter and he clenched his jaw tight.

'I'm not asking for much,' Casavettes said in the same calm, reasonable tone. 'Just a bit of a head start. You're closest to Lawson. When he makes a move, I want to know.' He paused. 'I pay well.'

'I don't want your fucking money!' Barton snarled.

'Up to you, Phil, but with Tumbletots on Tuesday and nursery fees Wednesday to Friday and you wanting to buy a second car to give Fran a bit more mobility, I'd've thought you needed it.'

It was too much to take in. Casavettes knew everything about Fran's routine. He even knew she was hoping to buy a car. Did he have people at the nursery? People like the man in the car outside, just doing their job, gaining Fran's confidence. *Dear God!* Had she invited them home? Brought them, smiling, into their house? Barton swallowed. He remembered what Lawson had told him about Tom Porter. He had gone to prison, rather than cross Casavettes. What had Lawson said? *He gets you right where you live.*

'What—' His mouth dried and he had to cough before he could begin again. 'What do you want?'

'I'll be in touch.'

The line went dead and Barton fumbled the handset back in the cradle, his hand shaking violently. All was quiet except for the rich rumble of the actors' voices and the bursts of laughter from the audience. There wasn't a sound from upstairs. Neither of them had stirred. The phone ringing, his running back and forth had roused neither Timmy nor Fran.

He ran for the stairs, heedless of the rain driving in through the open front door and stumbled up the steps, falling heavily on one knee, praying incoherently, scarcely aware that he was sobbing.

Timmy's bedroom door stood open. The night light rotated slowly, casting images of moon and stars on the walls. Fran was slumped in a chair, her hand caught between the bars of Timmy's cot. Timmy lay on his side, one fist bunched, his pyjama-top rucked up showing his toddler's pot-belly. His mouth was open and a silvery trail of mucus shone on his cheek. He wasn't moving.

Barton fell on the cot, lifting the boy out. Timmy flung his arms wide in a startle reflex and his eyes opened. He gasped, took a breath and screamed.

Fran stirred. 'Phil?' she murmured groggily.

Barton hugged Timmy to his wet shirt, kissing his hot face.

'What the hell are you playing at?' Fran demanded, now fully awake and furious. 'He's not been asleep half an hour!'

Timmy leaned towards her, flinging himself away from his father, still screaming, frightened and angry.

'Phil, you're scaring me!' she said. 'Give him to me.'

He handed the child to her.

'My God, he's drenched! *You're* drenched – what's the matter with you?'

'I'm sorry Fran,' Barton said. 'I thought—Ah, Jesus, I don't know what I thought!' He wiped his face with his hand, trying to get himself under control. He reached out to stroke Timmy's face with one finger, but the boy squirmed and screamed more furiously, burying his face in his mother's shoulder.

'For God's sake! Can't you see you're making it worse?' Fran jiggled the child, rubbing his back, shushing and comforting him.

Barton took a step back, unsure what to do.

'Why's it so cold in here?' Fran demanded. 'Is the front door open? Bloody hell, Phil! Can't you hear the rain?'

There was a dark patch of sodden carpet near the door. He

heard an engine fire up, then the Lexus disappeared into the rain-lashed darkness. He closed the door and checked every room, every cupboard, all the locks on every door and window before he began mopping up.

Chapter Twenty Six

Clara breathed in the scent of wild thyme. Long grass swished against her trouser legs as she walked through the meadow. A playful wind rippled the grass, buffeting it so that it dipped and danced like water on a lake, shifting its colour and tone: now blue-green, now bright and metallic in the sun. She spun full circle until she fell dizzily to the ground and lay watching a single cloud turn lazily in the perfect blue. She closed her eyes. A bee hummed nearby, seeking out nectar in a cool clump of clover. She felt the fat pink flower-heads flatten beneath her shoulders, cupped them in the palms of her hands.

Something tickled her face and she focused on the dainty purple-brown heads of quaking grass, trembling in the wind. The sun was hot on her face and head, burning, fierce.

Then a rogue thought: *This isn't right.* She clutched the clover stems until they tore. Frightened to let them go, she used all her powers of imagination to will herself to stay where she was, but it began to fall away from her and instead of grass and the soft sweet clover, she felt dirt and stone under her hands.

'No!' she moaned, still half-asleep.

A pale glimmer of dull grey light from the open door at the top of the stairs tormented her with the possibility of what lay beyond: freedom, family, home.

The pictures of the girls were just discernible in the gloom, smiling down at her and she looked hastily away, moving involuntarily into a crouching position. The chain tugged savagely at her right ankle and she gave a shout of pain. Her foot was swollen and discoloured, but she couldn't get her jailer to loosen it. Her craving for food was way beyond hunger now; she felt weak and debilitated to the point of apathy.

Her eyes and nose began to prickle; she knew that if she started to cry she would not be able to stop, so she wrapped her arms tight around her knees and stared with sullen determination at the wall opposite.

The uneven plaster was almost lost in the shadows, but one picture was visible, faintly luminous; it seemed to flicker in and out of her vision, like a ghostly apparition. The cold, though not intense, was relentless; an insinuating subterranean chill.

How or when the transition happened, she could not say, but in the logic of dreams, she accepted that she was no longer chasing the elusive image of a girl in a newspaper photograph, but instead was looking at her husband; a real, flesh-and-blood person, standing in the darkness.

'Hugo!'

He remained in the shadows, smiling sadly, perhaps a little reproachfully.

She struggled to her feet and inched forward, one hand outstretched, but he was beyond her reach and she fell to her knees sobbing with frustration. Hugo shimmered and faded momentarily, his features distorting like melting wax, but then he returned, as real to her as the aching chill and the awful unrelenting fear she had felt ever since waking in this terrible place.

'Hugo, please . . .' she whispered.

When he spoke, no mist of condensation formed around his face. She didn't question the fact, any more than she questioned how easy it was to see Hugo in the dark, almost as if a saintly glow shimmered around him.

'You should never have taken the case,' he said.

When she came to, her heart was thudding, beating against the walls of her chest as if it wanted to get out. A dragon was coiled in the corner of the room; she could hear its fiery snore. *It's a dream*, she told herself, remembering with an almost wistful sadness the field of clover and meadow flowers. *There is no dragon.* And yet she *could* hear its stentorian breath and feel its heat. She took a careful peek. A single red eye stared back at her. The source of the roar. Beneath the eye, a gas bottle. He had brought her a heater! She didn't move, afraid that this dream, too would vanish. She lay on a mattress. She was wearing a cardigan; thick, prickly wool that smelled of cigarettes. Blankets covered her. She wriggled her toes and discovered that there were socks on her feet. She sat up, then slumped forward, almost blacking out with the exertion.

'Back with us, are you?' He sat on the top step, masked, watching her, as before.

'Who's "us"?'

He smiled, twitching the black-rimmed mouth-slit. 'You were raving,' he told her.

'Well, that makes two of us, doesn't it?' A spiteful, childish snipe, but it was liberating, just having the courage to say it. Her brain felt seared. It was as if she had woken from a high fever, weak, but cleansed from whatever had infected her. *Fear infected you, Clara. Fear and despair.*

She huddled closer to the heater's glowing mantle, turning automatically to her right, to lift the chain so that it wouldn't chafe her ankle. It was gone. He had switched it to the left ankle and had looped it a little looser – only by one link, but it was more comfortable.

'Where's my jacket?'

'You were hypothermic,' he said in reply. 'You'd stripped off – thought you were too hot.'

Clara blushed, pulling the blankets closer around her shoulders. 'You haven't answered my question.'

He paused, seemed almost offended by her tone. It would have been more prudent to let him go on, telling her how he had taken care of her, brought her back from the brink. Well to hell with prudence.

'Am I supposed to be grateful?' she sneered. 'Is that it?'

He stood, brushing the dust and splinters from his hands, then he walked away.

You bloody idiot, Clara! She had missed a chance to communicate with him as a man instead of victim to abductor. She should have used his apparent considerateness as a lever – tried to get more from him. *Would it have hurt to let him show what a warm human being he really is?* She knew what she *should* do, the theory was relatively straightforward, but in practice she would have to fawn over the man who had kept her in this filthy, freezing pit, with no food and barely enough water. She couldn't help herself. She hated his guts and given the chance she would kill him.

She heard a footfall outside. He came in, closing the door again so that only a thin sliver of chilly light was visible. He crouched in front of her, a flask in his hand.

'You're blocking my heat,' she said, eyeing him sullenly. He looked at her for perhaps half a minute and she wondered with growing alarm if he would simply leave again, taking whatever was in the flask along with him. Even so, she couldn't bring herself to be pleasant to him, still less, to apologise. Then, quite unexpectedly, he moved a little to one side and she felt again the glorious warmth from the gas heater.

As she stared at the glowing red mantle, basking in the heat, intensified by its silvered cone reflector, he unscrewed the lid of the flask and poured out hot, creamy liquid. Clara's stomach cramped in response to the steamy aroma of chicken and vegetables, and she couldn't stop herself looking avidly at the cup.

He glanced at her and she looked away. If this was another of his sadistic games, she wasn't playing. But her stomach knew only that it was starved; it churned and gurgled despite her resolve, and her mouth flooded with saliva.

He handed the cup to her.

She took it; the heat made her fingers tingle and the smell was maddeningly appetising. She should throw it in his face. But she didn't. She raised it to her lips and took a cautious sip.

'I'll leave the rest so you can have it whenever you want.'

She took another sip. It seemed he did want gratitude. 'Thank you.' It was intended to sound sarcastic, but she heard humility in her voice. Appalled, Clara felt tears spill onto her cheeks.

He stood abruptly. 'You always did make assumptions a bit too easily, Counsel.' His voice was hard with detestation. 'It's only a bowl of soup.' He turned off the gas. The heater choked, popped and was silenced. He took it with him.

What assumptions had she made that were so offensive to him? That he was willing to treat her with compassion – to allow her the basic necessities for survival? She blinked after him, surprised to feel hurt that he disliked her so much. *Why help me, then? Why doesn't he just leave me to freeze to death?* Because he's going to let me go!

For a moment the notion was almost too much for her. She felt a giddy light-headedness. Dare she hope?

The earring! Before hysteria had overwhelmed her, before delirium and hypothermia had deprived her of reason, he had taken her earring. She touched the naked earlobe, needing to convince herself that this part was real, that it wasn't another hallucination. That it had actually happened.

'They must have got back to you by now,' she said.

He turned. 'Who?'

'The police? My husband?' He stared blankly at her, and she gasped in exasperation. *Do I have to spell it out for him?* 'The earring,' she said. 'Why else would you want it?'

He smiled and the mouth stretched in a frightening parody of a circus clown's grin. He tilted his head. 'A memento,' he said. 'What do the psychologists call them? Trophies. That's all it is, Counsel. A trophy. Something to remember you by.'

She still doesn't understand, he thought. This isn't about money. It's about pain. It's about suffering — emotional and physical. It wasn't enough for her to suffer. He wanted Pascal to wonder — *Is she alive?* He wanted Pascal to think about another man's hands on his wife — touching her, hurting her, using and then discarding her.

He wants me alive, Clara insisted to herself, refusing to let her cruelly rational inner voice have its say. He gave me food and warmth. He could have let me die and he didn't.

He carried on to the top step, then turned as if she had spoken her thoughts aloud. 'There's any number of reasons why I might want to keep you alive a little longer.'

Chapter Twenty Seven

The Incident Room was steadily filling, ready for the evening debrief. The day had been mild and sunny after the dismal weather of the previous two days and although the team was frustrated with their lack of progress, their mood was optimistic, almost buoyant. The lack of rain made it easier getting from place to place, as well as infinitely more comfortable: it made a change to come back to base dry and reasonably warm.

Young stood close to Rayner, hoping to gain some protection from her proximity. She was in heated conversation with DS Tyrell; both talked quietly, but their tone was vehement.

'I'll do the other actions,' Rayner said. 'Just don't refer this one.'

'It's not *going* anywhere, Sal,' Dawn protested. 'You're wasting your time.'

'Maybe, but it's *my* time.'

'No, Sal—' Tyrell glanced round, aware that she had raised her voice. 'You're wrong,' she went on, more quietly. 'It's police time.'

'I've got results on all my other actions,' Rayner insisted.

'Yeah?' Tyrell gave her one of her steely looks.

Rayner had missed something or forgotten to do something, and she couldn't think what. She closed her eyes for a second. *I give up.* 'Okay,' she said. 'Hit me with it.'

'You didn't pick up your messages yesterday,' Tyrell said. 'There was one from the police liaison officer who's doing that trace for you.'

Shit! 'I'll get on to it.'

'You should have got on to it yesterday.'

'I was out on enquiries all day yesterday.'

Tyrell lifted one eyebrow. 'Enquiries?'

Plodding all over town looking for Laura Kelsall. Rayner's shoulders slumped. 'Point taken. I *will* get back to him. I'll do it now. I just need to see this through, Sarge.' Tyrell hesitated and Rayner pressed her point home. 'I know I can track her down.'

Tyrell considered for a few moments. 'All right,' she said. 'I'll keep the action open. But I want daily updates – you fill in a report, even if there's nothing *to* report. And don't expect to be let off lightly on new allocations.'

Rayner smiled tensely and turned to Young. 'Still enjoying surveillance?' she asked. 'You've been reassigned to Pascal, haven't you?'

Young blushed, embarrassed that Rayner might think she had been listening in to her conversation with DS Tyrell. She looked nervously across at Fletcher before answering. 'Yeah, it's okay.' *How can Sal be so calm after what's just gone on between her and Tyrell?*

'A hell of a lot nicer in the sunshine,' Rayner commented.

Fletcher grinned. 'I don't know – the rain has its compensations, eh, Babe?'

'Lay off, Fletcher,' Rayner warned.

'What's up, Sal – you after a bit of it yourself?'

'You really are despicable, Fletcher,' Rayner said. 'D'you know that?'

Thorpe came through the double doors in time to hear Tyrell ask, 'Did you find your *Daily Mail* man, then, Fletch?'

Thorpe laughed. 'Fletch here was throwing up his breakfast at seven on Friday morning.'

'Bad curry,' Fletcher said, glaring at him.

Thorpe was sceptical. 'You mean you were too arseholed from Thursday. Which means that action won't be completed till Monday at the earliest.'

'Now that's where you're wrong, smart-arse,' Fletcher said, unable to contain himself.

Thorpe threw his arms wide. 'You've found him!'

'He's a creature of habit. Gets his morning paper *every* day — weekends included.'

'And?'

Fletcher shrugged. 'It's no big deal.'

'That's not what you've been making out the past few days, mate,' Thorpe laughed. 'You had us convinced you were on the trail of a pervert taking snapshots of the local housewives in their scanties.'

'I heard a rumour he was *that* close to bringing in the bastard who snatched Clara,' Rayner said, pinching a sliver of air between her finger and thumb.

Tyrell seemed amused by Fletcher's discomfort. She caught his eye and he glowered at her.

'It's in my report,' he said with bad grace.

Rayner smiled. 'Am I right in thinking the words chase, wild and goose come into it?' she asked.

Thorpe shook his head in mock reproach. 'Aren't we a team, Fletch?'

'Yeah,' Rayner said, smelling blood. 'Cough.'

Tyrell swept past Fletcher's desk and scooped up a photo wallet. Fletcher took a swipe at her, but he was too slow.

'Take a look at these.' She tossed the photographs to Thorpe.

Thorpe shuffled through them with an expression of faint disgust on his face. 'What the hell's this?' he demanded.

'Thing is,' Tyrell said, evidently enjoying herself, 'While Fletcher thought he was tracking down his perv, he was in fact snouting out a man with an unhealthy obsession for dog shit.'

A few people laughed; the debrief was scheduled for five minutes time and the Incident Room was now almost filled to

191

capacity. 'Our photographer is a man who likes an early-morning walk and, at this time of year, that means in the dark. He's trod in it, slipped in it, trailed it through the house and frankly, he's had it up to here.' She drew a line across her forehead.

Thorpe slapped his friend on the back. 'Poor old Fletch,' he said. 'Thought he was going to get soft porn and what does he get?'

There was laughter and a few shouts of 'Soft shite!'

'Now, now,' Rayner said. 'Fair dos. It's an antisocial practice which carries a £1000 fine. Problem is – how do you prove which turd came out of which dog?'

'Thanks for your concern,' Fletcher said, with as much irony as he could muster. 'I'll manage.'

But Fletcher's jibe at her sexuality had rankled and Rayner wasn't going to let him off the hook quite so easily. She took some of the stack from Thorpe. 'As evidence,' she said, in all seriousness, 'These pictures stink.'

More laughter.

'Ha-bloody-ha,' Fletcher sneered.

She held up a picture of a Scotty dog. 'This one,' She shook her head. 'Seconds too early. He's ready, he's braced, but he's not actually committing the offence.' She held up the next. 'This – could have come from any animal. Now here—' She held out the picture for closer inspection. 'Interesting composition. We have evidence linked to the dog, but where's the owner?'

Someone jabbed her in the back, warning her that the senior officers had come in, and she tossed the photographs down on Fletcher's desk. Dawn gave him a solemn reminder to file the photographs in the exhibits room.

'What you going to file it under, Fletch?' Rayner asked.

While McAteer and Lawson set up at the far end of the room, a few people made suggestions. 'D for dog shit.' 'Keep it simple – S for shit.' 'Please, gentlemen,' one of the officers said. 'We're professionals – file it under F for fouling.'

'Works for me,' Rayner said, 'F for fouling and F for Fletcher — it has a nice balance.'

McAteer called the debriefing to order with a brisk, 'Thank you everyone.'

Rayner made one final aside under her breath. 'F for fuck-up.' There were a few sniggers and then silence and sobriety were restored.

'We've had a positive ID on the Lexus seen outside Pippa's school on Wednesday.' For the benefit of those officers who hadn't been in at the start, he added, 'It was damaged by the getaway vehicle, but nobody reported it.'

'They had to take it in for repair eventually,' Lawson said. 'It's registered to Michael Casavettes,' He glanced over at Barton. 'Ray Casavettes' brother.'

'I want him interviewed,' McAteer said. 'Tonight.'

The night team leader responded with a terse, 'Boss.'

Barton relaxed a fraction. Fran had not been convinced by his excuses the previous night. After she had finally got Timmy down, some time after midnight, she had refused to listen and, inspecting the damage to the carpet, had criticised his inadequate attempts to mop up, then set to work with towels to soak up the rest of the water. She completed the task in silence and in the end he had given up and gone to bed. She hadn't followed him.

He fretted all day, knowing that Casavettes' men would probably be watching her. At eight-thirty, after the debrief, unable to stand the worry any longer, he phoned on the pretext of checking that she had got Timmy off the sleep all right. Fran was cool, but less angry, and he risked asking her if she had seen anyone during the day.

'Mum came round, why?'

'Oh . . .' He drew one hand tiredly across his forehead. 'I just didn't like to think of you all alone.'

'It's never bothered you before,' she said, sharply.

He took a breath, but before he could speak, she said, 'I'm sorry, Phil. It's just that you've ruined the bloody carpet and I've had three hours' sleep and he's been grizzling all day.' She sounded at the end of her tether.

'I know,' Barton said. 'I'll make up for it. Once this case is finished, we'll—'

'Don't make promises you can't keep,' she interrupted.

He bit back a reply. He didn't want to start a row about this. Fran must have sensed his hurt in the silence, because she added more gently, 'I'll see you in a couple of hours.'

Barton retrieved the report he had been working on and began to write.

'It's you and me tomorrow,' Lawson said.

Barton's hand jerked, leaving a tick at the end of the word that almost tore the paper.

'Where?' he asked, fighting to keep his tone neutral, dreading the expected answer.

'Breck Moor Prison. See if Ray Casavettes can account for his brother following Clara Pascal.'

'Why me?'

'Hoping to go to church with the family tomorrow, were you, Phil?' The two men made eye contact. Barton was the first to look away.

'I thought the night team were dealing with it,' Barton said defensively.

'They're dealing with Michael,' Lawson corrected. 'Ray is mine alone.'

'You're welcome to him.' When Barton looked up, Lawson was still gazing at him, quietly appraising him.

Barton smiled quickly. 'Come on, Boss . . . He's not going to give us anything – what's the point of both of us wasting a morning?'

'You know him,' Lawson said. If he saw the pained look flash fleetingly across Barton's face, he didn't show it. He lowered his voice. 'And you know about my past . . . association with him,' he added. 'I don't want to have to explain this to someone I don't trust, Phil.'

'I just don't think—'

'What?'

What could he say? *I don't think I can meet Casavettes face-to-face without grabbing him by the throat?* He had condemned Porter as a coward, but Porter had watched a man die – and Casavettes had virtually crucified him. Porter had a far better excuse for bottling out than Barton could claim. Rolling over because of a few slightly fuzzy photographs of his wife and baby paled by comparison with what Casavettes had done to Porter.

His shoulders slumped. 'Nothing, Boss,' he said. 'When d'you want picking up?'

'We'll go after the morning briefing,' Lawson said. 'You got much more to do?'

'No, why?' Barton was instantly wary.

'Just wondered if you fancied a pint, that's all.'

Barton checked his watch. 'Look, Boss . . .'

'I know,' Lawson said. 'You want to get home.' He squeezed Barton's shoulder. 'Give Fran my love.'

Chapter Twenty Eight

Assumptions, he had said. *You were always too quick to make assumptions.* Clara poured herself another cup of soup and savoured it as she had never before savoured food. He always calls me Counsel. Which means he's either an ex-client or someone I prosecuted. He believes I made assumptions about him, which means he must consider himself hard done by. Had he been wrongly convicted? Or maybe he felt she just hadn't tried hard enough for him?

His parting statement kept coming back to her. She kept setting it aside and it kept bouncing right back into her thoughts. *Any number of reasons to keep you alive.* Well she was glad of that, because she could think of only two. And of the two, the only one that she was willing to contemplate – ransom – seemed highly unlikely.

So, you're here with a madman. She stopped short. He wasn't mad – at least not by any standards she understood. He seemed able to reason, to control his impulses. *To control you, Clara.*

As an undergraduate, she'd had a boyfriend who was studying psychology. 'There's an experiment,' he told her. 'A classic. You offer the subject one chocolate bar now or three chocolate bars later. Your more intelligent, less impulsive subject will wait for the bigger reward.'

'Deferment of gratification' he called it. *So what gratification is the man in the mask deferring in order to savour the moment more sweetly?* Her inner voice tormented her with these questions. *What do you think, Clara? Why do men snatch women off the street?* She tried to make ransom a plausible motive, but every time she came back to it, she had to admit that if he wanted to ransom her, he would have done it well before now.

Oh, God! Her mind skittered away from the dark thoughts that plagued her awake or asleep. her pulse throbbed dully in her throat and her eyes itched to weep.

'This is not helping.' She found the sound of her own voice strangely comforting; it steadied her and enabled her to think more lucidly. It was no good letting her imagination run wild. *If he's going to hurt you, he will — unless you think of a way to dissuade him.* 'This isn't random,' she said aloud. 'He *chose* you. Now think why.'

There were prosecution cases — only a two or three in a year — which she found unsettling. Generally, she could approach them with equanimity, knowing that the defence counsel was more than capable of finding any flaws or weaknesses in the prosecution's case. But there were some, perhaps only four or five in her career to date; cases where the defence had been inadequate — even incompetent — and these troubled her even years later. The most recent involved a young drug addict who had been severely beaten. A neighbour heard screams and called the police. An intruder, she told them. Her boyfriend, Warren, had fought him off. But while she was being treated at the hospital, she confided to one of the nurses that it was Warren who had attacked her.

The evidence was compelling. he had her blood on his clothes and hands. His knuckles were bruised and scraped and his face scratched. Of course he said that his injuries were the result of defending his girlfriend and then comforting her while he waited for the ambulance to arrive, but she was adamant; she was willing to testify that Warren had laid into her with his fists and feet, after he discovered that she had stolen from him to buy drugs.

The police investigated his story of the attacker, but none of the neighbours had seen anyone enter or leave the house except for Kali and Warren. Nevertheless, Clara was uneasy. Although Kali denied it, Clara suspected that she was funding her drug habit with prostitution. Clara wondered if the 'mystery' attacker was in fact Kali's pimp or drugs supplier.

She could hardly blame Warren if he held a grudge against her.

Thinking back through her cases of the past year, she realised just how many of them were alleged rapes or violence against women. More often than not she would defend the case. She knew that Hugo didn't like it: he felt that she was being manipulated by men who made manipulation of women a way of life. Just the thought of Hugo made her weak with loneliness and she felt a tugging ache in her chest.

'Cases,' she muttered sternly. 'Think about your cases.' If she focused, perhaps she wouldn't succumb to the destructive urge simply to give in and accept whatever he had planned.

Aside from Casavettes, who had made her feel threatened? Mostly, she denied such vulnerability when she felt it, because the men she represented were sensitive to frailty; they latched on to it like barnacles to a boat. She had worked hard at convincing herself that she wasn't troubled by their poorly masked aggression.

Now Clara re-examined those barely acknowledged feelings of unease and came up with a name: Farrell Smith. His was the charm of the serpent: mesmeric, but ultimately repugnant.

Again and again she'd had to deflect Smith's impertinent questions about her home life, her family, her feelings. She had tried to believe his dismissal of his ex-girlfriend's claims, but at each conference Smith tried to insinuate himself into her life, crowding her physically and emotionally.

She had told herself, even after it became clear to her that Farrell Smith was capable of all that his ex-girlfriend had accused him of, that even the guilty have a right to the best legal representation. She took the coward's way out, retreating behind her desk, but he would find some excuse to come around and lean over her, standing too close, being too familiar, sometimes even touching her, and despite what Michaela had said about having the protection of a solicitor's clerk as witness, Clara had felt intimidated.

Finally, she asked for the case to be reallocated, but Smith wouldn't hear of it. Of course, Julian Warrington's belief in client as king meant that she had no choice but to see the case through to trial. At their next meeting it was plain that Smith revelled in her discomfort; his attitude, the sparkle in his eyes, the way he smiled all had feral, sexual overtones.

His self-satisfaction set her resolve hard against him. He stroked the back of his hand and smiled insultingly at her.

'Well, Clara,' he said. 'Looks like you're stuck with me.'

'I'm your lawyer, Mr Smith,' she replied sharply. 'Not your friend. In future you will address me as Ms Pascal.'

His eyebrows shot up, but he seemed amused rather than offended, as if he had half expected this feeble display of stick-wielding. But Clara wasn't finished.

'I am interested in your private life only insofar as it relates to your defence — and you certainly have no reason to become acquainted with my personal and private affairs.'

Still smiling, if a little more fixedly, he said, 'Whatever you say.'

'During consultations,' she pressed on, determined to set the ground rules, 'you will remain seated, keeping to your side of the desk as I keep to mine. Do I make myself clear?'

She had waited, insisting upon his acquiescence before continuing with the business of the meeting. Smith had taken that little humiliation very badly. From that moment he watched her with seething resentment and although he never said it, she thought he blamed her for his conviction. She thought with revulsion how he had held out his hand after the verdict was announced and she had been forced to shake it; the slow, almost languid way in which he had gripped her hand, the lingering contact had made her feel sick.

God, yes . . . Farrell Smith. But this man — the man who had abducted her — was older. Smith was in his thirties, but her abductor . . . It was difficult to tell just by his voice and the way he moved, but she would guess mid-forties. Anyway, Smith was still in prison, as far as she knew. *And what if Smith persuaded a cellmate — a friend — to help him? What then, Clara?*

Chapter Twenty Nine

Eight a.m. and it was still dark. People gathered in the Incident Room, shivering and complaining, their faces pale after five days of working fourteen hours straight. The makeshift office was too small to accommodate the additional personnel that had been drafted in over the last few days, but nowhere suitable could be found nearby for briefings, so they made do, crammed into a room that had seemed over-large on the first day of the investigation.

McAteer allocated a team to work through Eleanor Gorton's Filofax, trying to find out who of her acquaintances or clients had seen her last and who could give them useful background information on the victim. A neighbour had complained of a prowler in her garden two weeks before, but after searching the area, the local police had put it down to urban foxes. Officers were despatched to interview the complainant and check out Mrs Gorton's garden for signs that she had been stalked by her murderer prior to her abduction.

The rest was routine: new actions to be allocated, old ones to be followed up. A couple of deferred actions had come to the top of the pile again – sightings of the Lexus car damaged by the getaway van, now known to be linked with Ray Casavettes. Lawson and Barton would interview Casavettes in prison and McAteer wanted anyone who had seen it reinterviewed: since it was seen in the vicinity of the van and, given Casavettes' particular interest in Clara's abduction, it could be that the Lexus would lead them to the abductor.

Two teams were still on house-to-house. Sarah Kormish from the Child Protection Unit was sent to talk to Pippa to find out if the girl had remembered anything more since the event.

Fletcher was picking up his notebook, ready to report to the HOLMES room for his next action, when Thorpe limped up to him and dropped an evidence bag on his desk.

'What's this?' Fletcher demanded.

'Evidence.'

A few faces smiled over the tops of computer monitors.

Fletcher picked up the bag and turned it over. It contained Thorpe's left shoe.

'Trod in a bloody great steaming dollop of it on my way in this morning,' Thorpe said, deadpan. 'It being your specialism, like, I thought you'd want to investigate.'

Fletcher looked at him for a long moment, then he stood. 'It's good you've still got your sense of humour,' he said. His demeanour was unusually quiet and reflective. 'A woman's been dragged off the street, raped, murdered and dumped, another one, for all we know, is indulging the same sick bastard's fantasies – but you can still see the funny side.'

The observers disappeared behind their monitors as Fletcher walked to the door. His calm, reasonable tone made them ashamed of themselves. 'Back in a tick,' he said.

Thorpe turned to the few officers who remained in the room. 'What'd I say? What'd I do?'

'Aren't you going after him?' Rayner asked.

'You're joking me? With the boss on the rampage? How'm I going to explain my shoe missing?' Nevertheless, after a couple of minutes, he did hobble to the door and peer out. Fletcher stood chatting in the queue at the HOLMES room.

'Er, Fletch,' Thorpe called, smiling a little nervously.

Fletcher looked around, mildly irritated at the interruption.

'Where's my shoe, mate?'

Fletcher frowned, mouthing, 'Shoe? Shoe?' Then his brow cleared. 'Ah, the *evidence!*' he exclaimed. 'You'll have to see the Exhibits Officer about that.'

Thorpe was appalled. 'You haven't . . .' He ducked back inside the Incident Room. 'He's only gone and bloody logged it!'

There was a burst of laughter. 'If I was you,' Rayner advised, 'I'd leave it there, Chris. DS Tilby's a bit of a stickler and if McAteer gets wind of it, he'll go ballistic.'

Casavettes stared at him and Lawson returned the stare. It wasn't a hard-man act: Casavettes was curious; he seemed to be waiting for something. Perhaps he thought Lawson had come to haggle. After a while, he relaxed and sat back.

'What was brother Michael doing parked outside Pippa Pascal's school the morning Ms Pascal was abducted?' Lawson asked.

Casavettes shrugged. 'You'll have to ask him.'

'We have.'

'What did he say?' He seemed genuinely interested.

'Let's just say we weren't convinced,' Lawson said.

'So why ask me? I know as much about it as you do.'

'I doubt that,' Lawson said. Let him take that however he wanted.

Casavettes spread his hands, the picture of injured innocence. 'I was here last Wednesday, looking forward to my day in court. Deciding which suit would hit the right note of respectability – nothing too flash – picking out a tie—'

'Nothing happens in the Casavettes household without you knowing about it, Ray,' Lawson said.

Casavettes seemed mildly amused, even flattered. 'What are you saying?' he asked. 'I sent him after Clara?'

'Did you?'

'You never know who you're rubbing shoulders with, Mr

Lawson,' Casavettes replied, ignoring the question. 'You're not married, so it wouldn't bother you so much, but Sergeant Barton here, he must wonder who the bloke sitting next to his wife on the bus really is.'

Barton braced himself against a shudder as Casavettes' eyes slid over him.

'Thieves, junkies, nutters, hard men, hit men – they're all out there, breathing the same air, walking in the park, feeding the ducks with their kids.' He laughed.

'Well, not *with their kids* as such – there are limits, even for the mad and the bad – but you get my drift.'

Barton did, only too vividly. He saw the car outside his house, heard the click and whirr of a camera motor, the sound of breaking glass, Fran's startled scream—.

He made as if to stand, his chair scraping loudly on the floor tiles, but Lawson placed one hand on his arm, restraining him.

'Are you threatening us, Casavettes?' he asked, his tone deceptively mild.

Casavettes waited a second or two. 'I'm making an observation, Mr Lawson. Look at Clara's husband. He waves her off in the morning – normal day, she's off to court and little Pippa's looking forward to her birthday party in the afternoon; half an hour later, the police are on his doorstep.'

Barton jerked his arm away from Lawson and stared hard at Casavettes. Lawson gave him the chance to say something – anything – but Barton remained silent.

'Let *me* make an observation, Casavettes,' Lawson said, keeping his anger carefully reined in. 'The longer Clara's missing, the longer you'll stay here, sharing a cell that reeks of shit, with the stink of sweat in your clothes. Something tells me you're the sort that never gets used to that kind of thing.'

Casavettes smiled, but Lawson could see that he had struck home. Vanity was Casavettes' only real weakness.

Did Casavettes really believe he had something to gain by implying that he knew Clara's whereabouts or was he simply trying to frustrate their investigation for the hell of it? He hadn't mentioned the earring — and Lawson was sure that the information had been passed on. Was he saving it for later? Casavettes wasn't going to walk away from the drugs charges no matter what; so what did he have to gain, playing these games with them?

There again, what did he have to lose?

Lawson stood and turned away so he didn't see Barton dip into his trouser pocket and slip a folded piece of paper across the table. Casavettes palmed it and watched Barton's back until he disappeared through the door and was gone.

Chapter Thirty

Clara watched the man light the gas heater. Staring at the crown of his head, she felt a rising outrage that almost choked her. *Hit him!*

A timid voice she was fast coming to despise spoke up: I can't!

Of course you bloody can! This monster has beaten you, suffocated you, starved and frozen you — he's chained you up like an animal. Grab the damn flask and smash it down on his sick sadistic head. Beat his bloody brains out!

The man adjusted the gas flow and still she stared at him with loathing and fear. She wasn't strong. What if I don't hit him hard enough?

You have the advantage of surprise — just do it!

And what about the key. What if he doesn't have it on him?

You know he does. Jesus, Clara, you're as big a coward as he is! She hesitated too long. Perhaps he sensed her fleeting resolution, because he shifted suddenly and looked at her through the black-rimmed eye-slits.

Her breath caught in her throat, remembering the first time she had seen that fearful mask. Pippa would be having nightmares and Hugo wouldn't know how to calm her. She ached with longing, to see her little girl again, to hold her, to smell her hair, fresh, silky to the touch.

The man crouched opposite her, warming his hands, his blue eyes cold with dislike.

It was enough to spark a little of her accustomed fight. Who the hell was he to judge her – to judge and dismiss her. She confronted him, forcing the words out, finding the courage to speak, where she could not act, and in confronting him, she confronted her worst fears. 'You said there were reasons why you might keep me alive.'

'I said there were *other* reasons.' He made a small, oddly grotesque sideways movement, still at a crouch, bringing him closer to her. The action was deliberate, intended to intimidate.

She met his gaze. 'If you were going to rape me, you'd have done it long before now.'

He moved closer still, brought his lips to her ear. 'Are you sure?' he whispered.

She cringed, despite her resolve not to. *I will not cry.* He was taking the conversation where he wanted it to go. She couldn't allow that. *Bring it back, Clara.*

'The *other reasons* I can think of—' Her voice wavered, but she made herself go on, 'Are money, revenge, punishment . . .'

'Or . . .'

'What?' He had seen through her. Her nerve had failed her on this one point.

'Or delay. Isn't that what you were going to say? It's all in the news. Speculation. The tabloids are full of it. And it *has* caused a delay in the trial.'

She bit her lip. 'All right,' she said. 'Or delay.' He had neither confirmed nor denied any of her suggestions. She was no closer to knowing. 'Have I missed anything?'

He opened the matchbox and slipped the spent match inside, pocketing the box. 'Interesting theories,' he said. 'You might want to give them some thought.'

'I have,' Clara said. 'There's not much else to do. But I'm no mind reader.'

'You surprise me.'

Her reserve slipped and she spoke earnestly. 'If I knew what you wanted, we could move forward—'

'*Move forward?*' He snorted. 'Are you trying to *progress* the case, Counsel? We're not in a court of law and you're not in charge, Ms Pascal.'

She lifted a few links of the chain and tugged at the loop of metal embedded in the wall. 'I have no illusions about who's in charge,' she said. 'But why do I get the feeling I'm on trial?'

He didn't reply and she raised her voice. 'Don't you think I've a right to know the charge? Shouldn't I be given the chance to refute the evidence?'

'Full disclosure.' He shrugged. 'That's for the police, not me.'

He was certainly someone who had been through the system. Clara took a breath. What she was about to say was a calculated risk. 'I know that we've met. Your voice is familiar – don't worry, I don't want to know who you are—'

'I'm not the one the one who needs to worry,' he interrupted. 'And who do you think you're kidding? Of course you want to know who I am. Because you think if you know who I am, you'll be able to reason with me, use that persuasive patter you're so famous for. But you don't want *me* to know that you know, because then the magic won't work – and anyway, then you'd be dangerous to me.'

She had no answer for him. He had seen through her and he had summed up the situation as concisely as she could have herself.

He nodded, seemingly satisfied that he had hit home. 'Whoever said knowledge is power got it all wrong,' he said. '*Secret* knowledge – that's where power really lies.'

'Is that why you wear a mask?'

'You want to see me? Can you *handle* that knowledge, Counsel?' He reached over the top of his head and lifted the cloth at the nape of his neck.

'No!' Clara cried. 'Please – I didn't mean . . . I meant that there must be a reason why you don't want me to see your face.'

He smoothed the cloth back in place. 'There you go again. Applying reason. Everything obeys the laws of logic.' He seemed angry, agitated. She had pushed too hard. 'People can't just do things for the hell of it — they've got to have a *reason.*'

'So *tell* me,' she pleaded. 'Explain to me why you're doing this to me — to my family.'

His hand snapped out and he jerked the chain hard. Clara fell backwards, banging her head for the second time in days. Her ears boomed and she saw stars. She brought both hands to the back of her head. He grabbed them, pinioning them above her, straddling her, bringing his face close to hers.

'Maybe it's *sexy* seeing a woman totally helpless — totally reliant. Making her beg for the smallest thing. Watching her tremble and cower.'

Clara turned her head away. Tears squeezed from under her eyelids, she felt sick with fear and the throbbing in her head, but through the fog of horror and nausea, she focused on two words: *A woman.* Why did he keep referring to her as 'a woman'? Was this what Michaela, with all her experience of marital abuse, called objectification? Was he fashioning her into some*thing* rather than some*one*, removing the obligation to treat her with as a human being?

'Is this what it takes to make you feel like a man?' she demanded, her voice hoarse with fear and disgust. His weight on her repulsed her. He was breathing raggedly, his breath hot on her neck. He leaned away from her and looked into her eyes. For all he had said, he wasn't enjoying this. He let her hands drop.

'You aren't nearly as clever as you think you are, Counsel,' he said.

Chapter Thirty One

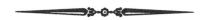

Monday saw Rayner back at Marjorie Kelsall's bungalow. A high, powder-blue sky, empty except for the vapour trails of jets skimming unheard above the traffic noise, promised a fine morning. The mushy paintwork of the window frames looked even sorrier in the exacting light of a clear November day.

The prison liaison officer had finally tracked Farrell Smith down to HMP Dunnings Wood, Devon. Rayner wondered ungraciously why he hadn't told the civilian operator this in his call, instead of leaving a message for her to contact him: it would have saved her a lot of aggravation with Tyrell. There was an up side: now that he was out of the equation, Rayner had the time to follow up another lead, as a result of which she had several further questions to ask Miss Kelsall.

She was dressed, ready for work as before and, as before, she was engaged in housework. She answered the door carrying bright yellow rubber gloves and wearing an irritated frown.

'Can I come in?' Rayner said.

For a moment, she thought Miss Kelsall might shut the door and leave her standing on the doorstep, then she exhaled irritably and opened the door wide. 'Wipe your feet,' she said. 'I've hoovered the floor.'

She left the rubber gloves on the meter cupboard and showed

her into the front room – it seemed that coffee was not on offer on this occasion. The room was chilly and bare: a three-piece suite and a coffee table, a mirror over the mantelpiece; no pictures. The carpet was green, in a swirling leaf pattern that Rayner remembered from the seventies.

'I've just come from Crewe,' Rayner said, watching Miss Kelsall with close interest. 'After the rail crash, a Casualty Bureau was set up to establish the identity of the victims,' Rayner went on. 'I spoke to the Senior Investigating Officer.'

Miss Kelsall's features twisted momentarily and she put her hand out, feeling for the arm of a chair to lower herself into it. She made a jerky gesture inviting Rayner to be seated.

It took her a few moments to compose herself. Rayner watched dispassionately: she didn't like being lied to.

'I heard it on the news,' Miss Kelsall said, reluctantly, the memory evidently still raw. 'I was listening to the radio while I did my housework.'

Now Rayner understood the breathless silence of the house, the absence of music or radio chatter: you hear news like that once in your life and you never want to risk hearing anything like it again.

Miss Kelsall carried on, her gaze unfocused, reliving the horror. 'I tried to phone him on his mobile.'

The senior investigating officer was experienced, nearing retirement, but what he had seen that day had shattered him. 'The eeriest, the most gut-wrenching sound was the chirrup of their mobile phones,' he told her. 'You'd be stretchering out the carbonised remains of some poor bastard and you'd hear *The Ride of the Valkyries* or the *Mission Impossible* theme. The awful thing was, you knew that behind that bloody silly tune was someone frantic to know what had happened.'

Miss Kelsall broke in on Rayner's thoughts. 'I phoned him again and again. It just rang and rang.'

What else could they do, Rayner thought, when it was impossible to tell who the dead were. 'Miss Kelsall,' she said, forcing herself to be detached, objective. 'Is there any reason to think – to hope – that your brother might be alive?'

Miss Kelsall stared at her as if she had made a particularly insensitive and cruel joke. 'You saw the photographs, Constable. My brother was in the first carriage – the one that was so badly burned. I saw him into it myself. I waved him off and—' Her face contorted in a spasm of pain.

Rayner waited and Miss Kelsall made an effort to collect herself, sitting stiffly upright and staring stoically ahead.

'Maybe he changed carriages,' Rayner suggested gently. 'Or maybe he went down to the buffet car. He might not have been in that carriage when—'

'Do you know how they identified the bodies, Constable?' Miss Kelsall interrupted sharply. 'By their dental records. What was left of them wasn't fit for their families to see. A husband wouldn't know his own wife.'

'Yes,' Rayner said firmly, 'But they *were* identifiable.'

Miss Kelsall turned her pale blue eyes on Rayner, eyeing her with contempt. 'You're saying that Brian walked away from his family? That he left a comfortable life, a good pension – he did very well out of the sale of his business.'

'It was a traumatic experience. Maybe he was in shock.'

Miss Kelsall shook her head. 'He was going to buy a house in the country, somewhere Laura wouldn't have to be around people. He wouldn't abandon her. Laura was his whole *life*.'

Rayner didn't speak immediately. She studied Miss Kelsall's face and thought that in happier times it would have had a pleasant, humorous expression. 'I haven't been able to trace your niece,' she said at last.

Miss Kelsall looked at her hands. 'I'm not surprised,' she said. Rayner took a breath to speak, but Miss Kelsall cut across her. 'I told you, after what happened, she couldn't stand to be around people.'

'Even her family?'

'What do you want me to say?' Miss Kelsall demanded

angrily. 'That we failed her? All right then, we failed. We let her down. We didn't know what to say to her – how to comfort her. And she—' Miss Kelsall jumped up and paced the room. 'We drove her away and now I know what I should have said and I've no one to say it to.' She stopped suddenly and covered her face with her hands.

Rayner watched, uncertain whether to put a comforting hand on the woman's shoulder. In the end, the woman's distress decided her. She reached out, but Miss Kelsall stiffened, twitching away from her, and Rayner let her hand drop. Miss Kelsall made that same conscious adjustment that seemed to reflect an effort of will, pulling herself upright and straightening her shoulders.

Rayner hesitated, then with some misgivings she offered Miss Kelsall her card. 'If Laura does get in touch, ask her to ring me,' she said.

The look on Miss Kelsall's face told Rayner that she despaired of ever seeing Laura again.

Chapter Thirty Two

Many of the faces were vaguely familiar. A few she knew almost as well as her own reflection in the mirror – notorious murders, the majority of them unsolved crimes. Clara experienced a moment of stark, unreasoning terror. *He killed them! He killed all of them.* Her fear threatened to spiral out of control and she clamped both hands over her mouth. *Don't scream, Clara. Please don't scream.* She tried not to think about how they had died, about what had been done to them, and for the first time in her life, she had reason to curse that facility of memory which had made passing exams so easy for her.

Gradually, as the frantic eddies and currents of her thoughts were calmed, she saw that the murders could not have been the work of one man: for one thing, the earliest murders chronicled in his bizarre gallery were from the nineteen-sixties, while the latest recorded the discovery of a girl's body near a Brighton night club, only months before. Four decades of abuse and murder. These girls were victims of the kind of lust that Clara had seen in dozens of cases, some of which she had prosecuted. But there were others she had defended. Men like Farrell Smith, who felt that they had a God-given right to control, to mistreat, to sexually torture women.

So the girls in the photographs represented a generality: unpunished crime; her jailer was revelling in the unheard cries of the victim. It was hard to take, but at least now she could see there was some degree of warped logic behind the man's actions. When she accepted that much, she began to see other things: not all of the murders were unsolved. The victims of Fred West, the Moors Murderers and the Yorkshire Ripper took their place amongst photographs of Rachel Nickell and Suzy Lamplugh.

Was he celebrating the sheer volume of atrocities against women? Did this man revel in the vulnerability of women as a sex? Clara's eyes darted from one section of wall to another and although she could not see her hand in front of her face, she saw the pictures as clearly as if they were spot-lit.

He's trying to tell me something. Is it subtle — something I'm missing — or is it a crass threat? You're next . . .

Peter Sutcliffe, Ian Brady, Fred West and John Duffy. Between them, how many had they killed? It took a hell of a long time to bring them to justice and they carried on killing until they were caught. Is that what he was trying to tell her — that he would kill and kill until he was stopped?

The door bolt slammed back and Clara gave an involuntary cry. He stood in the doorway, his size distorted by her terror; he seemed huge, a hulking figure, blocking out the light, staring down at her as she prayed silently, trying to control her trembling, trying so hard to appear brave, fighting the urge to beg with all her strength of will. *Not now. Please, don't let it be now.*

This man had taken her freedom, snatched her from her family, destroyed her daughter's trust in human kindness and decency, but she was determined he wouldn't rob her of the last remnants of dignity she had remaining.

'Take off the cardigan,' he said.

Clara instinctively clutched the lapels, pulling them tight around her neck.

'I want it back, take it off.'

He was serious. Arguing would only enrage him. *And you don't want that, Clara. He's your only link with the outside world and you don't want to piss him off — God, no.* She stood up, decreasing the psychological advantage he had over her by standing above her on the steps, and fumbled with the buttons, her fingers numb with cold and nerves.

He walked slowly down the steps and took it, squeezing it, briefly holding it to his masked face. 'Mmm . . . still warm.' He had something draped over his arm. 'You'll be cold. Put this on.'

Clara took it, then looked at him in question. A new refinement of his mental torture. A new game.

'What are you waiting for, Counsel?'

'I won't do this. What do you——? Why are you——?' She was in danger of breaking down and from the glint in his eye it seemed that he was hoping that she would. He had handed her a black gown, the sort she wore in court. She dropped it to the floor.

He shrugged. 'Suit yourself. But you'll get no heat and no food until you do as I ask.'

She didn't respond.

'I went to the robing room specially to fetch it.'

She looked at him, wide-eyed. Had he really walked into the Crown Court, past court ushers, police, barristers and solicitors?

'I don't know if it's actually yours,' he said. 'It doesn't *smell* of you, but then it might not. Nobody challenged me. Nobody noticed me. People like me are invisible to people like you. Until we make you notice.'

She looked at the robe, black and ugly, puddled on the floor.

'I don't see what the problem is,' he went on. 'It's your uniform, what you wear every day. You should feel right at home in it.'

What was her objection? Why *was* it humiliating to be made to wear an item of clothing that normally gave her confidence, a sense of belonging? *Because he's ridiculing everything it stands for.* And if she complied, what would follow? She thought she knew. Nevertheless, the trembling was becoming a palsied shaking: fear and cold combined. She was too weak to go through the debilitating fever of hypothermia again. She bent and picked up the gown, setting it on her shoulders, reassured by the weight of the broad shoulder pads and the thick twill. She wrapped its folds around her and felt instantly more secure.

'Now then, Counsel, he said, 'What do you make of your companions?'

She felt a thud of sick fear. 'My companions?'

'You've been with them for days.' He walked around the small space, trailing one finger over the pictures on the wall. 'Let's hear what you think.'

'About what?' Did he want her to tell him that she expected to be next? Was that it?

'You're all kitted out, ready. Let's hear your judgment.'

Is he mad? 'I don't make judgments,' she said, haltingly at first, then, more firmly: 'It isn't my job. I just present the best case I can for my client.'

He looked at her for a long minute. Clara made herself return his stare. 'All right,' he said, his eyes never leaving her face. 'Let's imagine you're defending one of the killers. You defend guilty men on a daily basis, so it shouldn't be that hard. Your job is to protect your client. Assess the situation. Decide how much blame the girl should accept.'

'Blame?' She blinked. 'For what? These girls were attacked. Murdered. How can they be to blame?'

'So, in your opinion, as counsel for the prosecution, they're innocent. They bear no burden of guilt.' He tilted his head. 'Congratulations, Counsel, you've just made a judgment. In their favour, admitted, and against your client. But a judgment nonetheless.'

'In the eyes of the law, murder is always wrong.'

'And what would you say if a girl went out in a skirt up to here and her tits hanging out?'

'The way a girl dresses doesn't justify rape and it certainly doesn't justify murder.'

'All right,' he said. 'Different scenario. What if she got tanked up, went back to his flat, started having sex, then changed her mind – put up a fight. He tried to calm her and she got crazy. He couldn't shut her up. Put his hand over her mouth to stop her screaming . . .'

Frantically, Clara tried to recall a recent case like the one he described, one that she had prosecuted, but there wasn't anything Nothing that even came close. He was trying to tell her something and she was missing it. What did he want from her? What did he want her to say? He was becoming agitated and it seemed he was waiting for a reply. 'There could be mitigating circumstances,' she said, 'I might suggest he pleads manslaughter.'

'I thought you said killing was always wrong.'

'I said murder is always wrong.'

'And manslaughter?'

'There are degrees of culpability—'

'A lawyer's answer!'

'In the eyes of the law—'

'I'm not talking about the *law*, Counsel.' He seemed determined not to let her speak. 'I'm talking about right and wrong.'

Then why force me into court dress? She tried again. 'The law helps us to make sense of the complexity of different situations—'

'Okay,' he interrupted again, pacing up and down excitedly. 'Here's a *situation* for you. He's taken a what – a nineteen-year-old girl off the street. She's not used to drinking, but he's taken her, knowing she's too pissed to know right from wrong, he fucked her and when she struggled, he killed her. What's your judgement on him?' He faced her, his eyes glittering – *with tears?*

Her mouth dried. She coughed and made herself answer. 'I thought this was a hypothetical situation.'

His gaze slid away from her. 'Hypothetical or not, I'm asking your opinion as a lawyer.'

'I told you, I don't judge my clients,' she answered, doggedly determined that he wouldn't trick her into taking that dangerous path. She was convinced more than ever that he was building to a confession and if he was trying to get her to condemn him, she wasn't falling for it.

'Are you saying you've no opinion of this man – of what he's done? You just present the case and let the court pass judgment?'

'My opinion of him doesn't matter,' she said carefully. 'That's why we have a jury system – so the decision isn't left up to one person.'

'And what about all those things he did to her? Don't they count for anything with you?'

'The case isn't tried on the circumstances, it's tried on the evidence.'

'Didn't you just say something about mitigating circumstances?'

She had walked into that one. She started composing an answer: contributory factors, diminished responsibility – anything to placate him – but she was tired and cold; her wits had been dulled by the privations of her imprisonment and she could not marshal her thoughts quickly enough.

'No answer?' he said, triumphantly. 'All right. Let's look at the evidence of a case much closer to home.'

Clara felt a detached interest in what was happening. The constant drub of her heart against her ribs was dizzying. Perhaps she was hyperventilating. She felt the kind of disoriented distance she sometimes experienced when she was sickening for flu. She thought she knew where he was heading and she thought that maybe she could get something from it: information, an admission. Something more than she had, anyway. He wanted to talk about himself. Maybe he wanted her absolution. Maybe she'd give it, if she thought it would get her out of this place.

'I'm listening,' she said.

'A mother drops her daughter at school. She walks back to her car and she's attacked. No provocation.'

Clara broke out in a sweat. In the days that she had been here, her family had become shadowy to her and this man, and the monstrous existence he had created to torment her, had become the only reality she knew. Her calm detachment was deserting her. She clenched her teeth and concentrated on her breathing.

'She's gagged and bound and thrown in the back of a van while her little girl – oh, hell, why be coy? – while *Pippa* sobs her heart out by the side of the road.'

The mention of Pippa's name was a shock, but he didn't say that Pippa was injured. He didn't say that. If Pippa was hurt, he would have told me, wouldn't he? Or did he prefer her to wonder, to fret about her safety? Pippa was fine. After all, she had heard her shouting after the van.

No, Clara. You heard her screaming. *You didn't see her.*

'He half suffocates her,' he went on, 'and she wakes up in a hole in the ground, chained to the wall like a dog. She's freezing, half starved, frightened for her life.'

She swallowed and with an effort of will she spoke calmly. 'Those are the facts so far.' Maybe he had lost a little time between bringing her, tied with the velcro bindings, into the cellar and later chaining her to the wall. She wasn't about to correct him.

'So?' he demanded.

'So what?'

'What's your defence?'

'Why would I defend you?'

'Now *you're* being coy, Counsel. You defend men like me every day. Everyone is entitled to representation, right?'

He stood in front of her, inches from her, and she knew he could see the beads of sweat on her face. He saw her fear and he revelled in it. She wanted to lash out at him, to shatter his complacency. But she needed to understand why she was there – why he had chosen her – so she said, with a composure that almost frightened her, 'I can't construct a defence without all the facts.'

'Can you ever say you really have all the facts?'

Clara smiled. She looked into his eyes and smiled. 'It's possible to know every detail of what happened, but *none* of the facts.'

'Ah,' he said. 'You mean the background.'

She nodded, not trusting herself to speak, afraid that if she said the wrong thing, he would clam up again and she would be no wiser than when he had started this charade.

'You're a respected lawyer, going about your legitimate business and BAM!' He slapped the wall next to her. She flinched, but forced herself to maintain eye contact with him. 'What excuse could there be for treating you like this?'

He wasn't a fool, he knew she couldn't excuse him what he'd done, so she said, 'Maybe not an excuse, but there may be . . . things I don't know that might cast a different light on events.'

'We're back to mitigation again.' He was mocking her. 'Maybe you did something to me that made me want to do this to you?' He paused and subjected her to a raking scrutiny. 'Whatever you did, it must have been *bad* — I mean, look at you.'

Clara heard the contempt in his voice and felt suddenly painfully aware of her appearance. She was filthy, dishevelled and red-eyed, and she stank, and he was taking all of this in. In a moment's insight she understood how someone could disregard the humanity of a degraded human being, even though they themselves had brought about that degradation.

She frowned, refusing to succumb to self-pity.

'If there are reasons . . .' she said, avoiding his gaze.

He gave a shout of laughter and she shuddered violently.

'You can't switch off, can you?' he exclaimed. 'It's a reflex for you, like breathing.'

'I'm just trying to—'

'I know what you're trying to do. Get this into your head, Counsel: I don't *need* your understanding.' He punctuated each point with a jab of his finger. 'I don't need your approval and I certainly don't need *justification* for bringing you here.'

He moved closer and – she couldn't help herself – she cringed.

'You want to know why you're here?'

I just want to go home! But that wasn't going to happen, unless she could persuade him, and to do that, she had to understand him, so she said, 'Yes.' Her voice a toneless croak.

His eyes gleamed. Was he smiling? 'You're here,' he said, 'because *I want you here.*'

Chapter Thirty Three

Trish had heard the key in the door and was standing in the hallway waiting for him.

Her annoyance quickly turned to concern. 'My God, Hugo . . .' He looked grey and his hand trembled as he pushed his fingers through his hair.

'Where's Pippa?' he asked.

'She's upstairs. In her room.' Trish gestured unnecessarily in the direction of the stairs.

He went straight into the sitting-room without taking off his overcoat and lowering himself slowly into an armchair, as if he were bruised and aching, he put his head in his hands. 'God, Trish, what have I done?'

Trish's heart hammered hard. 'Hugo . . .' She touched him lightly on the shoulder. 'What is it?'

'It's all my fault.'

She pulled up a chair and sat opposite him, waiting until he was ready to talk.

When he raised his head, his eyes were deep-shadowed and he had a haunted look. 'I hired a private detective.'

'Hugo—'

He shook his head impatiently. 'The police wouldn't listen! They're not interested in Casavettes.'

'You don't know that.'

He took both her hands. 'It doesn't matter now, because . . .' He paused and a fleeting moment of anguish flitted across his face. 'Melker – he's a – a what? A *business associate* of Casavettes.'

Trish took a moment to absorb what he had said. 'That doesn't mean—'

'I told him about her!' he burst out. 'Her work, the trial, Pippa, her birthday – everything. I let him in to our family. And he was passing it on to that vicious . . .' He balled his hands into fists and choked, unable to go on.

'What makes you so sure it's him?'

'Who else, Trish? Who else would do such a thing?'

'Wouldn't the police have arrested him by now if they thought that Casavettes had taken Clara?'

'They say they need evidence,' he said bitterly.

She looked wordlessly at him.

'Please don't say it, Trish.' He knew what she was thinking: if Clara had been taken by some lunatic – a random kidnapping – what chance had they of finding her alive? In his heart, he could see that this was becoming more and more likely, but he couldn't bear to hear it said – couldn't bear even to think it. He had to keep on believing that Clara would come back. As long as it was possible to believe that, he had to.

His eyes searched her face, reading her resignation. 'At least if Casavettes has her, it makes some sort of sense – doesn't it?'

'And you think Mr Melker told him where to find her?'

She could see that he was too muddled with lack of sleep, too intoxicated with grief to think straight.

'Hugo!' She took his face in her two hands. 'Casavettes knew about Clara months ago, when he was committed for trial. You can be sure he found out then which chambers she works out of, what car she drives, her family situation – even where she lives.'

He sat up, taking her hands in his, weighing up the logic of what she had said. 'Is that what they do, d'you think?' Another terrible idea blundered into his befuddled thoughts. 'Trish – do you think she knows that?'

'I think she tries not to think about it,' Trish said drily. 'Now what are you going to do about Mr Melker?'

'I thought I might go to his office – have it out with him.'

'And if he *has* got some involvement, with Casavettes – some illegal involvement, that is – you'll warn him off.'

'I have to do *something!*' He seemed completely lost and her heart went out to him.

'Go to the police. Tell them what you know. Let them talk to the private investigators. They're the professionals, Hugo, let them do their job.'

He bowed his head and, planting one hand on each knee, struggled to his feet. She sensed that he had finished with running away: he was ready to face the outcome of this dreadful crisis, however it came out.

'Pippa's been worried about you,' she said, almost tentatively.

He lifted a hand as if to make some protest, then let it fall.

'She hasn't seen you for more than a few hours since it happened, Hugo. She thinks you're avoiding her.'

'Of course I'm not avoiding her! I've been trying to . . .' To what? Play the detective? Find Clara and bring her home, like they do in the movies? He saw the futility of all his subterfuge of the preceding days. He had left Pippa alone when his place was with her, when she needed him most.

His shoulders slumped. 'I've been a complete shit, haven't I, Trish? I've run away from my responsibilities and left you to cope and then I've given you a hard time over it.'

'You did what you thought was best,' Trish said kindly.

'Does she hate me?'

'She thinks *you* hate *her.*'

He stared at her, shocked. 'How could she think that?'

'She's trying to make sense of an insane situation. You haven't said more than half a dozen words to her in days. And then it's to tell her off. Hugo, she thinks you blame her.'

'Christ . . .' He turned to the door.

'I'll call her down, shall I?' Trish suggested.

'D'you think . . . She won't want to speak to me, will she?'

'Stop feeling sorry for yourself, Hugo.' She spoke harshly and he glanced at her surprised. She met him eye-to-eye and he nodded. She was right. He had been so self-absorbed that he hadn't even been able to see that his daughter was suffering.

Pippa was reluctant. She held Trish's hand and hung back in the doorway, frowning resentfully at the floor.

'Pippa,' Hugo said. 'I'm sorry I've been so . . .' He chose a word she would use. '. . . So horrible.' She nodded, unconvinced, still refusing to look at him. 'You know I love you.'

She looked up, piqued by the outrageousness of the statement.

'I – I know I haven't shown it just lately,' Hugo faltered, 'but –.' He began to cry, ashamed of his weakness, but unable to stop himself.

Pippa stared in horror at her father. Her eyes seemed to grow larger and for a moment she shrank back against Trish. 'Daddy?' She whispered, as if unsure that this really was her father. Suddenly she ran to him, flinging herself at him. He grunted at the impact, then, after an anguished glance at Trish, he placed his hand on his daughter's head.

'Daddy, don't cry!' she begged. 'Mummy's going to come home. She is!'

Chapter Thirty Four

Like finger-training a bird. Get it to take food from your hand and you're half way to taming it. He knew how easily darkness, dirt and hunger erode the human spirit. The cold had a primal effect: they would curl into the foetal position, trying to conserve as much heat as possible, arms crossed, hands tucked in tight. The spine initiated thousands of tiny muscular contractions, designed to generate heat and gradually the shivering became a shaking they could not control: arms, legs, even the jaw, rattling the teeth against each other. The muscles, tense with cold, would eventually go into spasm and they screamed in pain.

This one wouldn't wait for it to go that far. She was weakening – physically and mentally. When she first arrived she would get up when he came into the cellar. She had watched him as carefully as he watched her. But the more intelligent ones had a lower tolerance, perhaps they reasoned that a little humiliation was worth it, if they could avoid the worst excesses of what they would otherwise have to endure. Now, she barely twitched when she heard him return – perhaps hugged herself more tightly, whimpered a little . . . And when he took from her: material things or her dignity, she no longer fought – she hadn't even the courage to argue; she merely gave whatever he demanded, her eyes wide, fearful. Oh, yes, she would ask: for covering, for warmth.

'*Beg me* . . .' He said the words aloud, breathing them into the frigid air, and he saw her whole body seize for a moment, then relax. She mewled like a kitten and shiver of pleasure trickled down his own spine. He would make her perform some small favour. Not sex – not yet – but something sufficiently intimate to bring her in close contact with him. Some platonic gesture, such as a wife might perform, unthinking, for her man. He would make her think about it; she would realise that this was a foretaste – a primer – and he would expect much, much more from her in the days to come.

But as with an animal, you could take a step too far, move too quickly and set back the training by days. It was painstaking work, but he relished the challenge. He stared at her for a little longer, feeling real affection for her.

He moved in closer and she edged away. He crouched. In a little while, she would be distracted again by the bitter, punishing cold, and his proximity would be less offensive to her. Perhaps she would even gain a little comfort from his body heat.

'*Beg me* . . .' he repeated.

She turned huge, terrified eyes to him.

'Please . . .' she said, not knowing what she was begging for. Pavlovian response. She was coming along nicely.

There was a ritual to his preparation. He spread out the photographs in groups on the floor. He was selective: he would keep only the best, those which captured her essence. His aim was to refine and intensify. From now until the final moment, he would focus entirely on her – the other videos were stored safely, now he would allow himself to view images only of her. It was a kind of worship. And like the mystics, the shamans and the holy men, he needed to concentrate all his thoughts and invest a great deal of emotion to extract the greatest pleasure.

The first step was to rediscover his reasons for having chosen her. In the preceding days, she had become dirty, her smell was distasteful to him, and the necessity of providing for her sometimes left him feeling nauseated.

With the photographs as reference points, he was ready. He pressed *play* and the big screen lit up. She let herself into the house. A light went on in the hall. He imagined her taking off her coat, her breasts pushed hard against the restraint of her jacket. She would go first to the kitchen. He could work between the front and the back of the house without being seen: silent as a cat, his night vision acute.

The kitchen blinds were open; she drew neither blinds nor curtains. He took this as an invitation – she *wanted* him to make contact. He liked to watch her in the kitchen. His breathing rate increased; he was beginning to feel the original excitement. He made an effort to recall the details of the times he had followed her, photographed her, filmed her.

A shrubbery at the end of her garden provided both hiding place and shelter. In the dense, overplanted clump of conifers he was dry and warm. He concentrated, recalling every detail of that night. There: a whiff of mulch from the fallen leaves on the lawn, the patter of rain on the canopy above him.

He sat motionless for hours, the tape edits moving from front room to kitchen, and once, briefly the dining-room too. She sat at the piano and played. Something sad and slow; it is as if she played it for him.

Later, she heated milk in a pan, poured it carefully into a mug, sprinkled something on top. He was enchanted by her grace. She dipped her head and sipped the drink, staring at her reflection in the kitchen window, watching the raindrops trickle erratically down the glass. It seemed that she was reaching out to him: she stared straight into the camera lens. He was reminded of another night, when a city fox strayed into his territory, carefully picking its way across the lawn. It got scent of him and froze, lifting its snout to test the air. Then it turned and for one heart-stopping moment their eyes met. He saw recognition in its eyes, recognition for another night creature, a fellow predator.

Chapter Thirty Five

Lawson scanned the room, locating the key players among the fifty or so officers present. Young. She hadn't settled well into the team. Fletcher had a lot to do with it, he suspected. There he was, looking pleased with himself, despite the dog shit episode.

Sal Rayner, a look of furious concentration on her face, working the phones right until McAteer called the team to order, still trying to run Laura Kelsall to ground.

Phil Barton sat at the front, subdued, his shoulders hunched in an attitude that shouted resentment. He was still sore that Lawson had made him come along to interview Ray Casavettes. They had got nothing and Barton had come out of it looking anxious and somehow guilty. Lawson gave a mental shrug. He'd get over it.

Chris Thorpe sat near the back, his trademark woollen hat pulled low. He was chewing gum and talking into the phone.

'Okay, this is the situation,' McAteer said, calling the assembly to order. 'Mr Pascal has' – he chose his words carefully – 'come clean about hiring Safe Hands Detective Agency. The agency discovered a link between Casavettes and the property developer for whom he's designing a health club.'

A few officers made a note.

'He's wasted his time and money, I'm afraid,' McAteer went on. 'Operation Snowman checked out the connection months back. They had him under surveillance. Nothing. He advised Casavettes on setting up a gym over in Wrexham, but it appears it was all above board – at least as far as Melker was concerned.'

Someone asked, 'Is Pascal in the clear, now?'

McAteer considered for a moment; the tension was palpable. 'I think he's genuine.'

There was a faint rustle, like a sigh, the released tension of fifty officers willing the SIO to give the answer he had just given. No one wanted to believe Pascal was involved, not least because if he was, Clara would almost certainly be dead by now.

'But the surveillance stays,' he added. 'The abductor may still try to get in touch. And there's no telling what Casavettes might try.'

'Meanwhile,' McAteer said, 'I'm stepping up the search for the van. Local dealerships, car auctions, private sales of white vans in the last three months. It's a lot of leg work and a hell of a lot of mind-numbing paperwork, but it might just turn up something useful.'

Tyrell came in: 'There's nothing that matches on the stolen list, Boss.'

McAteer nodded. He hadn't really expected a result on that line of enquiry: if the van had been stolen, they would have expected it to turn up before now, maybe dumped somewhere, burnt out. The abductor wasn't likely to keep hold of a vehicle the police were on the look-out for as stolen.

Thorpe cleared his throat, uncharacteristically reticent. 'For what it's worth, Boss.' The meeting fell silent, all eyes on Thorpe's face. 'Word is, Casavettes' lot are working as hard as we are to find the van. And my bet is, he's not looking to exchange insurance details.'

There were a few low whistles and a murmur rose from the assembly. If Casavettes was looking for the van it meant two things: he hadn't arranged the kidnap and he wanted to use Clara as a bargaining tool.

After a moment's pause, McAteer asked, 'How close is your source?' Thorpe's evident unease at being asked to divulge details of his informant made him add, 'I mean what's the possibility of him getting the location to us, before Casavettes has time to act?'

Thorpe seemed doubtful. 'I couldn't get the index number out of him. To be honest, I don't think he knows it – he said Casavettes would break his legs if he knew he'd told me even this much.'

'If he can get the number to us or the location – if Casavettes gets that far – we might be able to offer a reward.'

Thorpe nodded. 'I'll pass on the message.' It was plain from his tone that he didn't hold out much hope.

'I don't need to emphasise,' McAteer finished, 'that if they find the van first, we could be in real trouble.'

There was a rumble of complaint and McAteer said, 'I know the chances of finding it are slim—'

'Bloody anorexic, if you ask me,' Fletcher muttered.

'But we've got to try,' McAteer said firmly. 'There's a woman out there relying on us to try.'

The meeting broke up. They would try, because Clara might be out there, cold and frightened and hurt. And they still might get to her in time, but the fact was unless the abductor bought it in the last few months, the van would be difficult to trace through local dealers – assuming of course he had bought it through a local dealer rather than a private sale. Assuming also that he had bought in the Chester area. Swansea was willing to do all it could, but without even a partial index, it was a non-starter.

Barton sneaked guiltily into the car park, like an office worker sloping off for a crafty fag. Casavettes sounded calm, but the phone line crackled with tension and Barton was left in no doubt that the man was treading a very narrow line between icy control and dangerous rage.

'*Don't tell me what I already know,*' he said, his voice barely above a whisper.

'I'm giving you everything I can,' Barton protested, despising the high-pitched, wheedling tone to his voice.

'Everything you can, maybe, but not everything you know.'

Barton felt a cold chill of fear touch his spine. 'Jesus, Casavettes! I'm risking everything just talking to you.'

'You think so?' Casavettes said. 'Think what you're risking by not telling me what I want to know.' There was a silence and Barton thought for a moment that Casavettes had cut the connection.

He stood stupidly, barely aware of the of the biting cold and the constant thrum of traffic on Grosvenor Road. He couldn't think. He couldn't move. *Just don't hurt Fran. Don't hurt Timmy.*

'Are you *thinking*, Phil?' Casavettes' voice startled him. He shuddered.

'What d'you want?' He heard the spineless, defeated helplessness in his tone.

'A name.'

The snout who had given Thorpe the nod about Casavettes looking for the van. A cold sweat had broken out on Barton's forehead and upper lip and he wiped his face with his handkerchief. If he gave Casavettes the name, he might as well go out and shoot the man himself. 'I can't—'

'Not even for Timmy?'

His breath caught in his throat. 'Thorpe is really close about his informants,' he protested.

'Persuade him.'

Young bounced into the Incident Room, having picked up her action for the day.

'You're looking pleased with yourself,' Rayner remarked.

Young nodded, unable to stop herself from glancing nervously in Fletcher's direction. 'Long as I'm nowhere near *him*. What are you doing?' she asked.

'I've got a lead on Laura Kelsall.' One of her last-minute phone calls before the briefing.

Young's eyes opened wide in astonishment. 'You still chasing that down?'

'This bloody action's driving me nuts! I mean what kind of girl doesn't show up to her dad's funeral? Why doesn't she get in touch with her auntie? I want to hear her side of the story. So until I'm pulled off it, yeah – I'm still chasing it down.' Rayner had been messed about too much to let it drop. She wanted to get to the bottom of Laura Kelsall's disappearance before Dawn Tyrell or McAteer yanked the plug on it.

It was too windy for frost, but cold enough for black ice. A couple of minor shunts had slowed traffic and congestion was even worse than usual clockwise on St Nicholas Street. Rayner edged into the inside lane, ready to cut left onto Watergate Street and take Sealand Road.

Laura Kelsall was taking a vocational course at Blacon College of Further Education. With a bit of luck, she might even be there this morning, Tuesday being one of her college days. The information had come, unexpectedly, from Mr Parks, Laura's ex-landlord and occasional bed-partner. He warned Rayner not to give advance notice of her visit:

'If Laura gets wind that a pi—excuse me, a *dibble* is looking for her, she'll quietly slip away.'

He knew which courses she was taking and even told Rayner the name of her best friend. Rayner had to adjust her assessment of the man – perhaps Laura did mean more to him than a young body and a healthy sexual appetite.

'Why didn't you tell me this when I came to see you?' She was grateful for the information, but it would have been more useful several days earlier, when she had first spoken to him.

He didn't answer immediately.

'Mr Parks?'

'I don't want her upset,' he said. 'But she can't run for ever, can she?'

'That's a bit paternalistic, isn't it, sir?'

He laughed. 'You're right — but as you noticed, I *am* old enough to be her dad.' He paused and she was sure there was something else he wanted to say.

'Sir?'

He exhaled. 'Stupid, really. She won't want comfort from an old guy like me, but, maybe you could tell her anyway — that I'm here if she needs me?'

The main college building was a monument to 1960s economy and unimaginative architectural design. Concrete stairs at either end of the oblong façade echoed and amplified the noise of hundreds of students beginning their college day.

Rayner stopped a couple of girls, giggling past a knot of boys at the foot of the east stairs and asked for directions to the main office. She found it on the first floor, equidistant between the clamorous stairways along a grey-tiled corridor that smelled of polish and rubber.

The secretary gave her a room number where she would find Laura's friend.

When Rayner first caught sight of Una Shellien, she was sitting at the end of one of the benches in the lecture theatre, a fresh-faced girl of no more than eighteen, bobbing her head to some music playing on her personal stereo and chipping into the conversation of two girls in the row in front of her.

Rayner tapped her on the shoulder and Una looked round, smiling, her ponytail still bobbing to the beat.

'Una?'

'Yeah?'

'Could we—' Rayner mimed taking the headphones off and Una complied with a good-natured grin. 'Could we talk?'

'I've got my lecture,' Una said, glancing for the first time to the front, where the lecturer was checking through her slides. 'She locks the door if you're late.'

'It's important,' Rayner said, not wanting to flash her ID in front of the girl's friends. Lowering her voice, she added, 'It's about Laura . . .'

The colour fled from Una's face. She wasn't smiling any more. A quick nod of the head, then she eased out of her seat and Rayner was surprised that the girl was tall and leggy, her height emphasised by four inch heels. There were only three boys in the group, but the two heterosexuals responded, eyeing Una appreciatively. She, however seemed completely unaware of their attention and, bending to whisper to one of her friends, exposed even more well-toned thigh. 'If she locks the door, slip the bolt, 'kay?'

Her friend replied ' 'Kay,' and returned to her conversation.

They found an empty seminar room and sat next to each other in the semicircle of chairs facing the broad expanse of a whiteboard. Rayner leant on the wooden pallet attached to one arm as she took notes.

When she had Una's address and contact phone number, she said, 'You and Laura were good friends.'

Una's reply was emphatic. 'The best.'

'So, what did you think when she told you she'd been assaulted?'

Una's open, innocent face clouded with confusion. 'What did I *think*? I don't get it——. It was terrible – awful. What he did to her——'

'So you believed her?'

Una jumped up, banging her legs on the wooden pallet. 'I thought you were here to *help*! I thought you were going to arrest that evil bastard!'

'Woah!' Rayner didn't want to lose this one. 'I'm just working on the paperwork, Una. I hoped you'd fill me in.'

The girl hovered uncertainly for a moment, rubbing absently at the livid line on her thigh, where she had caught it on the chair.

'I really would like to get to the truth,' Rayner added,

deciding that it would not be a good idea to mention Clara Pascal just yet.

Una sat down, this time swivelling the arm rest safely out of the way and perching at the edge of the seat as if in preparation for sudden flight. 'What do you want to know?'

'Just tell it how it was.'

For a moment, it seemed she didn't know where to start, then she gave a little shrug. 'She was coping — just about — up to the trial. He was in prison, you see. Off the streets. After the verdict, she cried and cried. For days. You know she gave up the course?'

'Her auntie said she couldn't stand to be around people.'

Una's lips pressed into a thin line. 'It was gross, what he made her do. And he made her *say things* like she wanted . . . you know.' She blushed.

'And she had some sort of breakdown?'

'Every time she went near a man, she got — I dunno, flashbacks, I suppose.'

Rayner gave a non-committal grunt.

'I tried to help.' It was an exclamation, as if Rayner had accused her of some omission. Una's mouth twisted, then she swallowed hard and, staring stoically at the whiteboard, she went on: 'She'd have been all right if they'd put him away. But that woman made it seem like Laura had — well, that *she* was the one in the wrong.'

'You're talking about the barrister, Clara Pascal?'

Una nodded. 'Malicious, she called her.' Una tore her gaze from the whiteboard and looked into Rayner's eyes. 'Laura was the kindest, most generous person I've ever met and that cow called her malicious! She just shrivelled up and died inside when they let him go.'

'Do you know where she went when she moved out of her flat?' Rayner asked gently.

'Home — to her dad's.' She raised her shoulders and let them fall in a curiously child-like gesture. 'He couldn't help her either.' A tear quivered like a small jewel on her lower eyelid.

'Her dad sold the house, Una,' Rayner persisted. 'Where did she go after that?'

'Go?' Una stared at her, shocked. 'What do you mean, "go"?'

The pieces started to slot into place and Rayner realised with a sudden jolt that she had got it all wrong. She closed her eyes momentarily. 'My God . . .' she breathed. 'She's dead, isn't she?'

Una nodded.

Laura dead . . . All she knew of Laura was what Parks had told her, but still Rayner felt her throat constricting.

'Killed herself.' She could barely get the words out.

Another slight nod. The girl was trembling from head to foot.

Laura had been a girl like Una. Still in her teens. Her whole life ahead of her and driven to suicide. 'How? When?'

'An overdose . . . Monday, September the twenty-fourth.' It was a date Una would never forget. Rayner took both her hands.

'I'm so very sorry,' Rayner said.

'*He* killed her.' Una almost spat the words, pushing Rayner's hands away as she spoke. 'If it wasn't for him, Laura would still be alive.'

'I know,' Rayner said. 'I know.' She got up to leave.

'You find him – you make sure he pays . . .'

Rayner stuffed her notebook into her pocket and tried to think of a way of reassuring the girl without lying to her. 'I'll investigate,' she said, knowing how lame it sounded. She shrugged, apologising again, hating herself for having misled the girl. Seeing in Una's face a recognition that she had been duped, she added, 'I'll do what I can but . . .'

'You *bitch!*'

It would have been easier if the girl had run from the room, but she didn't, she stood her ground, her hands balled into fists, her pretty face contorted with fury, and Rayner was forced to creep away under her contemptuous gaze.

*   *   *

'Laura Kelsall's suicide puts her father firmly in the frame for Clara's abduction.' Rayner said.

'Except we don't know if he's alive or dead.' McAteer's office was warm and he looked smart and unruffled in his grey suit.

'What does Miss Kelsall have to say?'

'She wasn't home.'

'What about her workplace?'

'I didn't get a place of work.' Rayner felt her face flush with unaccustomed warmth under his gaze. She told herself that she was overheated after her furious drive back to base.

'I'll try the tax office, Guv, see if they can find her through their records.'

'What makes you so sure she's lying?'

'I don't know . . .' Her aunt's shocked reaction when she had first asked, *How did Laura take it?* How's a girl supposed to take the news of her father's death, when she's already been dead a month?

Rayner knew that McAteer would expect sound reasoning, so she curbed the anger she felt at being lied to and made an effort to convince him. 'I've checked the dates, sir. Laura killed herself on September 24th, like her friend said.'

'So?'

'That's almost two weeks *before* the Crewe rail crash. Miss Kelsall made a big thing about Laura's dad having everything to live for. He was going to buy them a house in the country, nurse Laura back to health.' She shook her head, incredulous that she had ever fallen for it. 'She told me Laura had "gone away". She knew damn well she was dead. She's been lying to me all along.'

Chapter Thirty Six

He notices her noticing him. That is always the first step: they *notice*. Often their gaze will skim over and past, sliding over his contours and slipping away, as a bar of soap slips from the hand. Occasionally they will check, looking quickly back — realising they have missed something — and seeing what they have missed, they are intrigued, even amused by their oversight. There is some force of physical attraction, part visual, part pheromone. He feels their hungry examination as hot needles, pricking the skin of his face and neck.

This one is dark, shapely. *The type.* She looks at him over the sloping stands of underwear, her interest telegraphed from ten yards away.

He resents her intrusion. This time has been set aside for the final preparations. He has spent hours browsing Next and Principles, Monsoon and Jaeger, to find the dress, then sifting through the lingerie sections of half a dozen stores, trying to find exactly the right colour and shade, just the right look. He had found the dress he wanted: a dark, shimmering green, low on the shoulders, something that would show enough of her breasts to imply an invitation without making her look cheap. He fingers the silky fabric of the bra he has chosen to match and looks up again. The assistant gives him an arch look.

He has two smiles: one he uses as a baited hook to reel them in. The other has quite the opposite effect. At first she is startled, then she looks away, flustered, a pink flush washes over her face and is gone, as she falls pale under his stare. He continues to stare, but switches off the smile. Now she is frightened. He lifts his chin and snouts the air. He cannot smell her fear. Not yet.

He has lost the mood that has taken him hours to find; he is angry with her and decides to punish her. He lets her turn away and continue her task, checking stock, sorting panties from small to large, replacing bras women have hung out of order on the stands. He waits until she has forgotten him. She wanders into an alcove, out of sight of the main shop floor, tapping in orders on a hand-held stock control gizmo.

He is quick and silent. He appears at her elbow and asks, 'What's your cup size?'

She jumps and makes a small sound at the back of her throat. He has heard it before and it excites him. She turns, her eyes huge and she grips the little plastic hangers to her chest; they provide poor protection from his close scrutiny.

'What did you say?' She tries to sound indignant, but her face has a pinched look and her nostrils are flared.

He leans over her. Now he scents her. It comes in a flood, a wave of anxiety – not quite terror, not in this public place – but she is afraid.

'My girlfriend is about your size.' He stares intently. 'Up top.'

'I—' She looks around wildly. For a moment it seems she will tell him. He steps back, holding up the bra he has taken from the stand, matching it to her body, tilting his head as if making a mental comparison.

She opens and closes her mouth a couple of times, then scuttles off, disappearing through a door marked 'Staff Only' and he laughs and laughs. This is bad. This is dangerous: till now, he has always been able to blend in with the grey mediocrity of the rest of humanity, his invisibility enhancing his omnipotence. He has to get himself under control.

Think of something other than the look of horror on the shop girl's face. Think about—Think about *her. She is ready. Waiting for him because she has no choice. She is pliable, ripe.* When he hands over the underwear to the middle-aged woman at the till, his hands are almost steady.

She stinks, after the days and nights he has kept her, but although this repels him, it is also arousing. His life is full of these inconsistencies. Ambivalence the psychologists called it: the existence in one person of opposing emotional attitudes to the same object. He pauses, savouring the word 'object'. He can place her exactly where he wants her, like an ornament on a mantelshelf. She is there, while she lives, to perform a function which he determines, the boundaries of which are limited only by his imagination.

He hands over the cash – it's always cash – and smiles pleasantly, now fully in control. The woman slides the little bag over the counter to him.

He will not look at her while she bathes. He can wait. He will ask her to dress in the clothes he has chosen especially for her. She will be reassured: tasteful underwear, a beautiful dress. She will think he is preparing to let her go.

He walks out of the shop still planning their evening together.

He will take her to the bedroom. At first she will be confused, then, as she realises what is in store for her, dismayed, tearful. But that will pass, because she is ready. She will say anything – do anything – to secure her release. He smiles at the paradox: secure-release.

By the time he reaches the car park, he has been through the night's events from start to finish. He knows the order and the timing for each stage. But he is willing to improvise. Anything is possible. He looks around him, right and left, not turning his head, using his eyes only. Nobody notices him. He is a chameleon again, grey and unremarkable in a crowd.

Chapter Thirty Seven

Her terror had been attenuated by the hours and days. Now all she felt was a nagging ache of fear. But fear, although less intense, had its own destructive effect. At some point over the last two days she had felt something shift within her, as though some part of her had collapsed in on itself, unable to support the burden of what was happening to her.

How many times had she walked out from a consultation with a client in the cells beneath the courts thinking *How can they stand it? The loss of control. Being locked in* . . . She had convinced herself that if anyone tried to take her liberty, she would fight like a lunatic until she was free. She looked down to where her hands lay, limp, palms up against her thighs. She could not see them. The darkness was absolute. I can't fight, because I have no hands, she thought, and giggled, then clamped down hard on it afraid that she wouldn't be able to stop. The idea was tenacious, though. *Perhaps I'm not here after all. Perhaps I'm fading away into the black stone floor, dissolving into its dirty slime.* For a few seconds she entertained the insane notion that she was not really there. It threatened to overwhelm her. She gasped and heard her heart pulse in her throat.

She closed her eyes, trying to impose some discipline on her thoughts. *The police are investigating,* she told herself. *They're trying to find you.* She tried to imagine them searching for clues. But what she saw was a line of men and women, stretched like blue tape across an open field, moving forward step by painstaking step, searching tussocks of greying grass, treading on brittle nettle stems, picking debris out of a tangle of weeds like over-zealous park-keepers.

She forced her eyes open and stared into the dark, willing the vision away. It lingered a few seconds longer on her retina — a flash-bulb image of her own death.

The questions came despite her: *Do they think I'm dead? Have they given up?*

'Stop it, Clara!' her voice sounded stagy, unreal, flat and dull in the close space. 'They haven't forgotten you and they haven't given up.'

She had read somewhere that hostages formed a bond with their captors, but far from establishing a rapport with her, the man in the mask had hardened towards her. She tried to make sense of this: it was easy to hate in the abstract, to despise what you don't truly know. Isn't that what race hatred was about? See a person face to face, talk to them as a human being, and the bigotry was harder to sustain.

Who do you think you're fooling, Clara? her spiteful inner voice demanded. *Make a person less human and you can treat them exactly as you like.* She didn't need light to feel the ingrained filth on her hands and face. She put a hand to her hair: her carefully pinned chignon had come down during the struggle in the van and now her hair was tangled and greasy, coarse with grit and dirt. Her lips felt swollen and cracked.

'Less than human . . .' she whispered to herself. *From the Roman conquest to the rise of the Third Reich, people have excused their actions by depriving their victims of their humanity.* She was disgusted with herself. What had happened — what he had done to her — had reshaped her into something she could not recognise and could only despise; how could she expect more of him?

What was she thinking? Did she really want this monster to *like* her? What would Michaela make of that: her cool barrister friend who had always found that aggressive clients could be talked round. She knew that Michaela was too generous a spirit to take pleasure in being proved right, but even thinking about her friend made Clara's eyelids prick with tears.

She sniffed and wiped her eyes with the gown. *He hates me, that much is plain. I'm never going to be able to persuade him out of that. He has humiliated and starved me. He wants to hurt me; he told me that and he could do if he chose. So why doesn't he? What's stopping him?*

Time. Her inner voice told her. *Only time. Every second, minute, hour and day you've been here he's been building to it. So what now? The countdown?*

I won't sit and wait for it to happen.

She tested the chain. It held without give against her best efforts. *The lock is the weakest link*, she thought. *Right, and how are you going to pick it — with your fingernails?*

How many men had she defended who could spring open a padlock with a penknife, a hair-grip? *Oh my God!* Her hands trembling, Clara combed her fingers through her hair once more, searching the tangles and knots. A hair-grip. Was it possible that she might still have one caught in her hair?

Her exploration became frantic. They had fallen out. Every one of them. Clara felt the mattress in an arc around her. Nothing. She got to her feet, and the darkness around her seemed to seesaw wildly for a second, then her knees buckled; she fell back onto the mattress, pulling the chain taut and jarring her ankle.

Her breath came in jerky gulps. *Break down, Clara — why don't you just break down and start screaming again. That'll do a whole lot of good, won't it?*

This time, instead of demoralising her, the mean, taunting voice made her angry — biting, kicking, gouging mad. 'To hell with you!' she yelled. 'Why don't you sod off and leave me alone?'

It made her feel better. Michaela always said that if she swore a little more she wouldn't get so tense. She remembered a boozy girls' night out in their student days; Clara was angry over some patronising remark one of their tutors had made. Michaela had said, 'A good feckin swear'll get it out of your system.' Clara laughed. It was more of a sob, but it was a start. She wiped her eyes again on the hem of her gown, then stood, taking it slowly this time, and using the wall for support.

She stepped onto the hard stone floor and bent at the knees. The mattress was thin and light, but it took all her strength to lift it and tip it towards the wall: no sense in finding the damn thing only for it to skitter out of reach into the darkness. At least this way, it would be trapped between the wall and the mattress.

She held her breath, listening for a sound. *There!* a faint *click!*

She dropped the mattress and immediately regretted it. What if the air movement had shunted the hair-grip? What if she couldn't find it?

Shut up and look for it. She worked methodically from left to right, between the wall and the mattress, praying that it hadn't been caught underneath, or moved to the side, that she hadn't imagined that first faint *click*.

On the second pass, she felt something shift under her fingertips. It was caught part way under the ticking of the mattress. Her fingers were numb with cold and her brain was slow with lack of food and sleep. She tried two, three times before she realised that the pressure of her knee, holding down the mattress, was preventing her retrieving the hair-grip.

Finally, she had it. She held it tightly, afraid of losing it again. The chain was beginning to chafe her left ankle now; it wasn't as sore as the right, but she knew that if she ever got out of this place, she would be hobbling for weeks. *When, Clara. When you get out of here.* She inched along the chain to her ankle, for a few moments circling the bruised skin with one cold hand. Then she set to work, trying to imagine the lever inside the padlock, trying to rock the mechanism, or spring it — was that how it was done? She had never cared enough to find out. It was language that interested her. Language and how it could be manipulated in the interpretation of the law. Practical matters were of no interest. Until now.

For half an hour she tried, till her fingers ached and sweat ran into her eyes. Then the hair-grip snapped.

For a while she gave in to despair. Then, as she fell in to a kind of stupor, she saw a clear, perfect image of Pippa on her birthday, wearing the ribbons she had filched from her briefcase, giggling as she pressed the button on the musical badge pinned to her lapel.

During her captivity Clara had felt Pippa slip away from her, until she could no longer picture her face. Now she saw and heard her, as clearly as if she had been in the room and Clara felt a mixture of joy that she hadn't lost her daughter, and shame that she had been so ready to give up.

She felt along the folds of her gown but she couldn't find the broken piece.

'Wait wait wait,' she whispered. 'Not using your head, Clara.' She lifted the padlock and shook it. Something inside the casing rattled. Gently, she tipped it into the palm of her hand, then slowly, and with great care, she transferred the precious centimetre of broken metal to the seam pocket of the gown. Later, it might be all she had to work with.

With renewed determination, she followed the links of the chain to the wall and touched the icy hoop of metal. It was held in place by bolts. But if she could dig away enough of the sandstone to work it loose . . .

Using the longer piece of metal remaining from the hair-grip, she began scratching the sandstone along the edges of the hoop, taking it slowly, working rhythmically, pacing herself.

Chapter Thirty Eight

The police patrol unit pulled up outside Willowbank, Peacock Grove, at one thirty-five p.m. PC Trudy Morley stepped out of the car and put on her hat. Her body armour had ridden up under her weatherproof and she reached under her jacket to give it a sharp tug.

'Looks deserted.'

PC Pete Cotter nodded. They looked up at the old house. All the windows were closed and the curtains drawn. The wind had dropped and the light had a muddy quality, threatening snow. They walked up the drive, mounting the steps up to the front door, their footsteps ringing out on the cold stone.

Cotter pulled on his gloves before lifting the brass door knocker and rapping hard. The sounds rattled across the street, echoing back from the empty houses opposite. They were derelict and crumbling, but a ten-foot sign proudly announced that they had been 'Sold for Development'. Morley tried the doorbell. It was the old-fashioned type, with a hammer and a gong. It rang out loud and clear, but still there was no reply.

'I'll try the back,' she said, her breath forming puffs of condensation that vanished quickly in the frosty air.

The path at the side of the house was slick with ice and she slipped and nearly fell a couple of times, ending up using the house wall for support. She checked the wheelie bin parked just inside the back gate. It was empty. There were no lights in the windows and the back door was secure. She could hear the doorbell even though the kitchen door was closed.

As she returned down the path, she saw a figure at the bottom of the steps. 'Pete,' she called.

PC Cotter looked down and saw the woman, her arms crossed and tucked inside the sleeves of her coat.

'He's not there now,' the woman said.

'Who are you?' Morley asked.

'Mrs Jessop. I live next door. I'm the one who called you.' She was seventy or more and had probably lived in the area when it had last been fashionable. Morley wondered if she knew she was sitting on a gold-mine.

'There's not supposed to be anyone staying. I said I'd water the plants, fetch the mail in, but I'm not going near the place while he's prowling around.'

'You didn't tackle him?' Cotter asked.

The old woman raised her eyebrows comically. 'I haven't the build for rugby,' she said.

'I mean you didn't speak to him.'

'I know what you meant. You meant that I'm a silly old biddy wasting police time because I haven't the good sense to open my mouth and ask a simple question.' Morley covered a smile. 'Believe me, I'm more than capable,' Mrs Jessop went on, speaking over Cotter's protests. 'But this fellow is not the sort you'd want to "tackle" on your own.'

'Did you get his licence number?' Morley asked.

Mrs Jessop dipped her head apologetically. 'As you can see, there's a wall between us and I didn't like to walk round to take a look in case he caught me.'

'Do you have the keys with you?'

Mrs Jessop fished in her coat pocket and brought out a key ring. There were two keys: a Yale and a mortise. She handed them over and followed close at their heels.

Cotter called as he opened the front door. The house was

silent except for the soft, measured tick of a grandfather clock. The air smelled musty and a little damp, and it was bitterly cold. Mrs Jessop clicked her tongue.

'He hasn't even had the decency to turn the heating on for a couple of hours a day!'

Mail was stacked neatly on the hall chest. Cotter went into the sitting room while Morley checked out the room next to it. It was dark and very cold. A large dining table dominated the floor space; there was ample seating for ten.

'Good God!' Mrs Jessop rushed forward, her hands clasped to her face.

Morley jumped, her heart pounding. She peered into the dim corners of the room. 'What?' she demanded.

'Look at the *ficus!*'

'The what?'

'The weeping fig!' A tall plant with pale leaf margins stood next to the window. Scattered beneath it was a drift of leaves.

Mrs Jessop groaned. 'Wouldn't you think he could have watered the plants?'

Morley wondered whether she should explain that squatters generally didn't put the maintenance of the property high on their list of priorities. Mrs Jessop hurried out of the room, bumping into Cotter who had come to investigate the commotion. She stopped long enough to prod him in the chest.

'You'll *have* to speak to him,' she insisted. She pushed past and made for the kitchen, muttering, 'I dread to think how the tradescantia have fared.'

The two officers retreated upstairs for a little peace. 'Find anything in the front room?' Morley asked.

'Nice telly. A stack of videos.' He shrugged.

The bathroom had been used recently: the bath was still wet and the glass by the sink contained wet-shaving gear. Morley moved on to the front bedroom while Cotter poked his head round what turned out to be the door of the study. He called through to Morley, '*Serious* computer gear.'

'Pete . . .'

He found Morley in the master bedroom. The curtains were closed, but Morley had switched on the light. The surfaces were dusted and gleaming and the bed neatly made. There were two video cameras, both on tripods. One was placed at the foot of the bed, the other on the side nearest the window. A still camera and studio lights completed the set-up.

'Maybe he's a film buff,' Cotter suggested.

Morley did not appreciate the pun. She called in what they had found. The duty sergeant told them to check the man's ID, make sure he had permission to use the place, and if he did, they were to take no further action.

'While we wait, I might just have a squint at those videos,' Cotter said, leading the way back downstairs.

'Don't tell me,' Morley said, curling her lip in disgust. 'They all had girls' names written on them.' She shook her head. 'I'll move the car out of sight. Don't want to frighten off our friend, do we?'

Cotter wasn't listening, he was staring down the hall at Mrs Jessop who stood, slightly bent, holding a jug of water in both hands, in an attitude of intense concentration. 'Mrs Jessop . . .'

She looked anxiously at them. 'There's something down there.' She pointed to a low panelled door under the stairs. 'In the basement.' She paused, listening. 'It sounds like a cat.'

Morley reached for the door handle.

'It's locked,' Mrs Jessop said. 'I'm sure she never had a lock on that door.'

A stout padlock was fastened to a gleaming new hasp. Cotter listened for a few seconds. He frowned. Suddenly, he was running towards the kitchen.

'What?' Morley demanded.

'That's no bloody cat!' he yelled, returning with a bread knife. He worked at the hasp, levering it away from the door until the wood splintered and the door swung open.

All three of them recoiled from the smell. Cotter covered his mouth and nose and pulled the light cord just inside the door.

'What is it?' Mrs Jessop whispered.

Cotter ignored her. 'Radio for back-up,' he said to Morley. 'There's a woman down there.'

The Armed Response Vehicle was deployed immediately and DCI McAteer went through to the radio room to brief Cotter and Morley. 'Move your car,' he instructed Cotter. 'I don't want him being warned off. Where's the woman?'

'She's in the kitchen, sir.'

'Get her out of the house. The ARV will be with you in minutes.'

Cotter returned to the kitchen. There was a stack of take-away cartons and empty lager bottles on the drainer. Man food. They had been washed and the bottles inverted to drain. Trudy Morley sat at the kitchen table on one side of the woman and Mrs Jessop on the other. He couldn't look at the woman. He couldn't bear what he saw in her eyes. Morley looked up and Cotter jerked his head in the direction of the doorway.

He closed the door after them and gave her McAteer's instructions.

'He thinks it's the guy who murdered that woman they found in the Dee, doesn't he?' Morley asked.

Cotter raised his shoulders.

'We'll go next door,' she told him.

She heard him slam the front door as she explained to Mrs Jessop and the woman what they were going to do. The woman seemed not to understand at first and when Morley tried to help her to her feet, she cowered, pulling away from her, giving a high keening wail. 'I don't want to go down there. Please don't make me!'

Morley glanced in desperation at Mrs Jessop. The old woman looked into the younger woman's grimy face and took both her hands. 'We'll go to my house,' she said. 'Make a cup of tea.'

It sounded banal, but she seemed comforted. She stared at Mrs Jessop for some moments, then nodded.

Mrs Jessop smiled. 'And a nice slice of cake,' she added, as if she invited abductees round for tea every day.

Morley led the way. Half-way down the hallway, she heard the key in the latch. Her breath caught in her throat. The figure beyond the lights of the front door was the wrong shape, the wrong height. She signalled with the flat of her palm for Mrs Jessop to take the woman back to the kitchen. Morley slid her baton from her belt and stepped back into the shadows.

The man was carrying shopping bags and his face was creased with concern. He had locked the mortise on his way out. He paused, listening at the foot of the stairs.

Morley stepped out of the shadows and shouted 'Police!'

He roared and leapt at her, flinging the bags aside. She swung her baton and caught him on the side of the knee. He crashed to the floor screaming and she stood over him, simultaneously flicking open her handcuffs.

She grabbed his left hand and pulled it behind him, yelling his rights at him as she clicked the lock on his left wrist. He jerked his hand and she lost her balance. As she fell, he rolled, bringing his right hand round and up. She felt a shock as though she had been punched hard in the solar plexus. Her knees gave way and she crumpled.

Suddenly the house was thick with bodies. 'Armed police!'

The man hunched, his back to them.

'Put your hands behind your head. Do it NOW!'

He let them see that his hands were empty, moving slowly, linking the fingers loosely behind his head. The handcuffs dangling from his wrist clinked softly.

'Kneel down!' He hesitated and the officer screamed the command again. He complied. 'That's right. Now lie down. Keep your hands where I can see them. Keep them in sight at all times.' Seconds later he was fully handcuffed and lying flat on his face.

Morley fought for breath. She couldn't find her voice. *Just winded*, she told herself. She felt a fool lying on the floor, face-to-face with this sick fuck. She had to move before Cotter returned. Around her, people were shouting. Somebody put their hand on her forehead, gently coaxing her to lie back, but she couldn't — the pain in her stomach . . .

The man was taken away and the paramedics arrived. She tried to direct them through to the kitchen, but they kept talking to her, their voices loud, but incomprehensible. Then Cotter came and crouched next to her, crying.

'Jesus, Trudy. Jesus . . .' He looked up at the paramedics. 'I shouldn't have left her.' Someone hooked their arms under his and lifted him bodily.

Her eyes flitted from one worried face to the next, looking for reassurance, finding only fear. *Come on, fellas—You're scaring me. I'm wearing my stab vest. It can't be that serious, can it?*

Chapter Thirty Nine

DCI McAteer was in conference when Lawson tapped at his door and walked in.

'Ben Dalrymple,' McAteer said, standing to make the introductions. 'Ben's a forensic psychologist.'

Dalrymple may have been fifty; it was hard to say – his face seemed unmarked by the years. His broad forehead and pale, clear blue eyes betokened a cool, rather remote nature. Lawson nodded politely, then turned back to McAteer to ask, 'How's Trudy Morley?'

'You know her?'

'Not personally, but some of the team do.'

McAteer shook his head. 'It doesn't look good, Steve. Bastard got her under her body armour with a *bradawl*, for God's sake!'

'And the woman? Have we got an ID yet?'

'She's heavily sedated, but the neighbour identified her as Angela Hutton. She runs a homeopathy clinic from home. She was supposed to've gone away for a few days. She'd dropped her keys next door, her car was all packed up – he must've pounced on her at the last minute. Her car was in the garage,' he added, pre-empting Lawson's next question.

Lawson glanced over at the profiler. His expression was interested, but calm; a good sign: Lawson had worked with a couple in the early days whose eagerness to make a name for themselves had clouded their professional objectivity.

'What're the chances he abducted Clara as well?' Lawson asked.

Dalrymple thought about this for some time, his legs crossed at the ankles, and one elbow resting on the arm of the chair, totally relaxed and unhurried. When he looked up, Lawson was startled by the intensity of the psychologist's gaze. He spoke slowly, as though weighing every word.

'They are similar in appearance,' he said. 'And around the same age, which means that both Clara and Angela may well fit some model he is symbolically trying to destroy.'

'And Clara defended him in a rape case a few months ago,' McAteer added.

'Sorry, Steve,' McAteer said, seeing Lawson's puzzled expression, 'HOLMES threw up that little gem a matter of minutes ago.'

'So we've got a name?'

McAteer nodded. 'He's still not talking, but, yes, we've got a name. Alex Martin.'

It rang a bell. 'Wasn't that the one where the victim's father threatened Clara?' Lawson shook his head. 'I don't get it. Martin was cleared. Why would he have it in for Clara if she got him off?'

'Martin is a controlling personality,' Dalrymple began. 'He likes to call the shots. In his relationship with Ms Pascal, the roles were reversed. He almost certainly resented that. Men with monstrous egos often have a very fragile self-esteem.'

'So he was pissed off with her because she was in authority?' Lawson made no attempt to keep the scepticism out of his voice.

Dalrymple raised his eyebrows. 'I'm presenting possible scenarios,' he said mildly.

'Doctor, we've got one corpse already — there's a woman in the hospital who's never going to be able to lead a normal life

again. Another has been missing now for six days. I'd like to find
her before—'

'We'd all like to find her,' McAteer interrupted. He exchanged a look with Dalrymple.

'For what it's worth,' Dalrymple said. 'I don't think Martin is
your man, Inspector Lawson.'

If that's the case, Lawson thought angrily, why waste my time
with 'scenarios'? He swallowed the words and said, 'Because?'
Not trusting himself to say more.

'From what little I've seen of his criminal record, Martin
shows a typical pattern of escalation: minor offences – flashing,
indecent assault—'

'Building to more serious – and more violent – assaults.'
Lawson interrupted. 'I did the course, Doctor. I know what
escalation is.'

'Martin watches his victims,' Dalrymple said, unruffled by
Lawson's impatience. 'We know that from his previous form.'

'So who's to say he wasn't watching Clara?' Lawson said. 'A
white van has been placed near to the Pascal house over the two
week period before the abduction—'

'Hear him out, Steve,' McAteer cut in. He glanced at
Dalrymple, inviting him to continue.

'Martin fantasises himself into the victim's life. Imagines that
she wants him there – that she is responding to him. It's an
elaborate process.'

'And it takes time . . .' Lawson considered this. 'You're
saying the abductions were too close together?'

Dalrymple nodded.

'What if—' McAteer flipped a look of apology to Lawson.
'What if something went wrong? He abducts Clara, but she puts
up a fight?'

'And he kills her?' Dalrymple paused. 'Ahead of time?'

Again that cool, dispassionate examination of the possibilities.

'Martin follows a ritual,' Dalrymple said. 'A slow build-up:

selection of the victim, stalking, the snatch – which, by the way, was witnessed in neither the rapes, nor in Eleanor Gorton's and Miss Hutton's disappearance.'

'Whereas Clara was dragged screaming off the street,' Lawson put in.

Dalrymple nodded. 'Once he has the women, he keeps them. We know that Eleanor was alive for some days after he abducted her. He had Miss Hutton for five days, so it seems reasonable to assume that either he's raping them over a period of days or else he's . . . how shall I put it?' He searched for the right word. 'He's grooming them. He selects them. He prepares them. He enacts his fantasies, capturing them on videotape and then he kills them.'

He made it sound so simple. Lawson studied the man's face. There was nothing to show that he gained any kind of vicarious thrill from what he was telling them: this was no more than an interesting intellectual exercise for him.

'You're saying that he must have selected Miss Hutton weeks ago?' Lawson asked.

Dalrymple inclined his head. 'It's possible.'

'Miss Hutton wasn't raped,' McAteer said.

'No,' Dalrymple agreed, 'But he had clothing with him when he came back to the house. A dress, underwear – and he had the video cameras set up in the bedroom.'

'Why couldn't he have "selected" his next victim while he's . . .' Lawson couldn't think of a suitable phrase. Dealing with them, maybe. *Tormenting* was the word that most closely described his interpretation of what the man did, but he had seen the look pass between McAteer and the psychologist moments earlier; they thought he was taking this too personally.

'He would be entirely focused on his present victim,' Dalrymple reassured him, considerately interpreting the pause.

'And since Angela Hutton is his present victim, we have to assume he didn't take Clara.'

'No,' Dalrymple said. There was a hint of apology in Dalrymple's voice. 'I don't think he did.'

Lawson felt sick with disappointment: if Alex Martin didn't take Clara, they had no leads. They were worse off than when they started the investigation — at least then, the trail was warm.

McAteer turned to look at the charts behind him. 'You're right,' he said. 'Ms Pascal doesn't fit the MO. She's married, for a start. Mrs Gorton was widowed, Miss Hutton is single. Both of them lived alone.'

'It's a similar pattern for his rape victims,' Dalrymple added.

'So it's not random. How did he select them?' Lawson had attended a lecture by a criminal profiler a year or two ago. The phrase that came up many times was *Anyone can become a victim*. 'How did he know they lived alone?' Anyone might become a victim, but the killer often had criteria for selection; with these women it seemed it was their marital status.

McAteer shrugged. 'Maybe he took a fancy to them and followed them home, worked it out from watching them for a few days.'

'How many would he have to follow before he found women as vulnerable as those two?' Lawson was growing impatient again.

'Perhaps Martin will tell you his . . . system,' Dalrymple suggested.

'You think so?' Lawson was frankly amazed.

Dalrymple raised one shoulder. 'Sadists like to talk about themselves; forcing the listener to hear his endless chatter is a form of domination.'

Lawson took a moment to digest this. 'I'll bear it in mind,' he said. 'But I prefer to go in to an interview with a few theories of my own.'

'Until we've spoken to Miss Hutton — or to his previous rape victims — we'd be guessing,' McAteer said.

Dalrymple agreed. 'I'm puzzled that he could take two women off the street and nobody notice,' he said.

'Maybe he broke into their cars and waited for them,' McAteer suggested.

Lawson nodded slowly, mentally working through another possibility. 'Maybe nobody noticed because he trapped them in their own homes,' he said.

McAteer shook his head. 'The houses showed no signs of disturbance.'

'I bet Miss Hutton's wouldn't have either, once he'd cleaned up after himself.' Lawson turned to the psychologist. 'Martin's a fastidious boy, am I right?' Dalrymple nodded. 'I bet he even changes the beds before he leaves.'

Dalrymple's unlined forehead creased into a frown. 'You know where a person is most vulnerable?' he asked, his tone reflective, musing. 'In the street? On a lonely station at night? You'd think so, wouldn't you?' he shook his head. 'You'd be wrong. In those places we're on our guard. Wary of strangers, alert to potential danger. The place where we're most vulnerable is at home. Because home is where we feel safest.'

McAteer reached for the phone. He pressed the direct line to the HOLMES Room. 'Find out if Eleanor Gorton's house has a basement,' he said.

Physically, Alex Martin was an unremarkable man. Neither tall nor powerfully built; he lacked the aura of danger that Lawson always sensed in Ray Casavettes. His fair hair was slightly receding; he cut it short, not trying to hide the fact. His face was bland, nondescript – perhaps too still for a person to be entirely at ease around him. Lawson gave a mental shrug. The same could be said for most ex-prisoners, as well as many police officers. But he sensed that this lack of expression was not learned behaviour – a survival strategy for a man who had done time: it was part of Martin's make-up. He could not respond as others do. Even a smile had a tariff, a cost to be calculated and exacted.

What *was* remarkable was the man's ability to shut them out of his thoughts. They could ask the same question a dozen times in as many different ways and he would stare at them without embarrassment or remorse, even without rancour: they had ceased to exist.

Lawson had interviewed suspects before who had exercised their right to silence, but there was always a reaction: either they hardened their expression, gritting their teeth against the hours of interrogation or else they sweated and fidgeted, moving things around the desk. They would push an ashtray or lighter away from themselves or stack their lighter on top of the cigarette packet when they were asked a particularly relevant question — one that struck home — and Lawson had learned to place one or two of these props within easy reach of the suspect. These nervous types mostly avoided eye contact; it was the accomplished liars who brazened it out.

For a full hour, Martin never spoke once — not even to confirm his name. But he didn't have that slippery, half-ashamed look that some had. This man didn't feel he had anything to be ashamed *of*. He was, however, royally pissed off that he had been caught.

Just as Lawson was about to give up, there was one flicker — a single moment when he felt he got a reaction.

'You're not doing yourself any favours, Alex.' He was careful to keep any hint of judgement out of his tone: Dalrymple had advised on that and Lawson agreed with him. 'A jury's going to look at your silence and think, "he's got something to hide".'

'My client has a *right* to silence,' his solicitor insisted. Adding officiously. 'It's in the wording of the caution your colleague read out at the commencement of this interview.' The solicitor was a tidy, meticulous man, who was given to verbosity, when nervous.

Lawson spread his hands. 'It's only human to wonder why he kidnapped these women.'

'Imprisoned and raped them,' Barton added, as if reminding him of a couple of items he'd left off a shopping list.

Lawson nodded. 'A jury's going to wonder, just like us. It's so—' He raised his shoulders. 'Unusual. How many suspects do we get who refuse to speak?' he asked Barton.

'It's very rare. Most — ninety-nine percent — want to explain. It makes them feel better, makes it easier for the jury to understand.'

No response. Martin stared fixedly at Lawson, registering nothing — not even boredom.

'Juries are made up of ordinary people. They want to hear both sides of the story — to play fair. Man refuses to speak, they come to their own conclusions.' He switched his attention to the solicitor. 'D'you think he understands me? If there's a problem in that respect, he is entitled to have an appropriate adult present during interview.'

Anger flared and was gone, almost before Lawson had the chance to register it. He had hit home — Martin's pride had been injured.

'Your tone is offensive, Inspector,' the solicitor warned, but Lawson's attention was fixed on Martin. The anger was replaced by a superior look; he held every man in the room in contempt, his solicitor included.

'I understand you perfectly well, Inspector,' Martin said quietly. 'I just haven't heard anything worth responding to.'

'Until now,' Lawson shot back. Martin looked at him, into him, through him, and Lawson felt a thrill of something akin to fear. It was quickly dispelled, but he had felt it: looking into Martin's eyes for that brief moment was like looking into the abyss.

DC Young knocked at the door. Martin's eyes darted away from Lawson's face. For one brief moment his tongue appeared, pink, moist, obscene, trapped between his upper and lower incisors. A second later Young was gone, but Martin had registered her age, height, weight all in the short time it took her to call Barton out of the room. Lawson continued, asking the questions they had agreed on, avoiding mention of Clara's name, at least for the time being.

Barton's return was announced for the tape. He placed three small bags on the table.

'Items of jewellery, removed from your house, Mr Martin, during the search which was witnessed by your solicitor.'

Martin's attitude changed: he became alert, almost hungry-looking. His hand moved a fraction – no more than a twitch of a finger, as if he would like to pick up the evidence bags.

'Don't touch them!' Lawson snapped.

Martin made eye contact, signalling his disdain for Lawson and his commands. Then he sat back in his chair, as if the bags of trophies he had kept from the women he had raped, the woman he had murdered, meant no more to him than worthless pebbles on a beach.

'These items have been identified as the property of Angela Hutton and Eleanor Gorton,' Lawson said, touching the first two bags in turn. 'We also have the videotapes you made – we're working through those and further charges may follow. In addition, there is the charge of the attempted murder of a police officer.'

Martin watched him coolly. Lawson was no more than background noise.

'Is there anything you'd like to say. For the record?' The tape whirred quietly for half a minute. Martin never even blinked.

Lawson nodded. It was no more than he had expected. Pushing forward the third bag, he said, 'We haven't been able to identify the owner of these two rings.'

Alex Martin looked down at the bag and Lawson saw something flit across his face. Nostalgia? Affection? It was too fleeting to be sure.

'Who did they belong to, Alex?' Lawson asked. They were quality rings: an emerald and diamond cluster, and a sapphire of the darkest blue Lawson had ever seen.

'My client exercises his right to silence,' the solicitor repeated, but his voice was hoarse. The man was pale. If he found looking at the victims' jewellery upsetting, what would his reaction be to the videos?

271

Lawson terminated the interview. The police officers met with Dalrymple in McAteer's office immediately afterwards.

'He's a cool bastard,' Lawson said.

'No signs of weakness?' Dalrymple asked.

'You were right about the fragile self-esteem. That may be the way in.' Lawson described Martin's reaction to his jibe about refusing to speak.

Dalrymple nodded. He showed no gratification in being proved right; this was simply a useful piece of information that he would use to help them crack Martin.

'I'm surprised he's persisted in his refusal to speak,' Dalrymple said. 'I thought he would – if only to bolster his ego. He's been caught and that must be a severe blow to a man like Martin, who had, in all probability, convinced himself that he was invincible.'

'You might want to review the videotapes of the interview,' Lawson said. 'See if there's something we missed. But right now, I'd say the monstrous ego has the edge,' Lawson said. 'He despises us so much that it'll take more than the odd taunt to shake his self-belief.'

'Meanwhile,' McAteer suggested, 'Clara's husband should see these.' He handed over the third evidence bag containing the two rings.

Someone had to tell Hugo Pascal, Barton knew that. He just wished it didn't have to be him. He was having enough trouble holding it together without having to watch someone else fall apart.

He stood in Pascal's sitting-room and wondered what the hell had ever made him want to be a police officer. He had just told Pascal that the woman they had rescued earlier that afternoon was not his wife. Pascal stared at Barton.

'Not Clara?' he repeated.

'We didn't want you to hear it on TV.'

Pascal seemed unsteady on his feet. 'Do you want to sit down, sir?'

'No.' He looked shattered.

'There's something else, sir.'

Pascal's head jerked up. He thought the worst.

'No – it's all right. I mean, we've arrested a man – at the house where we found Miss Hutton.' Pascal stared. 'Sir, you should know . . . The man we've arrested – your wife defended him.'

'What's his name?'

'Alex Martin.'

Instant recognition. Pascal's knees seemed to give way. He sat down heavily in one of the chairs.

'Sir,' Barton said, forcing Pascal to concentrate on what he was saying. 'We do *not* think Martin abducted your wife.' Somewhere in the confused swirl of emotions on Pascal's face, Barton thought he saw a glimmer of hope. 'Do you understand me?'

Pascal responded as if he was interpreting a foreign language. He stared at Barton for a few seconds then, frowning, he seemed to make sense of the words.

He nodded and Barton took a breath. 'Okay. Keep that in mind. They're going to say on the news that Martin has been arrested in connection with the murder of Eleanor Gorton.'

Pascal's breath caught in his throat.

'But, as I said, we *don't* think your wife is a victim.'

'You don't think,' Pascal repeated slowly, looking at his hands. 'But you're not sure?'

Oh, Jesus . . . This was the question Barton had been dreading. 'We think she was abducted by someone else, for some – other reason.' It was tactless and he regretted it as soon as he had said it.

Pascal's head swivelled up to him. 'You mean *some other reason* than rape and murder? Is that what you mean, Sergeant?' His eyes were red-rimmed. Pascal would not hold on to his sanity for much longer.

273

'Sir, I—' Barton couldn't lie to the man. 'We're doing everything we can.' He thought of Fran. He had telephoned her half a dozen times a day since Casavettes had made his threat. It had got to the point where Fran accused him of suffocating her; the fact was, he couldn't believe her to be safe even though he saw her every evening, slept next to her every night. He thought he had some inkling as to how much worse it must be for Pascal.

The evidence bag in his suit felt so heavy in his pocket that he was surprised his jacket wasn't pulled out of shape. This was the second time he'd had to ask Pascal to identify jewellery that might belong to his wife and he wasn't sure Pascal was up to it. 'Is Mrs Markham here, Mr Pascal?' he asked.

'You want me to come to the station — see if I recognise him?'

'Maybe later, sir. But you might want to call her.'

Pascal blanched. 'For God's sake, whatever it is, *tell* me!'

'We searched Martin's house,' Barton said. 'I want you to look at these and tell me if you recognise them.' He drew out the evidence bag and Pascal snatched it from him, poring over it with a complicated mixture of eagerness and dread.

After a few moments he handed the bag back to Barton. It slipped from his fingers and Barton had to catch it.

Pascal shook his head. 'Not hers,' he said. His mouth twitched convulsively and he had to clear his throat before he could repeat, 'Not Clara's.'

Chapter Forty

How long? How long since he left? An hour? Two? The walls press in, stone grinding massively on stone.

Christ! I'm suffocating! Drowning in this fetid air!

Get up. Walk. Calm yourself. Do you want him to see you like this?

What's taking him so long?

One, two — two-and-a-half paces. Turn. One, two. The steel door scowls, half a pace away, solid, immovable.

What if there's a fire? What if nobody comes? Panic rushes up like a tidal wave.

Stop. Stop thinking like this. Stop thinking. Thinking does no good. Walk. Empty your mind. One, two paces. Turn. One, two paces. Breathe in. Hold it. Breathe out. Pacing, pacing, trying not to see the walls, the close, hard proximity of stone.

A noise.

Footsteps?

The grate of metal on metal. Turn. *Don't let him see your fear.*

The hatch opens. Cold grey eyes stare unblinking at him. Martin stares back. Calm, now. Unreadable.

He remembers the policewoman standing over him. The faint *pop!* as the point of the bradawl punctured her skin. How easily it slid to the hilt once in. The custody sergeant looks away. He looks away *first*.

'Visitor,' he mumbles, rattling the bolt back and opening the door.

His solicitor seems nervous and this gives him confidence.

'Can't they find an interview room for this consultation?' he demands.

'All occupied.' The solicitor says, with an apologetic grimace.

'I'll bet.' Martin steps back to let him in. 'Leave the door.' His voice sharper, more urgent than he had intended.

The solicitor takes his hand from the door as if the steel is superheated. 'I only thought . . . for privacy,' he stutters.

He is pale, though whether this is natural or the result of his nearness to a killer, Martin cannot say. He is neat, to the point of fussiness, like a school swot trying to impress his teachers. He doesn't know how to proceed and Martin has a sudden insight.

'They've been showing you edited highlights,' he says, amused by the idea.

The solicitor swallows. In this light, his skin has an almost green tinge. Martin watches him idly to see if he will faint.

'We have to prepare a defence,' the solicitor says weakly.

Martin looks at him. He shifts from one foot to the other. His left hand moves restlessly. He is rotating his wedding-ring with his thumb, as if the action will guard him from evil. Is he thinking, *What if it had been my wife?* Is he wondering what kind of monster he is representing?

'What do you suggest?' Martin asks.

The solicitor notices Martin's quick glance at his left hand and thrusts both his hands into his pockets.

'I recommend that you co-operate, Mr Martin.'

'Now why would I do that?'

The solicitor frowns. He had not expected this response. He pretends not to have heard the question and blunders on: 'If, for instance, you have any information regarding the disappearance of Clara Pascal . . .'

Clara Pascal! Of course — why not? The coincidence was

striking, her disappearance, then the discovery of Eleanor's body. Martin feels a flash of anger that his solicitor has agreed to act as errand-boy for the police.

'Where do you think it'll get me, this *co-operation?*'

The solicitor flushes slightly. He is embarrassed to say. Martin laughs. 'You don't really expect me to co-operate out of remorse!'

The solicitor struggles to find a coherent argument. 'It . . . it wouldn't harm your case if—'

'Will it, for instance, guarantee me a lighter sentence?'

'Of course, I couldn't guarantee—'

'Of course . . . But would they view Eleanor Gorton's death in a more *favourable* light?' The solicitor opens his mouth, but closes it as Martin continues. 'I mean they have the video—' Another laugh. 'A whole library of videos! And they've found my little mementoes, too. They hardly need a confession.'

The solicitor coughs politely. 'Things do look fairly black, but—'

'Perhaps we can call on Angela Hutton as a character witness.' He is enjoying himself now. Enjoying making the solicitor squirm. 'Angela knows me quite well by now. Think she'd take the stand for me?'

The solicitor is sweating. Exhilarated, Martin beckons for him to lean in closer. 'Tell you what,' he says. 'There must have been half a dozen police saw me spike that policewoman. Maybe *they'd* put in a good word.'

The solicitor recoils.

'Do you find me repellent?' he asks, just to hear the pathetic little man deny it.

'No, of course not, I—'

Martin leans forward again. 'Liar.' He sits back and smiles, and the solicitor's shoulders slump.

'So you won't co-operate?'

Martin smiles. He looks even more like a schoolboy in his

disappointment. 'Tell them I'm ready to talk,' he said. 'I'm ready to talk to them about Clara.'

It's the girl again. The one who brought the jewellery – his mementoes. Martin feels a tingle of excitement. They've sent her with some big thug – pretend the girls can do the job, but make sure they've got someone there to protect them. She's not bad. The right build; the hair is right: brown, long, a slight wave in it. She's young – but he has been known to make exceptions . . . The heavy guy takes his arm to lead him to the interview room; Martin offers no resistance. His eyes are on the girl. She doesn't have the confidence he favours in his companions. Nevertheless . . .

She raises her right arm to push through a fire door and in doing so swings a little towards him. Her jacket falls away from her body and – almost without thinking – he reaches out and touches her breast.

Pain explodes in his arm, she grabs, twists, slams him into the wall. *Bitch is breaking my arm!* He yells and she pushes harder, mashing his face into the wall. She's shouting.

'Fucking pervert! What the *fuck* d'you think you're doing?' She puts on a bit more pressure.

'Okay, Cath.' It's the burly guy. He sounds nervous. 'You can let him up now.'

'You heard him, you stupid bitch!' Furious, he resists, but pain rips through his shoulder. 'Let go of me!'

'What?' She twists until he feels his flesh will tear. 'Did you *say* something, arsehole?'

'Get her off me!'

'Come on, Cath. Don't take it out on him.'

'Take *what* out on him? He just grabbed me, Thorpe!'

'Okay, and you've restrained him. Now let him up.'

'Get this straight,' she says, increasing the pressure a little more. 'I don't have to take this kind of shit from pervs and murderers. Got that?'

'Let him go, Cath.' Thorpe's voice, cajoling.

'I can't hear you, Martin.'

'All *right*.' If he ever gets her in a room by herself, he'll make her sorry for this.

She lets him up slowly, releasing his hand at the last possible moment. He straightens, supporting his right arm with his left. 'You could've broken my arm!' he snarls.

She smiles at him. Looks him in the eye and bares her teeth right back at him. 'Try that again, it won't be your arm in a splint — wanker.' If he wasn't in so much pain he would put his hand around her throat and squeeze.

Lawson came in to the interview room looking sombre. He might be a bank manager in his grey suit and unimaginative tie. Martin tried to think of him in that way: pushing paper, keeping the cogs turning, the wheels running smoothly. The strain was telling; despite his neat appearance, the inspector looked poorly rested and harassed.

Barton, he thought, was nursing some grievance or guilty secret. Martin, who was attuned to vulnerability in others, picked up this much, but Barton was hiding it — from himself? Perhaps. From Lawson, certainly.

'You said you had information about Ms Pascal's whereabouts,' Lawson began, instinctively avoiding using her first name in front of Martin. Using her given name to Martin would only add to the insult.

'Where is my solicitor?' His voice was calm. He kept it flat, almost toneless. If they knew how much he feared that cell, they would use it — he would, if their positions were reversed.

'He'll be along shortly,' Lawson told him.

Along shortly! What was he paying the little shit for? Martin debated a moment. He could refuse to speak to them until after he had lodged a complaint with his solicitor over the manhandling he had been subjected to, in which case he would be taken back to the cell. Or he could talk.

'So,' Lawson said. 'Shall I start the tape or would I be wasting my time?'

Martin lifted one shoulder. Up to you. He yawned through the introductions and time-recording, even smiled a little at Lawson's careful explanation that he had given Martin the opportunity to wait until his solicitor returned.

'Can you tell us Ms Pascal's whereabouts, Mr Martin?'

Martin's smile broadened. *Mr* Martin. So, co-operation conferred a new respectability and reinstated his right to courtesy. He wagged his finger at Lawson. He wasn't going to make it that easy.

'She feels the cold,' he said. 'Well, she would, wouldn't she? She was dressed for the courtroom, not a basement cell. A suit. Good quality. Black's not to my taste, of course—'

Barton interrupted. 'No, you go in for green satin, don't you, Mr Martin?'

Martin eyed him coldly. His choice of evening wear for Angela was a private matter.

'She'll be wondering by now,' he went on, ' "Is he ever coming back?" Can you imagine what it's like desperately wanting the man you most fear in all the world to return?'

'Why would I want to imagine something like that?'

He wanted to tell Barton to stop interrupting. His answers were not required. But he sensed that Barton would interrupt all the more if he said anything, so instead, he immersed himself in a fantasy. In this, he reached down the sergeant's throat and, seizing his tongue by the root, he tore it out. While he stared at the sergeant, he visualized the blood welling up in his throat, surging like molten lava and bubbling from between his lips, red, thick, hot.

'She's hungry,' he said, as though he had never paused. 'No – she's starving. Literally starving. She's way past hunger. Past ravenous. She can barely stand now. Her legs tremble if she tries her weight on them. They won't support her.'

'Why are you telling us this?' Lawson asked. He knew the answer – Dalrymple had given him the answer during their debrief: this was another manifestation of the man's sadistic need for control. For Martin, domination and cruelty were substitutes for strength.

Martin's eyes flicked quickly to him, then away. 'At first, she craved food – even begged for it – but the brain switches off the craving after a time. You need food, but you're not going to get it. What's the point of driving yourself crazy with hunger and stomach cramps and flooding the system with digestive juices if all you've got to digest is your own stomach wall?'

He was looking slightly to Lawson's left. His nostrils were flared and his skin flushed. Lawson felt a wave of revulsion. *He's getting off on this!*

'I can see that this . . . reminiscence is all very pleasant for you, Alex,' he said. 'But it doesn't convince me that you have Ms Pascal.' He smiled. It came almost as a surprise that his skin didn't crack with the effort.

A look of petulant annoyance crossed Martin's face and he looked directly at Lawson. '*You* don't have her, do you, inspector? And you don't know where to look, otherwise you wouldn't be talking to me.'

'So where should we look?' Lawson asked. 'Where will we find her?'

'Look below ground.' Martin slid a nasty look from Lawson to Barton. He wanted them to think of the graveyard. He wanted them to see a rotting corpse when they thought of Clara Pascal. 'I doubt you'll ever find her. Of course, someone might chance upon her some months or years from now – a demolition team, maybe. Schoolboys on a treasure hunt.'

'Is she in a derelict house, Alex?'

Martin wasn't listening. 'Maybe the schoolboys will keep her a secret. Visit her again and again.'

'Is that what *you* do, Alex?'

'She'll become part of their initiation rites. They'll dare each other to touch the bones. To poke their fingers into her eye sockets . . .' His breathing was fast and uneven.

'These are *your* fantasies, Alex,' Lawson said, intruding more forcefully into Martin's thoughts this time. 'Decent people don't do what you're suggesting.'

Martin closed his eyes. He wouldn't listen. He shut out the inspector's voice, returning to what he had been saying earlier. Rewind . . . Pause . . . Play.

'Hunger pains fade after a time,' he began again. 'But thirst doesn't.' His eyes were bright and hard. 'First it's just a dryness — a bit of a click when you swallow. But she's been there a long time. By now her tongue will be swollen, her lips cracked. She'll feel feverish, despite the cold.'

Does he have her? Lawson wondered. *Is Clara suffering like this?*

The door opened and Alex Martin's solicitor came in.

'You should not be interviewing my client,' he said.

'Mr—' Lawson realised that he didn't know the solicitor's name. 'Sir, Mr Martin agreed to be interviewed in your absence. It's all recorded.'

'For the tape,' Barton said. 'Mr Calvert, Mr Martin's solicitor, has just entered the room.'

Calvert. Yes, of course, Lawson thought. Mr Neville Calvert.

'I demand that this interview is terminated until I have had the opportunity to consult with my client.'

'You heard what the officer said.' Martin's voice was silky, but they all sensed a danger behind it. 'I gave my consent. Now sit down.'

The solicitor opened and closed his mouth a couple of times, then he folded into the chair next to Martin. *You spoiled his big moment*, Lawson thought. *He won't forgive this easily, Mr Calvert.*

Lawson felt the pressure build. Something had changed. Martin's cool facade was crumbling. He detected a deterioration in Martin's emotional state. As if behind the eyes something had been shunted off-kilter. He got a mental image of a mountainside, grey and glinting with scree, the treacherous little shards of flint shifting underfoot. Lawson saw that behind Martin's icy control, beneath his arrogant disdain for everyone but himself, was hate and fear.

'If you know where she is, tell us,' Lawson said.

Martin stared again, a little off to Lawson's left, but this time there was a determined, grim set to his face. He was no longer enjoying himself. 'She'd do anything for a sip of water.' His tongue appeared between his teeth, a quick flick and then gone again; he closed his eyes and exhaled. 'Anything.'

'I don't think you have her,' Lawson said.

'It's damp in there. She could lick some of the seepage off the walls. But she'll be wondering how long she can hold out. Tempted to drink her own urine. Of course that only makes things worse – hastens the end – but would she know that?' He smiled across at Lawson. 'Would she care? You get to that point, you really couldn't give a shit.'

'I'm terminating this interview,' Lawson said.

Martin continued in a stolid, expressionless tone, defying Lawson to stop him. 'She's looking for relief now. She thinks she can't stand any more. She can, of course. If you're still capable of thought, then you can stand it. Because when your body really can't stand another second, it shuts down.'

Lawson recorded the time and flicked off the tape, trying not to listen to the filthy, destructive words coming out of Martin's mouth. He opened the door and called in the two DCs he had left on guard outside the interview room. 'Take him down,' he said. 'I can't stand to look at him.' The solicitor – he had forgotten his name again – made no complaint.

'She might choke on her tongue,' Martin said. If Lawson was going to send him back to that disgusting hole, he'd give him something to think about.

He resisted as the two DCs led him away, a half frightened, half vicious smile on his face. Lawson understood, for one fleeting moment, the terror that Martin's victims had felt. The man was evil. In Martin, evil manifested itself as pure selfish need, an unembarrassed, uncritical desire to fulfil that need no matter how much it hurt others. He hurt women to make his own fear go away.

'Sometimes the tongue swells so big it just blocks the airway. Or she could swallow it on purpose – finish it quickly.'

'Mr Martin!' the solicitor exclaimed. 'You said you'd help!'

Martin stared in cold fury at the man, torn between a desperate desire to stay out of the cell and a need to remain dignified, to appear in control. 'I said I was ready to talk about Clara. I'm talking.' He was almost at the door. The officers had him by the elbows. His shoulder hurt where the stupid bitch had twisted him arm. He couldn't go back to that cell. He wasn't ready. He shouldn't *be* here.

'You want to know where she is . . .'

Lawson stopped the two officers with a tiny movement of his head. They turned Martin to face him.

'I can tell you.'

You and Casavettes, both, Lawson thought, holding Martin's flat stare. 'I don't believe you,' he said quietly, watching for Martin's reaction.

I should have given him something – anything – to make him feel he had to go on listening. 'A Victorian house,' Martin said. 'Red brick. Double-fronted.'

Lawson smiled. 'I could have guessed as much myself. If you're looking for a house with a cellar around here, it's bound to be Victorian. And red brick.'

'Who said it was around here?' He felt a little kick of excitement in his chest. He had Lawson's interest. A response.

'All your victims have been from Chester,' Lawson said. If he had taken Clara outside the city, all their enquiries so far would have been for nothing. Angela Hutton was held in her own house. Would he take Clara far from that? Wouldn't it make more sense to keep them within easy travelling distance of each other?

'The Wirral is thirty minutes' drive from here,' Martin said, talking fast, knowing that although he had Lawson's attention he was far from being convinced. 'We're forty minutes from Birkenhead. Another ten minutes on top, you could be in the centre of Liverpool.' He paused for effect. 'There's thousands of Victorian houses to choose from in Liverpool.'

Lawson jerked his head and the two officers pulled Martin towards the door. He struggled.

No! This isn't supposed to happen! 'Send me back to that shit-hole, I won't co-operate,' he warned, his voice rising in anger and alarm.

'Call this co-operation?'

Martin flushed. 'I'll refuse to talk. Clara can rot, for all I care.'

He was almost through the door when Lawson called them back. 'Send for tea and a sandwich if he wants it. But I want two officers on this door at all times. Inside the room if his solicitor isn't here with him. If he needs a toilet break, you both go with him and the door stays open.' He glanced at Barton and they both walked out.

'He knew what she would be wearing in court. He's been in court often enough – he knows the dress code,' Lawson said, striding along the corridor towards the staircase. 'Clara even represented him. He's guessing, Phil.'

'What about the cellar?' Barton asked. 'Think he's right about that?'

'It's where *he* would keep her. I don't believe he can think beyond his own fantasies – his own methods. She could be in a garage, a derelict house, an empty workshop – if she's drugged, she could be in some tatty flat in Blacon, for all we know, tied to a bed.' He ran one tired hand over his face. 'Jesus, Phil, she could be dead by now.'

Barton looked at him. He didn't need to say it. They had to carry on as if Clara were alive until they had irrefutable proof that she was dead.

Lawson nodded, as if the sergeant had spoken the words.

'Eleanor's place had a cellar. Forensics are re-examining to see if there's anything they've missed. But I think he's telling us about Eleanor Gorton and Angela Hutton: what he did to them, how they reacted. I think Dalrymple is right. I don't think Alex Martin ever had Clara.'

'Trouble is, Boss, we can't be sure.'

And until they were, Lawson knew they would have to waste their time listening to his sickening fantasies and allowing Martin to relive the torture and rape of his victims, with them as his unwilling audience.

Chapter Forty One

Parks had been smoking dope just prior to Rayner's arrival. The sweet smell of it filled the landlord's basement flat. Middle of the afternoon and he was pleasantly stoned. Rayner gave him a hard stare and he grinned apologetically.

'If I'd known you were coming . . .'

'You'd've baked a cake. Yeah, right, but that's illegal, an' all.'

He winced. 'Am I busted?'

'*Busted?*' Rayner shook her head. The guy was living in a time-warp. 'No, Mr Parks,' she said. 'I've come about Laura.'

Suddenly he was dead serious. 'You found her.'

'I know where she is,' she said, choosing her words carefully. She didn't have to say any more. He peered at her, as if the cannabis fug still clouded the room, but she knew from his dismayed expression that he understood.

'Figures,' he said, after a long silence. He lit a cigarette, his hands shaking. He noticed her watching him and said, 'Carcinogenic, antisocial, but boringly legal.'

Rayner ignored the attempt at humour. 'You knew.'

He took a long, damaging drag on his cigarette and the tobacco flared and hissed. He held his breath, then slowly exhaled through his nostrils.

'When she cleared out, I thought she needed time to get her

head together, be with her family. But she was away too long . . .
I had a bad feeling.' His eyes filled with tears.

'I'm sorry,' she said, and meant it.

'So am I.' A tear brimmed onto his cheek. He looked up at
her, unembarrassed. 'Laura was a girl who made people feel *good*
about themselves.'

She nodded, trying to understand. As she left, she asked him
the question that she had made the journey to ask. 'Did Laura
ever mention her auntie?'

He nodded, perplexed. 'Yeah, sometimes.'

'What does she do for a living?'

He shrugged. 'She never said.'

'Shit!'

'What's up?' He seemed genuinely concerned.

'Not your problem,' she said. She had been back to Miss
Kelsall's house, but it was empty, shivering and damp in the
gathering gloom of late afternoon. Time. It was all time and it
was running out for Clara Pascal. She returned to base and
checked again with the tax office.

'Mr Lynott is out on his tea break at the moment, but I'll
leave a message for him to contact you,' the receptionist said.

Great! Her knuckles whitened as she gripped the receiver.
'Well why don't you go and find Mr Lynott and remind him that
while he's dipping his digestive biccy in his coffee, a woman's life
hangs in the balance. Okay?'

She took a breath and exhaled before giving her direct line
and mobile number, in case he had misplaced them, as well as the
Incident Room fax number. For a few moments after she had
hung up, she sat looking at the phone. Unguarded comments.
You're losing it, Sal, she told herself. *Why the* hell *didn't you ask Miss
Kelsall where she works?*

The mention of a tea break reminded her that she hadn't
eaten since breakfast and she decided to fill the time by grabbing
something from the canteen downstairs. It had been fitted out
with museum visitors in mind and the room was bright and

modern. She considered and rejected the healthy options on offer, plumping instead for a bacon-and-egg sandwich, which would at least be portable if Mr Lynott eventually got back to her.

She was just settling down to it when Fletcher breezed in.

'Sal!' he exclaimed. 'What are you doing here? Skiving?'

She gave him a sour look. 'You seem to be "between actions" a lot, Fletcher.'

He smirked. 'I was born efficient, me.'

'Yeah. Remind me – how many days did it take you to work out that your "stalker" was actually the local dogwatch?'

He shrugged, piqued and went to the counter. Rayner checked her watch. Five minutes and she would phone the tax office again. Fletcher returned with a mug of tea and an Eccles cake.

'Aren't you supposed to be out looking for that van?' she asked, irritated that he had intruded on the only five minutes she had managed to scrounge for herself all day.

'Everyone's entitled to a break,' he said.

'Well mine's over.' Rayner abandoned the half mug of coffee she had remaining and took her sandwich with her.

'Where're you off to?'

She resisted the temptation to tell him to mind his own business, reminding herself that they were supposed to be a team and exchanging information was part of the process. 'I'm going to interview Laura Kelsall's auntie.'

He laughed. 'You're not still on that? Where've you been, Rayner?'

'What do you mean?'

'It's all over, bar the shouting. They've arrested someone. He had his next victim all lined up for her fifteen minutes of fame. Lights, cameras, the lot. Must think he's Stephen bloody Speilberg.'

'She's alive?'

'The most recent, yeah. Clara – who knows?'

'When did they find her?' She sat back down.

'Around lunch-time. He'd had her for a few days, by all accounts. Lawson's been in conference with McAteer for the past half hour.'

'Shit! You mean he snatched two in a week?' She felt sick. Clara was dead. If they had found this woman alive and no sign of Clara, she must be dead. It didn't matter what she did now, she wasn't going to help Clara.

'He's a greedy boy, our Alex,' Fletcher commented.

'Who?' Rayner started to her feet.

'You're not telling me you know him?' Fletcher mumbled through a mouthful of pastry and currants.

'I'm not telling you bugger all — I'm *asking* you his name.'

The fierce glint in her eye warned Fletcher against telling her not to get her knickers in a twist and he said, 'Bloke they've arrested is called Alex Martin.'

She headed for the door.

'Hey,' Fletcher called. 'You've forgotten your sarnie.'

'You have it,' Rayner answered. 'I've lost my appetite.'

She didn't wait for an answer to her knock. McAteer looked up from his conversation with Lawson. Sergeant Barton was there, too.

'Is it true?' she demanded.

McAteer's grave expression changed to annoyance. 'We're in conference, Rayner,' he said.

'Sir. If you've arrested Alex Martin, he's the man who allegedly — listen to me, "allegedly"! He raped Laura Kelsall and he got away with it and she killed herself because of him.'

'Laura Kelsall is dead?' Lawson asked. He hadn't had time to catch up on the day's events since interviewing Martin.

Rayner nodded jerkily, not trusting herself to speak.

'Have you spoken to Kelsall's sister, yet?' McAteer asked.

'I was going to, but what's the point?'

'If her brother is dead, then let her prove it, otherwise he's the prime suspect in Clara Pascal's abduction.'

Rayner stared from McAteer to Lawson. 'I thought you'd charged Martin.'

'With Eleanor's murder, yes.'

'Sir,' Rayner said, 'I'm sorry. I was told—' It went against the grain to land Fletcher in it, even though she despised the man, and she corrected herself. 'I thought . . .' She shook her head. 'I got the wrong end of the stick. I'll go and talk to Miss Kelsall.'

McAteer called her back. 'Emergency briefing at six,' he said. 'Don't be late. And I'd like a result on Miss Kelsall.'

'Sir.' She retreated.

As she left, Lawson jerked his head, indicating that Barton should go with her.

'Sal!' Rayner turned. 'Wait a sec,' Barton called. 'I'll come with you.'

Rayner tried to keep the suspicion from showing on her face. 'I can manage, Sarge.'

'I know you can.' Barton slowed down and fell in step with her as she continued the walk back to the Incident Room. 'But this could be our best line of enquiry to date – God knows we're getting nowhere with the van.'

'What about DI Lawson? Won't he be needing you?'

Barton's eyebrows lifted. 'We're not joined at the hip. If he needs me, he'll call.'

'Okay,' she said, giving in gracefully: she knew that Barton was being tactful, asking her permission to tag along. In reality, she had no choice in the matter. 'Let's see if we've got an address to go to, shall we?'

'You go ahead,' Barton said. 'I'll meet you in the car park in five minutes – I've got to make a phone call.'

There was a fax waiting for her from the tax office when she returned to the Incident Room. Miss Kelsall worked at a nursery and garden centre off the A41. She just hoped Mr Lynott didn't take it into his head to make a complaint. They arrived at four-thirty to find the place locked up.

'Winter hours,' Barton said. 'Ten till four.'

On the drive out to Miss Kelsall's bungalow – Rayner's third that day – she filled him in on the background.

'So if it wasn't for this friend of hers, you'd still be none the wiser?'

Rayner shook her head. She tried to shift the image of Una Shellien, her pretty face ugly with rage. 'She looked at me like I'd crawled out of a sewer . . . . You know what made it so hard to take?'

Barton glanced across at her.

'She was right. I'd manipulated her. Instead of asking straight out, I let her think that I was investigating Martin. I felt like the worst kind of sewer slime.' A little puff of air escaped from between her lips. 'I still do.'

'I know what you mean – they always want to see the best in you, kids, but if they find you out . . .' He sucked air between his teeth. 'Still, she'll be glad to hear he's been arrested.'

'Cold comfort.' Barton glanced across in question. 'Well,' Rayner said. 'It's not like we caught him before he did any more harm.'

Barton felt an answering pang of guilt. What harm was Casavettes capable of doing with the information he had passed on?

Thin needles of icy rain sliced almost horizontally as they drew up outside Miss Kelsall's. Rayner was hugely relieved to find her at home.

She scowled at Rayner, then flipped Barton a derisory glance. 'Brought reinforcements?' But she let them in without the usual quibbles about being busy, showing them to the front room and inviting them to be seated. Barton took the chair adjacent to Miss Kelsall, leaning forward, his elbows on his knees. Rayner remained standing. Neither spoke and for a while they listened as freezing rain hissed like blown sand against the windows.

'You've been lying to me.'

Miss Kelsall looked up at Rayner.

'Have I?'

'You know you have.'

She could see Miss Kelsall wondering how much she knew — which lie to admit to and which to deny.

'Let's start with Laura.'

Miss Kelsall's face tightened as she clamped down on her emotions. At least her grief for her niece wasn't counterfeit.

'I said I hadn't seen her for some time. That was the truth.'

'It's true that she didn't go to her dad's funeral, either, but you weren't honest about it.'

'I should have told you, but I couldn't — it was just too painful to. . .' Her voice trailed off and she cleared her throat.

Rayner was beginning to feel sorry for her. *No,* she thought. *Not this time.*

'What did you do with the money?' she asked.

Miss Kelsall was shaken. 'What money?'

'Your brother sold his house, his business. You told me he'd done well out of that. The insurance money might take a bit longer — after all, there's no body — but the rest must amount to a tidy sum.' She looked around her, taking in the fading colour on the walls and the green leaf pattern of the carpet. 'You look like you could do with a few house improvements, Miss Kelsall. I mean, when was this place last decorated?'

'What the *hell* business is that of yours?' Miss Kelsall demanded angrily.

'It's obvious you haven't used your brother's money. Why not?' Rayner was just as angry and she intended to get a straight answer.

'Maybe it's because you don't feel it's yours to use,' Barton suggested, kindly. Bang on cue. It had the right effect. Miss Kelsall was grateful for Barton's more gentle approach and she felt the need to explain herself to him.

She drew herself up, composing herself. 'It didn't — it still doesn't — feel right, benefiting from my brother's death,' she said.

'Oh, yes . . . Your brother's death,' Rayner repeated. 'Did I tell you, Sarge, Miss Kelsall went to the crash site and knew — just *knew* — he was dead.'

Miss Kelsall eyed her with cold dislike. 'I hope you never have to go through anything like it, Constable Rayner.'

'Thank you for that kind sentiment,' Rayner said, ladling on the sarcasm. 'I've had to break the worst news to people more times than I care to count. And d'you know what's strange?' She saw Barton wondering whether he should interrupt and shot him a warning look to keep quiet. 'What's strange is they *never* believe it — not really — not until they've seen the body. It's never wholly real until they have . . .' She paused, staring at Miss Kelsall who resolutely avoided her eye. 'But not you,' she finished. 'You just *knew* he was dead!'

She turned and stalked to the window, leaving Barton to take his turn. The traffic on the A51 was a steady stream, slowed by the foul weather, but still noisy through the leaky windows.

'Thing is,' Barton said, injecting an intimation of apology into this tone, 'We could prosecute you with conspiracy to defraud the insurance company.'

Miss Kelsall looked up at him, her eyes wide with alarm. 'I've never even spoken to the insurance company!' she protested.

'Oh,' Barton said. 'Why?'

She seemed flustered. 'Because . . .'

'Because he's not dead.' Rayner separated the words, enunciating them quite clearly. She watched Miss Kelsall's reflection in the glass. She looked edgy; her hands clasped and unclasped in her lap and she shot a pleading glance at Barton.

'If that's true,' he said. 'If you've been claiming money he's not entitled to, knowing he's still alive, it's conspiracy,' he paused. 'Conspiracy is a very serious charge.'

'I didn't conspire to do anything!' Miss Kelsall exclaimed.

Rayner turned to face the room. 'You told me that your

brother was going to take Laura away, let her convalesce in the countryside.'

'He *was!*'

'You told me he wouldn't walk away from the crash and abandon his daughter.'

Miss Kelsall was distressed. 'He sold up so that he could take her away. He *did!*'

'Laura had been dead two weeks when the rail crash happened,' Rayner insisted.

Miss Kelsall wept quietly. 'I know,' she groaned. 'Don't you think I *know* that?'

Barton caught Rayner's eye: he would take it from here. 'Miss Kelsall, if Clara Pascal dies, it won't just be conspiracy to abduction you'll be facing – it'll be conspiracy to murder.'

She turned to him, shocked. 'I didn't know,' she said. 'I *swear* I didn't know!'

'Then help us,' Barton urged, leaving aside for the moment that she must, at some stage have realised what her brother had done. 'Tell us what you know.'

She shrugged, heaving a massive sigh.

'I really did think he was dead. I couldn't believe he would let me think that – and so soon after Laura . . .' She shook her head. The memory was still painful to her.

'But he got in touch,' Barton prompted.

She nodded. 'End of October – no, the beginning of November. He just turned up on the doorstep.' She looked from one to the other, inviting them to share in her astonishment.

'What did he want?'

She grimaced. 'Money. I completed the sale of the house after –' She frowned, then braced herself to say, '– after the railcrash. He'd already sold the business. 'It's gone to probate, but the house sale . . . I'd done all the negotiations, you see. I told the solicitor to pay it into my account. But I couldn't touch it.'

'So you gave him money,' Barton prompted.

She glared at Barton. 'It is his, after all.'

'How much did he want?'

'Fifteen thousand.'

'How did you pay him?'

'Cash.' She saw the look on Barton's face and protested, 'He didn't say why he wanted it!'

'And you didn't think to ask,' Rayner said.

'He looked so awful,' she appealed to Barton. 'If he wanted to disappear, who could blame him?'

'Except it wasn't just anonymity he wanted, was it?' Barton said softly.

She looked away, her face working.

'Where is he?'

Her voice was barely audible. 'I don't know.'

'He didn't even give you a phone number?'

'He said he would be in touch.'

'What was he driving?'

She frowned at the leafy swirls in the carpet.

'You say you didn't know what he was planning—'

'I *didn't!*' Miss Kelsall interrupted.

'I believe you. But now you do know. You know that your brother abducted Clara Pascal. You know he's keeping her against her will. And you can help us, if you want to.'

She closed her eyes and tears welled from under her lashes.

'You didn't see what that man did to Laura, she was such a happy girl before he . . . It destroyed Brian, watching her fade away a little day by day.' She swallowed, then went on, almost in a whisper. 'It was Brian found her. She'd taken pills – it wasn't a picturesque death. It was ugly and cruel. He should never have had to see his own little girl like that—'

'Do you want to see him charged with murder?' Rayner broke in, her voice harsh, unyielding. 'The court might understand his actions so far, but if Clara dies—'

Miss Kelsall clasped both hands in front of her. It took a few moments, but neither officer tried to rush her. 'A van,' she said at last. 'He was in a van.'

'What sort of van?' Rayner said, scarcely daring to breathe.
'A white Ford Transit.'

If there had been any lingering doubt in their minds, it was banished: Brian Kelsall had abducted Clara Pascal.

The team's curiosity was evident in the hush that fell when the officers present saw a stranger with McAteer and Lawson. Five-nine or -ten — only average height by their standards — but he was strongly built. He stood in front of the whiteboard, calm, unembarrassed by the attention. His eyes, a pale, glacial blue, skimmed the room, lighting on one or other of the officers and remaining there as if he had seen something in them that required explanation or investigation. He moved on only when it seemed he had resolved the problem, extracted the information he sought.

'Doctor Dalrymple lectures in forensic psychological studies at St Werburgh's, here in Chester and –' McAteer paused and made pointed eye contact with a few of the team whom he knew were less than sympathetic to criminal profiling as an investigative tool '– I should point out that he is an ex-police officer.'

A few people actually sat up and picked up pens in response to this piece of information.

'He retired at the rank of DI six years ago with twenty years' service in the force. Originally I asked him to help us narrow down the range of suspects in Clara Pascal's abduction, but since this afternoon we have someone in the frame.' He nodded and Rayner stood up.

'Oh, *what*?' Fletcher exclaimed.

'Where've you been, Fletcher?' Rayner muttered, taking a childish pleasure in throwing his words back at him.

It didn't take long to explain the situation. 'His sister believes he abducted Clara with the intention of frightening her and putting her family through what he'd gone through,' she went on. 'She doesn't believe he intends to hurt her.'

McAteer noticed Dalrymple shift slightly. 'Doctor?'

Dalrymple frowned. 'He's had Clara for a long time. Now, we're told she's persuasive, so it could be in her favour — she might have had time to build up a relationship with him. However, he has almost certainly heard by now that Alex Martin has been arrested.'

'But with Martin in custody, isn't he more likely to let Clara go?' Young ventured.

Dalrymple shook his head. 'A woman is known to have been murdered by Martin since his release. Another is under heavy sedation in hospital, after several days imprisoned and terrorised in her own home. Kelsall may well blame Clara.'

'Surely the sister knows where he is?' Fletcher interrupted.

'He didn't give her a contact address,' Rayner said.

'And you believe her, do you?'

'Yeah, Fletch, I do as a matter of fact.' She maintained eye contact a second or two longer to reinforce her point. 'She confirmed that he is driving a white Ford Transit. No registration,' she added quickly, before they could get their hopes up.

'We've got Miss Kelsall under covert surveillance,' Lawson said. 'If he goes to see her, he'll be followed.'

McAteer noticed Thorpe sitting near the back of the room and asked, 'Anything from your source, Thorpe?'

'He's in hospital, Guv.'

'Why am I only hearing this now?' McAteer demanded, sharply.

Barton turned and stared at Thorpe.

'I got the call as I arrived here. His girlfriend. Three men broke into their flat in the early hours.'

'Is he badly hurt?'

'Sounds like.'

'See him directly after this meeting. If he knows the vehicle registration, I want it.'

Thorpe raised his eyebrows. 'It's not gonna happen, Guv.'

Lawson thought Thorpe was probably right, but he said, 'Do what you can, Chris.'

McAteer scanned the assembly. 'Okay. We've got the colour, make and model of the van. We've got an ID on the main suspect. Now, Kelsall must be holding Clara somewhere. He was looking at country properties around Tarvin before his daughter's suicide and we know he's got the money to rent.

'The HOLMES team has been working on reassigning actions, so check with them. We're shifting the focus on a blitz of estate agents. Photos of Kelsall will be available when you pick up your new actions. It's too late tonight, but I want an early start in the morning.'

'Lucky break,' Fletcher muttered as he picked up a copy of the Brian Kelsall photograph on his way out. He didn't mean it as a compliment.

Rayner gave him an amused look. 'You know, the harder I work, the luckier I get,' she said. 'This didn't just fall into my lap, Fletcher. I had to go out and find it. Anyway, the suspect's vanished and he might have Clara with him right now. I wouldn't call it an unqualified success, would you?'

'I'm off to see Martin — want to tag along?' Lawson was elated. With Martin out of the frame, Clara's chances of survival were much better.

Barton picked up his notebook and stuffed it in his jacket pocket. *Casavettes has put a man in hospital.* Until this week, Barton had thought himself pretty much inured to the effects of violence: he had seen enough of it in his years on the force. He thought he understood its indiscriminate nature, its callous unpredictability. He had been in personal danger many times and he could handle that, but now his wife and his son were under threat and this was an entirely unknown situation. He didn't know the rules of engagement, he didn't know how to act, and he was more terrified than he had ever been in his life. If Fran knew what he was doing, could she ever forgive him? Would she understand that he was doing it to protect her and Timmy?

'You know what?' Lawson went on, buoyed up by the news they had just delivered to the team. 'I think Martin's claustrophobic. And you know what else? I'm going to enjoy sending that sick bastard back to the cells.' He grinned. 'Maybe he's not the only sadist around here.'

Barton glanced at his watch. 'I've got a few calls to make, Boss.'

Lawson shrugged. 'Suit yourself. I'll catch you later.'

Martin sensed a shift in the balance of power. Lawson seemed calm, almost relaxed. The change made him nervous. He licked his lips. For a long time, Lawson said nothing. He leaned against the door frame with his arms folded, staring down at Martin.

'What are you looking at?' Martin knew he had given Lawson the upper hand, breaking the silence like that, but he couldn't stand it any longer – Lawson staring at him with that smug look on his face.

'I'm looking at a man who's going back to the cells for the night.'

'No!'

Lawson crinkled a little around the eyes. 'Take him down,' he said.

'I told you – I won't talk.'

'Lawson smiled. 'Well, that'll be a blessing.'

'I mean it,' Martin warned.

Lawson pushed away from the door frame. 'We don't need your help,' he said. 'And we've got plenty on you with Miss Hutton's statement and the video tapes. You needn't say another word. Ever.'

Chapter Forty Two

It was impossible to count the hours in the solid darkness and silence. She found it impossible to work for more than a few minutes, scratching a thin line in the sandstone with the hair-grip before collapsing, sick with exhaustion, on to the mattress again. Her fingers were swollen and sore and the wetness she felt was as likely to be blood as sweat. She thought that night had passed, but how could she be certain in this emptiness crowded with fear?

Time seemed to distort, stretching like a thin thread of silk, seemingly interminable and yet devastatingly fragile. Clara sat shivering on the mattress, huddled in the legal gown he had given her, taking occasional sips of the rapidly cooling soup from the flask to keep warm.

In her waking moments she was constantly afraid. Fear followed her like a creeping shadow, invading her dreams, so that she could snatch only minutes of nightmarish sleep, waking breathless and afraid. He had been away so long and the darkness felt so close, so oppressive, she could almost feel it *give* when she stretched her hand out into its depths.

Why worry, so long as he leaves you alone? As she relaxed, vivid images — waking dreams — flashed across her vision: people dressed in bright summer colours. She felt her body spin lightly and her breathing became slower, deeper.

A bolt of horror tore her from sleep. *Oh, God! What if he doesn't come back?* Her heart pounded, filling her ears with sound. *Where is he? What if something has happened to him?* She would not last long in this cold. She tried to estimate the lapse of time, using her state of hunger and the use of the bucket as a guide. Eight – perhaps ten – hours had passed. He had never before left her for so long. *What if he's had an accident?* She found herself willing him to return, praying for his safety. Sharp points of light danced in the darkness, dizziness flooded her senses, threatening a blackout and she forced herself to slow her breathing.

After a minute or two, she felt a little better. 'If he doesn't come back, you'll have to find a way out, that's all,' she told herself. *Good idea, Clara,* her cynical self chipped in. *How do you propose to do that?*

Her fingers closed around the jagged point of metal and she squeezed the hair-grip into her palm. The darkness was impenetrable. She had to feel along the chain to find the loop that fixed it to the wall. *Brilliant, Clara. What d'you think this is – the Great Escape?*

'Shut up,' Clara said, quietly, but quite distinctly. Her inner voice had become as real to her as a person. As real anyway as the nightmare she was living.

She took a breath, then began again the torturously slow process of etching into the wall either side of the stay, drawing a line, one two, three, four, five times, on and on, up to twenty, using her index finger to check the indentation she had made before switching to the other side.

Two more scratches and the hair-grip snapped; Clara scraped her knuckles on the rough stone and broke a nail. She cried out in anger and dismay. She searched for the broken section, but it had disappeared. Sullenly, she turned back to the wall and began scratching again along the thin ridge she had already made.

She saw occasional flashes in the tarry blackness: the little points of light had returned. Her brain trying to relieve the monotony of thick night, or exhaustion and lack of food? She did not stop to think but worked on, in a trance, not feeling the bruises forming deep purple weals on her fingers and the palms of her hands. She tasted grit on her teeth; it coated her lashes, but she continued, sweat sending the dirt stinging into her eyes, consoled by the scrape of metal on stone.

The door crashed open. Clara turned, quickly hiding the hair-grip in the folds of the gown. He stood in the doorway, breathing heavily. She blinked, screwing her eyes up against the light. Her heart raced; she was more afraid now that at any time since this had started. Something had gone disastrously wrong. *Please God, don't let him kill me! Not now.*

As he walked down the steps, he seemed weighted down by something; the risers seemed almost to give under his heavy tread. Clara stared wordlessly at him. *I won't plead.* He had taken so much from her already, he wouldn't take the last vestiges of her dignity. He carried a newspaper in his hand, which he rolled and threw at her feet. It uncurled, revealing the banner headline:

SICK

She stared at it, unable to move.

'Read it,' he ordered.

The headline took up a third of the page. Below it were pictures of two women. Clara's eyes prickled and the text swam out of focus. She shook her head.

'Please . . .' she whispered. *Don't do this, Clara. Don't beg.* She wanted some explanation, needed to know why he had chosen her.

'*Read it!*'

The threat in his voice shocked Clara out of her distress. She sniffed and wiped her eyes with the heel of her hand. Sandstone grains scratched her eyelids and she saw that there was blood on her hands. Which meant it would be on the wall, too. Keeping her eyes on him, she thrust her hands into the sleeves of her gown and moved a little to hide the damage to the stays in the wall.

The newspaper subheading read:

Woman rescued from underground Hell

This was surreal. Another hypothermic hallucination? She struggled to make sense of the text, skimming it as she might a verbatim record of a police interview.

'Woman held prisoner . . . Policewoman stabbed . . . videos . . . photographs . . . depraved . . . arrested . . .' She stopped, went back, found 'arrested' and read the sentence in full.

'Police have arrested a thirty-five-year-old man in connection with the incident.'

Clara looked up into the masked face of her tormentor. If they had arrested a man, why was she still here? Why was she chained to the wall, frightened, cold, hungry to the point of collapse?

'I don't understand,' she said, staring stupidly at the text.

He slipped a hand into his pocket and Clara gave an involuntary cry. A knife? Yes, a knife . . . She watched in horror. But it wasn't what she thought. He drew out a tape recorder and she almost whimpered with relief. He pressed a button and placed the recorder on the floor between them, out of her reach.

'A man was arrested earlier today in connection with the stabbing of a policewoman in the south of the city. Police have confirmed he has been charged with a number of offences, including kidnapping and murder. The man, named as local travel agent Alex Martin . . .'

'Alex Martin,' Clara whispered.

He clicked the machine off. 'All those lives. The women he

humiliated, raped – and now he's murdered because you let him go free.'

In an instant of clarity, she recognised his voice. 'Dear God . . .' *Brian Kelsall – Laura's father.*

How could she have been so wrong? She had thought he was revelling in unsolved killings, in the helplessness of the victims, when in fact he was asking her to listen to them.

'You judged me as a father,' he said. 'And you judged Laura, but you never judged him. Why was that? Because he was paying your fee – is that the only thing that matters to you?'

'Laura,' she said. 'Is she . . .?'

He didn't have to tell her. She could see in the anguish in his eyes: Laura was dead. She wanted to tell him that she was sorry, but no apology could atone for the loss of his daughter.

'Nine weeks he was out on the streets after you got him off. Nine weeks.' He picked the newspaper up from where Clara had let it fall. 'Look at them.' Eleanor Gorton and Angela Hutton. Kelsall pulled off the mask and she expected to see hatred in his face, but he seemed drained of all emotion, immeasurably tired. 'Do you think my Laura is in his vile gallery?' he asked. 'She said he filmed her, but you laughed at that, didn't you? Said it was ludicrous.'

'The police investigated!' Clara protested. 'They searched his house.' What was she doing? Still trying to justify her actions? Appalled though she was, she couldn't stop herself from adding, 'They found nothing—'

'They found something this time.' His voice was low and firm.

She bowed her head.

'I wanted *you* to suffer, not them – I never wanted this.'

He climbed the stairs slowly, holding the rail as if to prevent himself being dragged back.

Chapter Forty Three

'Pascal will receive a package in about one minute.'

'Casavettes?'

'I'll get back to you when you've had time to think.'

The line went dead and Lawson immediately called surveillance to warn them.

Thirty minutes later, Young stood in front of his desk, looking sorry for herself. Between them, a sealed plastic bag, containing a photograph of a white van.

'You failed to follow even basic procedures to prevent contamination of the evidence,' he said.

'I tried to stop him, sir, but he kept going on about it being news of Clara — he wouldn't listen.'

'If you want to stay in the job, Young, you'd better find a way to *make* people listen.'

'Boss?' Barton poked his head around the door.

Lawson scowled a moment or two longer at Young, then switched his attention to the sergeant.

'The courier service checks out,' Barton said, coming into the room. 'The bloke who dropped off the package gave a false name and business address, but from the physical description, I reckon it's one of Casavettes' heavies.'

'How come you're so sure?'

Barton glanced at Young. 'I've . . . had dealings with him

recently.' *Outside my house in a rainstorm.* The man in question had been handing over pictures on that occasion, too. Only they had been of Barton's wife and child.

'You can go,' Lawson told Young. 'But stick around. Make yourself useful. I'll want to discuss this further.' He picked up the bag containing the photo. A small oblong had been cut, neatly excising the number plate. The van was parked next to a house with weedy block paving and two shallow steps to a black-painted front door. There was a large bay window on one side of the door, with new brickwork showing beneath it.

'A cellar,' Barton commented.

Lawson nodded.

'I've put every available officer on tracing the van,' he said, 'But it looks like we've got no choice — we're going to have to talk to Casavettes.'

'Think it is Kelsall's van?' Barton asked.

Lawson shrugged. 'The point is, it *could* be. And I don't see Casavettes trying to bluff on this one.'

Barton didn't either. Casavettes had put a lot of time and manpower into tracking down the van. Why would he bluff now? But he asked the question anyway: 'There's no doubt this really *is* from Casavettes?'

Lawson gave a brief shake of the head. 'He phoned me *before* the package was delivered.' Which meant he had sent it to the courier service. 'And you said yourself, the description matches one of Casavettes' thugs.' Even if he didn't have Clara under lock and key, he certainly knew who did. And he knew where she was.

Barton asked, 'What are you going to offer him?'

'He's in prison, Phil. We're not in a position to offer anything.'

'He's on remand,' Barton corrected.

'He's had every application for bail knocked back.'

'There's always a JC bail application.'

'A Judge in Chambers application? You've got it all worked out, haven't you?'

The phone rang and Lawson picked up before Barton could respond.

'You wanted proof.'

Lawson recognised the slightly nasal drawl. 'Casavettes. Where is she?'

'I'm only guessing, mind – you're the detective – but my money'd be on her being in that cellar under the front window.'

'I don't like having to repeat myself.'

'Then don't bother. You're wasting your breath anyroad.'

'All right,' Lawson said. 'Give me the registration of the van.'

Casavettes laughed. 'You're joking me!'

'As a gesture of good faith.'

There was a pause.

'Casavettes?'

'I'm thinking about it.'

Lawson closed his eyes, willing Casavettes to comply. Casavettes sniffed. 'Thought about it,' he said. 'Tell you what, Mr Lawson, I'll take you to her.'

'We're not going down that road, Casavettes.'

'You want her back.'

'Yes.'

'If you want her back, it's on those terms.'

'It's not open for discussion.'

'I think it is. Now I don't know what McAteer has given you to negotiate with, but I know he won't have left you empty-handed.'

Lawson didn't answer.

'I'm not asking much,' Casavettes said. 'Bit of fresh air and decent food before the trial. It's not like I'm asking you to drop the charges.'

'Forget *that* idea, Ray. Put it right out of your mind.'

'I'm a realist, Steve,' he said. 'I know what's feasible and what isn't.'

'Your case isn't a police matter any longer,' Lawson said.

'You're not our responsibility. There's the prison service, the courts to consider.'

'This is a kidnapping, Steve. Normal rules don't apply.'

It was true. They would do anything to ensure the safety of the victim in abduction cases. *Almost* anything.

'Arrange bail, I go with you, show you where she is, everyone's happy.'

'You've had every bail application turned down. Face it, Casavettes, you're not going to make bail.'

Casavettes laughed softly. 'Who made sure my bail applications failed, Steve? We both know it can be done. Fix it.'

Lawson took a breath. He had run out of objections.

'A case like this can make a superstar of the investigating officer or it can put him in the outer reaches of nowhere,' Casavettes said into the silence. His voice had a sharper edge, even a hint of desperation. 'Get me out of here or you'll spend the next five years working on Clara's abduction.'

This is what Lawson had feared most: Clara was now doubly at risk. 'I'll have to talk to my—'

'Now you're really pigging me off,' Casavettes cut in. 'I found her and I can make her disappear. Don't give me any excuses – you want her? Get me out of here and you can have her. Piss me about, I swear you'll never find her.'

Justice Adrian Walker had a full morning: at ten a.m., he would present his summing up in an assault case; while the jury considered its verdict, he would preside over a closed session discussing points of law with the lawyers trying an embezzlement case.

He was reading through his summation when a court usher interrupted to give him a hand-delivered bail application from Ray Casavettes' solicitor.

Judge in Chambers bail applications weren't often made – never for men like Casavettes – and Justice Walker was astonished that it had been made at all. He set it to one side with an irritated sigh and continued skimming his notes. Minutes later, DI Lawson was shown into his chambers.

He explained the purpose of his visit and Walker squinted again at the solicitor's application. After a moment or two he fixed the inspector with a steady, unflinching gaze. Lawson resisted the temptation to shift from one foot to the other under it.

'You are asking me to approve an application from a violent criminal — a drug trafficker — who has orchestrated the intimidation of witnesses even from within his prison cell,' Walker said.

Yes, Lawson thought. *That's about the size of it.* He considered: his options were nil. He had to get Clara out or he would risk one of two things: Kelsall killing her or Casavattes' men moving in to take her away from Kelsall. He decided to come clean.

'We think he knows where Ms Pascal is,' he said.

'If his release is prerequisite to his co-operation, all the more reason to decline his application.'

'Your Honour—'

'Inspector,' Justice Walker cut across him testily. 'If I establish a precedent in this case, it could open the floodgates. Give in to this kind of coercion and you run the risk of subverting the entire judicial system.'

'We don't believe he abducted Ms Pascal,' Lawson said, trying to sound firm without giving Walker reason to think he was being confrontational. 'We *do* believe he knows where she's being held. We think he can take us there.'

While he sweated it out, waiting for the paperwork, in the cramped café near the entrance of the building, Lawson put together the outline of a scheme to take to the meeting he would go on to at HQ. They would need to cover all eventualities, but time was short and Clara's life depended on their foresight and planning.

He picked up the paperwork and after eyeing the clouds to gauge the likely imminence of rain, decided to leave the car parked in front of the courts and walk the short distance to Cheshire Constabulary Headquarters across the road. Half-way across the car park, his mobile rang.

'Something for you to think about in your meeting with the top brass.'

Lawson began walking slowly towards the arch leading out onto the main road. 'I'm listening,' he said.

'I've got a condition.'

'You want to see the prison doctor about that.'

'That was nearly amusing, Steve. See if this tickles your funny bone.' He paused and Lawson felt a mixture of irritation and curiosity. 'I don't want no poxy gate arrest.'

'You are joking,' Lawson said. 'You expect us to let you just walk out of there? How are we supposed to keep tabs on you?'

'You'll just have to rely on my goodwill.'

'Not a chance.'

'You seized my passport, Steve. Where am I going to go?' Lawson laughed. 'And you said I was a comedian.'

'I didn't say *no one* could be there. We've known each other a long time. You can come along for the ride. I'll take you to her, like I said.'

Lawson couldn't believe the man. 'You haven't got a snowball's chance in hell,' he said.

'Neither has Clara, without me.'

Lawson's skin prickled as if stung by a thousand tiny ants.

'Think of it as a — what did you call it? A gesture of good faith,' Casavettes cajoled. He was trying to be reasonable — as close as Casavettes ever got to being reasonable.

'I can't do it,' Lawson said. 'Take us to Clara, then we'll negotiate.'

'Not good enough.' Lawson sensed that Casavettes' patience had been tested to its meagre limits. 'It's just you and me or the deal's off.' He cut the connection.

Lawson looked over at the drab grey tower block that housed Cheshire Area Constabulary. McAteer would be there, as would a detective chief superintendent, and members of the Firearms Support Unit. They weren't going to like this.

Barton stopped by Lawson's office as he strapped on his body armour.

'You all miked up?'

Lawson nodded: they could not talk frankly.

'I want in on this one, Boss.'

'You are, as far as you can be, Phil.'

'Minding the shop!'

Lawson shrugged into a waterproof jacket. 'I need you here.'

'Doing *what?*'

'Co-ordinating. We have to find Kelsall.'

'I thought that was what Casavettes promised.'

'I'd rather not put my trust in Ray Casavettes' word of honour,' Lawson said, drily.

'I've earned the right to be on this one.' Barton's voice was low, charged with emotion.

'You'd be a liability.'

Barton looked shocked, hurt. 'What the hell does that mean?'

'You're known by Casavettes *and* his men,' Lawson explained. 'You recognised the description of the guy who dropped off the photos to the courier service. Chances are, he'd recognise you. We can't take that chance.'

Barton began to object, but Lawson cut across him. 'You know what you have to do, Phil. Do it.'

Barton waited for Lawson to leave, then he went outside to his car, gathering his coat collar against the biting wind. He got in and shut the door, checking the car park for prying eyes before he took out his mobile. It was freezing, even inside the car. But it wasn't the cold that made his fingers tremble as he keyed in the number.

A cruel wind whipped up, sending surges of dust and litter along the pavement. Lawson pulled in to the kerb and watched as Casavettes stepped, blinking, into the light. Instinctively, he looked up at the sky, which was low and grey, but he smiled to himself, nevertheless.

As Lawson waited, a Chrysler Voyager swept past and pulled in at an angle, blocking Lawson's car. Two men got out.

'What's this?' Lawson demanded.

'Security check.' Casavettes was still smiling. He jerked his head at the shorter man. 'Okay Lenny.'

Lenny began searching through Lawson's pockets, stuffing Lawson's mobile phone and wallet into his own pocket, before opening his outer jacket. He glanced over his shoulder to get Casavettes' reaction.

'Expecting trouble, Steve?'

'You're pushing your luck, Casavettes.'

'I just want to make sure we're alone. Take it off.'

Lawson complied, removing his jacket and body armour and bracing himself against the icy wind.

'Now the shirt.'

'For God's sake!'

'Do it,' Casavettes said.

Lawson stared at Casavettes for some moments. Reluctantly, he removed his shirt.

Casavettes tutted. 'Never trust a copper.' He pulled at the straps which held the covert radio to Lawson's body and ripped the wire out of his shirt sleeve. Lenny handed him Lawsons's car keys from the ignition. Casavettes opened the boot and threw the body armour inside.

'We'll take the Chrysler,' Casavettes said. 'It looks cleaner than your car.'

Lawson had half-expected this. He slipped into his shirt and began putting on his jacket.

'U-uh,' Casavettes scolded. 'Not the jacket.'

'It's bloody freezing!' Lawson protested.

'Should've thought of that before you got wired up.'

Lenny tossed Lawson's wallet into the boot of his car and his mobile phone after it.

'Woah, woah, woah!' Casavettes shouted, as Lenny moved to shut the boot. 'I could use that.' He fished the phone out and hefted it in his hand. 'Bloody hell, Steve, how long've you had this antique?'

Lawson shrugged, indifferent.

'You wanna get yourself one of them new lightweights,' he said. 'This must play hell with your suits. Still, beggars can't be choosers.' He grimaced. 'Couldn't get my mobile through security.' He pocketed Lawson's mobile and led the way to the Chrysler.

Chapter Forty Four

You let him go free, Clara. You let a rapist loose on the streets. You made his victim despair so the only way out was to kill herself.

The evidence was flimsy, she told herself. It was his word against hers.

And you took the word of a rapist.

The police investigated her story. There was nothing in his flat — no recording equipment, nothing.

You took every word she said and twisted it, made it look like she was lying.

I thought she was!

Did you? Did you really care who was telling the truth and who was lying? He was wrong about the money — it isn't money that motivates you. It's the need to prove you're the best. Putting forward the best argument. Being better than your opponent. Persuading the jury. What is a jury after all, but twelve people deciding who has the best lawyer? You wanted to be the best — no, you wanted to be acknowledged *as the best. That's what really matters to you.*

It mattered even more in The Crown v. Martin, because you didn't want to lose to Peter Telford.

I fight every case with equal vigour, she came back indignantly.

Do you? Peter Telford has everything that you aspire to: success, high profile cases, a career path that will lead to the bench in a few years' time. But more than anything you envy his reputation, because you're ambitious, aren't you, Clara?

The criticisms, Clara knew, were at least in part justified. Why else was she always the first to arrive in Chambers? Why else had she accepted any case the chambers clerk had offered, in her early days? Why, she thought, with aching regret, had she been so unwilling to take her own daughter to school on her birthday?

Because you put career — no, you put winning *— above family, above conscience, even above what you know to be right.*

Clara sank to her knees and put her head in her hands. Had she caused Laura's suicide, Eleanor Gorton's murder because of her own greed for status?

Chapter Forty Five

The Incident Room was busier than it had been for days. Officers made phone enquiries about the sale of a white van, while others out on foot tried to track down Kelsall's visits to estate agents. Dawn burst into the room, waving a slip of paper. Telephone message.

'We've had a positive ID,' she said, grinning all over her face. 'One of the estate agents came up with a name – Kieran Laurence. Laura's initials, reversed. We need to inform all the officers out in the field. We've already asked for a PNC check, but anyone doing the garage and car dealer ring-round, make sure you use the name.' She went to the whiteboard and wrote it up with a flourish. The atmosphere in the Incident Room was electric: the investigation was finally going somewhere.

Young flitted unhappily amongst the activity, carrying a black bin-liner, steadily filling it with rubbish. It would have been kinder if Lawson had sent her back to uniform division. At least if he'd sent her away she wouldn't have to face the rest of the team.

Thorpe rescued a half-eaten Snickers bar from her and replaced it on his desk. 'Haven't you got anything better to do?' he demanded grumpily. His visit to the hospital had proved fruitless – his informant refused to speak to him. Young murmured an apology. He crossed one more estate agent off his list, then picked up the phone handset and dialled the next.

'She's been demoted, Chris,' Fletcher called from his station – a desk piled high with newspapers, loose sheets of paper, empty coffee cups and sweet wrappers. 'Class prefect to litter monitor in a day.' He shook his head sadly. 'I had such high hopes of you, Babe.'

'Don't call me that,' Young snapped, more in the tone of a plea than a demand. *It was bad enough having to do this. Couldn't they have the decency to ignore her?*

'Don't take it to heart, Babe,' Fletcher said. 'It's the nature of the job: one minute you're in line for a commendation, the next your on your arse, picking out the splinters, wondering how you got there.'

Young moved away to the farthest corner of the room. Rayner looked up as she went past. She concluded her telephone call and hung up, crossing another one off her list.

'Hang on.' She threw an apple core into the bin bag.

'I don't see why he has to be so mean,' Young exclaimed.

Rayner leaned back in her chair and scrutinised Young. 'You ask for it,' she said bluntly.

Young was outraged. 'I didn't *ask* for him to treat me like this!'

'Didn't you? Listen to yourself, Cath. "He's so mean!"'

Young blinked. Even Sal had turned against her. 'Well it's true,' she said stubbornly. 'And I've never been anything but nice to him.'

Rayner shook her head, incredulous. 'There's no point in being pleasant and expecting idiots like Fletcher to be *nice* to you. He doesn't know the meaning of mutual respect.'

'I do my job.'

'And you think Fletcher should respect you for that?'

Young looked bewildered. What else should she expect?

Rayner softened a little. 'That's not the way it works, Cath. Do things right, Fletch'll say you're sucking up to the boss. Make a mistake and he's all over you like a rash.'

'That's harrassment,' Young said. She was upset before and hurt. Now she was angry. 'I could take it to the union.'

'Not wise,' Rayner said quietly, separating the two words and injecting enough conviction to make Young tear herself from staring resentfully at Fletcher and focus instead on her.

'But I'm being victimised!'

Rayner shook her head. 'There are no victims, Cath. Only volunteers.'

Young frowned. She knew what Rayner was saying. There were natural victims: she had met them even in her few years on the force. Sal was telling her that she was one of them. How could things have turned out so badly? She had come to this enquiry optimistic, brimming with confidence. She was going to establish herself as a good team-player, to quietly impress her superior officer with her thoroughness and determination. Well, she'd impressed them all right. They thought her weak and lacking authority and her anticipated slow-burn to a distinguished career in CID would be no more than a camera-flash. Blinking back tears, she made a move to continue.

'Look,' Rayner said, 'Lawson is pissed off right now – he's making a point. Give him a few hours to simmer down, he'll put you back on proper duties. God knows we're desperate.' She realised how that sounded and began to back-track, but Young moved on, offended, refusing to listen.

She had to return to Fletcher's desk eventually. He was two-thirds the way down his list. He yawned and stretched as she approached.

'I'm just off for a coffee,' he said. 'I like my notebook on the left, pens on the right.'

Young bit her lip and said nothing.

He eyed the mess on his desk critically. 'That phone cord looks a bit tangled – and see what you can do about those coffee stains, eh, Babe?' He walked away, whistling and Young started dropping biscuit wrappers and old newspapers into the bin bag.

She checked every item before ditching it: she wouldn't put it past Fletcher to lay a booby trap – get her to throw something out that should be filed. DS Tyrell, impatient for news, had returned to get a verbal round-up from the team. As she passed Fletcher's desk, Young asked, 'What do I do with these?'

Tyrell didn't even glance over. She waved a hand, dismissing her. 'Ask "Soft Shite".' Tyrell had taken to Fletcher's new nickname and used it at every opportunity.

Young shuffled through the set of photographs Fletcher had dumped on his desk the previous Saturday. The dog photos. It gave her a certain satisfaction to see how Fletcher had wasted his time, inflating 'the man with the camera' investigation to one of vital importance.

Each snapshot: dog turd, dog squatting, dog walking away – gave her greater confidence. If Fletcher called her Babe once more, she might just try calling him Dog Shite, see how he liked it.

She stopped, tilted one of the pictures to the dingy overhead lights. It wasn't enough. Her hand trembling, not daring to look away from the photograph in case it vanished, she felt for the lamp switch and clicked it on.

'Hey, Sal . . .' Her voice was no more than a breath and Rayner swept past, preoccupied in her own work.

Young lowered herself into Fletcher's chair, her knees weak.

'You all right, Cath?' Thorpe, whose desk faced Fletcher's had glanced up from his list of car dealers. She looked from the picture to Thorpe and back again to the picture.

'It's this . . .'

Fletcher heeled open the door. He was holding a coffee cup in one hand and sandwiches and a Mars bar in the other. 'Bloody hell!' he complained. 'I'm not gone five minutes and she's in *my* chair at *my* desk.' He clumped over to Young. 'Come on – shift.'

Young didn't move.

'This picture.' Her voice was weak, breathless.

'Pop 'em on top of that pile,' he said. 'I'll get to 'em.'

Young continued to stare at the picture on top of the stack.

'What's up with her?' Fletcher asked, his voice rising in irritation. 'Got a fetish for dogs in the number two position?'

Thorpe flipped Fletcher a disparaging look. 'Thought that was you, Fletch.' He liked Young and Fletcher's continued vendetta against her was beginning to bug him.

Young cleared her throat. 'This picture,' she said, her voice stronger this time. 'There's a van.' The room fell quiet. Officers muttered apologies into their phones and cupped their hands over the mouthpiece, listening to her.

'A rusty, white Ford Transit,' she said clearly and distinctly. Was this what DI Lawson meant by making people listen? She looked up. They were all watching her.

Fletcher dropped his snack on the desk and made a grab for the photograph, but she snatched it out of his reach.

'Registration's readable,' Young said. 'I'll put a call through, shall I? Do a PNC check?'

'I'll do it,' Fletcher said.

She heard the desperation in his voice. Heard it and relished it. 'Like *hell* you will.' Her voice was gaining strength with each utterance. She lifted the rubbish bag and placed it carefully on his desk. 'Better finish clearing up,' she said as she walked away. 'You never know what else you'll find under this crap.'

Fletcher appealed to his fellow officers. 'It was just a load of snapshots of dogs taking a dump!' He was sweating.

Thorpe looked at him with disgust. 'You logged my bloody trainer, but you didn't even check through the pictures. Fletch, you're unbelievable.'

Casavettes insisted on Lawson riding in the back of the car with him. 'Where I can keep an eye on you,' he said. He slouched in the far corner, staring out of the window for several minutes, greedily drinking in the colour and light.

'Aren't we heading the wrong way?' Lawson asked.

'Know where she is, do you, Steve mate?'

'You're supposed to be telling us that, Ray. That was the deal.'

'I said I'd take you to her.'

'I remember. But she isn't in Lancashire, is she, Ray?' Lawson stared at Casavettes, but still he refused to make eye contact, continuing instead to gaze at the countryside flashing past. 'We're half-way to Ormskirk and you're wasting my time.'

'Carry on like that, I might think you're still wired, Steve. Passing messages to your boss.' He moved his head slowly, giving his full attention to Lawson. 'I start thinking that, I might have to kick you out and me and the lads go looking for Clara without you.'

Lawson couldn't risk that. He had to stay with Casavettes no matter what.

Ten years ago, Casavettes had been wild, impulsive, but he was capable even then of restraint and – as both Lawson and Porter knew to their cost – of planning. So what had he got planned for today?

In prison he seemed pent-up, dangerous, but the threat was contained, *confined* by the prison regime, the physical limits of its walls and bars, and the constraints of its rules. Here, in his leather upholstered car, backed up by his bodyguards, he had a predatory aura, like a lazy cat that might strike out of malice or for the excitement.

After five minutes Lawson could stand it no longer. 'We're wasting time, Casavettes,' he said. 'If you know where she is, stop pissing about and take me to her.'

The two men locked gazes and Lawson saw amusement beneath Casavettes' contempt. Still engaged in an unblinking battle of wills, he fished in his coat pocket and took out Lawson's phone, only looking away to punch in a number.

'It's me,' he said. 'You got them car regs for me?' He clicked his fingers and Lenny, who was sitting in the third row of seats, took out a pen and notebook.

Casavettes dictated the vehicle identification numbers of the four cars assigned to covert surveillance, watching for Lawson's reaction.

'What's that mate?' Casavettes asked. 'Lawson? He's sitting about three feet away from me. Want a word?' He laughed. 'Hung up on me!' he said, pressing the 'end message' key. 'Must be hard, being so popular, Steve, mate.'

Lawson made the mistake of glancing at the mobile in Casavettes' hand, a fraction of a second only – there and then away.

'What?' He looked at the handset. 'This? Think you'll get it back and do a number trace? Forget it, Steve. Tell you what, though, I'd be doing you a favour, stamping on this piece of shite – they might replace it with some serious gear.'

Lawson looked away, shaking his head.

'Now—' Casavettes punched in another number, then handed the phone to Lawson. 'Call them off.'

Chapter Forty Six

The pace was frantic. Every desk was occupied and the room was clamorous with voices. Phones rang and the central heating pipes groaned and clanked from time to time in the background. There had been numerous confirmations from estate agents that Kelsall had viewed houses in and around Chester, but he had neither signed a lease, nor put in an offer on any of the properties they had traced so far.

Officers were telephoning again the car dealers and garages they had crossed off their lists that morning, this time asking the managers to check the vehicle registration on the photograph Young had unearthed. Young was back on the team, brimming with energy and new-found confidence.

Tyrell came into the Incident Room and rapped loudly on one of the desks. 'Trudy Morley,' she said, when she had their attention. 'They think she's coming out of her coma.' There were exclamations of relief. 'She's not out of the woods yet, but she's more responsive, anyway.'

'Any chance of a visit, Sarge?' One of the trainee detectives had spoken up. 'We were on the same watch.'

'Sorry, Dave. Family only.'

He shrugged. 'Just thought it might help, knowing we're thinking about her.'

Fletcher muttered a remark about mates backing up their

colleagues as Young walked past. Normally, she would have blushed, cringing inwardly at the implied criticism. This time, instead of pretending she hadn't heard, she stopped, went back, planted her hands palm down on his desk and leaned over him.

'If you'd given me one break — that much leeway.' She pinched a micron of air between her thumb and forefinger. 'I'd've bailed you out. But ask yourself, Fletcher — would you have covered for me if I'd fucked up the way you did? I don't think so — you'd've given me a hard time, like you've been giving me a hard time since this investigation started.'

Someone called her. She turned and saw DS Barton standing in the doorway.

'Boss wants a word,' he said, his eyes flitting from Young to Fletcher, evaluating the situation. He walked with her to McAteer's office.

'Is Fletcher giving you grief?' he asked.

'Not so's you'd notice.' She caught his eye and smiled.

He was startled for a moment: the smile transformed her from an apologetic, nervous novice to a confident self-aware woman. In that moment he saw beyond her shyness and anxiety and saw her potential as a member of the team. He smiled back. 'I was going to say I'd have a word, but . . .'

'Thanks,' she said. 'I can handle Fletcher.' She paused outside McAteer's door to straighten her blouse and fluff her hair.

McAteer rose to greet her. 'Constable Young. Good work on the photos.'

Barton came in and closed the door.

'Just doing what I was told, sir.'

McAteer exchanged a look with Barton. Evidently she still resented being allocated the task of cleaning up the Incident Room. The sergeant shrugged — she was entitled to a little mild truculence.

'Nevertheless,' McAteer said. 'As a result of your discovery, we've just received a fax from the DVLA.'

Her eyes glowed with excitement. He placed a printout on

his desk. 'The driver's licence photograph,' he said, tapping the sheet. 'I had it enlarged. And this is a picture Miss Kelsall gave DC Rayner and DS Barton yesterday.'

She compared the two photographs carefully. 'Same man, no doubt about it,' she commented mildly, but could not disguise the eagerness in her voice. 'What's the address?'

'We need to establish that it's genuine,' McAteer said, tacitly warning her that there might be fresh disappointment to face.

'Sir, I can—'

They were interrupted by a sharp rap at the door. 'Guv?' Rayner glanced at Young and Barton. 'You sent for me.'

'I want you to check out an address,' McAteer began.

'But sir!'

McAteer's look was enough to silence Young's protestations, but when he spoke, his tone was conciliatory. 'I need an experienced officer, Young,' he said. 'It's not a reflection on you. But I need someone who's done this before.'

Young took a breath. Held it. *Shit!* He was right. *He's telling you to your face, so you don't go thinking you're marked down as a fuck-up.* She nodded. 'It makes sense.'

'I wanted you to be clear about my reasons,' McAteer said, maintaining eye contact.

She relaxed a little, even smiled. 'Hey,' she said, 'We're a team, aren't we?'

As Rayner turned the corner of the street she felt suddenly exposed. The address on Kelsall's licence might be as bogus as the name he had given, but until she walked past the house and saw it for herself, she couldn't be sure.

She walked at a strolling pace down the broad and leafy curve of Meadowsweet Drive, every sense alert. It was misty and cold. The milky swirl of cloud above her head seemed flimsy, insubstantial, and yet the sun had not broken through all day. Number seventeen was at the far end of the road. She walked on the opposite pavement, watching for movement, checking out the cars parked at the roadside, without turning her head or even seeming to pay much attention to her surroundings.

'Just walk straight down the road,' McAteer said, and his voice boomed in her earpiece. She resisted the reflex to poke a finger into her ear and carried on walking. 'Just act naturally.'

She almost laughed. *Act natural!* She was having trouble making her legs work normally and she'd given up trying to get a relaxed swing into her arms and instead, jammed her hands into her pockets.

A shadow in a car a little further down the road set her skin tingling. It was a Lexus — one of Casavettes' fleet cars? She made the muscles of her neck and shoulders loosen and walked past the Lexus without so much as a sideways glance, managing, nevertheless, to get the vehicle identification number and to notice that there were two men in the car.

They were parked a few doors down from number seventeen, which meant it would be difficult to clock the van's licence plate without turning her head. She took a deep breath and with a cursory glance over her shoulder to check for traffic, crossed the road diagonally, just after the Lexus, and ended up almost facing number seventeen. The van was there, parked in the driveway. The plate checked out with the index number the DVLA had given them and she recognised, almost without thinking, the weedy block paving and the bricked-up cellar on the photograph Casavettes had sent to Hugo Pascal.

It was all over in seconds and she walked on, feeling an unpleasant burning sensation between her shoulder-blades, imagining the two men watching her to the end of the road, pausing their conversation until she turned the corner and disappeared from sight.

A little further down the road a dark green Sierra pulled in beside her. 'Fancy a lift?' Thorpe, for once minus the hat that made him look like a photofit of an armed robber. Rayner feigned surprise and smiled, making a chatty remark about not expecting to see him, just in case Casavettes had more of his men watching. She climbed in and waited until they had moved off before pressing the connection mounted in the dash.

'The van's there,' she said. 'A metallic grey Lexus is parked opposite.' She gave the ID number.

The firearms support unit moved men in within minutes. Two rounded the corner in a battered van and pulled up outside number nineteen. One man strolled up to the door, whistling, while the other began unloading the van: pots of paint, boxes of wallpaper. The house owner opened the door, as they had arranged by phone, and grumbled quite convincingly about having expected them that morning.

A minute or two later a Transco van pulled up at the end of the road and a man in overalls jumped out, clipboard in hand. In the next street, armed officers knocked at the two houses immediately behind number seventeen Meadowsweet Drive and set up surveillance on the rear of the property.

The Incident Commander radioed McAteer. 'The premises are secure,' he said. 'It's confirmed we have two men in the Lexus saloon car outside.'

'Ray Casavettes' men,' McAteer said.

'If they try to make a move on the house, we'll cuff'n' stuff'em.'

'Anything on Clara's condition?' McAteer asked.

'We've got Technical Support in the adjoining house. They'll put in fibre optic cameras and covert listening as soon as.'

'How long will that take?' McAteer asked.

'They're drilling through from the basement, since that's where we think she's being held. They say the mortar's damp, which will speed things up, but the walls are thick and the drills have to go slow. It could still take hours.'

Chapter Forty Seven

Lenny watched out of the rear window while they criss-crossed the flat, featureless countryside between Lydiate and Aughton for half an hour, until Casavettes was satisfied that they really were free of police surveillance. He leaned forward and tapped the driver on the shoulder. 'Okay,' he said. 'We're clear. Head for Delamere.'

He gave further instructions as they got closer to their destination, guiding them to a thin finger of tufty grassland, bordered by whippy birch saplings, at the edge of the forest. The sun was a dull red orb, slipping behind the trees. It would be dark in less than an hour. The grass was almost as dull and grey as the sky, but above, the cloud was thinning and in places was no more than a thin mist, just above the canopy.

At the end of a narrow metalled road, just wide enough to take one car, they turned into a semicircular driveway. Ahead, a sandstone cottage with red and yellow polyanthus planted in the borders and winter-flowering pansies and ivy in hanging baskets either side of the door.

'Very nice,' Lawson commented. 'Thinking of taking a winter break?'

'I had somewhere warmer in mind,' Casavettes said.

'This isn't the house in the photograph,' he said, stating the obvious, keeping the patter going, to hide the fact that he was gearing up for a fight.

'I'm having her brought here,' Casavettes replied, glib. Untrustworthy.

Lawson bunched his hand into a fist. He wasn't sure if he could take the driver out with a left-handed punch, but he was prepared to try. The driver first, then Casavettes. That still left Lenny, in the seat behind him, but if he could get Casavettes in a head lock—

Two more men came out of the cottage and walked towards the Chrysler.

Shit! 'What the fuck are you playing at, Casavettes?' Lawson demanded.

'Relax, Steve. Just the welcoming committee.'

The driver touched a button and the window next to Lawson slid down. Lawson felt a cold shock — the barrel of a gun, just touching his neck. The pulse of his carotid artery hammered against it.

'Get out of the car,' the man said, sliding back the door. 'Do it slowly.'

Lawson moved with infinite care.

Once he was safely outside the car, the man took a step back and Lawson let out a gasp of pure relief as the gun barrel was moved a foot or two distant from him.

'Nice one, Jeff,' Casavettes said, grinning.

Lawson glanced around at the five men surrounding him. Two were armed, as far as he could see. Across a lawn, to the right of the cottage, was a picket fence and beyond it, a well-cropped paddock. Birdsong trilled from woods at the back of the building, the rap of a woodpecker echoed across the clearing and in the distance, a faint buzz.

Casavettes cocked an ear to the sound. 'Hear that? That's my first-class ticket to freedom.' A helicopter. 'Drugs are like e-commerce,' he went on. 'You can set up anywhere and make a fortune.'

Lenny glanced doubtfully at his watch. 'He's a bit early yet, Boss.'

'Seen the weather, Len?' Casavettes said. 'He probably thought he'd have trouble finding the place.'

'Where's Clara?' Lawson demanded. The cold bit through the thin fabric of his shirt and he had to clench his jaw to stop his teeth chattering.

Casavettes gave him a slow, considering look. 'Where she's always been. With Brian Kelsall.'

'I want the address,' Lawson said.

'I'm a man of my word, Steve,' Casavettes said, feigning offence. 'I've just moved the goalposts a bit. This is how it goes: two of my men are outside, keeping an eye on Kelsall's place.' His eyes glittered with malicious enjoyment. 'Me, I'm a belt-and-braces sort of bloke, so you, Steve, are coming with me. When I'm at my destination – if I'm happy with how things have gone – I'll make two calls: one to your Incident Room and one to my men outside Kelsall's. Call it my insurance policy: I'm safe – she's safe.'

'No,' Lawson said. 'That wasn't the deal—'

Light and pain exploded in the side of his head. He fell to his knees. He hadn't even seen it coming. The buzz of the helicopter suddenly magnified, then the noise and the light retreated and he thought he would pass out. They hauled him to his feet and he stood for a moment, swaying, fighting dizziness and nausea.

Casavettes gave his head a little shake. 'I don't like being interrupted, Steve.'

Lawson felt a warm trickle of blood run from his temple down the side of his face. The slice of the chopper blades clattered in the little clearing, and Lawson thought he could make out a dark shadow through the thinning cloud cover as the other two manhandled him towards the paddock at the side of the property.

Suddenly, Casavettes was screaming. 'Shit! Get him inside! Do it *now!*'

Jeff let go of Lawson. He stumbled, recovered, looked up. A police helicopter. Jeff raised his arm to shoot at the chopper.

Lawson yelled, punching the guy who still had hold of him, then barging sideways at Jeff. The shot went wide and the gunman lost his balance.

The helicopter tannoy clicked in and the co-pilot barked an order for Casavettes and his men to throw down their weapons. Casavettes grabbed Lawson. They struggled. He heard cars screeching up the road. Gunshots.

'Get him!' Casavettes screamed.

Lawson landed a punch that sent Casavettes staggering. He regained his balance, grabbed Lawson's shirt and launched himself into a head-butt. Lawson jerked back and Casavettes connected with his chin. In one flowing movement he slid his right leg behind Casavettes' right hip, gripped him by the lapels and twisted. Simultaneously, a shot rang out and Casavettes screamed as he smacked into the ground.

Jeff stood, staring stupidly at Lawson. The gun hung limply from his hand.

'Drop the gun!' Lawson shouted. 'Drop it! NOW!'

More voices joined his. A car tore across the turf and armed officers swarmed after it.

The gunman blinked at them for a few moments, then, with a start, he seemed to realise he still had the gun and with almost comical care, he set it down on the grass.

'Turn around!' the officers yelled. 'Kneel down!'

A hand touched Lawson's shoulder. 'You all right, Guv?'

Lawson put his fingers to his temple; they came away sticky with blood. 'I'm okay.'

The officer looked down at Lawson's shirt-front. The pale blue cotton was soaked with blood. *Jesus! Was I shot?* Lawson felt his side. Nothing. 'I'm fine,' he said, hearing the surprise in his voice.

Casavettes lay on the ground, with two armed officers pointing guns at him. He was pale as wax, panting, an expression of astonishment on his face.

'Medic!' Lawson yelled.

The ambulance pulled up next to the unmarked car on the lawn. Lawson delayed the paramedics taking Casavettes away. 'I'll be needing this,' he said, fishing his mobile phone out of his pocket.

'I was gonna get you a new one, mate,' Casavettes said. A weak smile played about his lips. From the radio in an unmarked car, a faint crackling echo of his voice: '. . . new one mate.'

Casavettes closed his eyes briefly. 'Aw, fuck.'

'It's got a little radio transmitter,' Lawson explained. 'You talked this lot through the route, all the way here.'

Casavettes plucked at Lawson's shirt sleeve, struggling to say something, and Lawson bent down to listen. Casavettes smiled. 'She's dead, Lawson,' he croaked. 'You just killed Clara, you sad fucker.'

Chapter Forty Eight

Exhausted, Clara had slept for a few hours. She woke feeling sick. *She's dead, Clara. Laura's dead. And Eleanor. You killed them both.* The voice insinuated itself into her every waking thought. But she couldn't forget her remorseless pursuit of Brian Kelsall during the trial.

You told the jury that he was in some way jealous of his daughter's sexual freedom, that he had found out about his daughter's affair with a much older man and Laura, rather than admit to him that she had been a willing partner in Alex Martin's sex games, had screamed rape. And they believed you, because you're so persuasive. Jesus! you had them feeling sorry *for Alex Martin! 'I believe him, members of the jury — don't you?' And because you're an attractive, intelligent woman, they think, 'Of course we believe you, Ms Pascal. You wouldn't defend a guilty man, would you?'*

But the evidence! *What about the evidence?* It was no good saying there was no evidence. It was there, but Martin had successfully hidden it. Clara tried to tell herself that finding the videotapes and photographs had been the prosecution's job, that it was their failure, not hers.

They had all the evidence they needed in the transcripts of the interviews. Verbatim. Laura's halting account to the woman police officer. The cameras, Martin's stage directions, the repeated violation and humiliation of a teenage girl.

Martin was entitled to competent defence — even the guilty

are allowed representation. *Yes, but you were never content with mere competence, were you, Clara? You always had to dazzle.*

I thought she was lying! But if that was the case, why had she refused prosecuting counsel's suggestion that she watch the original interview tapes? Was it because, faced with the video evidence, she would be unable to misread Laura's torment? Was she afraid that Laura's distress would affect her – that it would weaken her ability to defend a man who, in her heart, she knew to be dangerous?

Clara groaned. What she had put that girl through in the witness box! The endless questions, gently put, of course, because the jury's sympathies were always with a potential rape victim. *And you're far too clever to alienate a jury, aren't you, Clara?* When Laura broke down, she took it as an admission of guilt, an admission that she had lied and, more unforgivably, she had persuaded the jury of it.

Because of her clever arguments, her bamboozling of the witnesses, her careful coaching of Alex Martin, a woman was dead – two, counting Laura – and of course Laura *did* count. Another woman had been destroyed by sadistic, calculated humiliation and terrorisation: Angela Hutton would never be what she had been before.

The steel door stood ajar. Kelsall had left the light on, the newspaper on the floor. Clara picked it up and forced herself to read. She would not spare herself. Martin had suffocated all of his victims in the same way. Kelsall had used the same method on her, pinching her nose, holding her mouth closed. He had tried to tell her all along, why she was there, and she hadn't seen it. Laura had described it in detail in court. She had struggled, passed out. She had come to hours later in Martin's bed. Disoriented and in fear of her life, she had complied with his demands.

As she read and reread the horrors hinted at in the newspaper, Clara became dimly aware of something encroaching on her consciousness. Music. At first, it seemed distorted, like sounds under water, and Clara realised that she was close to fainting. She lay down on the mattress for a few minutes until the feeling passed and the music resolved itself into something recognisable.

Eric Clapton, 'If I saw you in Heaven.' Kelsall played it again and again in a constant loop. Clara was afraid. Did he intend to follow Laura – to take his own life? She called over and over until she was hoarse. He didn't come.

As Clara drifted into unconsciousness, the technical support team broke through into the cellar. There was little to see: the grey tip of the drill bit appeared briefly and then retracted; nothing much to hear, only the gritty fall of a few grains of sandy mortar onto the stone floor. But Clara was past listening. The sounds she heard were the voices of girls she had never known. She knew that they blamed her and she felt they were right.

After a breathless pause, DC Jim Tennant gently withdrew the drill.

The second officer handed him a probe. Slowly, achingly slowly, and with infinite care, Jim worked the fine audio-visual cable into the narrow channel. Both men donned headphones. Clara was just discernible as a grey outline on the monitor. They glanced at each other, both asking the same unspoken question. A shake of the head. Nothing. No movement, no sound, only the pulse of music beyond the cellar door. The record ended.

Seconds passed. Minutes, until the silence became a deafening roar. Jim raised a finger.

There. A beat of silence. *There* – again – a groan. They made eye contact and Jim grinned. *She's alive!*

When she came to, Kelsall was standing over her.

Her heart raced, but she felt groggy, unable to respond to the adrenaline coursing through her veins. She made an effort to sit up. Her head pounded, throbbing as though her brain would burst out of her skull.

Kelsall was staring at something in his wallet. A picture of Laura? She felt again that awful thud of guilty recognition: *see what you've done, Clara?*

Kelsall stirred, seemed to become gradually aware of her presence. 'Look after your little girl,' he said. 'Take good care of her. Because you only have to look the other way for one moment . . .'

It wasn't a threat and Clara felt it all the more keenly for that. Her eyes burned with anguish, but no tears would come.

He turned to leave.

'Mr Kelsall!'

He stopped and looked at her, through her.

'Mr Kelsall, don't . . . Please don't do anything . . .' *What, Clara? Were you going to say 'Don't do anything you'll regret.'? Look at him — you've torn the man's heart out. Death would be infinitely preferable to what he's going through now.*

'What's the matter, Counsel?' The mocking tone had returned to his voice. 'Afraid you'll be buried alive here?'

'I wasn't thinking of myself,' Clara said, scarcely able to get the words past the lump in her throat. 'Truly I wasn't.'

For a moment he seemed surprised that she might actually feel for him. He stared at the picture in his wallet, his face deeply lined with pain. Then he looked up and his eyes were flat and lifeless.

'You can't kill a dead man, Counsel.'

He walked away, his foot on the first riser of the steps, and Clara was afraid — very much afraid — that despite what he said, Kelsall planned to kill himself. She said the first thing that came into her head, the only thing that she thought might stop him carrying on up the steps and out of the house.

'Laura wouldn't—'

He rounded on her, his eyes blazing. 'Don't!' His voice rose to a tormented shriek. 'Don't you tell me what Laura would want!' He was trembling with anger, racked with grief.

All his senses were focused on her; neither he nor Clara were aware of the tiny hole that had appeared in the mortar on the far side of the cellar, nor could they see the pink crumbs of mortar on the grey stone flags. On the other side of the wall, the two officers watched them on the monitor. Thirty more, hidden in the gardens and houses surrounding the house, waited for their orders, prepared for the long haul, but primed for action. In the car opposite the house, Casavettes' men ate a packet of crisps and played Radio One at low volume.

Half a minute passed before Clara spoke again. 'I know it can do no good. And I know it isn't – it could never be – enough, but I really am—' She stopped. The words were inadequate. It seemed almost an insult to say them, but she went on anyway. 'I am sorry.'

Kelsall thought about it, looking at the pictures of the women and girls on the walls around them, coming back to the picture of his daughter in his wallet. When he spoke, his voice was gentle, full of regret.

'Yes,' he said. 'I can believe you. But it doesn't change the fact that you let a guilty man go free. You set him at liberty to terrorise and rape and murder. Can you forgive yourself?' Clara couldn't answer him. It was too soon for her to try to make sense of what had happened; all she knew was that at that moment, she hated herself.

'Can you live with it?' he asked. '*Can* you?' His eyes raked her face. She couldn't meet his gaze.

He took the photograph out of his wallet. Carefully, with a tenderness Clara found almost unbearable to watch, he taped Laura's picture to the wall alongside the others.

His hand slipped back into the pocket of his jacket and he bent his head for a moment, as if in silent prayer. Then he turned to face her. He had a gun in his hand.

Clara made a small sound in her throat.

*   *   *

Armed officers appeared as if from nowhere, moving at a run, swarming over the wall at the end of the garden, racing towards the house. In the street, more officers ran for the car. Casavettes' men looked at one another, then reached for their door handles simultaneously.

Immediately they were seized by police.

Confused sounds: the smash of glass — the frenzied barking of a dog further down the road — a dull boom—

And then the report of a gun.

Chapter Forty Nine

The excited chatter, audible from the foot of the stairs, exploded into a tumult of cheers and applause when Lawson stepped through the door into the canteen.

Someone shoved a plastic cup into his hand and he sipped it. Champagne. But he wasn't wasn't in the mood to celebrate. He scanned the room. McAteer stood near the far wall — not alone: under these circumstances, even the DCI was entitled to share in the punchy euphoria, the sheer relief of a successful outcome. He was set apart only by the amount of space he had to himself. In the crowded clamour of the canteen, DCs rubbed shoulders — literally — with DIs, but McAteer, out of respect for his rank, was afforded a larger-than-average margin; enough to raise his cup of bubbly without having his elbow jogged.

McAteer caught Lawson's eye and gave a slight nod. Even celebrating, the DCI maintained his standards of dignity and formality. Lawson edged through the crowd: surveillance officers, technical support, the HOLMES team, officers who had done the hard slog over the past week. Even the firearms support team were represented.

Cath Young, laughing and relaxed, was talking to Thorpe and Sal Rayner. Thorpe raised his glass. 'Nice one, Boss,' he shouted over the general clamour. Lawson noticed Fletcher slumped at a table within easy reach of Young, his eyes red-rimmed and bleary, and Lawson was struck again by the change in her. Only days ago, she would have avoided standing anywhere near Fletcher, fearful of some comment or a sly grope. Now she seemed barely aware of him.

He stayed for thirty minutes, exchanging congratulations, smiling, but feeling sick in the pit of his stomach. At the time, he had acted without thinking, but now he couldn't stop the thought recurring: he could have been killed. And this wasn't over yet: they still didn't know how many other women had been abducted and raped by Alex Martin. For the moment, it looked like Eleanor had been the only murder victim, but they were still working through the videotapes. And there were so many . . .

When the voices began to echo and he found himself frowning in an effort to understand, Lawson placed his champagne, barely tasted, on the canteen counter and left.

He slunk past the Incident Room and went straight to his office. Barton called in five minutes later, carrying two mugs of coffee. He handed one over and Lawson took a grateful sip. As he set it down, his hand trembled and he spilt a little.

Barton frowned. 'You all right, Boss?'

'Fine.'

'Yeah?' He wasn't convinced.

Lawson smiled tiredly and ran a hand over his face. 'I've been better, Phil.'

'I got your car from the prison.' Barton seemed awkward, unsure what to say. 'It's parked round the back.'

Lawson nodded. 'How're Fran and the baby?'

'Okay,' Barton said.

'You sound doubtful.'

He sighed. 'Fran's pissed off. We'll be in a safe house till after the trial. Taking precautions, police escort for her and Timmy. She likes her own space.'

'She'll get used to it.'

'Yeah . . .'

'How do *you* feel?' Lawson asked.

Barton shrugged. 'I know I'd be feeling a hell of a lot worse if I really had caved in.'

Lawson looked down at his own shaking hands. 'Sometimes that's the best you can hope for.'

Barton scratched the ridge between his eyebrows, suddenly embarrassed. 'The rest of the team,' he said. 'They do know I'm with the good guys?'

'Of course, why?'

'Just something Fletcher said.'

'Fletcher! He's not still trying to stir it, is he?'

'Stir it with who?'

'Look, Phil,' Lawson said. 'Don't take Fetcher so seriously. You know how the newspapers got hold of the story at the start of this?'

'Fletcher?'

'McAteer thinks so. He thinks he might have told them about the earring as well.'

Barton grunted. 'The press aren't likely to cough on their informant, and Fletcher isn't stupid. He'll just keep his mouth shut and wait for this to go away.'

'Right. But Fletch has had his arse kicked once already, and Fletch being Fletch, he's looking to divert attention from himself.'

'He went to McAteer, didn't he?' Barton asked.

Lawson thought about it: after what Barton had been through, he deserved to know all the facts. 'He put in a quiet word with the boss,' Lawson explained. 'Thought it might be worth checking your mobile account.'

Barton flushed darkly.

'Take it easy, Phil. He was just trying to score some brownie points after his cock-up over the photos. McAteer kicked him out of his office so fast, you'd think he had revolving doors. And you have to admit, you did give a great performance.'

Another shrug. 'Oscar material, me.' Only it was no act; the fear had been real. The pause lengthened into a silence and

Lawson realised that there was something more Barton wanted to say. He raised his eyebrows and Barton shrugged. 'About Porter—'

'It's all right, Phil.'

'No, it isn't. What I said about him bottling out. He was just protecting his family.'

'Like you did,' Lawson said.

Barton gave a perfunctory nod. 'I keep thinking did I do the right thing.'

'Of *course* you did the right thing!'

'Not for the job. For my family.' Barton gave him a searing look. 'I mean, what if he—'

'Phil,' Lawson interrupted. 'You can't think like this. Porter was on the inside. On the take. He set Casavettes up and Casavettes saw that as a betrayal. It was personal. With you, it was different. He took a calculated risk; it didn't pay off.'

Barton thought about it for a few minutes. It made sense and for the moment, he was comforted.

'With your testimony,' Lawson said, 'we'll have something extra to hang on Casavettes – when he's fit to stand trial, that is.'

The phone rang and Lawson picked up. 'Marie!' Barton signalled that he would leave, but Lawson shook his head, waving him to a seat. 'No, look, it's okay. No . . .' He grimaced at Barton. 'I'm fine.' There was a pause. 'You know how they exaggerate on the news . . . I should have, I know, I'm sorry, but I was only on the periphery. Hardly involved at all. No . . .' Then, 'Yes, we found her . . . She'll be fine.' There was a longer pause. He glanced at Barton, then away. 'Me too,' he said. 'I'll be home in an hour or so.'

When he hung up, Barton gave him a quizzical look.

'What did you except me to do?' Lawson demanded. 'Frighten her half to death with what really happened?'

'You could've been shot, Steve.'

'But I wasn't. Anyway, all the more reason not to tell her.'

'Your hands are still shaking.'

Lawson set down his mug. 'Thanks for pointing that out. Anything else?'

Barton pulled his earlobe.

'Well, go on,' Lawson said. 'You might as well say it.'

Barton shrugged. 'Why d'you think she called? It's all over the news, Steve. *You're* all over the news.'

Lawson gave him a crooked smile. 'You know how the press exaggerate.'

'Yeah, right,' Barton said. 'And while you're convincing her they got the wrong man, you might think of a reason why you've got a couple of stitches in your forehead.'

Lawson raised a hand to his head. 'Oh, shit.'

Chapter Fifty

Hugo held Clara's hand. She stared at him, hungrily taking in every contour of his face, grateful just to be near him. The warmth of his body, the smell of him reassured her.

She did not want to sleep, was fearful even of closing her eyes in case this, too, was a hallucination. Horrified by the prospect of waking up and finding herself in the cold and dark, she fought against exhaustion, but sleep crept up on her anyway, gently enfolding her. An image, sharp and clear, flashed across the back of her eyes: the ugly grey muzzle of the gun. Brian Kelsall raising it. Turning.

She twitched, opened her eyes.

'It's all right,' Hugo murmured, as he had done a dozen times already. 'You're safe. I'm with you.'

'Pippa . . .' She was breathing hard and Hugo stroked her hand, careful of the scrapes and cuts on her fingers.

'Pippa's fine. Remember? She's at home with Trish. She can phone me on my mobile.'

She was confused, distressed by her inability to retain these simple facts.

'It's the sedatives,' he reassured her. 'Nothing to worry about.'

'You shouldn't have brought her,' she said. 'She was so upset.'

'It was relief. Look, she's hardly slept a wink since you . . . I mean since . . .' He swallowed.

Clara reached up and touched his face. 'What I've put you through.'

He pressed her palm to his lips. 'Kelsall did that, not you.'

'No,' she said. 'I don't blame him, Hugo. I wish . . .'

She felt so weak, but she was determined not to cry.

Hugo brushed a lock of hair from her eyes. 'What, darling?'

'I wish I could have helped him – but there was no evidence. I really thought she'd made it up. There were no bruises. Nothing to show that he'd . . .' She heard herself, trying to justify herself to her husband, trying to excuse her behaviour in court, and at that moment she felt ashamed, of herself and of her profession.

'Shhh,' Hugo soothed, stroking her face, kissing her forehead. 'I know . . .'

She almost succumbed, but then, fighting against the cowardly impulse to excuse her actions, she said, 'There were no bruises because Laura was so terrified she did exactly as she was told.'

'Alex Martin fooled a lot of people,' Hugo said.

She shook her head. 'I sensed it. I felt uncomfortable with him, I just ignored it.'

'For God's sake, Clara! If you refused to represent every sleaze who made you uncomfortable—' He stopped abruptly, realising he had revealed more than he had intended.

Clara gazed at him, puzzled and hurt.

'I didn't know,' she said. 'I never knew that you felt that way.'

'Clara, I—' He began to apologise, but was interrupted by a soft tap at the door and a slim, grey-haired man looked in.

Hugo jumped to his feet. 'Inspector Lawson!' Embarrassment made him a little effusive. 'This is the policeman who—'

'Yes.' Clara smiled. 'I know.' She held out a hand to Lawson. 'Thank you. For both of us.' Infuriated with herself, she felt a tear spill onto her cheek.

'I just wanted to see for myself you were all right,' he said. 'I didn't realise . . .' He indicated the drip slowly emptying into her arm.

'This? I'm a bit dehydrated. Electrolytes haywire or something. I'll be right as rain by the morning.' She knew she sounded too bright. Brittle. An awkward silence followed. 'Hugo, could you . . .? I mean I'd like to——'

Hugo stood. 'Of course. I'll go and get a coffee.'

He went, closing the door behind him, and they were left alone. For a moment, they simply looked at each other, then Clara asked, 'Are you here to take a statement?'

'No,' he said. 'We got enough from what you told the officers earlier to piece together most of it. I'll send someone in tomorrow to take a formal statement. I couldn't really feel it was over until I saw you with my own eyes. It's difficult, you know? You work on a case like this, you feel you know the family by the end of it and yet I'd never met you.'

Clara nodded. It was hard to imagine just how much activity had gone on, how many people had heard her name, talked about her, speculated on her fate, while her world became a small room and one man who had the power of life or death over her.

'Inspector,' she said. 'They wouldn't tell me. Brian Kelsall, is he——?' She looked anxiously into his face, knowing the answer, but needing to hear it said. 'Hugo didn't know. He came straight here and——'

'He's dead,' Lawson said.

'I thought so.' She had watched Kelsall tape Laura's picture to the wall and then he had walked away. She couldn't stop him. Was powerless to comfort him. Could never make amends. She had looked into his eyes and seen nothing. Nothing at all. *You can't kill a dead man.* He was dead before the police burst through the door. Before even he had raised the gun. He had been dead since the morning Laura killed herself.

Even so, she wasn't ready for what happened.

For thirty seconds – it can't have been more, but it seemed

much longer – she stared at the gun in his hand. Her heart squeezed tighter and tighter, until she could hardly breathe. She heard glass shatter at the back of the house. He didn't react – or perhaps he did, because he did the strangest thing: he seemed to smile a little.

Then a dull boom she felt more than heard. The cellar door slammed with the force of it, she was knocked off her feet and for a moment darkness crowded in. Then she heard footsteps. The door flew open and sharp, white light blinded her. Kelsall was on the floor. He started to get up. There was shouting. She remembered confused yells, orders to lie down. *Did they mean her?* She was shouting, too.

'Don't shoot! *Don't shoot!'* Was she shouting at them or at Kelsall? It was hard to disentangle: her thoughts were slow and it had happened so fast.

Brian Kelsall stood, turning in an arc as he did so, sweeping his gun arm round, towards her, towards the police. Everyone was screaming. Then a roar, deafening in the confines of the cellar, two, maybe three shots.

He fell. First to his knees, then he keeled forward and she flinched as his face hit the floor.

She must have blacked out, because the next thing she recalled was a paramedic crouched next to her and with him a police woman. They were gentle. And kind. She could have borne anything but kindness.

She nodded, frowning. 'There's something else—' She swallowed. 'Mr Kelsall was worried about his daughter, you see. The papers said you'd found video tapes—'

Lawson didn't reply.

Clara nodded again. *Oh God!* 'I didn't believe her. I should have, but I didn't.'

'I'm sorry,' he said.

'Not as sorry as I am.' He seemed to understand her ambivalence towards Brian Kelsall and this gave her the courage to say, 'You've been honest with me, Inspector. I'm grateful for that. Can I ask you one more question? And will you promise to answer me straight?'

'Of course.'

'Do you ever get over something like this?'

Lawson looked down at his hands; they were still trembling. Clara Pascal hadn't been raped and she hadn't been shot at, but she had been starved and humiliated and terrorised. 'I wish you hadn't asked me that,' he said.

She looked at him, eager and yet dreading his answer.

He sighed. 'You get over flu. You get over mumps,' he said. 'This goes deeper.'

'Yes,' she said. She felt that what had happened to her had altered her, weakened her in some fundamental way. 'But do you learn to live with it?'

Lawson shrugged. 'What else can you do?'